My Little Pony
Legends of Magic

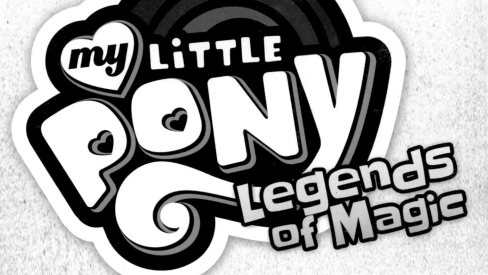

Become our fan on Facebook **facebook.com/idwpublishing**
Follow us on Twitter **@idwpublishing**
Subscribe to us on YouTube **youtube.com/idwpublishing**
See what's new on Tumblr **tumblr.idwpublishing.com**
Check us out on Instagram **instagram.com/idwpublishing**

ISBN: 978-1-68405-059-8   20 19 18 17 1 2 3 4

COLLECTION EDITS BY
JUSTIN EISINGER
AND ALONZO SIMON

COLLECTION DESIGN BY
RON ESTEVEZ

PUBLISHER
TED ADAMS

Originally published as MY LITTLE PONY: LEGENDS OF MAGIC issues #1–6.

Ted Adams, CEO & Publisher
Greg Goldstein, President & COO
Robbie Robbins, EVP/Sr. Graphic Artist
Chris Ryall, Chief Creative Officer
David Hedgecock, Editor-in-Chief
Laurie Windrow, Senior VP of Sales & Marketing
Matthew Ruzicka, CPA, Chief Financial Officer
Lorelei Bunjes, VP of Digital Services
Jerry Bennington, VP of New Product Development

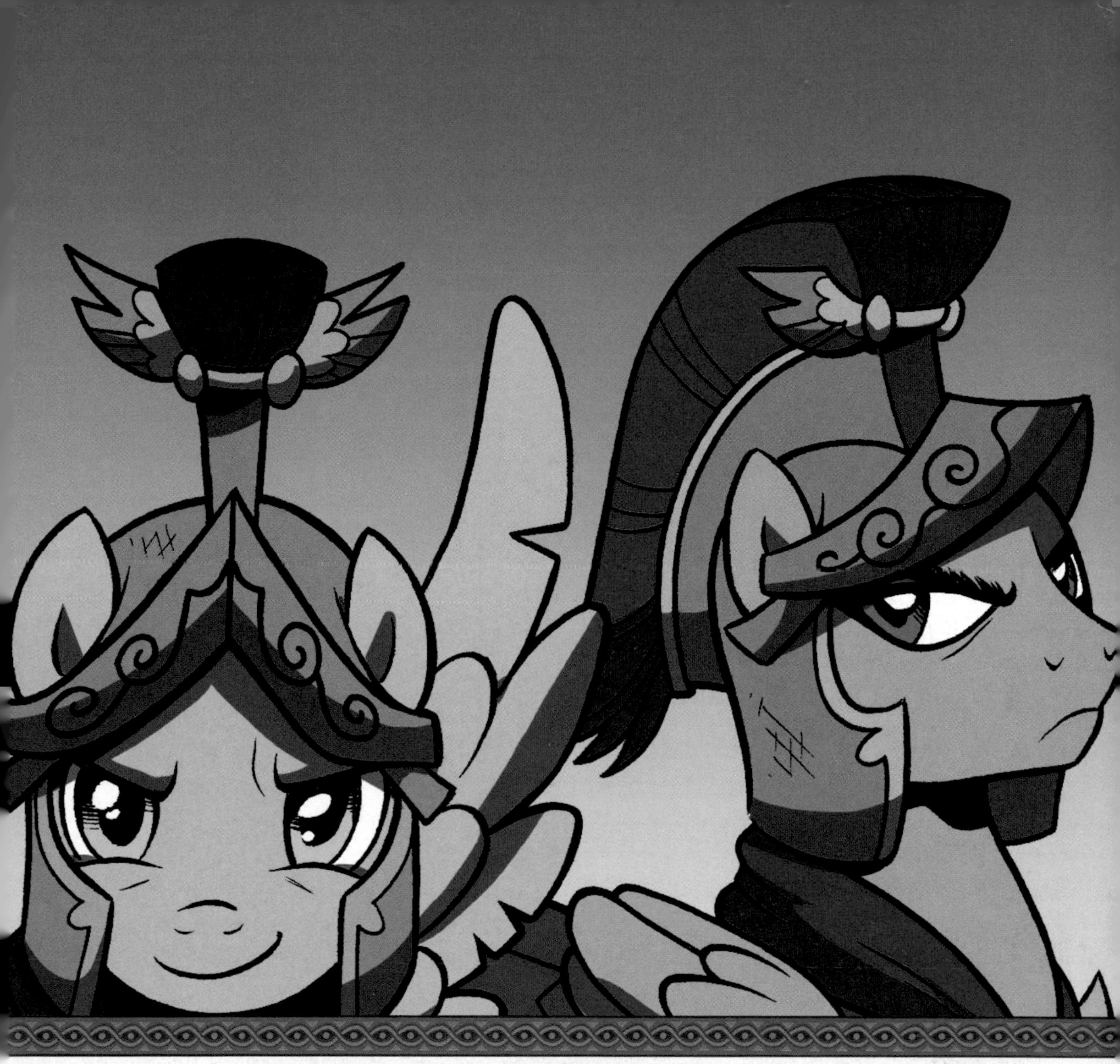

WRITTEN BY JEREMY WHITLEY

ART BY BRENDA HICKEY

COLORS BY HEATHER BRECKEL

LETTERS BY NEIL UYETAKE

SERIES EDITS BY BOBBY CURNOW

SPECIAL THANKS TO MEGHAN MCCARTHY, ELIZA HART, ED LANE, BETH ARTALE, AND MICHAEL KELLY.

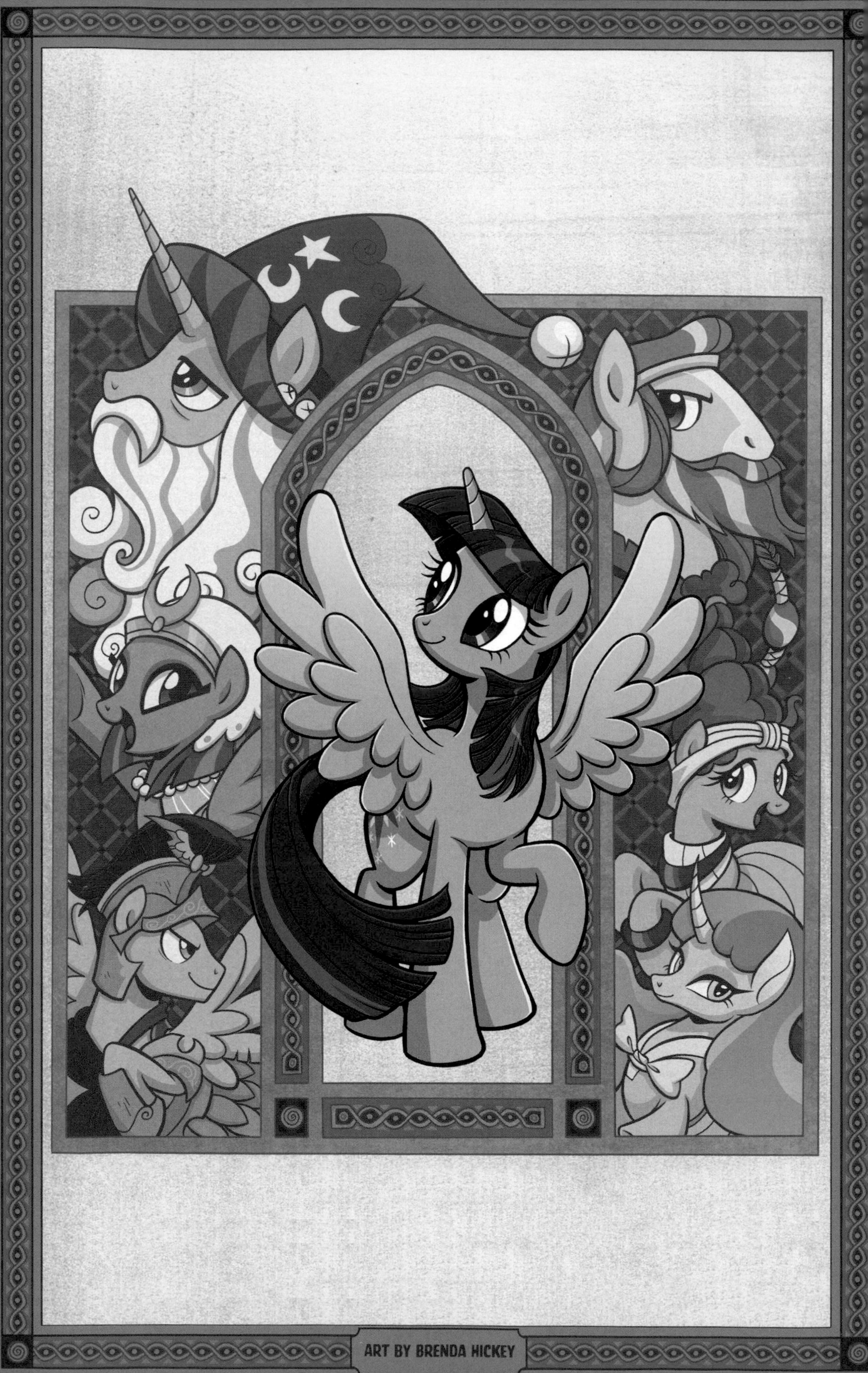

ART BY BRENDA HICKEY

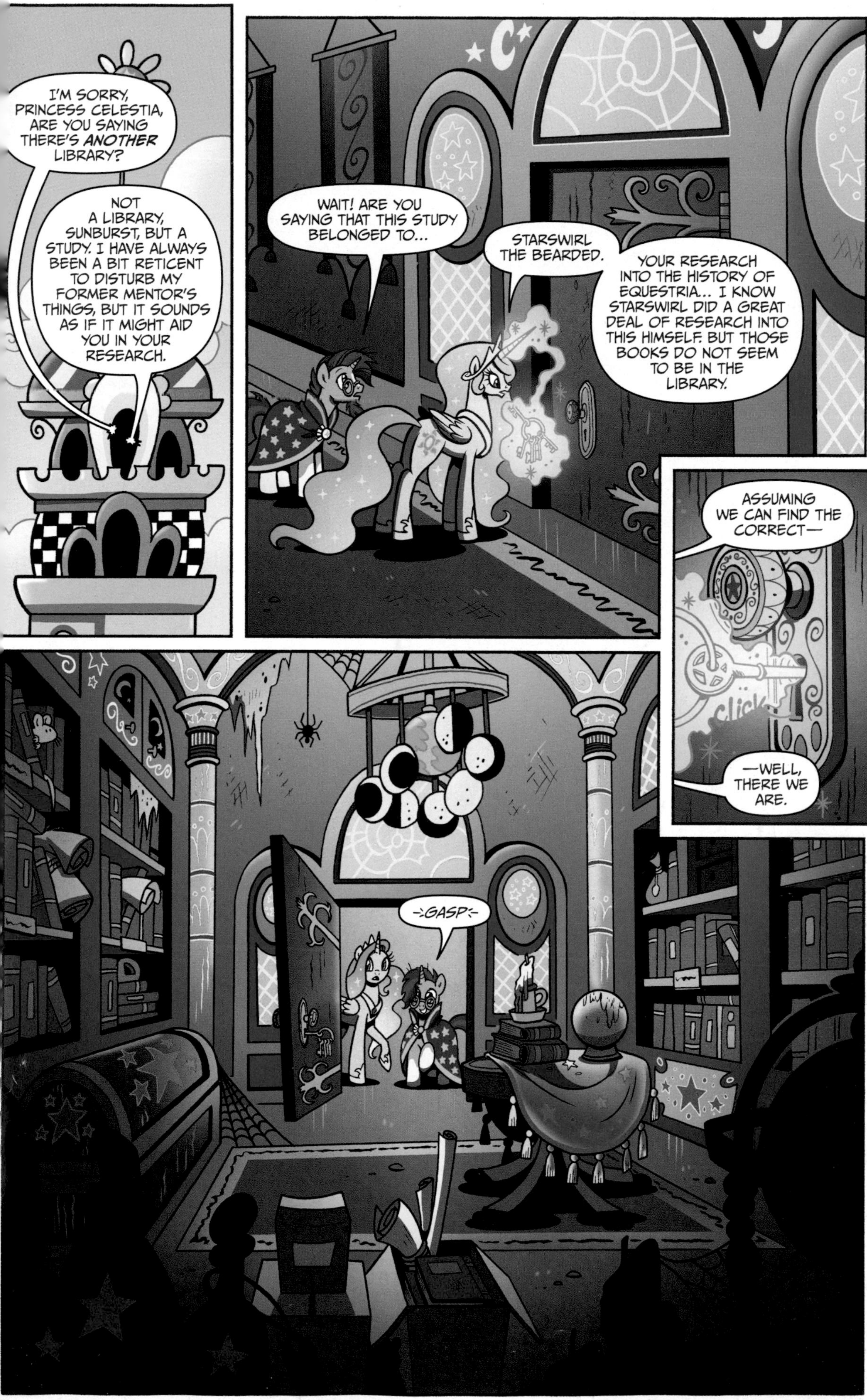
I'M SORRY, PRINCESS CELESTIA, ARE YOU SAYING THERE'S ***ANOTHER*** LIBRARY?
NOT A LIBRARY, SUNBURST, BUT A STUDY. I HAVE ALWAYS BEEN A BIT RETICENT TO DISTURB MY FORMER MENTOR'S THINGS, BUT IT SOUNDS AS IF IT MIGHT AID YOU IN YOUR RESEARCH.
WAIT! ARE YOU SAYING THAT THIS STUDY BELONGED TO...
STARSWIRL THE BEARDED.
YOUR RESEARCH INTO THE HISTORY OF EQUESTRIA... I KNOW STARSWIRL DID A GREAT DEAL OF RESEARCH INTO THIS HIMSELF. BUT THOSE BOOKS DO NOT SEEM TO BE IN THE LIBRARY.
ASSUMING WE CAN FIND THE CORRECT—
CLICK
—WELL, THERE WE ARE.
-GASP-

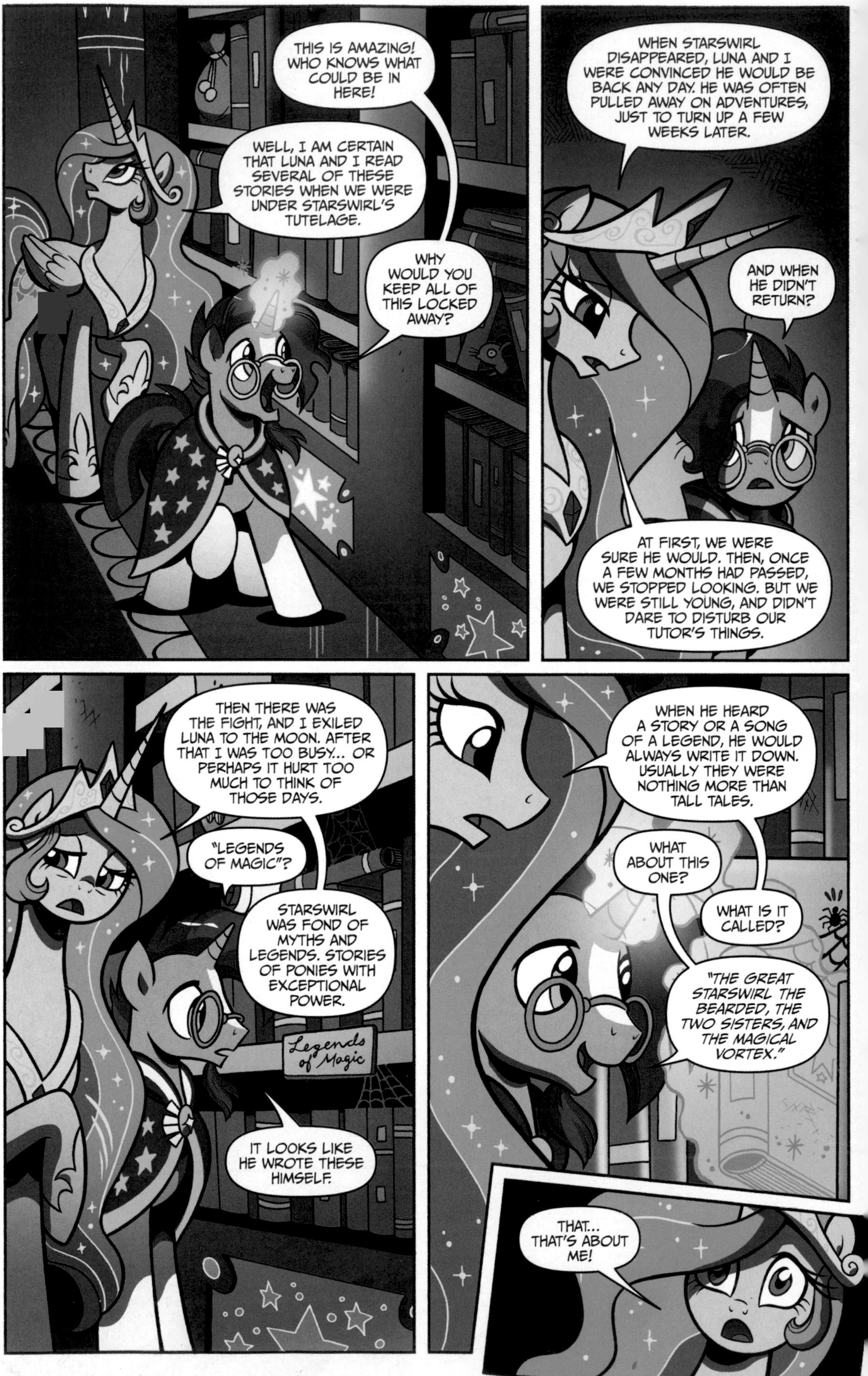
THIS IS AMAZING! WHO KNOWS WHAT COULD BE IN HERE!
WELL, I AM CERTAIN THAT LUNA AND I READ SEVERAL OF THESE STORIES WHEN WE WERE UNDER STARSWIRL'S TUTELAGE.
WHY WOULD YOU KEEP ALL OF THIS LOCKED AWAY?
WHEN STARSWIRL DISAPPEARED, LUNA AND I WERE CONVINCED HE WOULD BE BACK ANY DAY. HE WAS OFTEN PULLED AWAY ON ADVENTURES, JUST TO TURN UP A FEW WEEKS LATER.
AND WHEN HE DIDN'T RETURN?
AT FIRST, WE WERE SURE HE WOULD. THEN, ONCE A FEW MONTHS HAD PASSED, WE STOPPED LOOKING. BUT WE WERE STILL YOUNG, AND DIDN'T DARE TO DISTURB OUR TUTOR'S THINGS.
THEN THERE WAS THE FIGHT, AND I EXILED LUNA TO THE MOON. AFTER THAT I WAS TOO BUSY... OR PERHAPS IT HURT TOO MUCH TO THINK OF THOSE DAYS.
"LEGENDS OF MAGIC"?
STARSWIRL WAS FOND OF MYTHS AND LEGENDS. STORIES OF PONIES WITH EXCEPTIONAL POWER.
Legends of Magic
IT LOOKS LIKE HE WROTE THESE HIMSELF.
WHEN HE HEARD A STORY OR A SONG OF A LEGEND, HE WOULD ALWAYS WRITE IT DOWN. USUALLY THEY WERE NOTHING MORE THAN TALL TALES.
WHAT ABOUT THIS ONE?
WHAT IS IT CALLED?
"THE GREAT STARSWIRL THE BEARDED, THE TWO SISTERS, AND THE MAGICAL VORTEX."
THAT... THAT'S ABOUT ME!

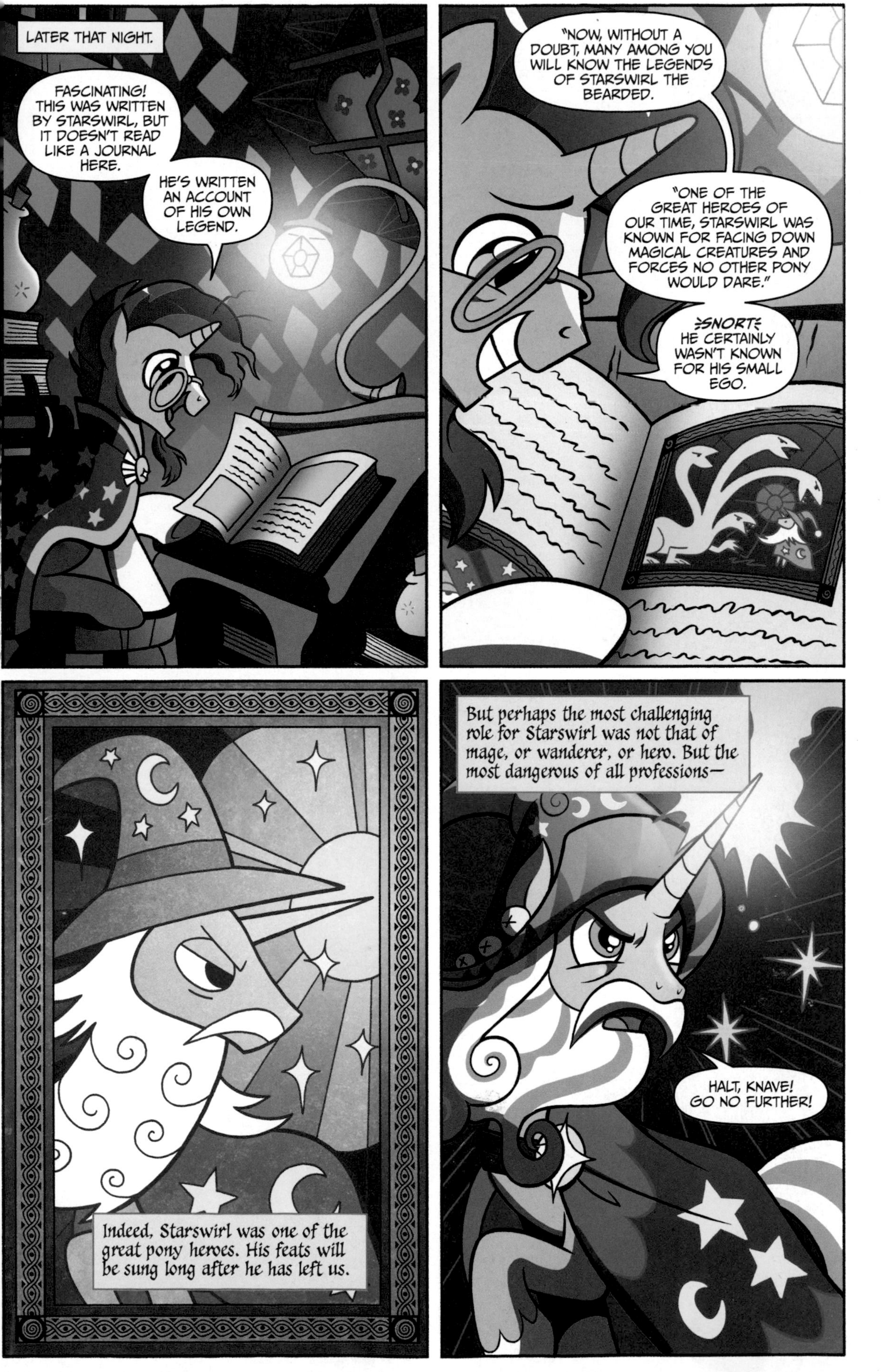
LATER THAT NIGHT.
FASCINATING! THIS WAS WRITTEN BY STARSWIRL, BUT IT DOESN'T READ LIKE A JOURNAL HERE.
HE'S WRITTEN AN ACCOUNT OF HIS OWN LEGEND.
"NOW, WITHOUT A DOUBT, MANY AMONG YOU WILL KNOW THE LEGENDS OF STARSWIRL THE BEARDED.
"ONE OF THE GREAT HEROES OF OUR TIME, STARSWIRL WAS KNOWN FOR FACING DOWN MAGICAL CREATURES AND FORCES NO OTHER PONY WOULD DARE."
SNORT HE CERTAINLY WASN'T KNOWN FOR HIS SMALL EGO.
Indeed, Starswirl was one of the great pony heroes. His feats will be sung long after he has left us.
But perhaps the most challenging role for Starswirl was not that of mage, or wanderer, or hero. But the most dangerous of all professions—
HALT, KNAVE! GO NO FURTHER!

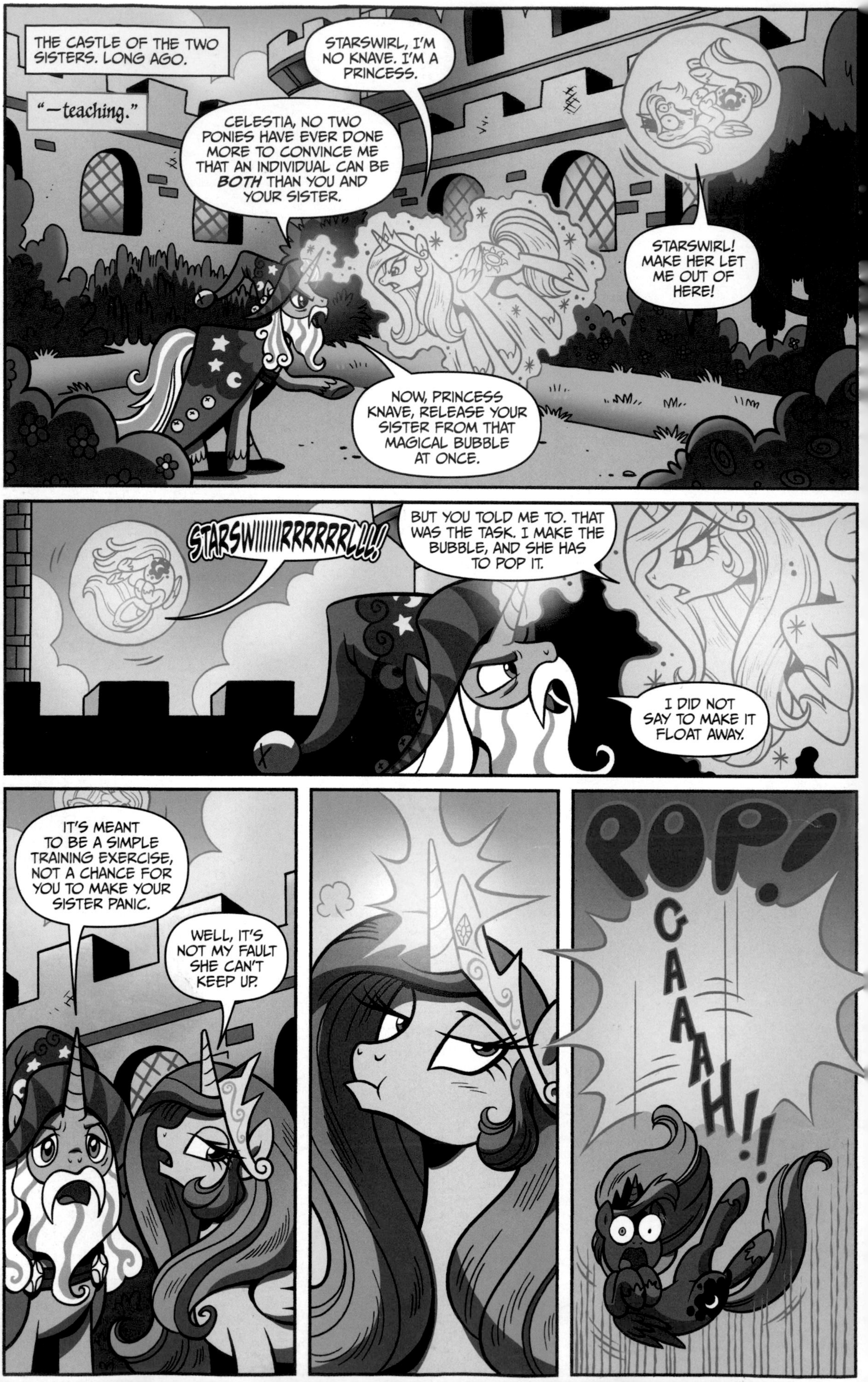
THE CASTLE OF THE TWO SISTERS. LONG AGO.
"—teaching."
CELESTIA, NO TWO PONIES HAVE EVER DONE MORE TO CONVINCE ME THAT AN INDIVIDUAL CAN BE *BOTH* THAN YOU AND YOUR SISTER.
STARSWIRL, I'M NO KNAVE. I'M A PRINCESS.
STARSWIRL! MAKE HER LET ME OUT OF HERE!
NOW, PRINCESS KNAVE, RELEASE YOUR SISTER FROM THAT MAGICAL BUBBLE AT ONCE.
STARSWIIIIIIRRRRRRLLL!
BUT YOU TOLD ME TO. THAT WAS THE TASK. I MAKE THE BUBBLE, AND SHE HAS TO POP IT.
I DID NOT SAY TO MAKE IT FLOAT AWAY.
IT'S MEANT TO BE A SIMPLE TRAINING EXERCISE, NOT A CHANCE FOR YOU TO MAKE YOUR SISTER PANIC.
WELL, IT'S NOT MY FAULT SHE CAN'T KEEP UP.
POP!
GAAAH!!

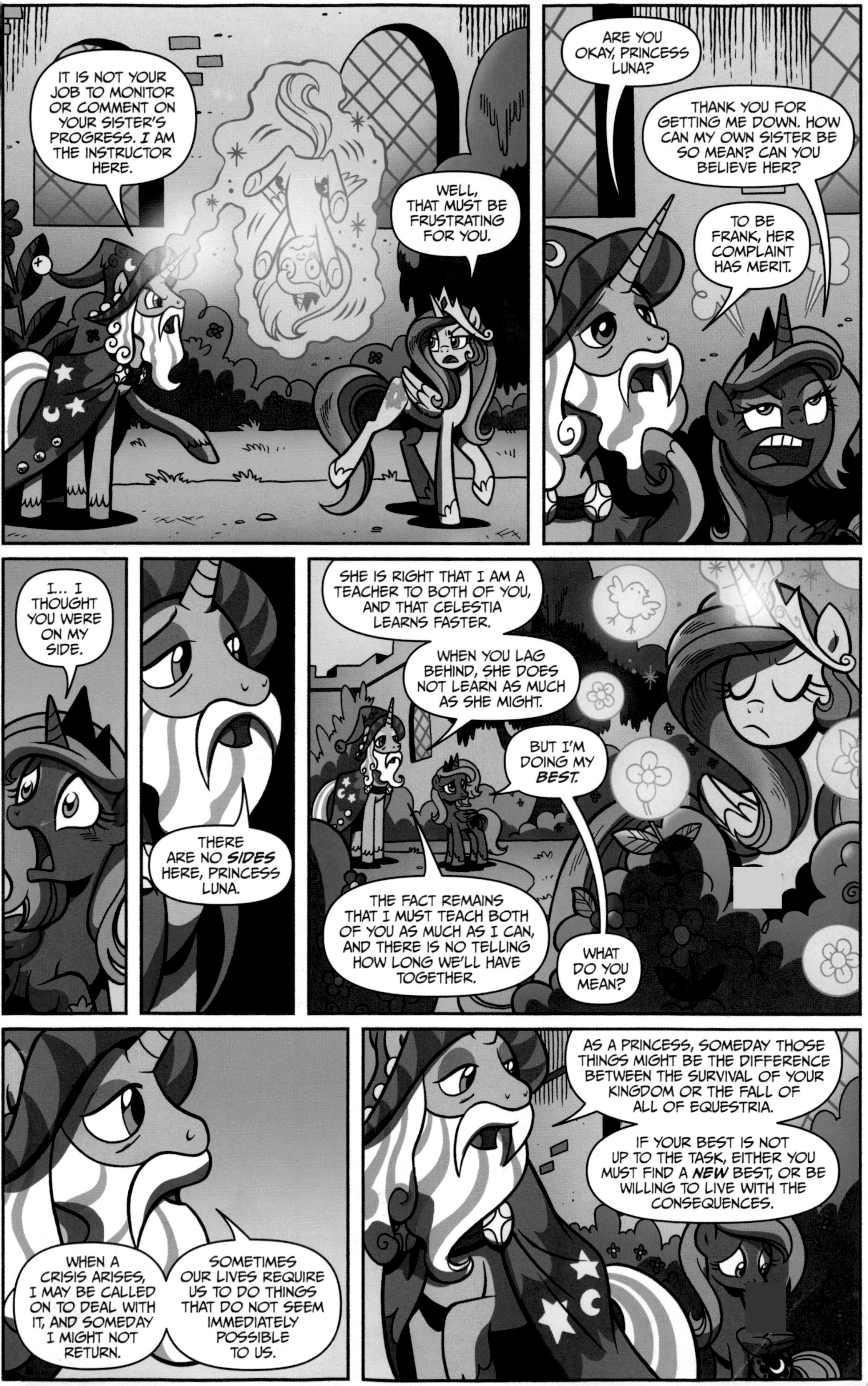
IT IS NOT YOUR JOB TO MONITOR OR COMMENT ON YOUR SISTER'S PROGRESS. *I* AM THE INSTRUCTOR HERE.
WELL, THAT MUST BE FRUSTRATING FOR YOU.
ARE YOU OKAY, PRINCESS LUNA?
THANK YOU FOR GETTING ME DOWN. HOW CAN MY OWN SISTER BE SO MEAN? CAN YOU BELIEVE HER?
TO BE FRANK, HER COMPLAINT HAS MERIT.
I... I THOUGHT YOU WERE ON MY SIDE.
THERE ARE NO ***SIDES*** HERE, PRINCESS LUNA.
SHE IS RIGHT THAT I AM A TEACHER TO BOTH OF YOU, AND THAT CELESTIA LEARNS FASTER.
WHEN YOU LAG BEHIND, SHE DOES NOT LEARN AS MUCH AS SHE MIGHT.
BUT I'M DOING MY ***BEST.***
THE FACT REMAINS THAT I MUST TEACH BOTH OF YOU AS MUCH AS I CAN, AND THERE IS NO TELLING HOW LONG WE'LL HAVE TOGETHER.
WHAT DO YOU MEAN?
WHEN A CRISIS ARISES, I MAY BE CALLED ON TO DEAL WITH IT, AND SOMEDAY I MIGHT NOT RETURN.
SOMETIMES OUR LIVES REQUIRE US TO DO THINGS THAT DO NOT SEEM IMMEDIATELY POSSIBLE TO US.
AS A PRINCESS, SOMEDAY THOSE THINGS MIGHT BE THE DIFFERENCE BETWEEN THE SURVIVAL OF YOUR KINGDOM OR THE FALL OF ALL OF EQUESTRIA.
IF YOUR BEST IS NOT UP TO THE TASK, EITHER YOU MUST FIND A ***NEW*** BEST, OR BE WILLING TO LIVE WITH THE CONSEQUENCES.

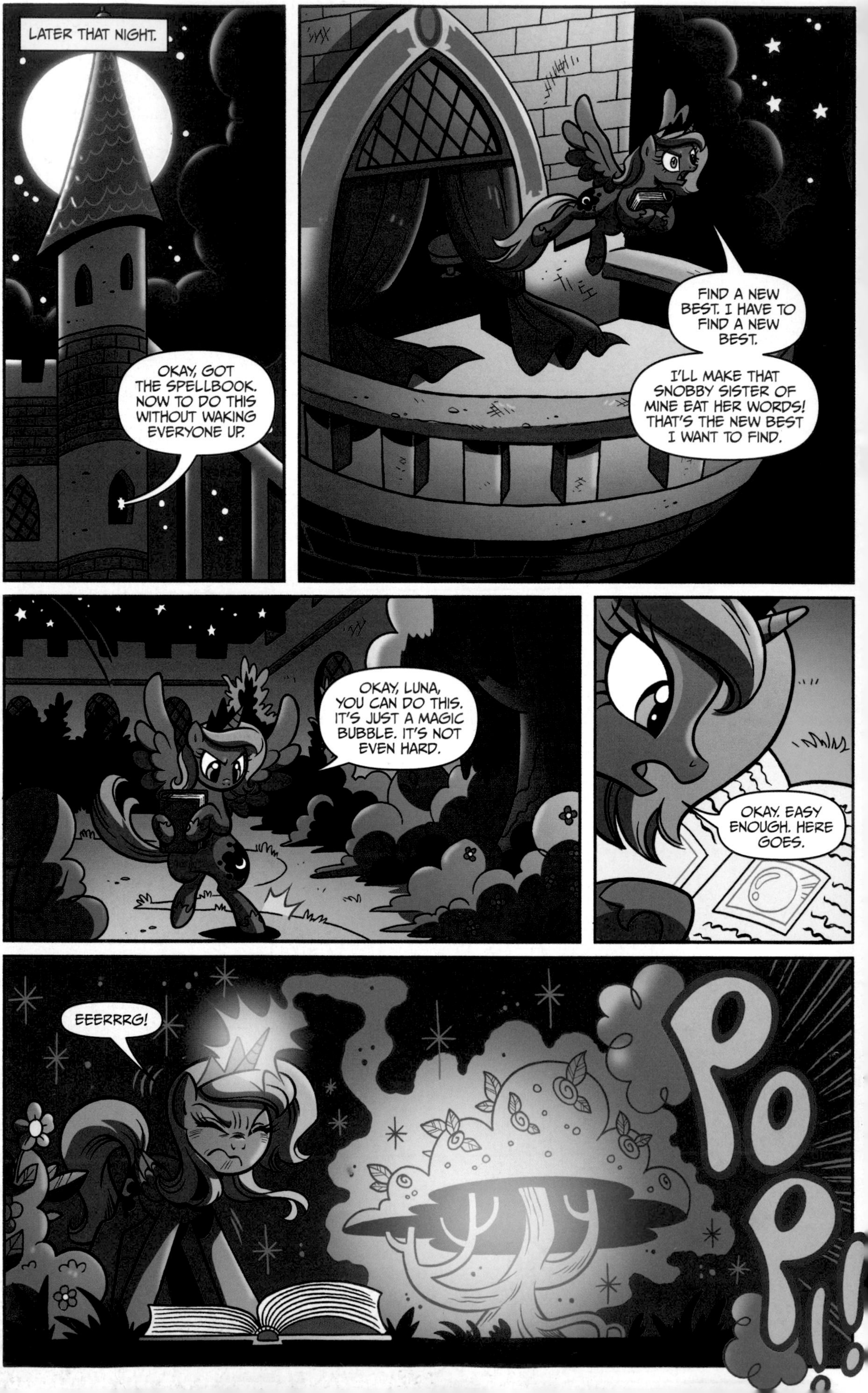
LATER THAT NIGHT.
OKAY, GOT THE SPELLBOOK. NOW TO DO THIS WITHOUT WAKING EVERYONE UP.
FIND A NEW BEST. I HAVE TO FIND A NEW BEST.
I'LL MAKE THAT SNOBBY SISTER OF MINE EAT HER WORDS! THAT'S THE NEW BEST I WANT TO FIND.
OKAY, LUNA, YOU CAN DO THIS. IT'S JUST A MAGIC BUBBLE. IT'S NOT EVEN HARD.
OKAY. EASY ENOUGH. HERE GOES.
EEERRRG!
POP!!

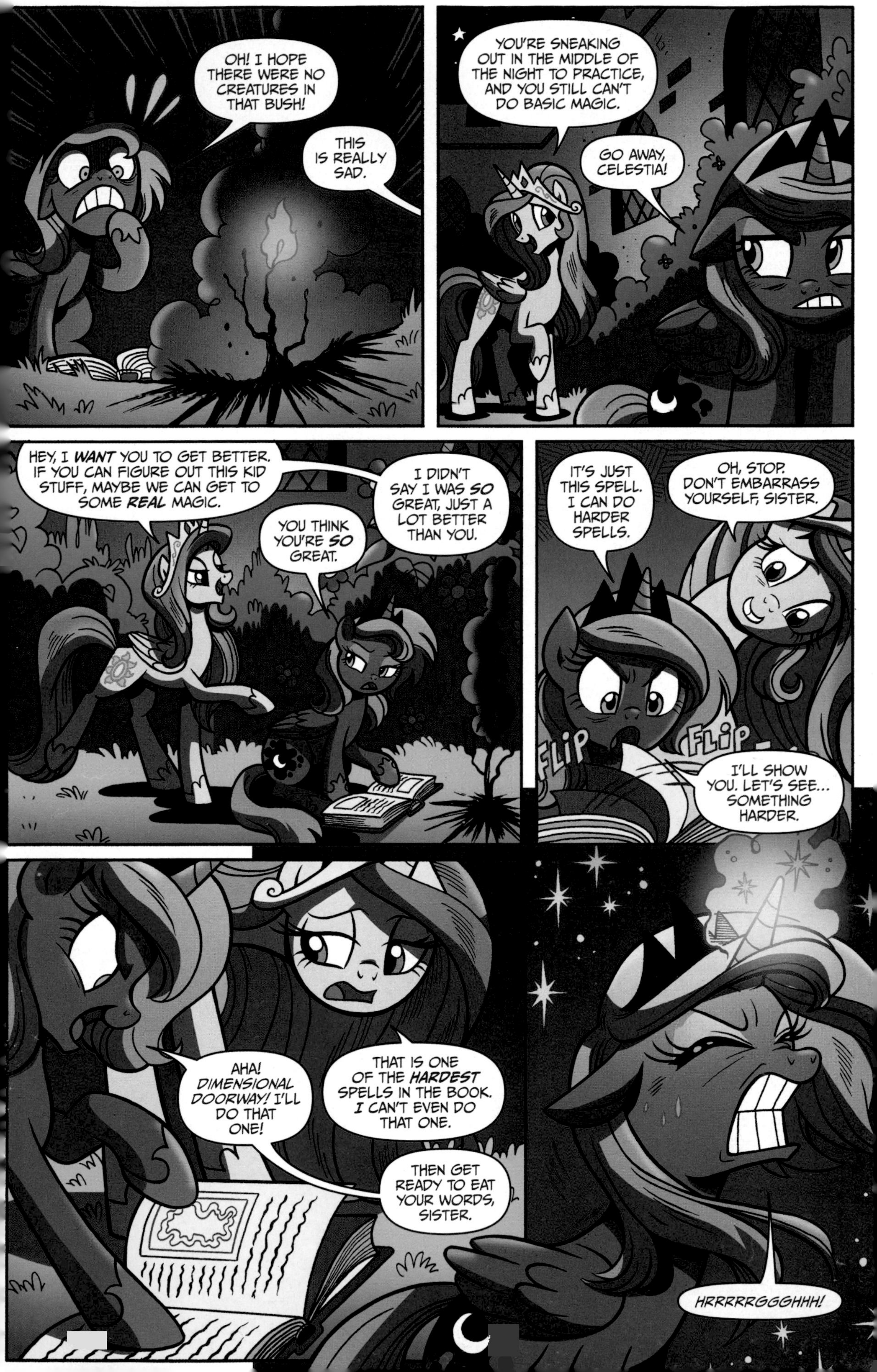
OH! I HOPE THERE WERE NO CREATURES IN THAT BUSH!
THIS IS REALLY SAD.
YOU'RE SNEAKING OUT IN THE MIDDLE OF THE NIGHT TO PRACTICE, AND YOU STILL CAN'T DO BASIC MAGIC.
GO AWAY, CELESTIA!
HEY, I WANT YOU TO GET BETTER. IF YOU CAN FIGURE OUT THIS KID STUFF, MAYBE WE CAN GET TO SOME REAL MAGIC.
YOU THINK YOU'RE SO GREAT.
I DIDN'T SAY I WAS SO GREAT, JUST A LOT BETTER THAN YOU.
IT'S JUST THIS SPELL. I CAN DO HARDER SPELLS.
OH, STOP. DON'T EMBARRASS YOURSELF, SISTER.
FLIP
FLIP
I'LL SHOW YOU. LET'S SEE... SOMETHING HARDER.
AHA! DIMENSIONAL DOORWAY! I'LL DO THAT ONE!
THAT IS ONE OF THE HARDEST SPELLS IN THE BOOK. I CAN'T EVEN DO THAT ONE.
THEN GET READY TO EAT YOUR WORDS, SISTER.
HRRRRRGGGHHH!

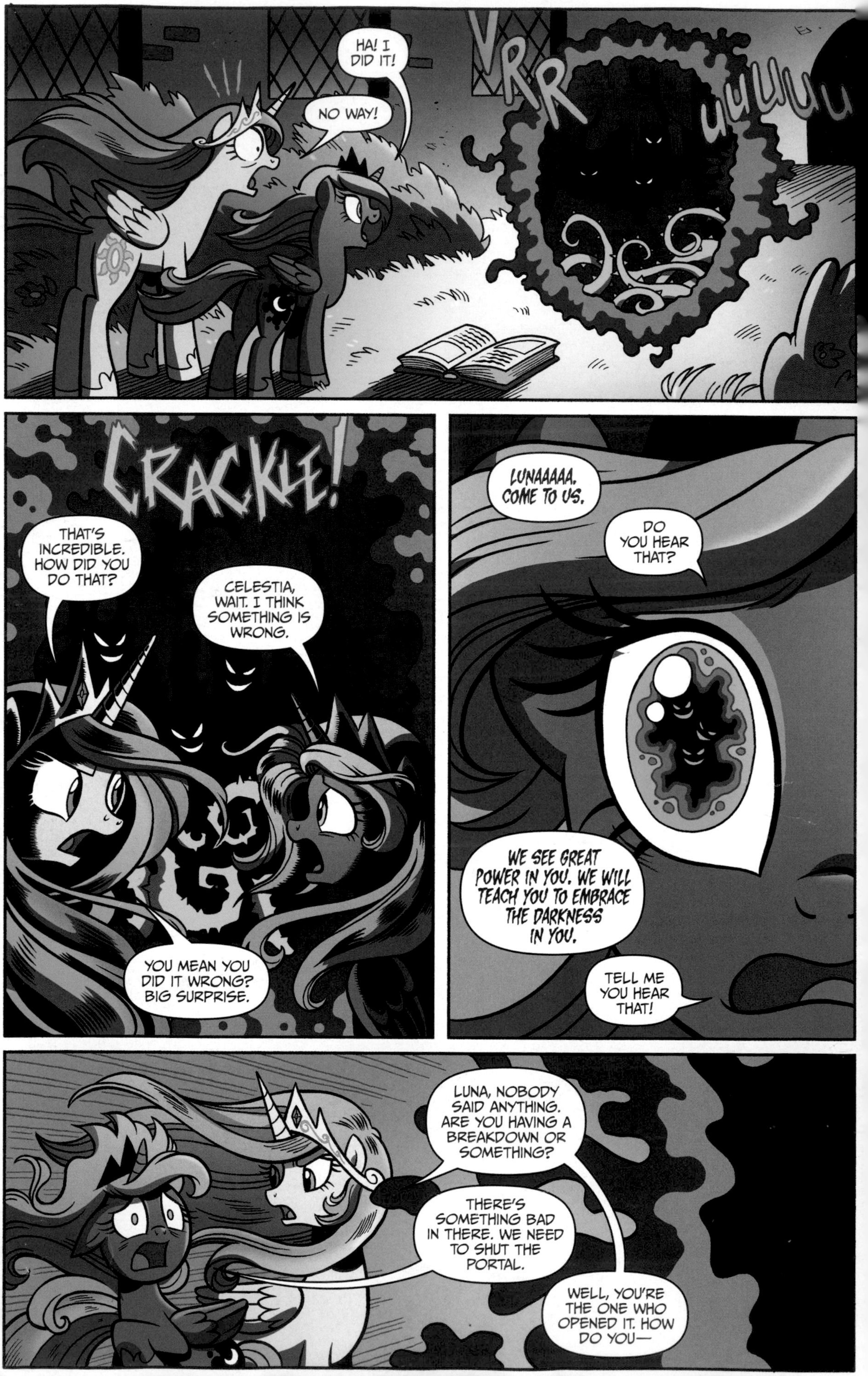
NO WAY!
HA! I DID IT!
VRRR
UUUUU
CRACKLE!
THAT'S INCREDIBLE. HOW DID YOU DO THAT?
CELESTIA, WAIT. I THINK SOMETHING IS WRONG.
YOU MEAN YOU DID IT WRONG? BIG SURPRISE.
LUNAAAAA. COME TO US.
DO YOU HEAR THAT?
WE SEE GREAT POWER IN YOU. WE WILL TEACH YOU TO EMBRACE THE DARKNESS IN YOU.
TELL ME YOU HEAR THAT!
LUNA, NOBODY SAID ANYTHING. ARE YOU HAVING A BREAKDOWN OR SOMETHING?
THERE'S SOMETHING BAD IN THERE. WE NEED TO SHUT THE PORTAL.
WELL, YOU'RE THE ONE WHO OPENED IT. HOW DO YOU—

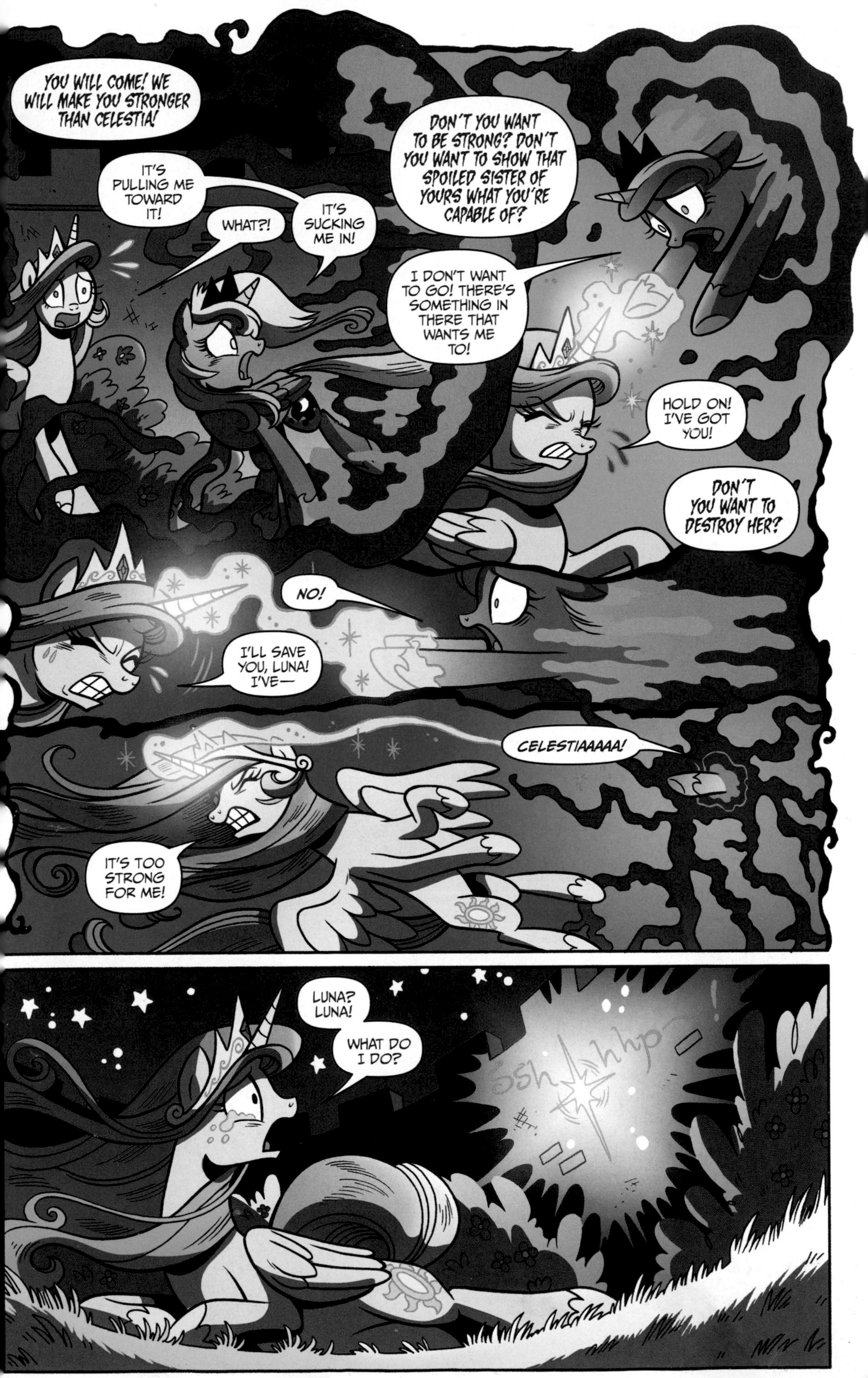

YOU WILL COME! WE WILL MAKE YOU STRONGER THAN CELESTIA!
IT'S PULLING ME TOWARD IT!
WHAT?!
IT'S SUCKING ME IN!
DON'T YOU WANT TO BE STRONG? DON'T YOU WANT TO SHOW THAT SPOILED SISTER OF YOURS WHAT YOU'RE CAPABLE OF?
I DON'T WANT TO GO! THERE'S SOMETHING IN THERE THAT WANTS ME TO!
HOLD ON! I'VE GOT YOU!
DON'T YOU WANT TO DESTROY HER?
NO!
I'LL SAVE YOU, LUNA! I'VE—
CELESTIAAAAA!
IT'S TOO STRONG FOR ME!
LUNA? LUNA!
WHAT DO I DO?
SShhhp

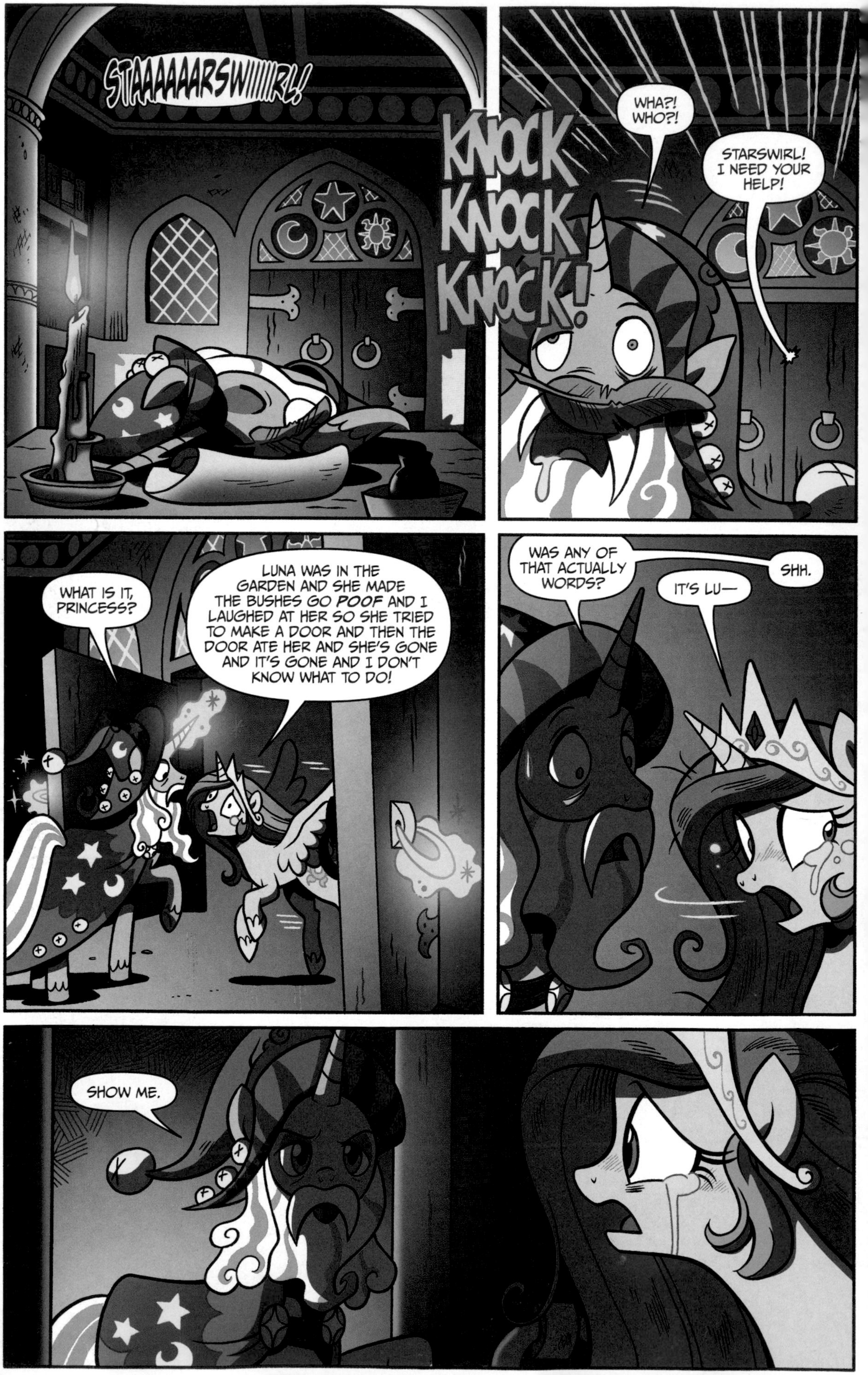
STAAAAAARSWIIIIIIRL!
KNOCK KNOCK KNOCK!
WHA?! WHO?!
STARSWIRL! I NEED YOUR HELP!
WHAT IS IT, PRINCESS?
LUNA WAS IN THE GARDEN AND SHE MADE THE BUSHES GO POOF AND I LAUGHED AT HER SO SHE TRIED TO MAKE A DOOR AND THEN THE DOOR ATE HER AND SHE'S GONE AND IT'S GONE AND I DON'T KNOW WHAT TO DO!
WAS ANY OF THAT ACTUALLY WORDS?
IT'S LU—
SHH.
SHOW ME.

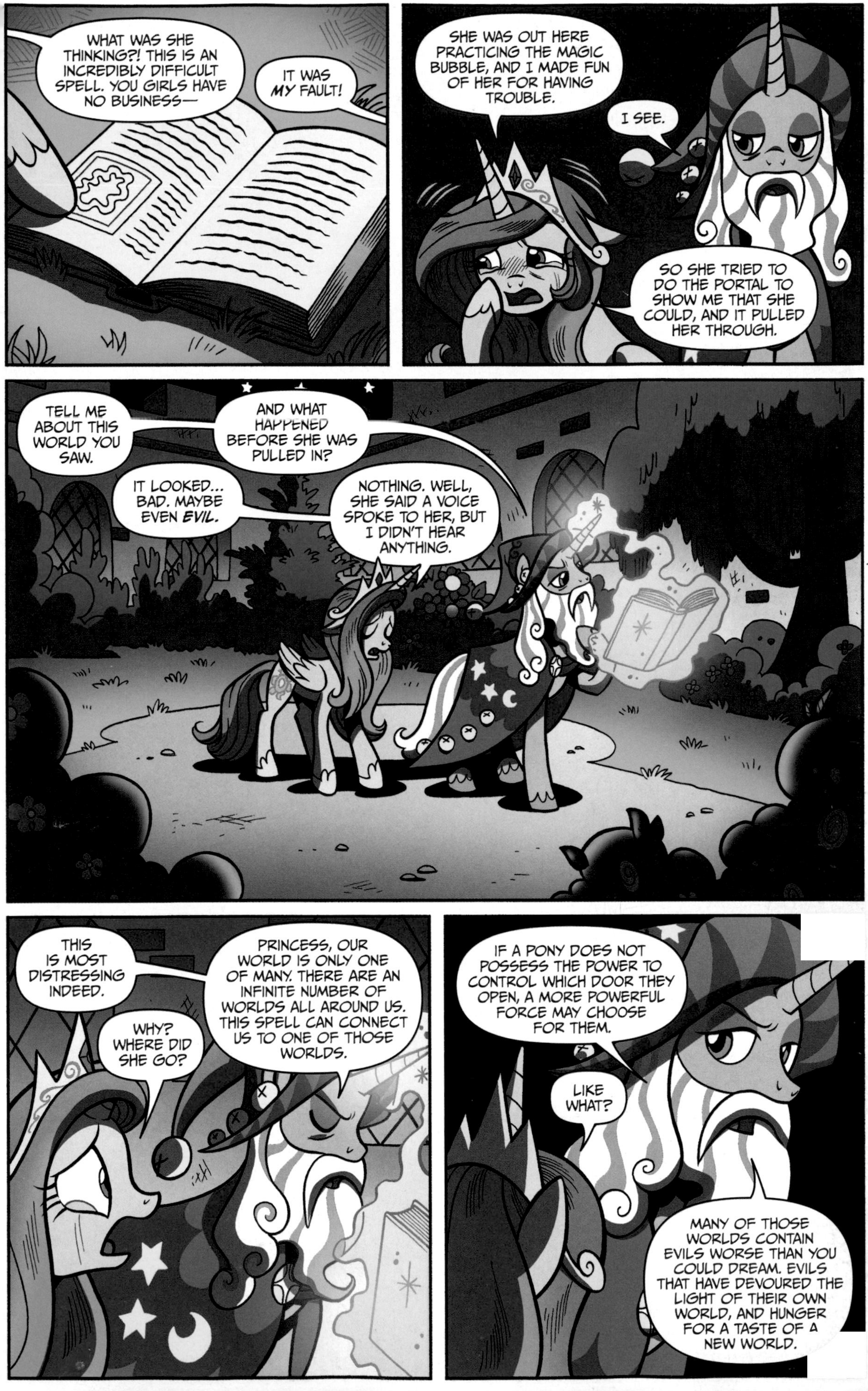
WHAT WAS SHE THINKING?! THIS IS AN INCREDIBLY DIFFICULT SPELL. YOU GIRLS HAVE NO BUSINESS—
IT WAS *MY* FAULT!
SHE WAS OUT HERE PRACTICING THE MAGIC BUBBLE, AND I MADE FUN OF HER FOR HAVING TROUBLE.
I SEE.
SO SHE TRIED TO DO THE PORTAL TO SHOW ME THAT SHE COULD, AND IT PULLED HER THROUGH.
TELL ME ABOUT THIS WORLD YOU SAW.
AND WHAT HAPPENED BEFORE SHE WAS PULLED IN?
IT LOOKED... BAD. MAYBE EVEN *EVIL.*
NOTHING. WELL, SHE SAID A VOICE SPOKE TO HER, BUT I DIDN'T HEAR ANYTHING.
THIS IS MOST DISTRESSING INDEED.
WHY? WHERE DID SHE GO?
PRINCESS, OUR WORLD IS ONLY ONE OF MANY. THERE ARE AN INFINITE NUMBER OF WORLDS ALL AROUND US. THIS SPELL CAN CONNECT US TO ONE OF THOSE WORLDS.
IF A PONY DOES NOT POSSESS THE POWER TO CONTROL WHICH DOOR THEY OPEN, A MORE POWERFUL FORCE MAY CHOOSE FOR THEM.
LIKE WHAT?
MANY OF THOSE WORLDS CONTAIN EVILS WORSE THAN YOU COULD DREAM. EVILS THAT HAVE DEVOURED THE LIGHT OF THEIR OWN WORLD, AND HUNGER FOR A TASTE OF A NEW WORLD.

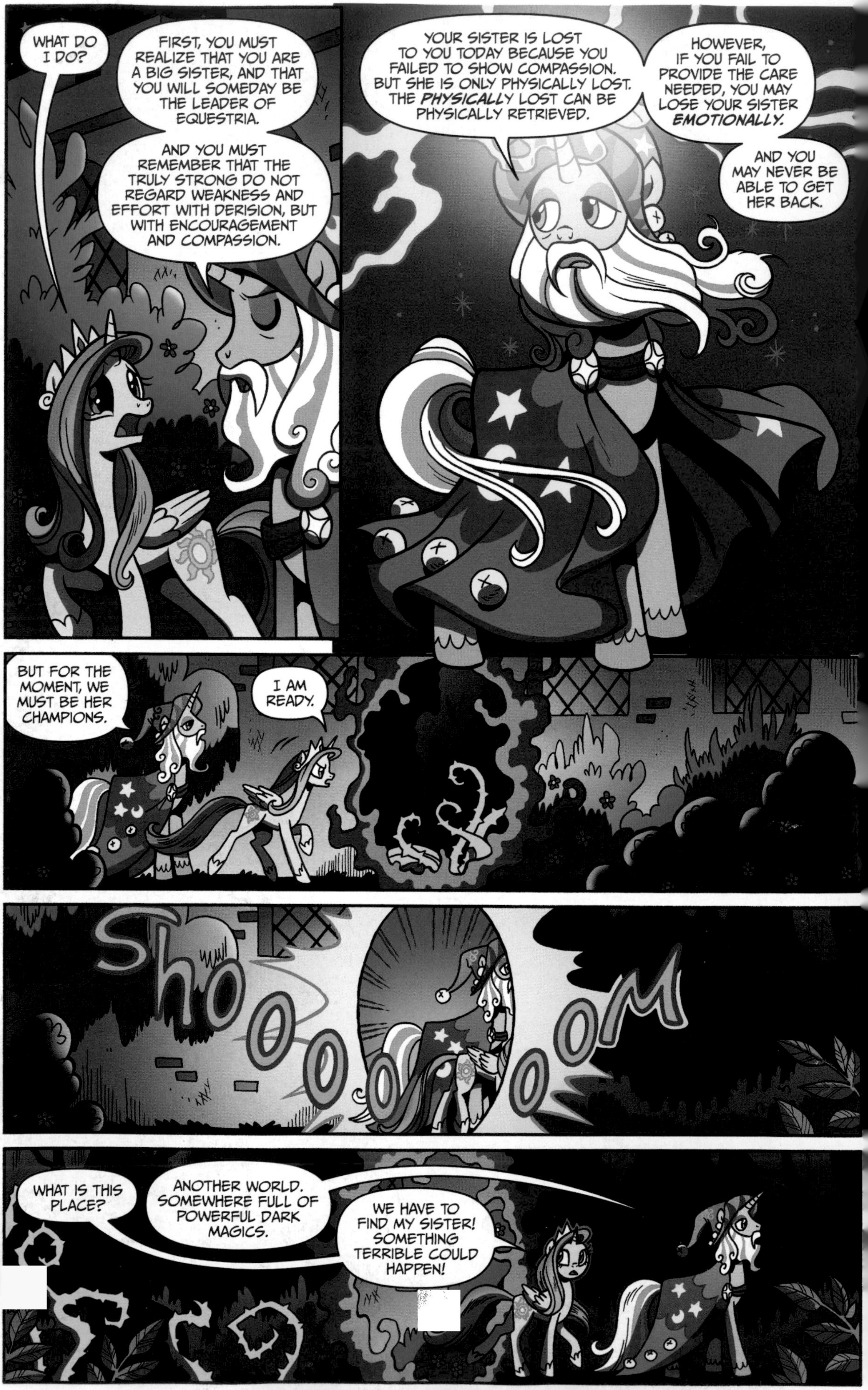
WHAT DO I DO?
FIRST, YOU MUST REALIZE THAT YOU ARE A BIG SISTER, AND THAT YOU WILL SOMEDAY BE THE LEADER OF EQUESTRIA.
AND YOU MUST REMEMBER THAT THE TRULY STRONG DO NOT REGARD WEAKNESS AND EFFORT WITH DERISION, BUT WITH ENCOURAGEMENT AND COMPASSION.
YOUR SISTER IS LOST TO YOU TODAY BECAUSE YOU FAILED TO SHOW COMPASSION. BUT SHE IS ONLY PHYSICALLY LOST. THE PHYSICALLY LOST CAN BE PHYSICALLY RETRIEVED.
HOWEVER, IF YOU FAIL TO PROVIDE THE CARE NEEDED, YOU MAY LOSE YOUR SISTER EMOTIONALLY.
AND YOU MAY NEVER BE ABLE TO GET HER BACK.
BUT FOR THE MOMENT, WE MUST BE HER CHAMPIONS.
I AM READY.
SHOOOOOOOOM
WHAT IS THIS PLACE?
ANOTHER WORLD. SOMEWHERE FULL OF POWERFUL DARK MAGICS.
WE HAVE TO FIND MY SISTER! SOMETHING TERRIBLE COULD HAPPEN!

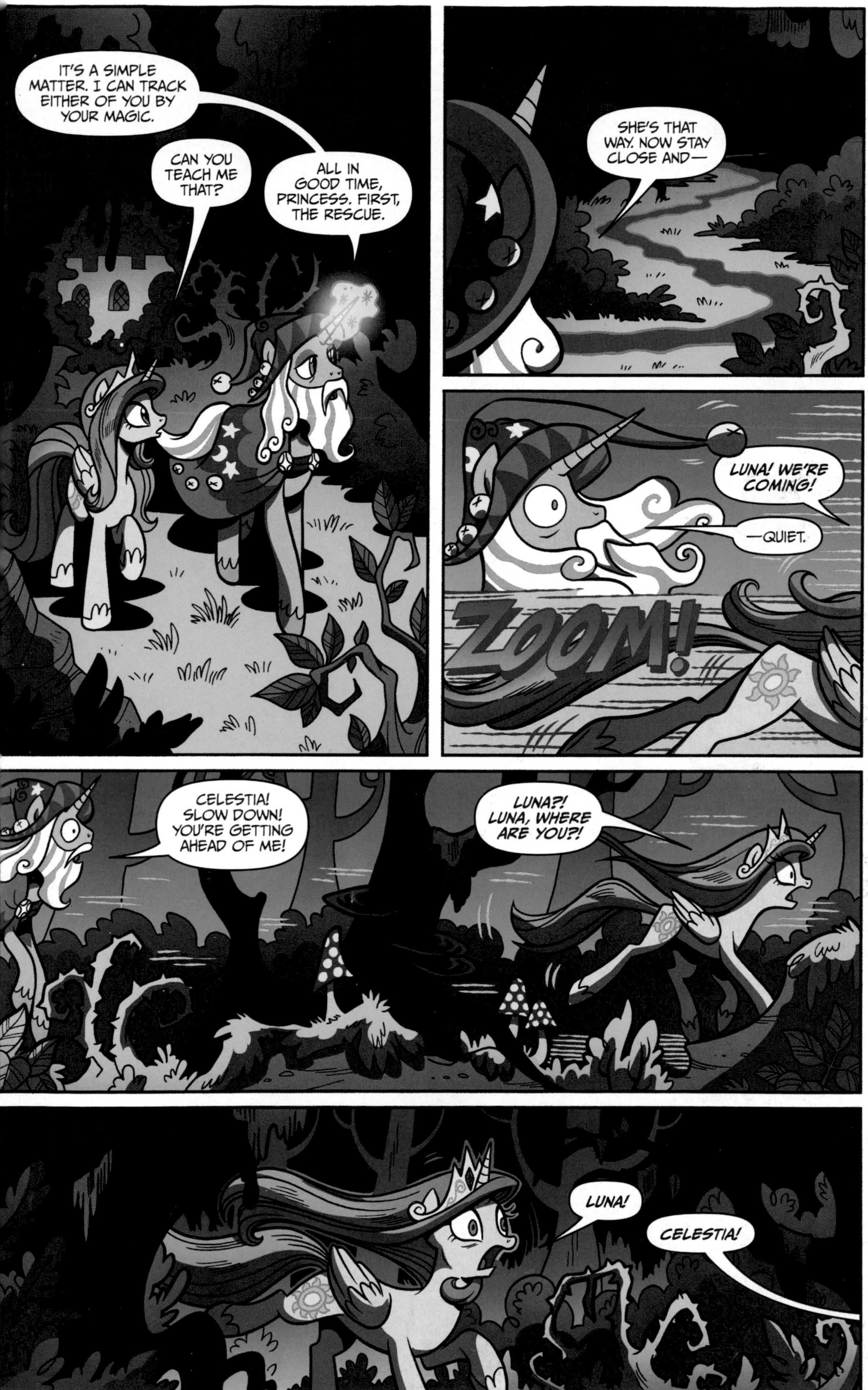
IT'S A SIMPLE MATTER. I CAN TRACK EITHER OF YOU BY YOUR MAGIC.
CAN YOU TEACH ME THAT?
ALL IN GOOD TIME, PRINCESS. FIRST, THE RESCUE.
SHE'S THAT WAY. NOW STAY CLOSE AND—
LUNA! WE'RE COMING!
—QUIET.
ZOOM!
CELESTIA! SLOW DOWN! YOU'RE GETTING AHEAD OF ME!
LUNA?! LUNA, WHERE ARE YOU?!
LUNA!
CELESTIA!

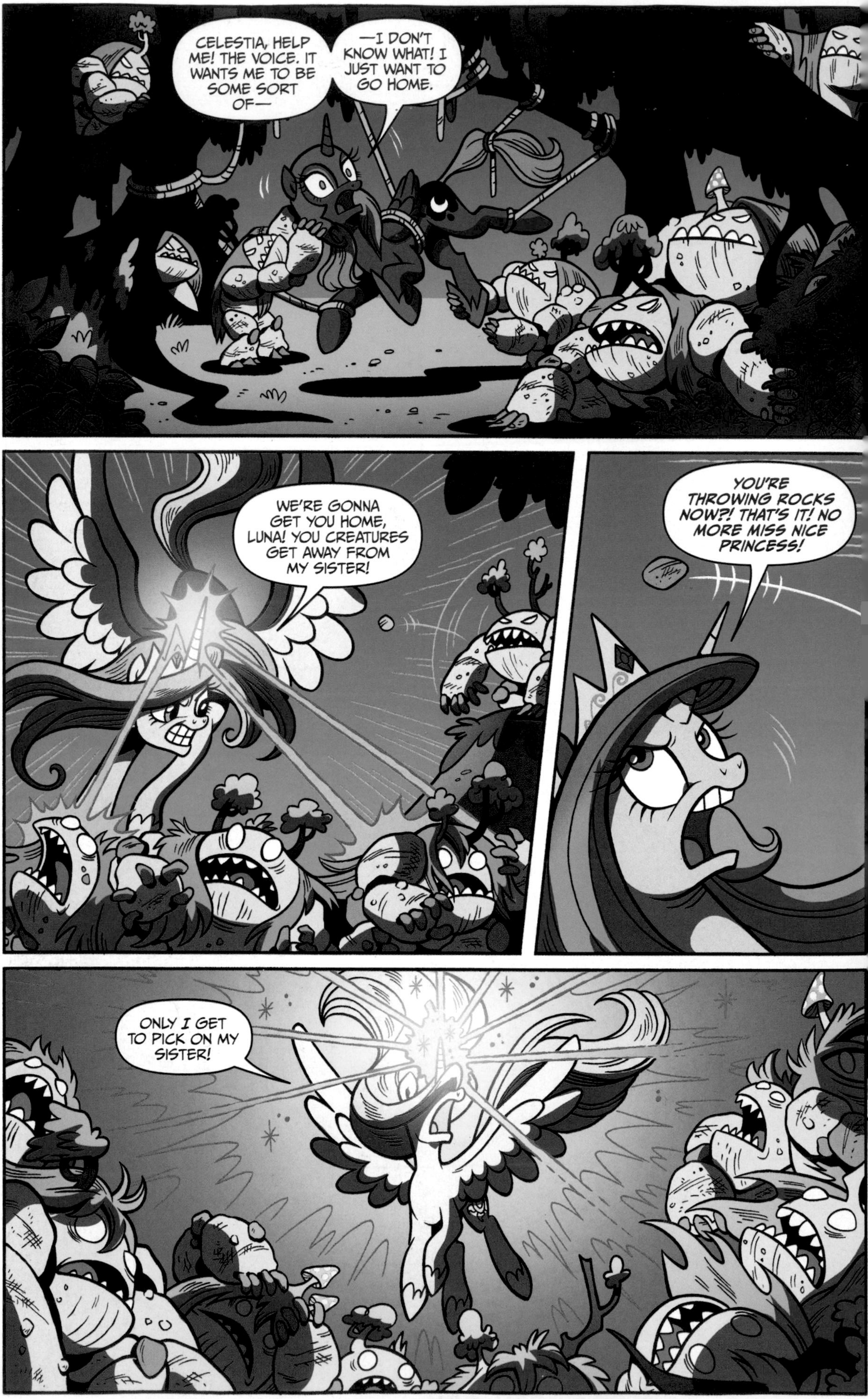
CELESTIA, HELP ME! THE VOICE. IT WANTS ME TO BE SOME SORT OF—
—I DON'T KNOW WHAT! I JUST WANT TO GO HOME.
WE'RE GONNA GET YOU HOME, LUNA! YOU CREATURES GET AWAY FROM MY SISTER!
YOU'RE THROWING ROCKS NOW?! THAT'S IT! NO MORE MISS NICE PRINCESS!
ONLY I GET TO PICK ON MY SISTER!

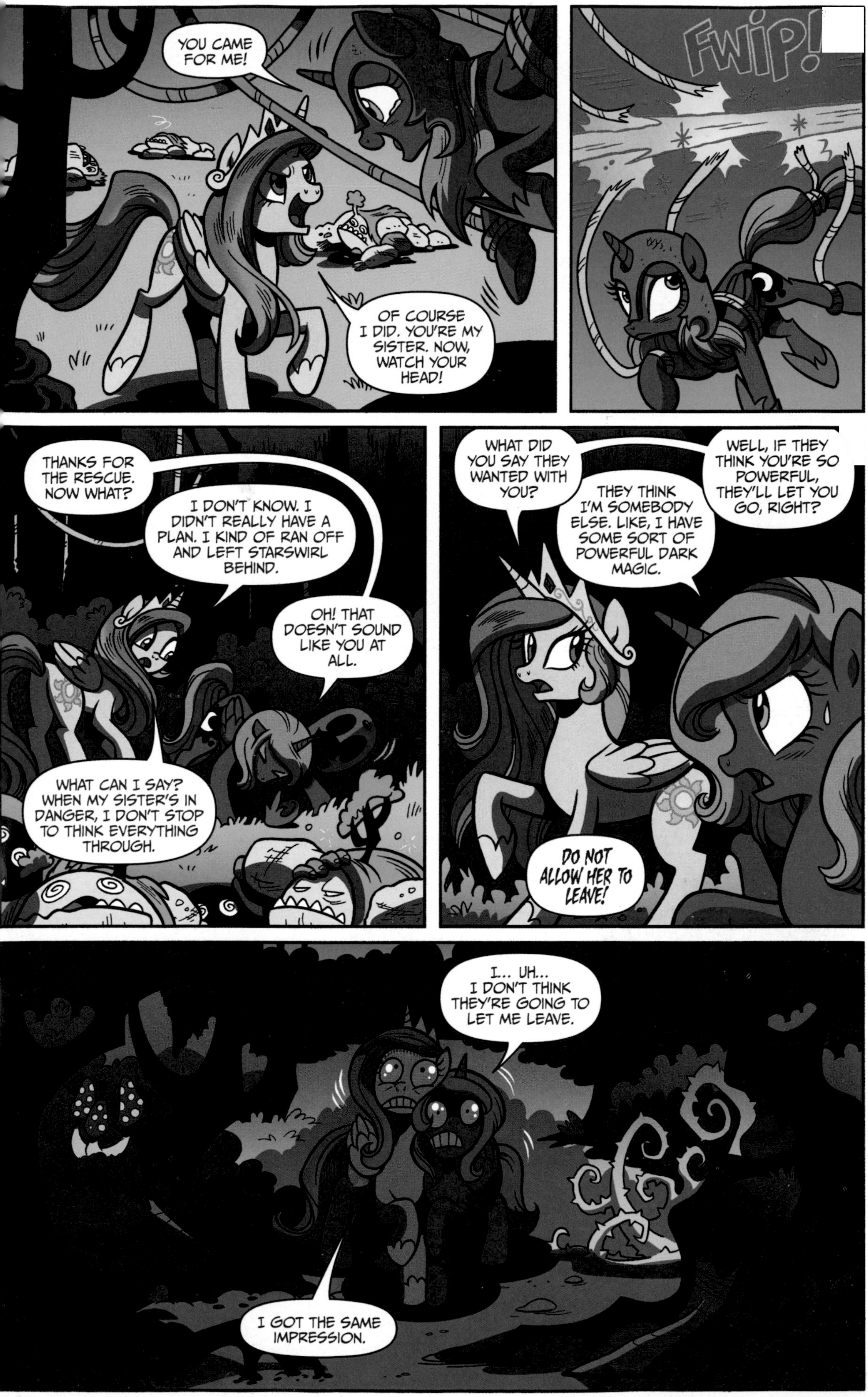
YOU CAME FOR ME!
OF COURSE I DID. YOU'RE MY SISTER. NOW, WATCH YOUR HEAD!
FWIP!
THANKS FOR THE RESCUE. NOW WHAT?
I DON'T KNOW. I DIDN'T REALLY HAVE A PLAN. I KIND OF RAN OFF AND LEFT STARSWIRL BEHIND.
OH! THAT DOESN'T SOUND LIKE YOU AT ALL.
WHAT CAN I SAY? WHEN MY SISTER'S IN DANGER, I DON'T STOP TO THINK EVERYTHING THROUGH.
WHAT DID YOU SAY THEY WANTED WITH YOU?
THEY THINK I'M SOMEBODY ELSE. LIKE, I HAVE SOME SORT OF POWERFUL DARK MAGIC.
WELL, IF THEY THINK YOU'RE SO POWERFUL, THEY'LL LET YOU GO, RIGHT?
DO NOT ALLOW HER TO LEAVE!
I... UH... I DON'T THINK THEY'RE GOING TO LET ME LEAVE.
I GOT THE SAME IMPRESSION.

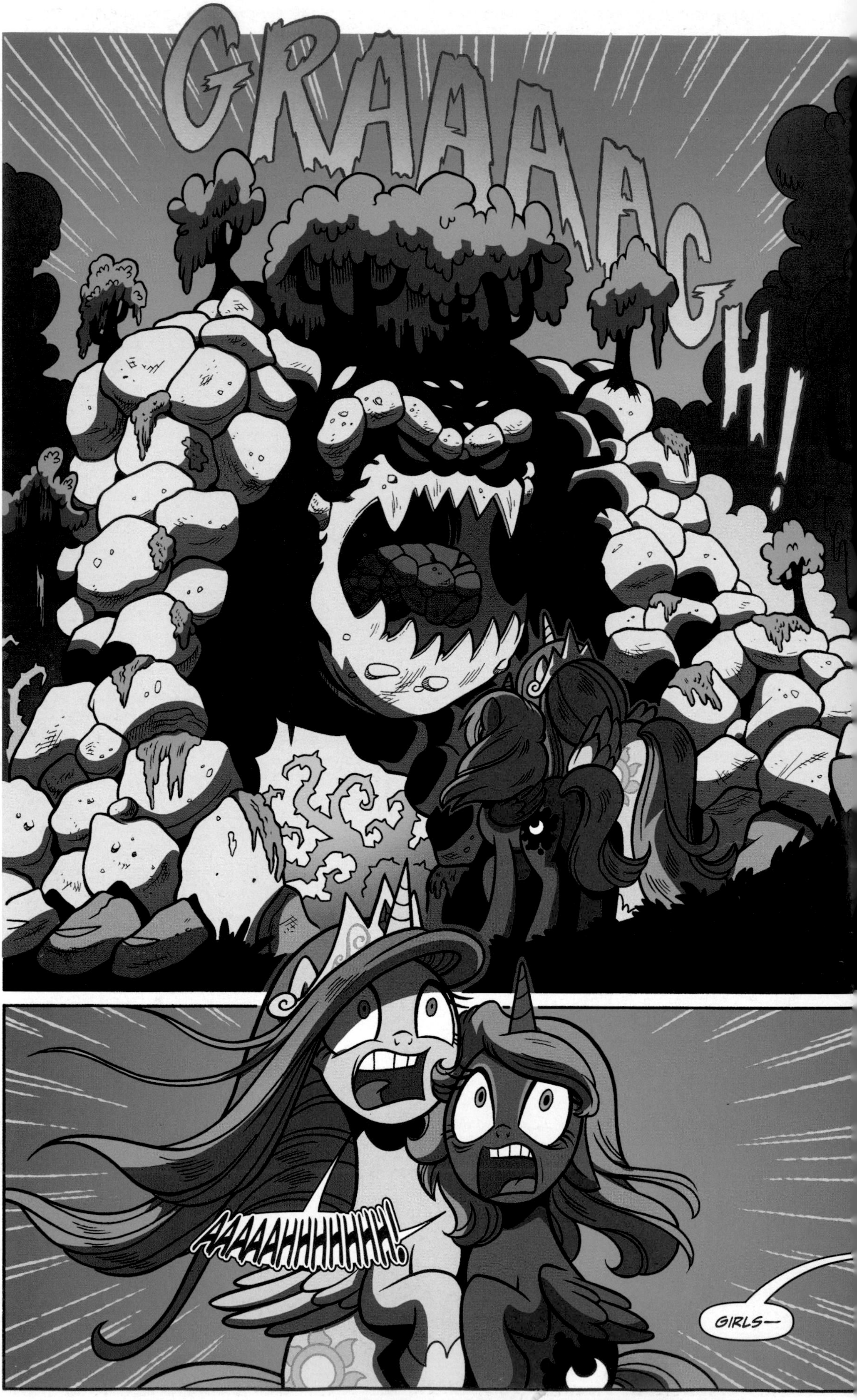
GRAAAAACH!
AAAAAHHHHHHH!
GIRLS—

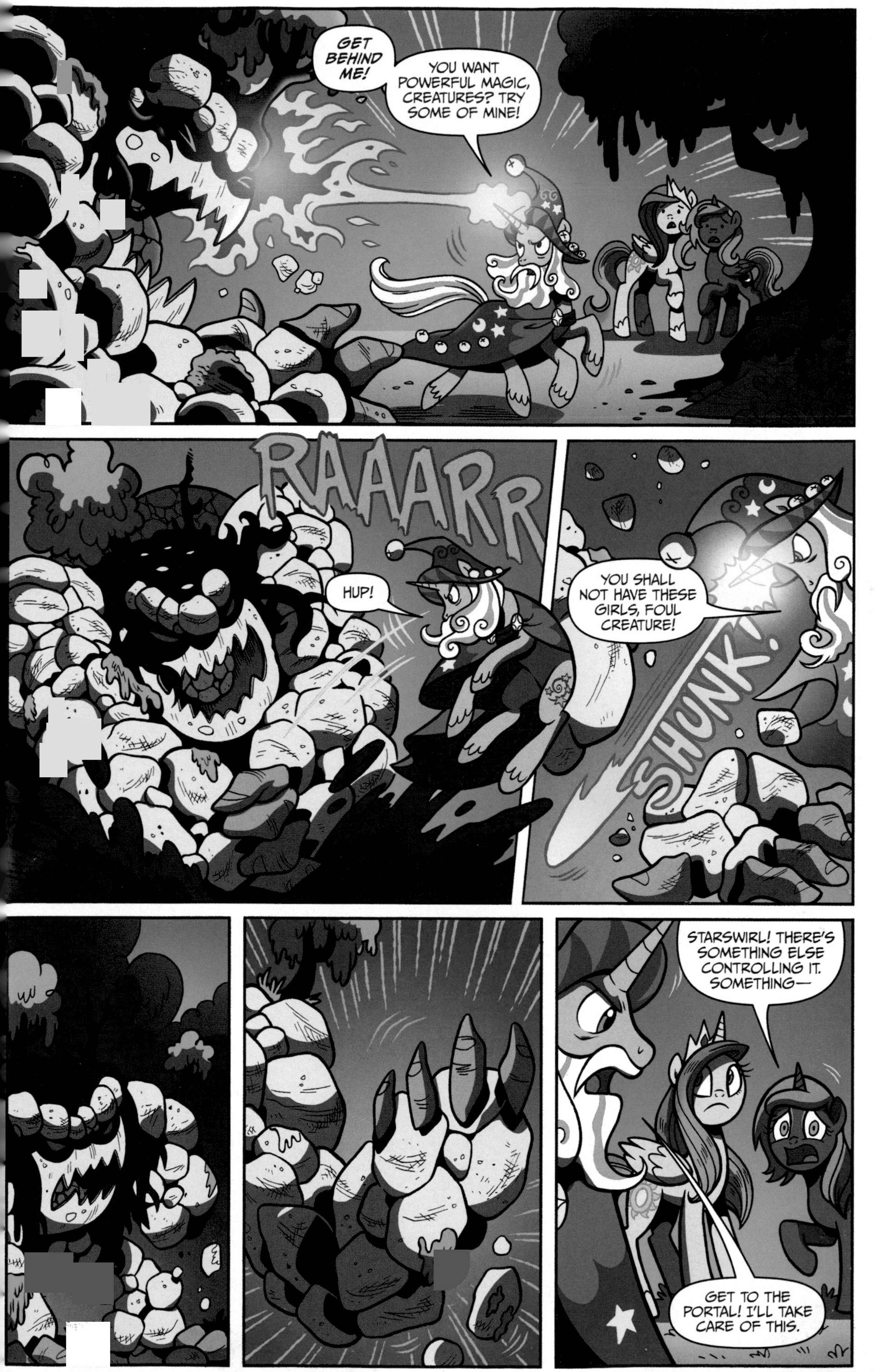
GET BEHIND ME!
YOU WANT POWERFUL MAGIC, CREATURES? TRY SOME OF MINE!
RAAARR
HUP!
YOU SHALL NOT HAVE THESE GIRLS, FOUL CREATURE!
SHUNK!
STARSWIRL! THERE'S SOMETHING ELSE CONTROLLING IT. SOMETHING—
GET TO THE PORTAL! I'LL TAKE CARE OF THIS.

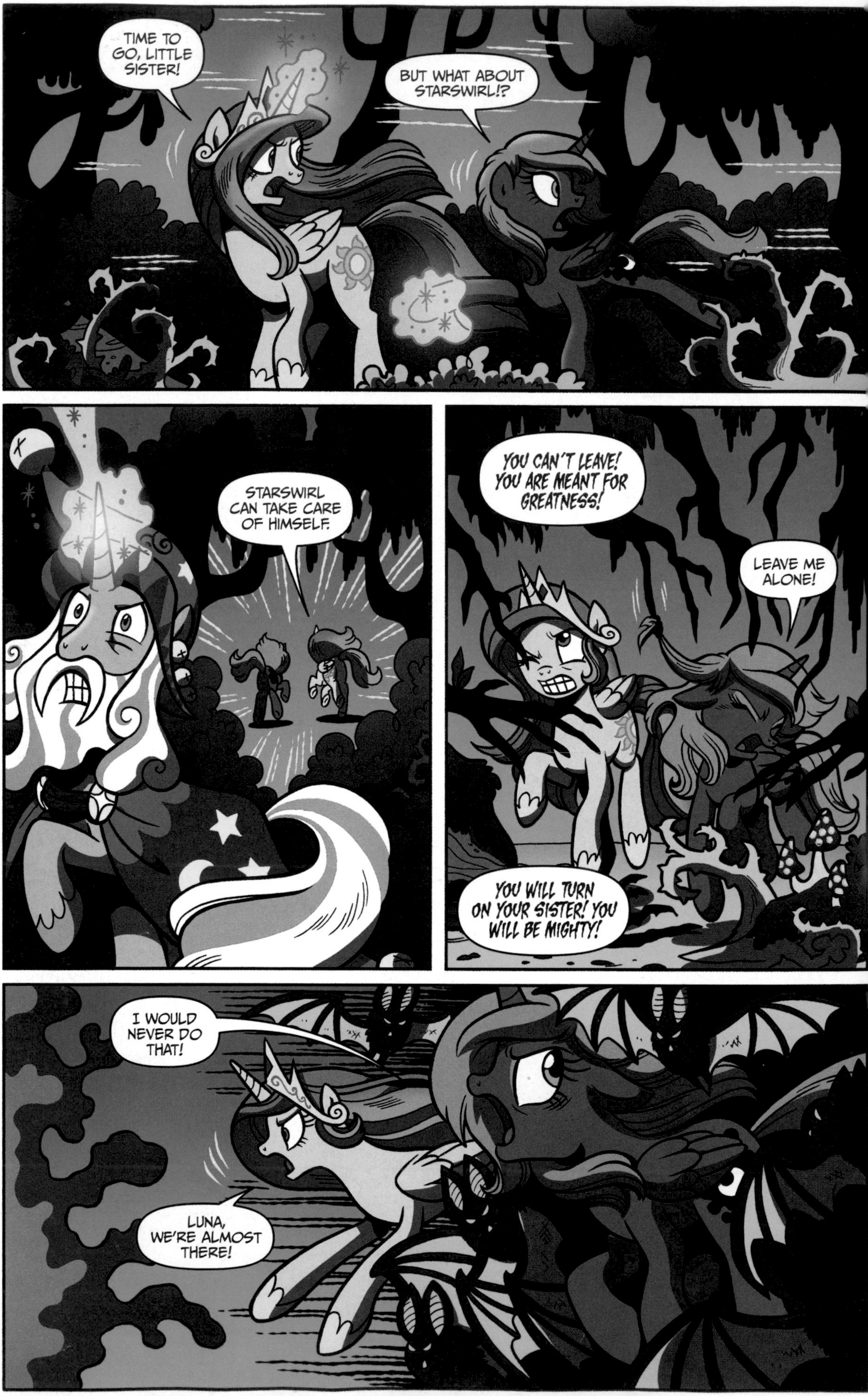
TIME TO GO, LITTLE SISTER!
BUT WHAT ABOUT STARSWIRL!?
STARSWIRL CAN TAKE CARE OF HIMSELF.
YOU CAN'T LEAVE! YOU ARE MEANT FOR GREATNESS!
LEAVE ME ALONE!
YOU WILL TURN ON YOUR SISTER! YOU WILL BE MIGHTY!
I WOULD NEVER DO THAT!
LUNA, WE'RE ALMOST THERE!

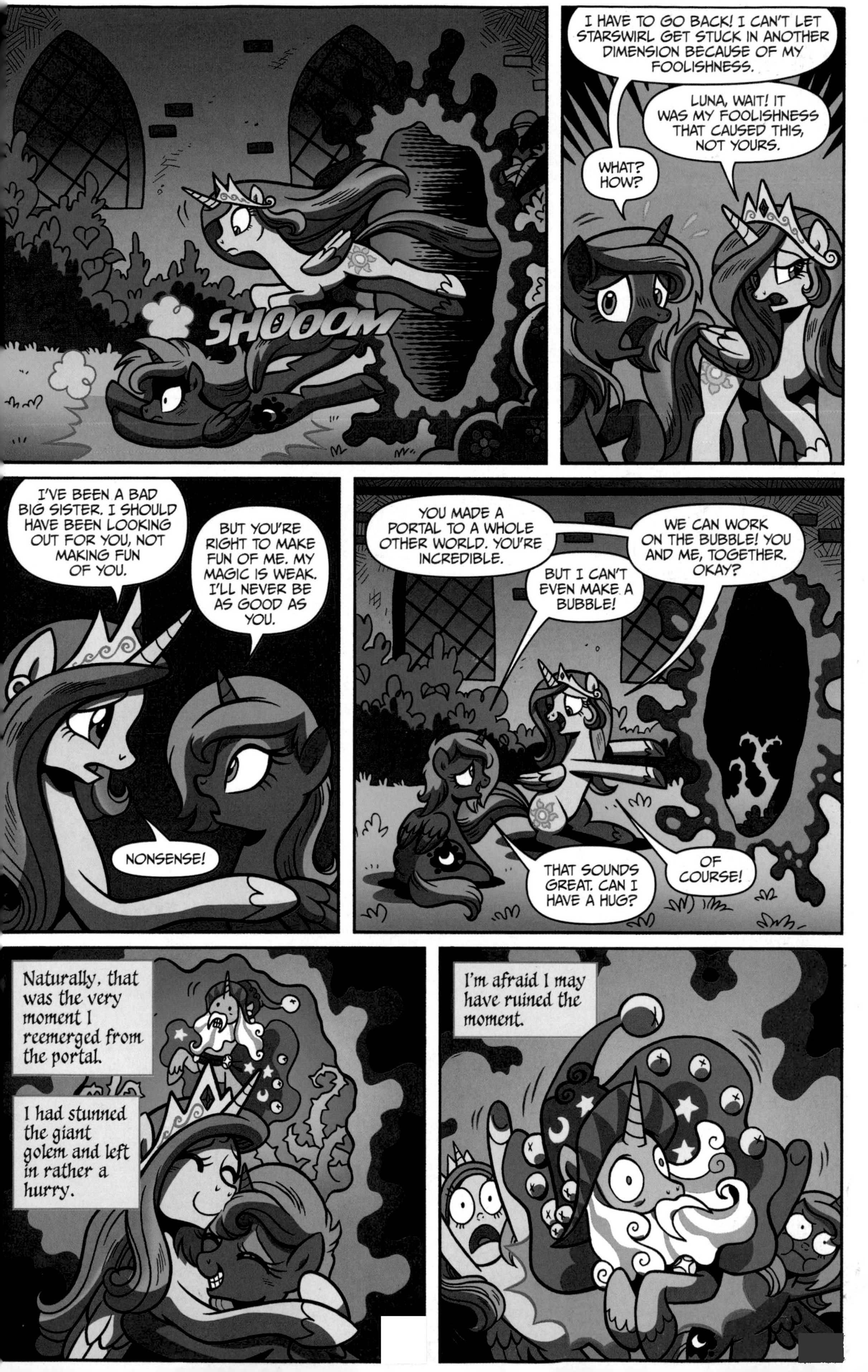
SHOOOM
I HAVE TO GO BACK! I CAN'T LET STARSWIRL GET STUCK IN ANOTHER DIMENSION BECAUSE OF MY FOOLISHNESS.
LUNA, WAIT! IT WAS MY FOOLISHNESS THAT CAUSED THIS, NOT YOURS.
WHAT? HOW?
I'VE BEEN A BAD BIG SISTER. I SHOULD HAVE BEEN LOOKING OUT FOR YOU, NOT MAKING FUN OF YOU.
BUT YOU'RE RIGHT TO MAKE FUN OF ME. MY MAGIC IS WEAK. I'LL NEVER BE AS GOOD AS YOU.
NONSENSE!
YOU MADE A PORTAL TO A WHOLE OTHER WORLD. YOU'RE INCREDIBLE.
BUT I CAN'T EVEN MAKE A BUBBLE!
WE CAN WORK ON THE BUBBLE! YOU AND ME, TOGETHER. OKAY?
THAT SOUNDS GREAT. CAN I HAVE A HUG?
OF COURSE!
Naturally, that was the very moment I reemerged from the portal.
I had stunned the giant golem and left in rather a hurry.
I'm afraid I may have ruined the moment.

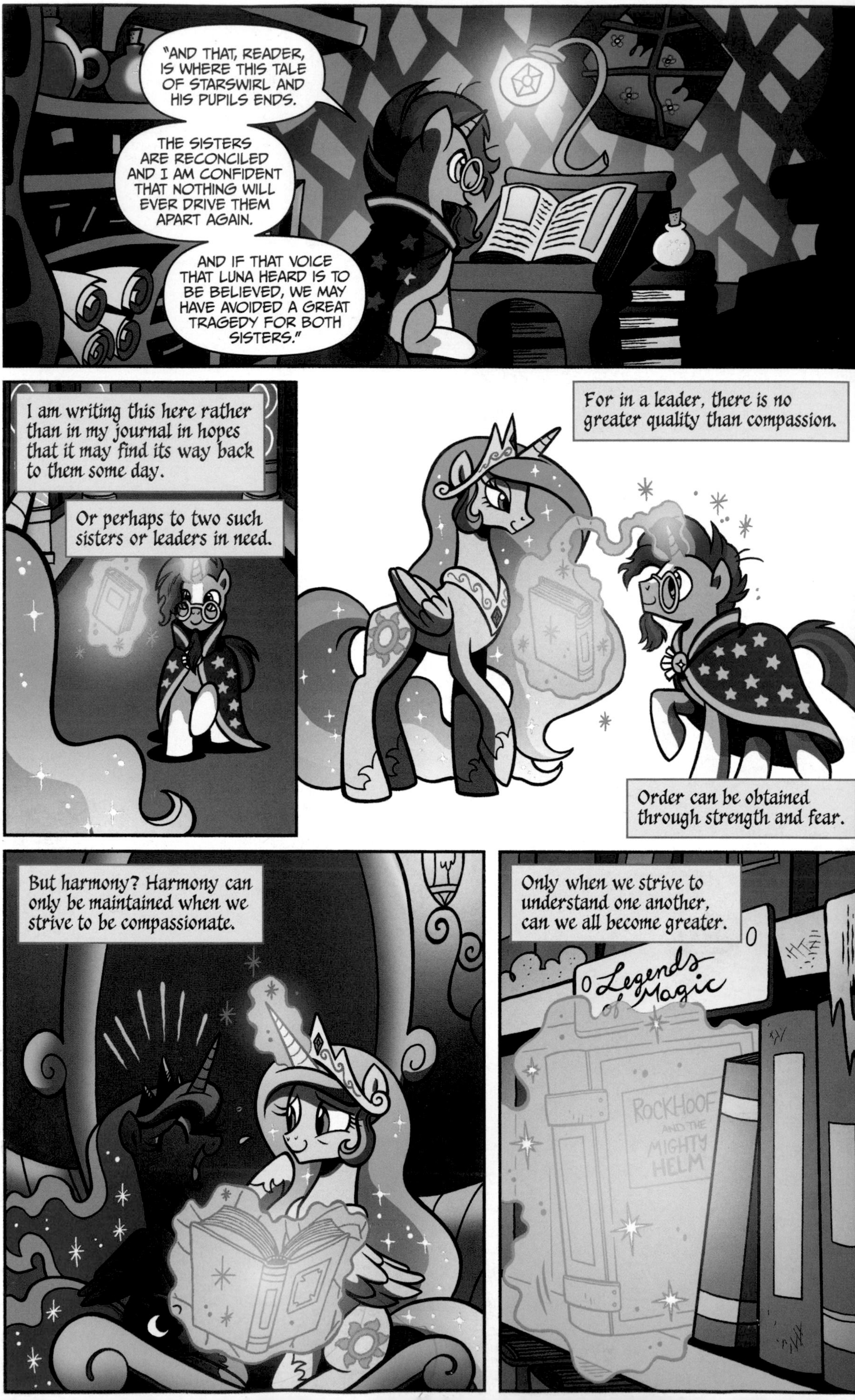
"AND THAT, READER, IS WHERE THIS TALE OF STARSWIRL AND HIS PUPILS ENDS.
THE SISTERS ARE RECONCILED AND I AM CONFIDENT THAT NOTHING WILL EVER DRIVE THEM APART AGAIN.
AND IF THAT VOICE THAT LUNA HEARD IS TO BE BELIEVED, WE MAY HAVE AVOIDED A GREAT TRAGEDY FOR BOTH SISTERS."
I am writing this here rather than in my journal in hopes that it may find its way back to them some day.
Or perhaps to two such sisters or leaders in need.
For in a leader, there is no greater quality than compassion.
Order can be obtained through strength and fear.
But harmony? Harmony can only be maintained when we strive to be compassionate.
Only when we strive to understand one another, can we all become greater.
Legends of Magic
ROCKHOOF AND THE MIGHTY HELM

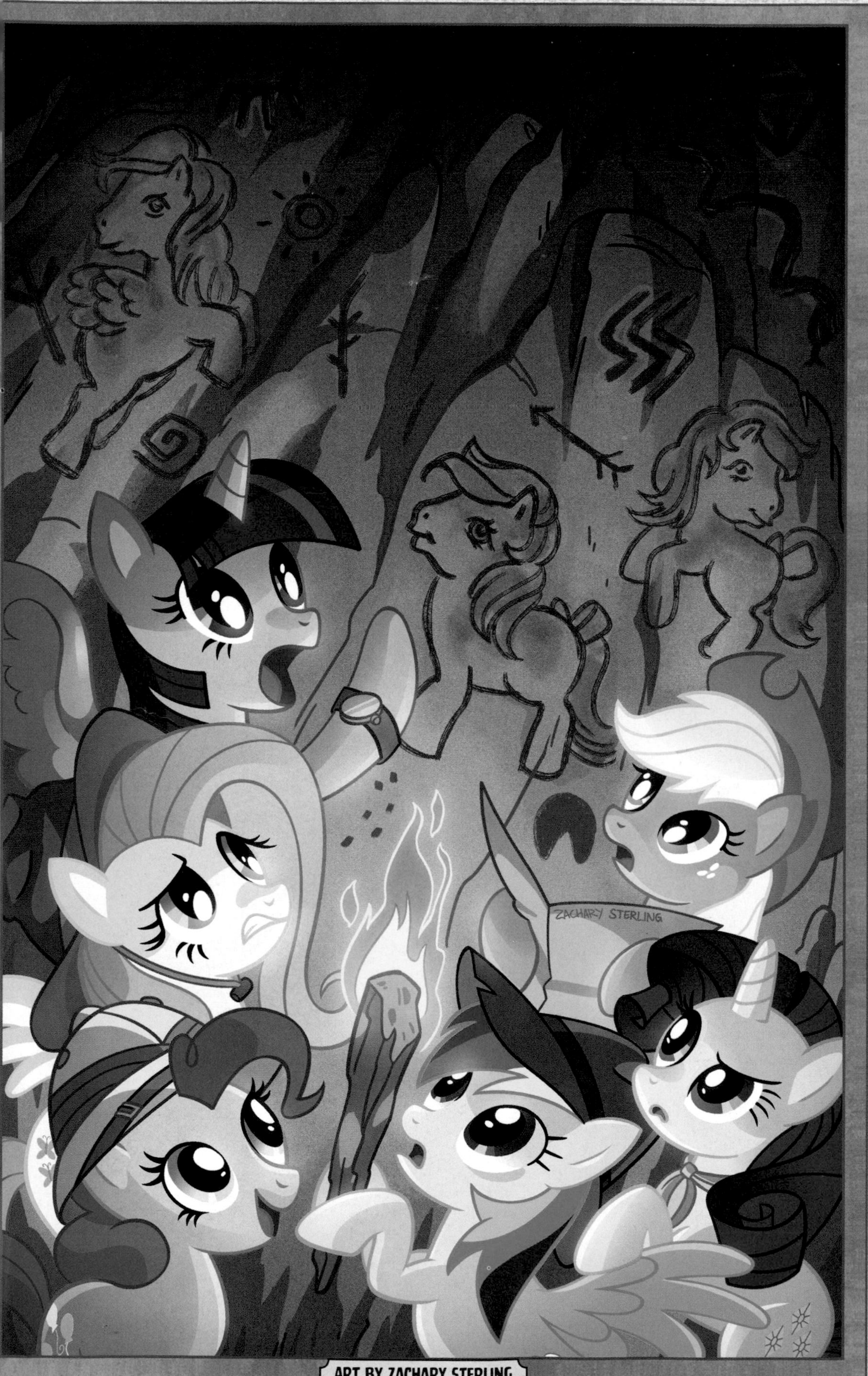
ZACHARY STERLING

ART BY ZACHARY STERLING

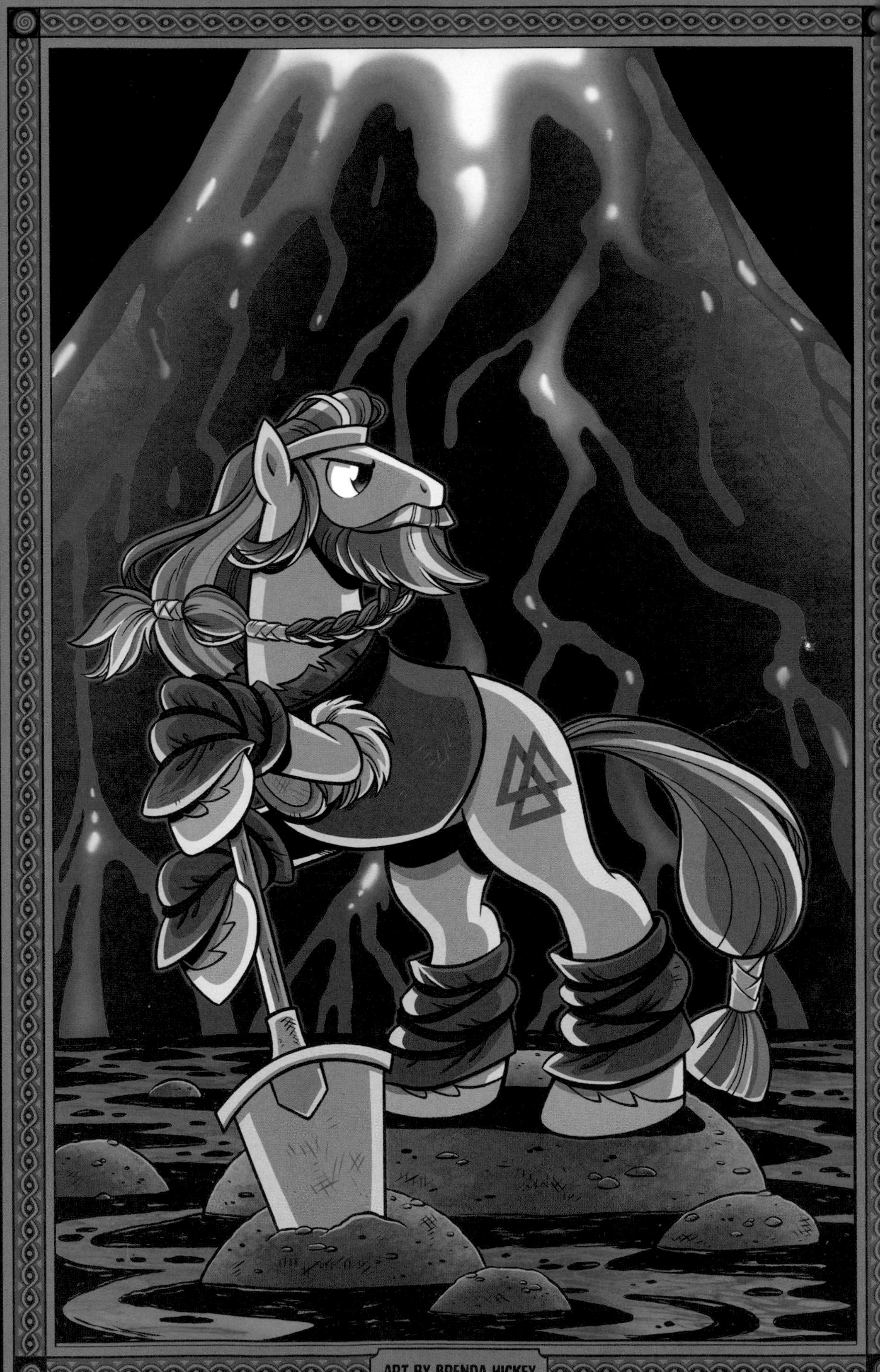

ART BY BRENDA HICKEY

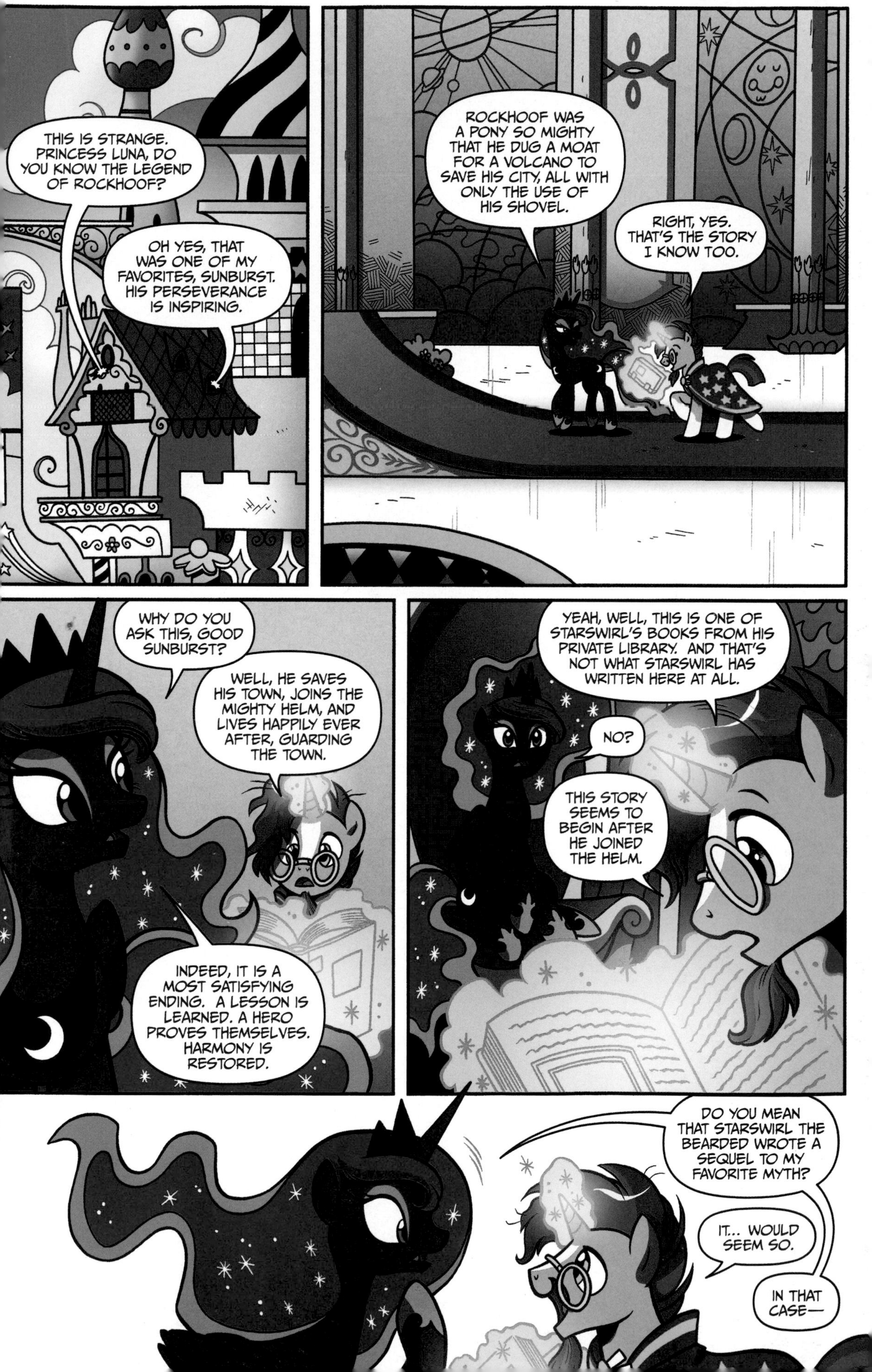
THIS IS STRANGE. PRINCESS LUNA, DO YOU KNOW THE LEGEND OF ROCKHOOF?
OH YES, THAT WAS ONE OF MY FAVORITES, SUNBURST. HIS PERSEVERANCE IS INSPIRING.
ROCKHOOF WAS A PONY SO MIGHTY THAT HE DUG A MOAT FOR A VOLCANO TO SAVE HIS CITY, ALL WITH ONLY THE USE OF HIS SHOVEL.
RIGHT, YES. THAT'S THE STORY I KNOW TOO.
WHY DO YOU ASK THIS, GOOD SUNBURST?
WELL, HE SAVES HIS TOWN, JOINS THE MIGHTY HELM, AND LIVES HAPPILY EVER AFTER, GUARDING THE TOWN.
INDEED, IT IS A MOST SATISFYING ENDING. A LESSON IS LEARNED. A HERO PROVES THEMSELVES. HARMONY IS RESTORED.
YEAH, WELL, THIS IS ONE OF STARSWIRL'S BOOKS FROM HIS PRIVATE LIBRARY. AND THAT'S NOT WHAT STARSWIRL HAS WRITTEN HERE AT ALL.
NO?
THIS STORY SEEMS TO BEGIN AFTER HE JOINED THE HELM.
DO YOU MEAN THAT STARSWIRL THE BEARDED WROTE A SEQUEL TO MY FAVORITE MYTH?
IT... WOULD SEEM SO.
IN THAT CASE—

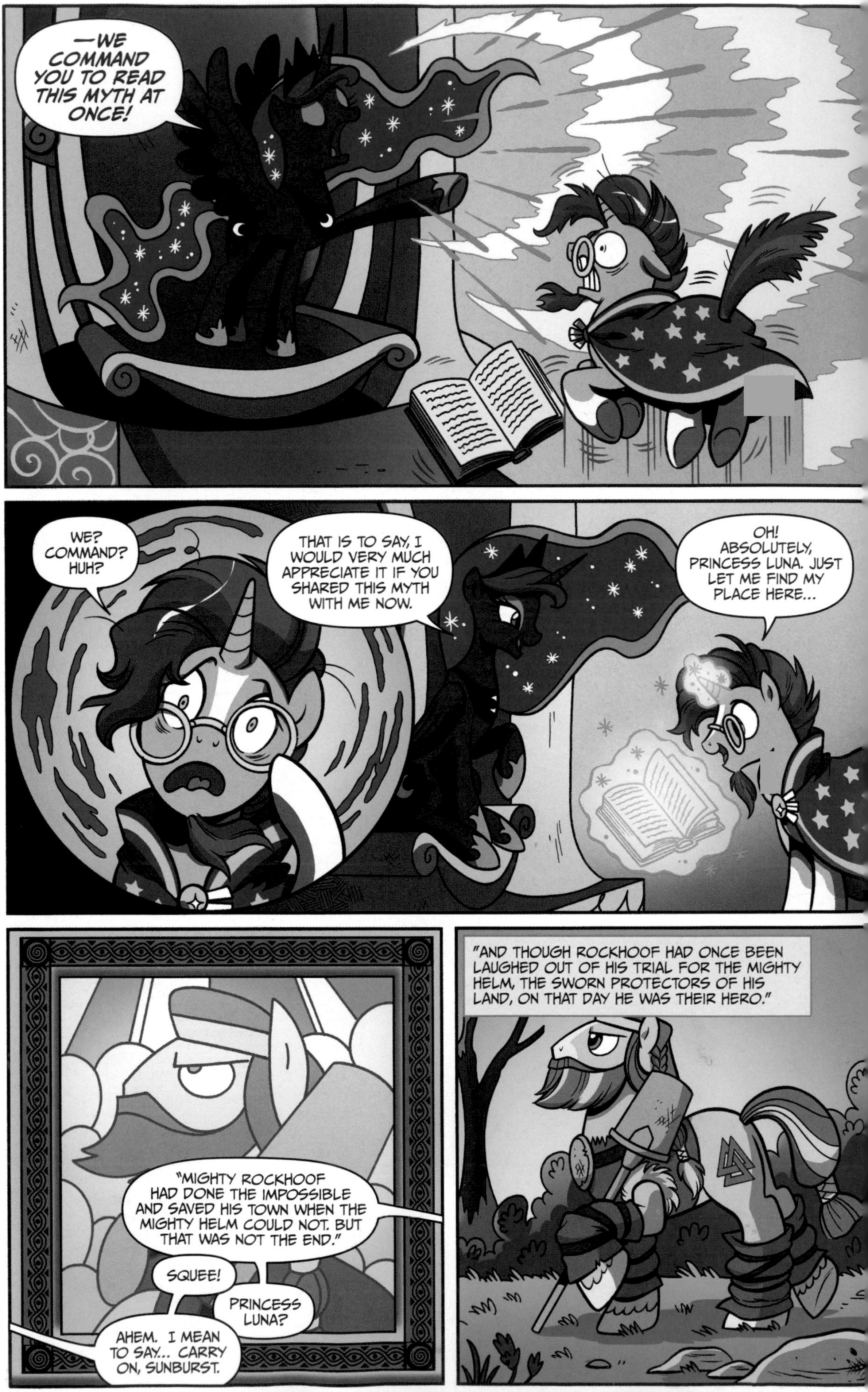
—WE COMMAND YOU TO READ THIS MYTH AT ONCE!
WE? COMMAND? HUH?
THAT IS TO SAY, I WOULD VERY MUCH APPRECIATE IT IF YOU SHARED THIS MYTH WITH ME NOW.
OH! ABSOLUTELY, PRINCESS LUNA. JUST LET ME FIND MY PLACE HERE...
"MIGHTY ROCKHOOF HAD DONE THE IMPOSSIBLE AND SAVED HIS TOWN WHEN THE MIGHTY HELM COULD NOT. BUT THAT WAS NOT THE END."
SQUEE!
PRINCESS LUNA?
AHEM. I MEAN TO SAY... CARRY ON, SUNBURST.
"AND THOUGH ROCKHOOF HAD ONCE BEEN LAUGHED OUT OF HIS TRIAL FOR THE MIGHTY HELM, THE SWORN PROTECTORS OF HIS LAND, ON THAT DAY HE WAS THEIR HERO."

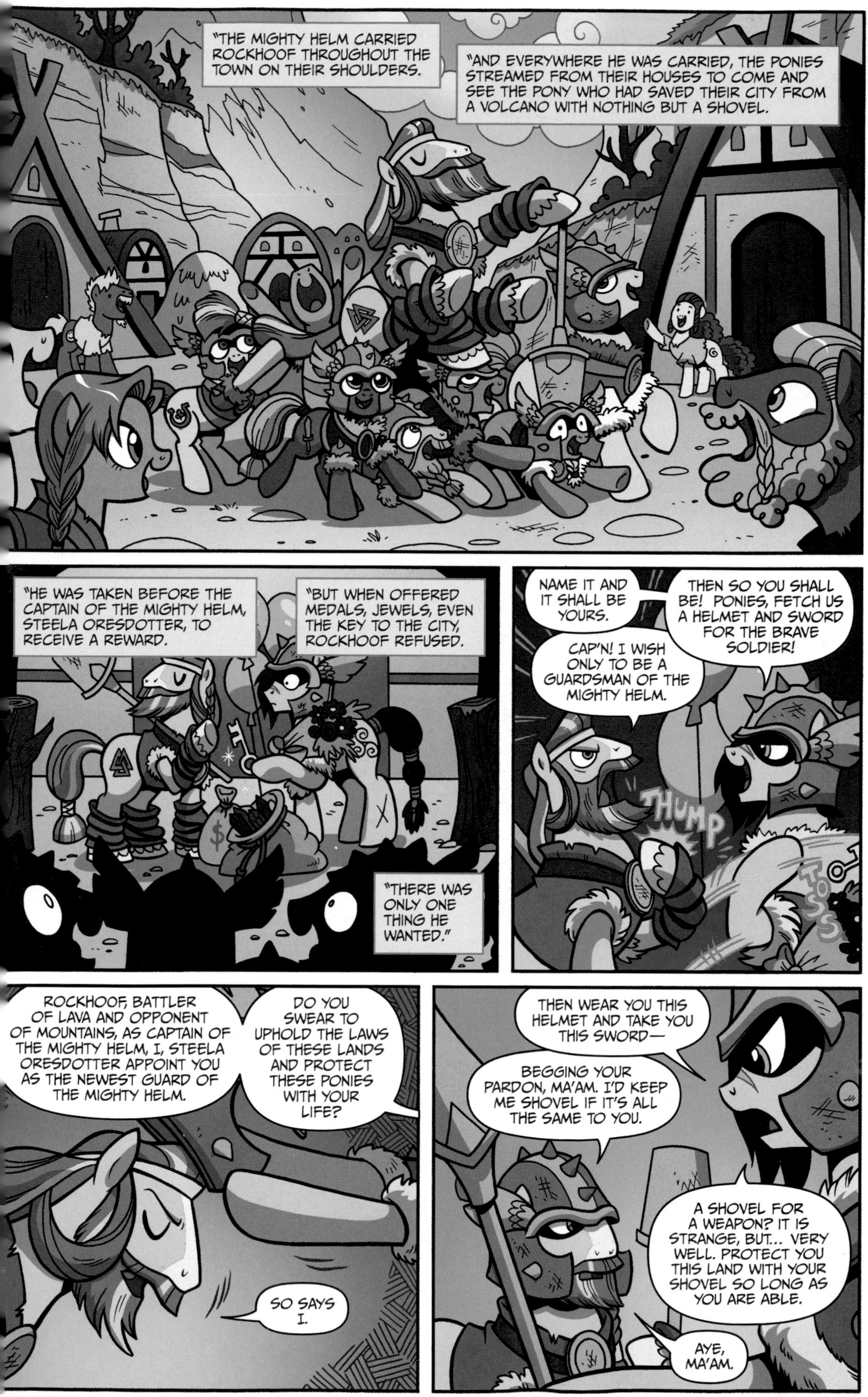
"THE MIGHTY HELM CARRIED ROCKHOOF THROUGHOUT THE TOWN ON THEIR SHOULDERS.
"AND EVERYWHERE HE WAS CARRIED, THE PONIES STREAMED FROM THEIR HOUSES TO COME AND SEE THE PONY WHO HAD SAVED THEIR CITY FROM A VOLCANO WITH NOTHING BUT A SHOVEL.
"HE WAS TAKEN BEFORE THE CAPTAIN OF THE MIGHTY HELM, STEELA ORESDOTTER, TO RECEIVE A REWARD.
"BUT WHEN OFFERED MEDALS, JEWELS, EVEN THE KEY TO THE CITY, ROCKHOOF REFUSED.
"THERE WAS ONLY ONE THING HE WANTED."
NAME IT AND IT SHALL BE YOURS.
CAP'N! I WISH ONLY TO BE A GUARDSMAN OF THE MIGHTY HELM.
THEN SO YOU SHALL BE! PONIES, FETCH US A HELMET AND SWORD FOR THE BRAVE SOLDIER!
THUMP
TOSS
ROCKHOOF, BATTLER OF LAVA AND OPPONENT OF MOUNTAINS, AS CAPTAIN OF THE MIGHTY HELM, I, STEELA ORESDOTTER APPOINT YOU AS THE NEWEST GUARD OF THE MIGHTY HELM.
DO YOU SWEAR TO UPHOLD THE LAWS OF THESE LANDS AND PROTECT THESE PONIES WITH YOUR LIFE?
SO SAYS I.
THEN WEAR YOU THIS HELMET AND TAKE YOU THIS SWORD—
BEGGING YOUR PARDON, MA'AM. I'D KEEP ME SHOVEL IF IT'S ALL THE SAME TO YOU.
A SHOVEL FOR A WEAPON? IT IS STRANGE, BUT... VERY WELL. PROTECT YOU THIS LAND WITH YOUR SHOVEL SO LONG AS YOU ARE ABLE.
AYE, MA'AM.

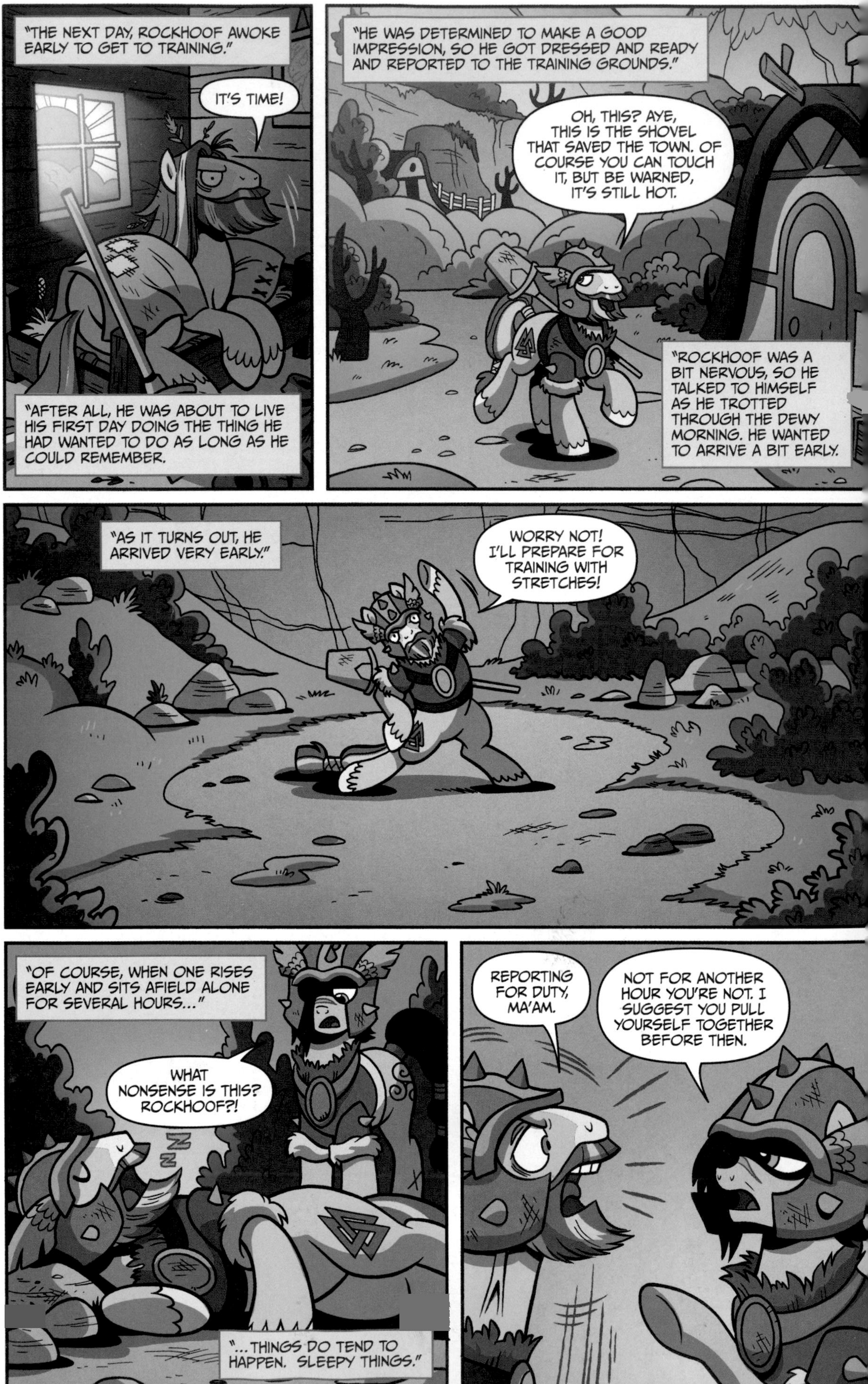
"THE NEXT DAY, ROCKHOOF AWOKE EARLY TO GET TO TRAINING."
IT'S TIME!
"AFTER ALL, HE WAS ABOUT TO LIVE HIS FIRST DAY DOING THE THING HE HAD WANTED TO DO AS LONG AS HE COULD REMEMBER.
"HE WAS DETERMINED TO MAKE A GOOD IMPRESSION, SO HE GOT DRESSED AND READY AND REPORTED TO THE TRAINING GROUNDS."
OH, THIS? AYE, THIS IS THE SHOVEL THAT SAVED THE TOWN. OF COURSE YOU CAN TOUCH IT, BUT BE WARNED, IT'S STILL HOT.
"ROCKHOOF WAS A BIT NERVOUS, SO HE TALKED TO HIMSELF AS HE TROTTED THROUGH THE DEWY MORNING. HE WANTED TO ARRIVE A BIT EARLY.
"AS IT TURNS OUT, HE ARRIVED VERY EARLY."
WORRY NOT! I'LL PREPARE FOR TRAINING WITH STRETCHES!
"OF COURSE, WHEN ONE RISES EARLY AND SITS AFIELD ALONE FOR SEVERAL HOURS..."
WHAT NONSENSE IS THIS? ROCKHOOF?!
Z
Z
"...THINGS DO TEND TO HAPPEN. SLEEPY THINGS."
REPORTING FOR DUTY, MA'AM.
NOT FOR ANOTHER HOUR YOU'RE NOT. I SUGGEST YOU PULL YOURSELF TOGETHER BEFORE THEN.

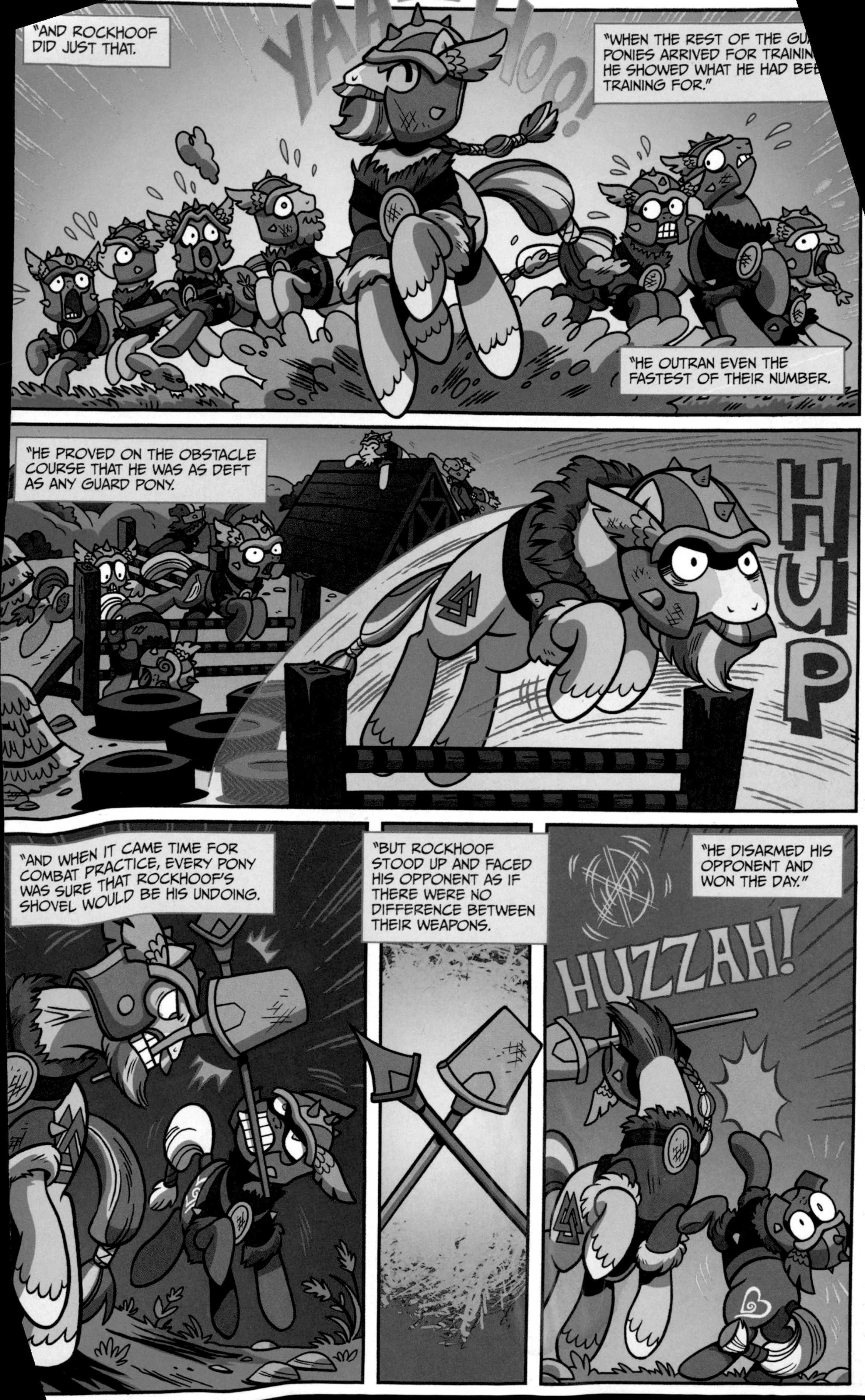
"AND ROCKHOOF DID JUST THAT.
YAA-HOO!
"WHEN THE REST OF THE GU PONIES ARRIVED FOR TRAININ HE SHOWED WHAT HE HAD BEE TRAINING FOR."
"HE OUTRAN EVEN THE FASTEST OF THEIR NUMBER.
"HE PROVED ON THE OBSTACLE COURSE THAT HE WAS AS DEFT AS ANY GUARD PONY.
HUP
"AND WHEN IT CAME TIME FOR COMBAT PRACTICE, EVERY PONY WAS SURE THAT ROCKHOOF'S SHOVEL WOULD BE HIS UNDOING.
"BUT ROCKHOOF STOOD UP AND FACED HIS OPPONENT AS IF THERE WERE NO DIFFERENCE BETWEEN THEIR WEAPONS.
"HE DISARMED HIS OPPONENT AND WON THE DAY."
HUZZAH!

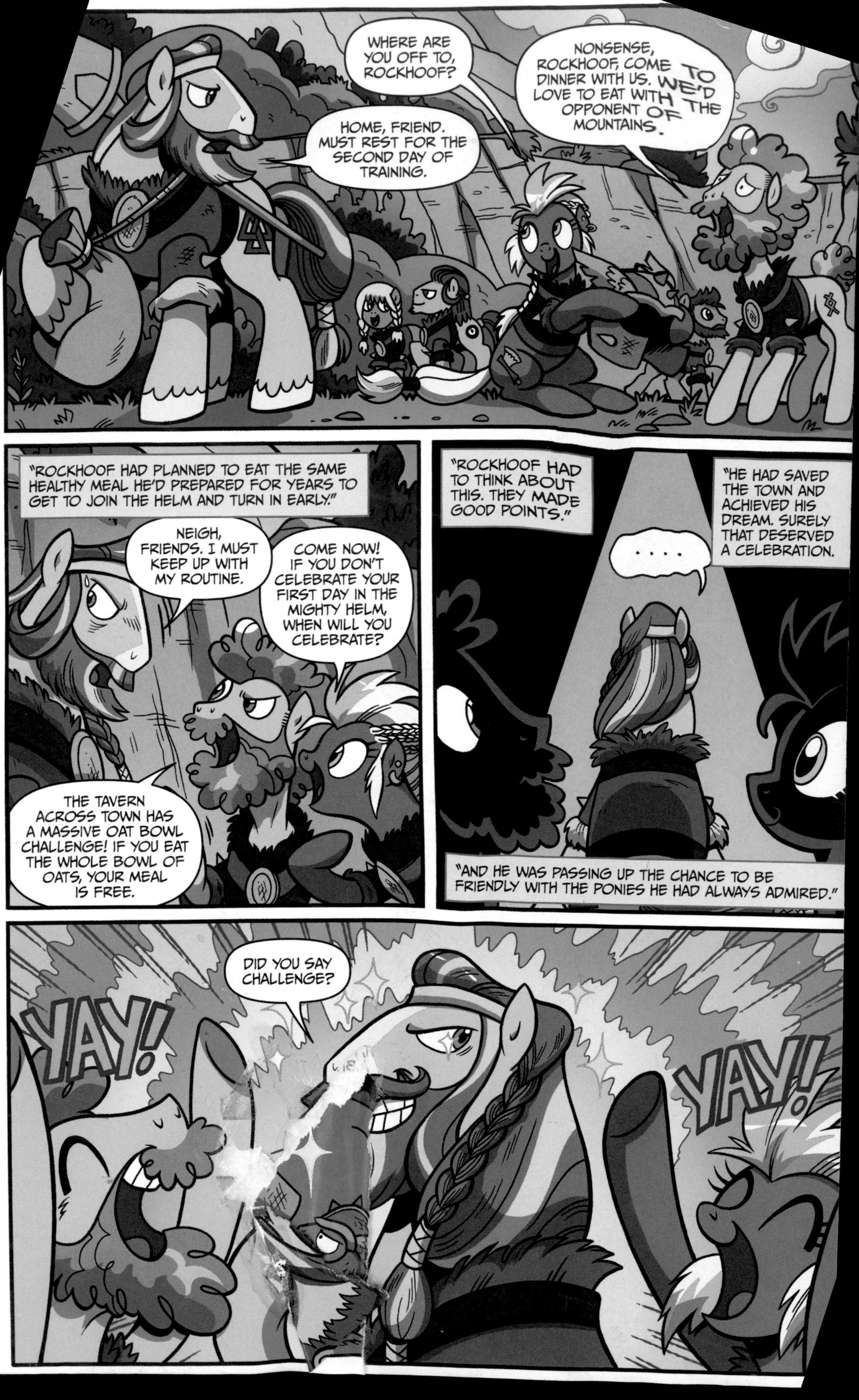
WHERE ARE YOU OFF TO, ROCKHOOF?
HOME, FRIEND. MUST REST FOR THE SECOND DAY OF TRAINING.
NONSENSE, ROCKHOOF, COME TO DINNER WITH US. WE'D LOVE TO EAT WITH THE OPPONENT OF MOUNTAINS.
"ROCKHOOF HAD PLANNED TO EAT THE SAME HEALTHY MEAL HE'D PREPARED FOR YEARS TO GET TO JOIN THE HELM AND TURN IN EARLY."
NEIGH, FRIENDS. I MUST KEEP UP WITH MY ROUTINE.
COME NOW! IF YOU DON'T CELEBRATE YOUR FIRST DAY IN THE MIGHTY HELM, WHEN WILL YOU CELEBRATE?
THE TAVERN ACROSS TOWN HAS A MASSIVE OAT BOWL CHALLENGE! IF YOU EAT THE WHOLE BOWL OF OATS, YOUR MEAL IS FREE.
"ROCKHOOF HAD TO THINK ABOUT THIS. THEY MADE GOOD POINTS."
....
"HE HAD SAVED THE TOWN AND ACHIEVED HIS DREAM. SURELY THAT DESERVED A CELEBRATION.
"AND HE WAS PASSING UP THE CHANCE TO BE FRIENDLY WITH THE PONIES HE HAD ALWAYS ADMIRED."
DID YOU SAY CHALLENGE?
YAY!
YAY!

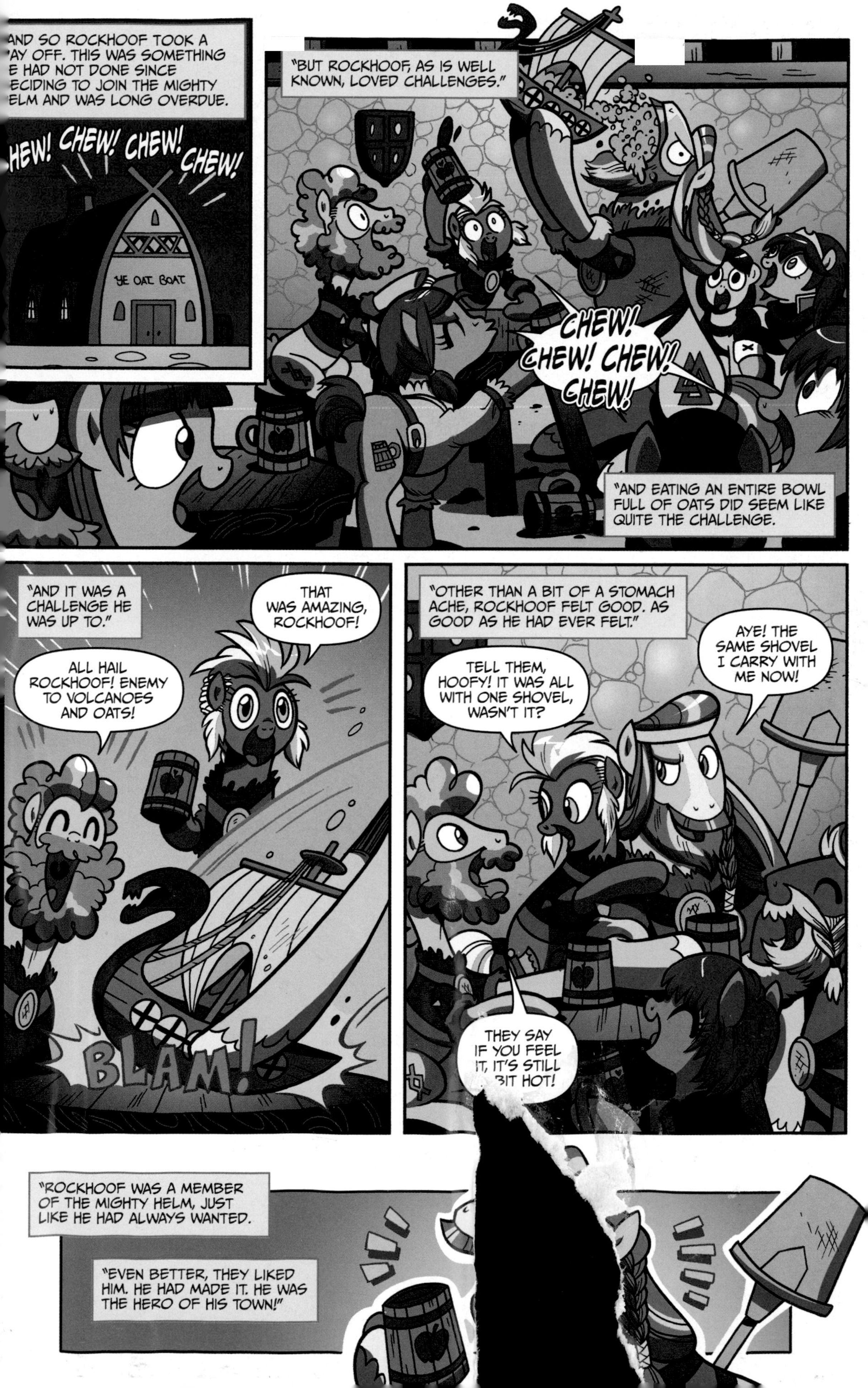
AND SO ROCKHOOF TOOK A
AY OFF. THIS WAS SOMETHING
E HAD NOT DONE SINCE
ECIDING TO JOIN THE MIGHTY
ELM AND WAS LONG OVERDUE.
HEW! CHEW! CHEW! CHEW!
YE OAT BOAT
"BUT ROCKHOOF, AS IS WELL KNOWN, LOVED CHALLENGES."
CHEW! CHEW! CHEW! CHEW!
"AND EATING AN ENTIRE BOWL FULL OF OATS DID SEEM LIKE QUITE THE CHALLENGE.
"AND IT WAS A CHALLENGE HE WAS UP TO."
THAT WAS AMAZING, ROCKHOOF!
ALL HAIL ROCKHOOF! ENEMY TO VOLCANOES AND OATS!
BLAM!
"OTHER THAN A BIT OF A STOMACH ACHE, ROCKHOOF FELT GOOD. AS GOOD AS HE HAD EVER FELT."
TELL THEM, HOOFY! IT WAS ALL WITH ONE SHOVEL, WASN'T IT?
AYE! THE SAME SHOVEL I CARRY WITH ME NOW!
THEY SAY IF YOU FEEL IT, IT'S STILL
BIT HOT!
"ROCKHOOF WAS A MEMBER OF THE MIGHTY HELM, JUST LIKE HE HAD ALWAYS WANTED.
"EVEN BETTER, THEY LIKED HIM. HE HAD MADE IT. HE WAS THE HERO OF HIS TOWN!"

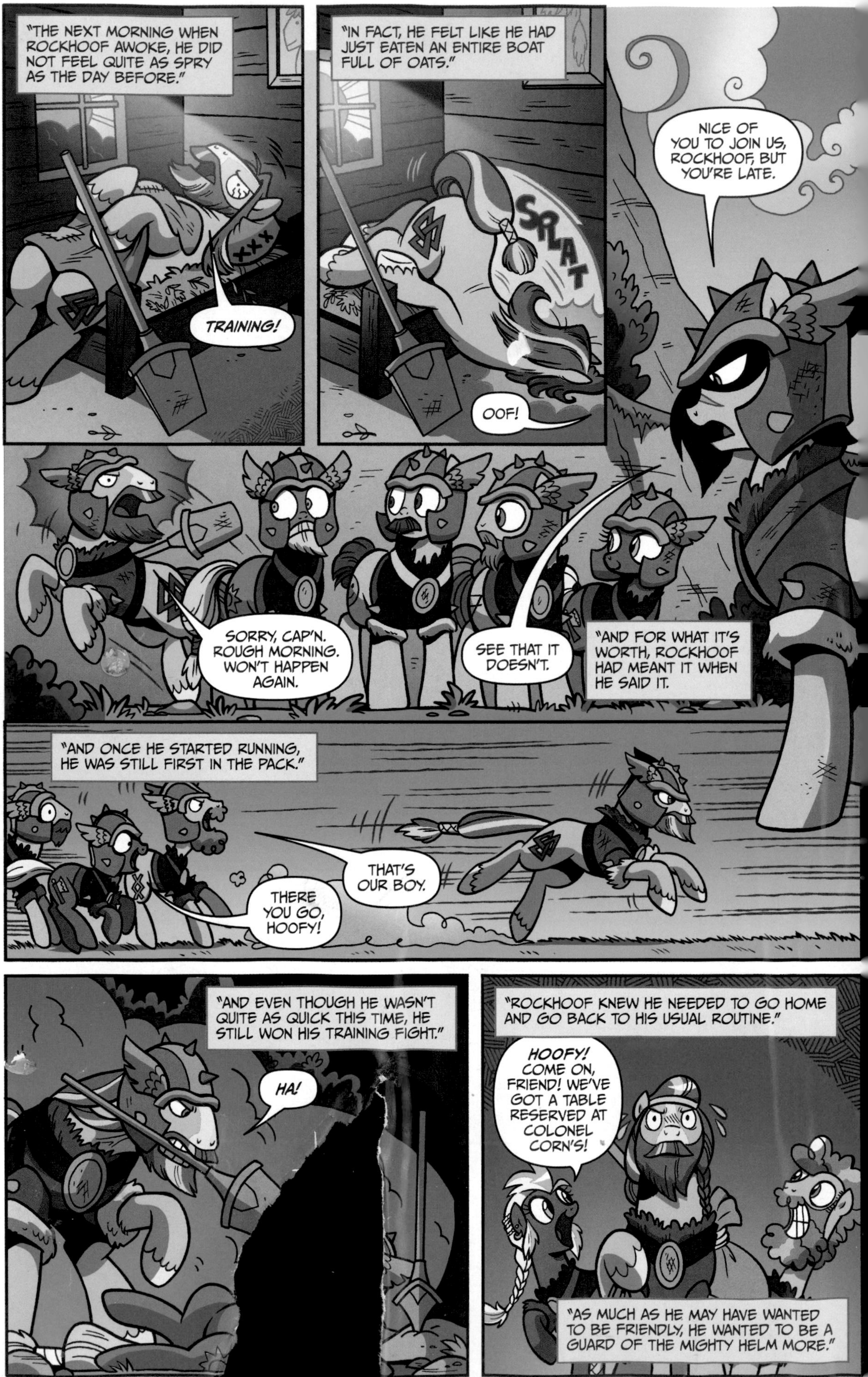
"THE NEXT MORNING WHEN ROCKHOOF AWOKE, HE DID NOT FEEL QUITE AS SPRY AS THE DAY BEFORE."
TRAINING!
"IN FACT, HE FELT LIKE HE HAD JUST EATEN AN ENTIRE BOAT FULL OF OATS."
SPLAT
OOF!
NICE OF YOU TO JOIN US, ROCKHOOF, BUT YOU'RE LATE.
SORRY, CAP'N. ROUGH MORNING. WON'T HAPPEN AGAIN.
SEE THAT IT DOESN'T.
"AND FOR WHAT IT'S WORTH, ROCKHOOF HAD MEANT IT WHEN HE SAID IT.
"AND ONCE HE STARTED RUNNING, HE WAS STILL FIRST IN THE PACK."
THAT'S OUR BOY.
THERE YOU GO, HOOFY!
"AND EVEN THOUGH HE WASN'T QUITE AS QUICK THIS TIME, HE STILL WON HIS TRAINING FIGHT."
HA!
"ROCKHOOF KNEW HE NEEDED TO GO HOME AND GO BACK TO HIS USUAL ROUTINE."
HOOFY! COME ON, FRIEND! WE'VE GOT A TABLE RESERVED AT COLONEL CORN'S!
"AS MUCH AS HE MAY HAVE WANTED TO BE FRIENDLY, HE WANTED TO BE A GUARD OF THE MIGHTY HELM MORE."

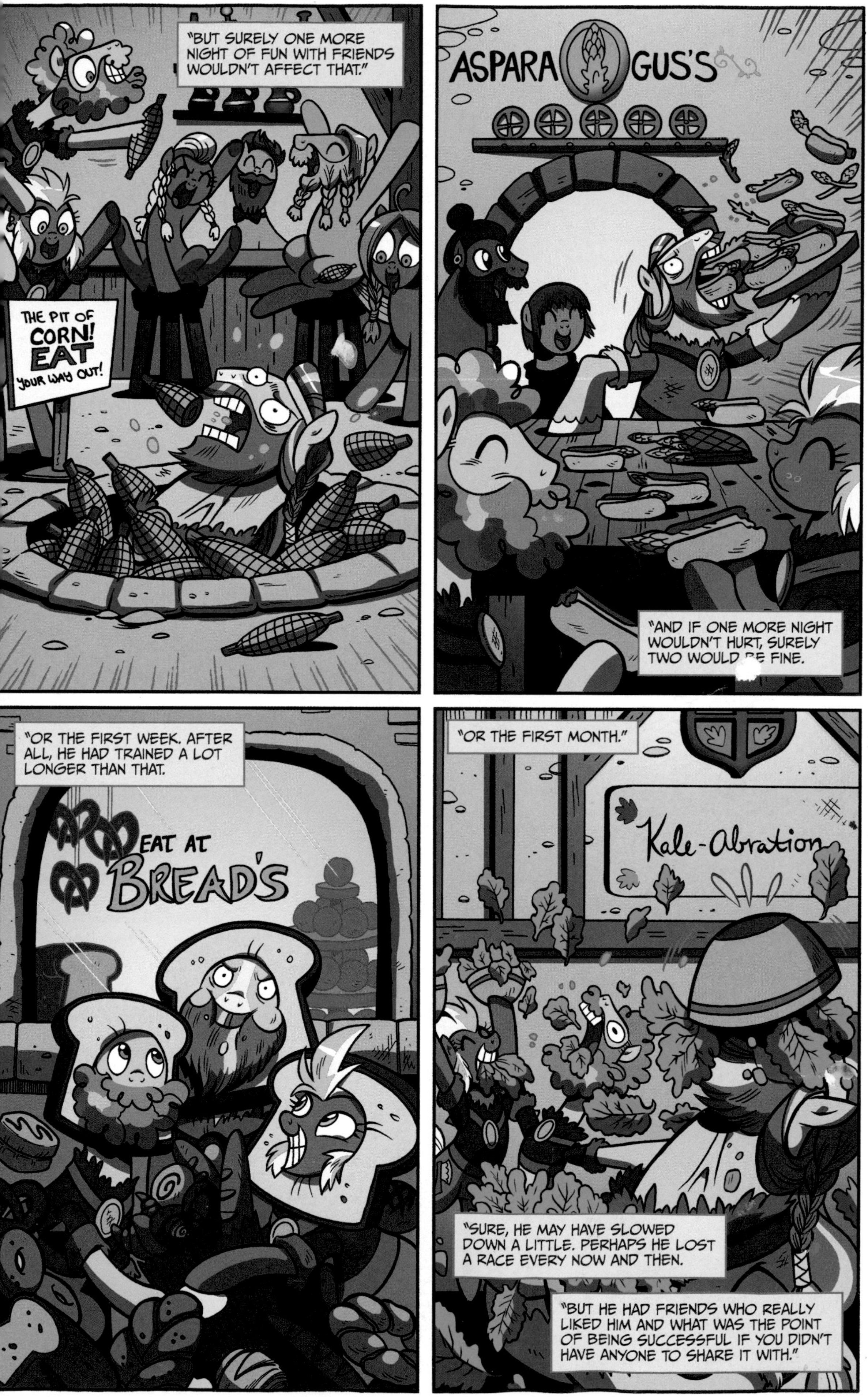
"BUT SURELY ONE MORE NIGHT OF FUN WITH FRIENDS WOULDN'T AFFECT THAT."
THE PIT OF CORN! EAT YOUR WAY OUT!
ASPARAGUS'S
"AND IF ONE MORE NIGHT WOULDN'T HURT, SURELY TWO WOULD BE FINE.
"OR THE FIRST WEEK. AFTER ALL, HE HAD TRAINED A LOT LONGER THAN THAT.
EAT AT BREAD'S
"OR THE FIRST MONTH."
Kale-abration
"SURE, HE MAY HAVE SLOWED DOWN A LITTLE. PERHAPS HE LOST A RACE EVERY NOW AND THEN.
"BUT HE HAD FRIENDS WHO REALLY LIKED HIM AND WHAT WAS THE POINT OF BEING SUCCESSFUL IF YOU DIDN'T HAVE ANYONE TO SHARE IT WITH."

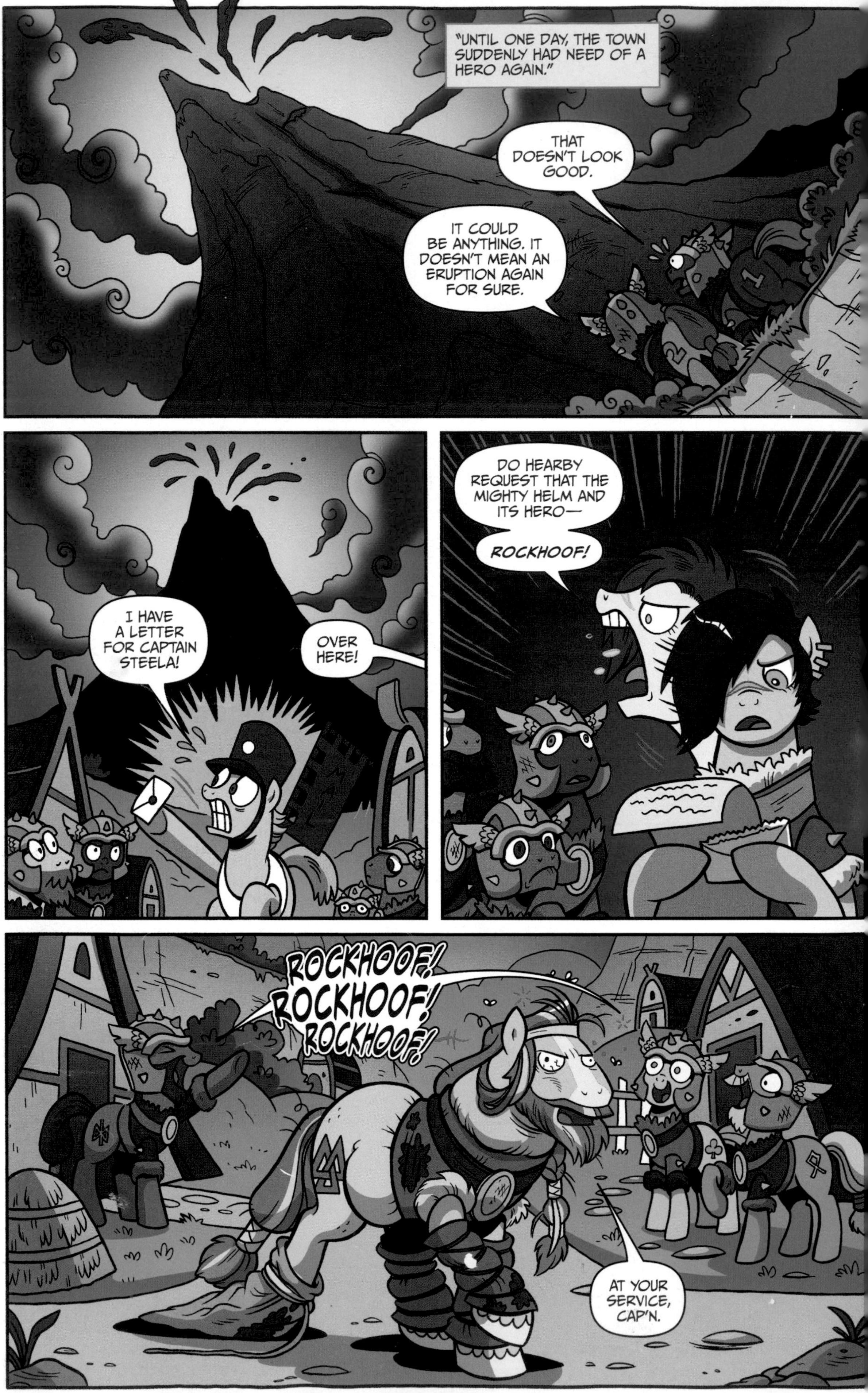
"UNTIL ONE DAY, THE TOWN SUDDENLY HAD NEED OF A HERO AGAIN."
THAT DOESN'T LOOK GOOD.
IT COULD BE ANYTHING. IT DOESN'T MEAN AN ERUPTION AGAIN FOR SURE.
I HAVE A LETTER FOR CAPTAIN STEELA!
OVER HERE!
DO HEARBY REQUEST THAT THE MIGHTY HELM AND ITS HERO—
ROCKHOOF!
ROCKHOOF! ROCKHOOF! ROCKHOOF!
AT YOUR SERVICE, CAP'N.

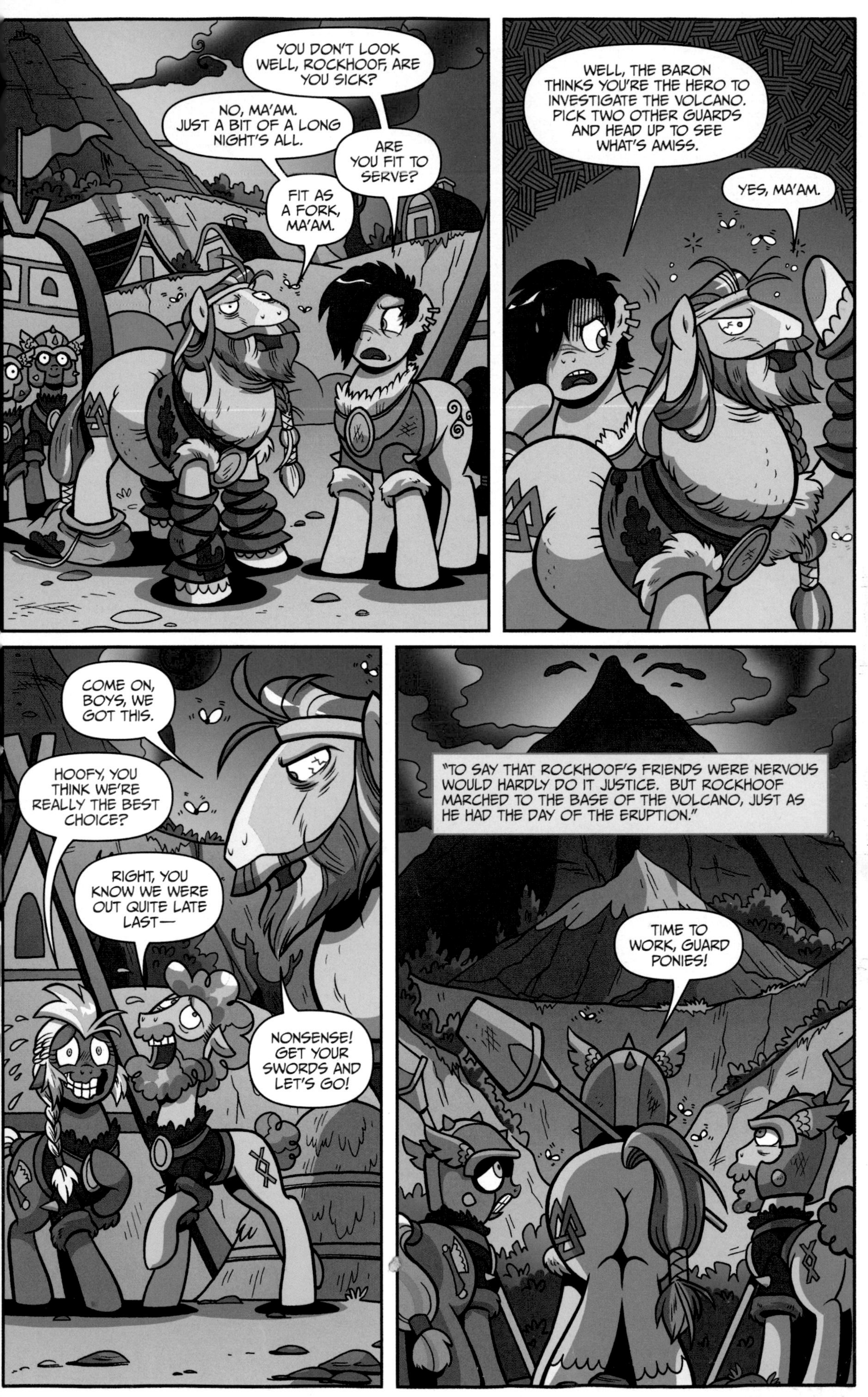
YOU DON'T LOOK WELL, ROCKHOOF, ARE YOU SICK?
NO, MA'AM. JUST A BIT OF A LONG NIGHT'S ALL.
ARE YOU FIT TO SERVE?
FIT AS A FORK, MA'AM.
WELL, THE BARON THINKS YOU'RE THE HERO TO INVESTIGATE THE VOLCANO. PICK TWO OTHER GUARDS AND HEAD UP TO SEE WHAT'S AMISS.
YES, MA'AM.
COME ON, BOYS, WE GOT THIS.
HOOFY, YOU THINK WE'RE REALLY THE BEST CHOICE?
RIGHT, YOU KNOW WE WERE OUT QUITE LATE LAST—
NONSENSE! GET YOUR SWORDS AND LET'S GO!
"TO SAY THAT ROCKHOOF'S FRIENDS WERE NERVOUS WOULD HARDLY DO IT JUSTICE. BUT ROCKHOOF MARCHED TO THE BASE OF THE VOLCANO, JUST AS HE HAD THE DAY OF THE ERUPTION."
TIME TO WORK, GUARD PONIES!

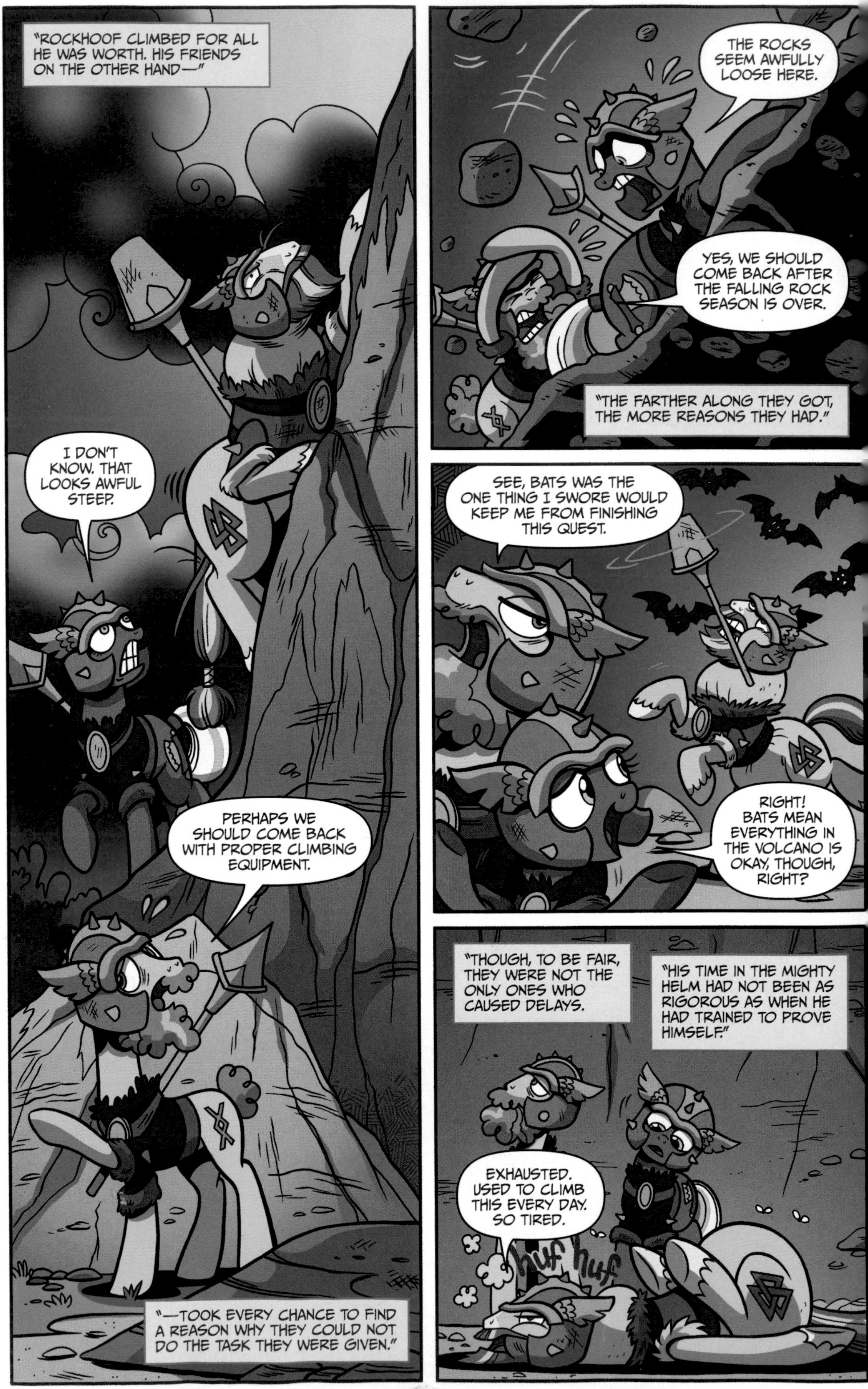
"ROCKHOOF CLIMBED FOR ALL HE WAS WORTH. HIS FRIENDS ON THE OTHER HAND—"
I DON'T KNOW. THAT LOOKS AWFUL STEEP.
PERHAPS WE SHOULD COME BACK WITH PROPER CLIMBING EQUIPMENT.
"—TOOK EVERY CHANCE TO FIND A REASON WHY THEY COULD NOT DO THE TASK THEY WERE GIVEN."
THE ROCKS SEEM AWFULLY LOOSE HERE.
YES, WE SHOULD COME BACK AFTER THE FALLING ROCK SEASON IS OVER.
"THE FARTHER ALONG THEY GOT, THE MORE REASONS THEY HAD."
SEE, BATS WAS THE ONE THING I SWORE WOULD KEEP ME FROM FINISHING THIS QUEST.
RIGHT! BATS MEAN EVERYTHING IN THE VOLCANO IS OKAY, THOUGH, RIGHT?
"THOUGH, TO BE FAIR, THEY WERE NOT THE ONLY ONES WHO CAUSED DELAYS.
"HIS TIME IN THE MIGHTY HELM HAD NOT BEEN AS RIGOROUS AS WHEN HE HAD TRAINED TO PROVE HIMSELF."
EXHAUSTED. USED TO CLIMB THIS EVERY DAY. SO TIRED.
huf huf

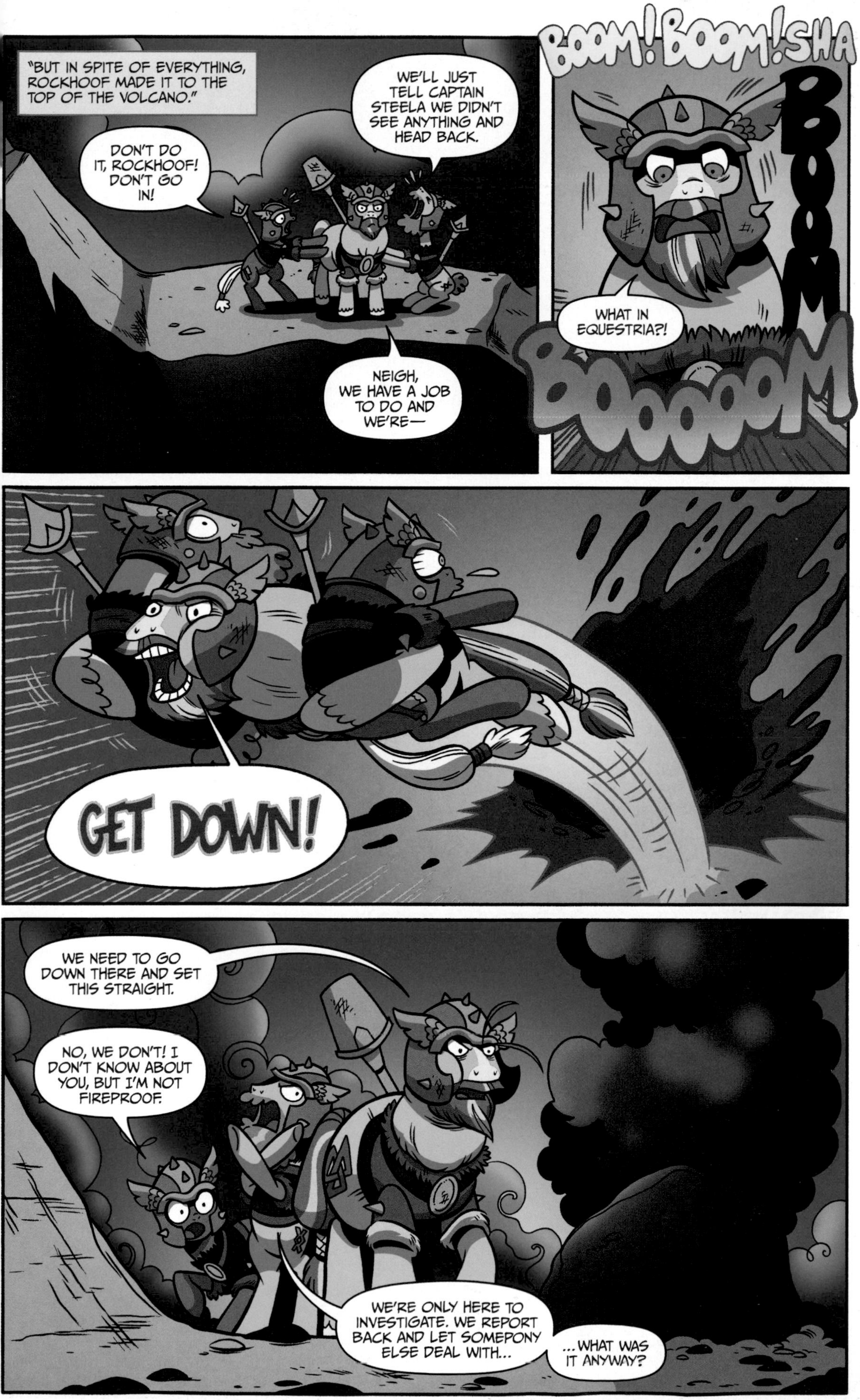
"BUT IN SPITE OF EVERYTHING, ROCKHOOF MADE IT TO THE TOP OF THE VOLCANO."
DON'T DO IT, ROCKHOOF! DON'T GO IN!
WE'LL JUST TELL CAPTAIN STEELA WE DIDN'T SEE ANYTHING AND HEAD BACK.
NEIGH, WE HAVE A JOB TO DO AND WE'RE—
BOOM! BOOM! SHA BOOM
WHAT IN EQUESTRIA?!
BOOOOOM
GET DOWN!
WE NEED TO GO DOWN THERE AND SET THIS STRAIGHT.
NO, WE DON'T! I DON'T KNOW ABOUT YOU, BUT I'M NOT FIREPROOF.
WE'RE ONLY HERE TO INVESTIGATE. WE REPORT BACK AND LET SOMEPONY ELSE DEAL WITH...
...WHAT WAS IT ANYWAY?

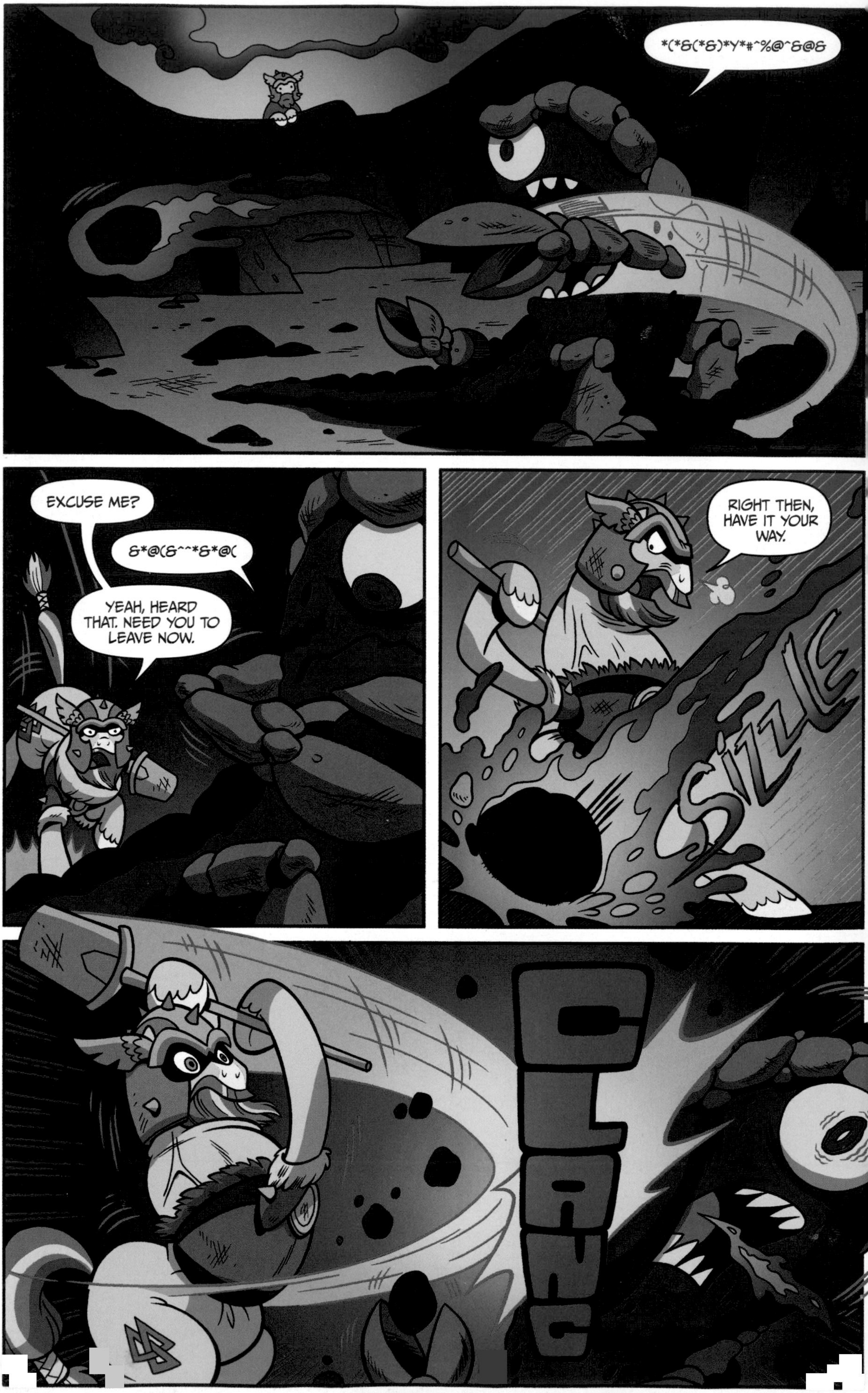
(&(*&)*Y*#^%@^&@&
EXCUSE ME?
&*@(&^^*&*@(
YEAH, HEARD THAT. NEED YOU TO LEAVE NOW.
RIGHT THEN, HAVE IT YOUR WAY.
SIZZLE
CLANG

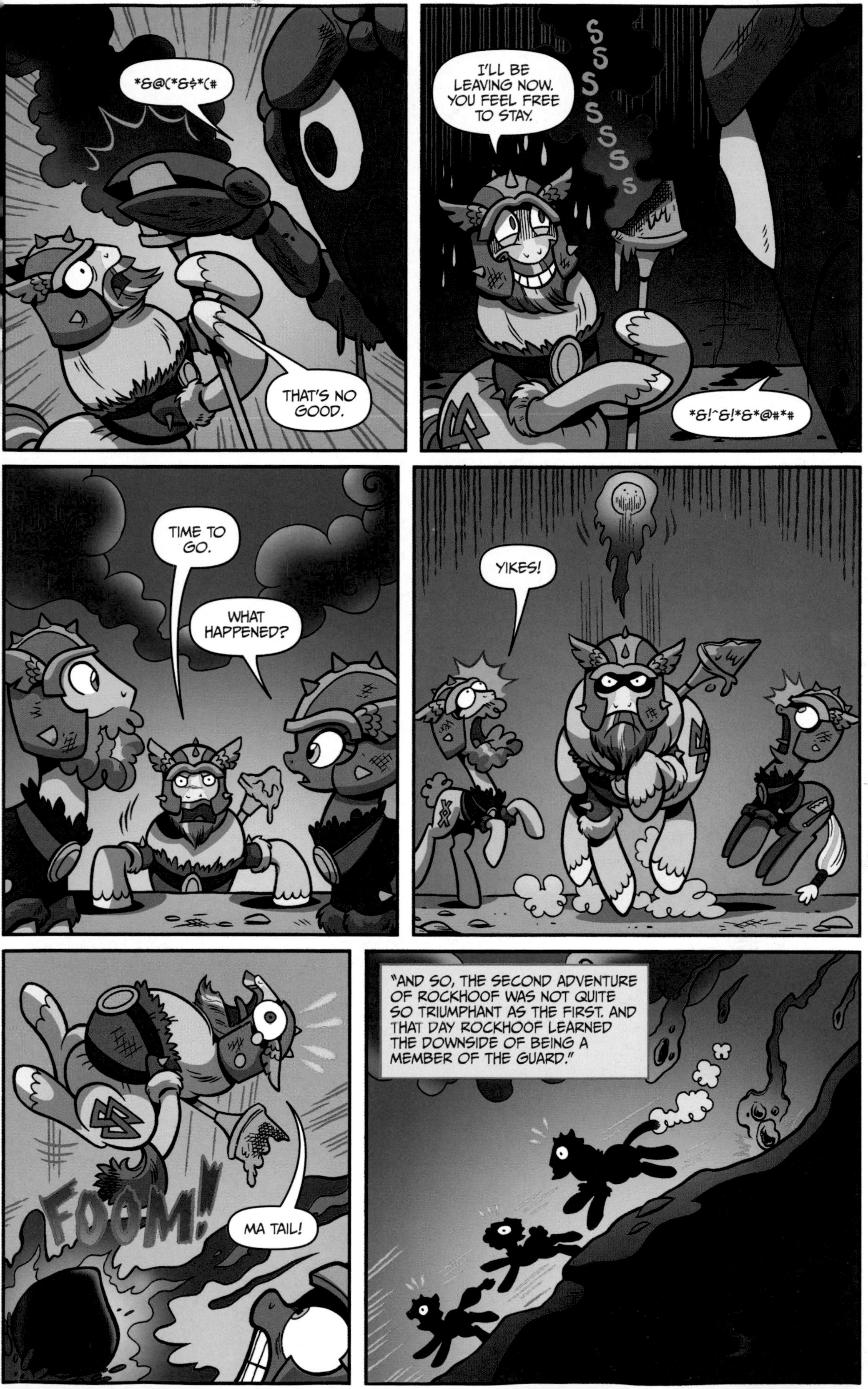
&@(&$*(#
THAT'S NO GOOD.
I'LL BE LEAVING NOW. YOU FEEL FREE TO STAY.
SSSSSSS
&!^&!&*@#*#
TIME TO GO.
WHAT HAPPENED?
YIKES!
FOOM!
MA TAIL!
"AND SO, THE SECOND ADVENTURE OF ROCKHOOF WAS NOT QUITE SO TRIUMPHANT AS THE FIRST. AND THAT DAY ROCKHOOF LEARNED THE DOWNSIDE OF BEING A MEMBER OF THE GUARD."

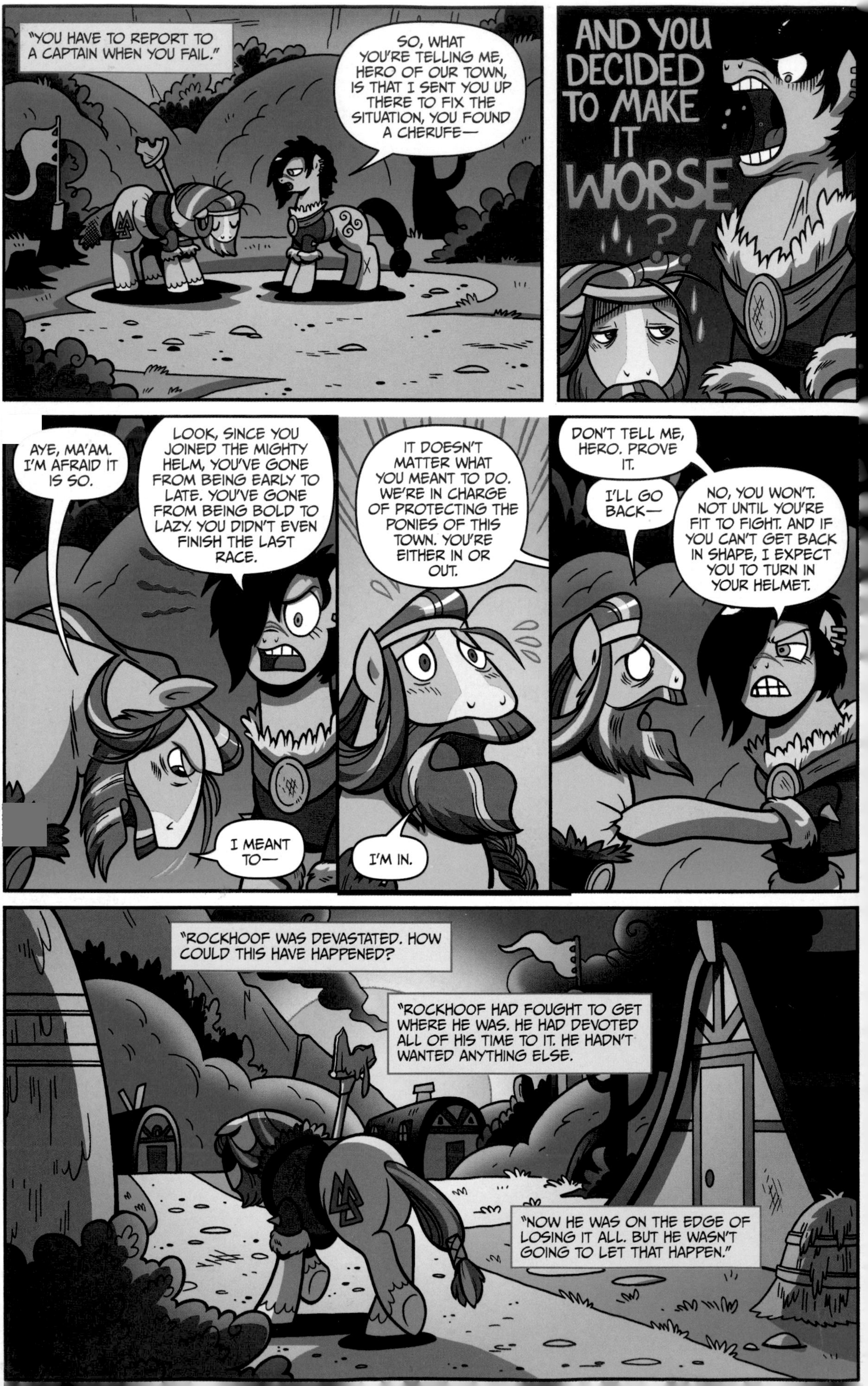
"YOU HAVE TO REPORT TO A CAPTAIN WHEN YOU FAIL."
SO, WHAT YOU'RE TELLING ME, HERO OF OUR TOWN, IS THAT I SENT YOU UP THERE TO FIX THE SITUATION, YOU FOUND A CHERUFE—
AND YOU DECIDED TO MAKE IT WORSE ?!
AYE, MA'AM. I'M AFRAID IT IS SO.
LOOK, SINCE YOU JOINED THE MIGHTY HELM, YOU'VE GONE FROM BEING EARLY TO LATE. YOU'VE GONE FROM BEING BOLD TO LAZY. YOU DIDN'T EVEN FINISH THE LAST RACE.
I MEANT TO—
IT DOESN'T MATTER WHAT YOU MEANT TO DO. WE'RE IN CHARGE OF PROTECTING THE PONIES OF THIS TOWN. YOU'RE EITHER IN OR OUT.
I'M IN.
DON'T TELL ME, HERO. PROVE IT.
I'LL GO BACK—
NO, YOU WON'T. NOT UNTIL YOU'RE FIT TO FIGHT. AND IF YOU CAN'T GET BACK IN SHAPE, I EXPECT YOU TO TURN IN YOUR HELMET.
"ROCKHOOF WAS DEVASTATED. HOW COULD THIS HAVE HAPPENED?
"ROCKHOOF HAD FOUGHT TO GET WHERE HE WAS. HE HAD DEVOTED ALL OF HIS TIME TO IT. HE HADN'T WANTED ANYTHING ELSE.
"NOW HE WAS ON THE EDGE OF LOSING IT ALL. BUT HE WASN'T GOING TO LET THAT HAPPEN."

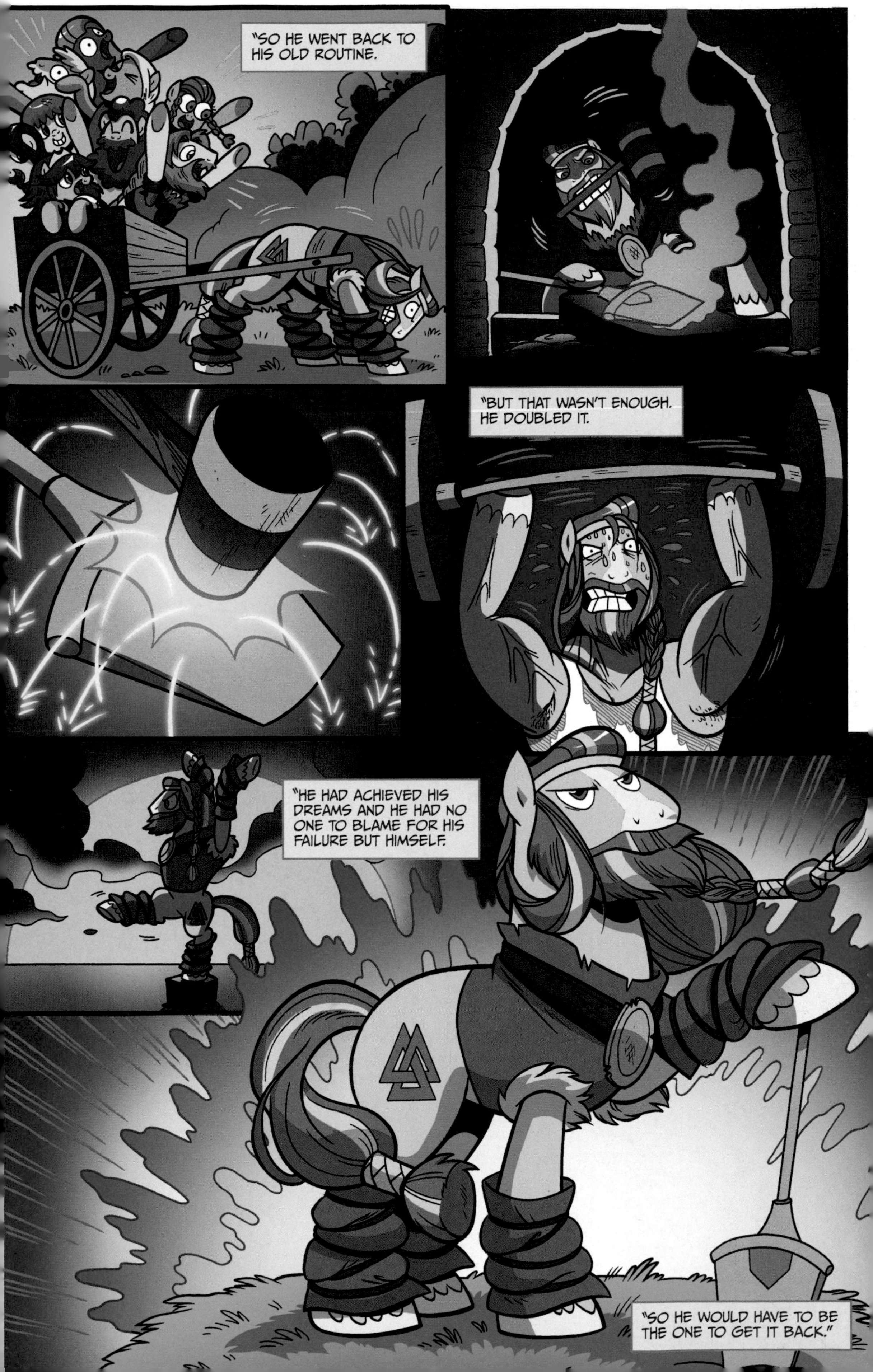
"SO HE WENT BACK TO HIS OLD ROUTINE.
"BUT THAT WASN'T ENOUGH. HE DOUBLED IT.
"HE HAD ACHIEVED HIS DREAMS AND HE HAD NO ONE TO BLAME FOR HIS FAILURE BUT HIMSELF.
"SO HE WOULD HAVE TO BE THE ONE TO GET IT BACK."

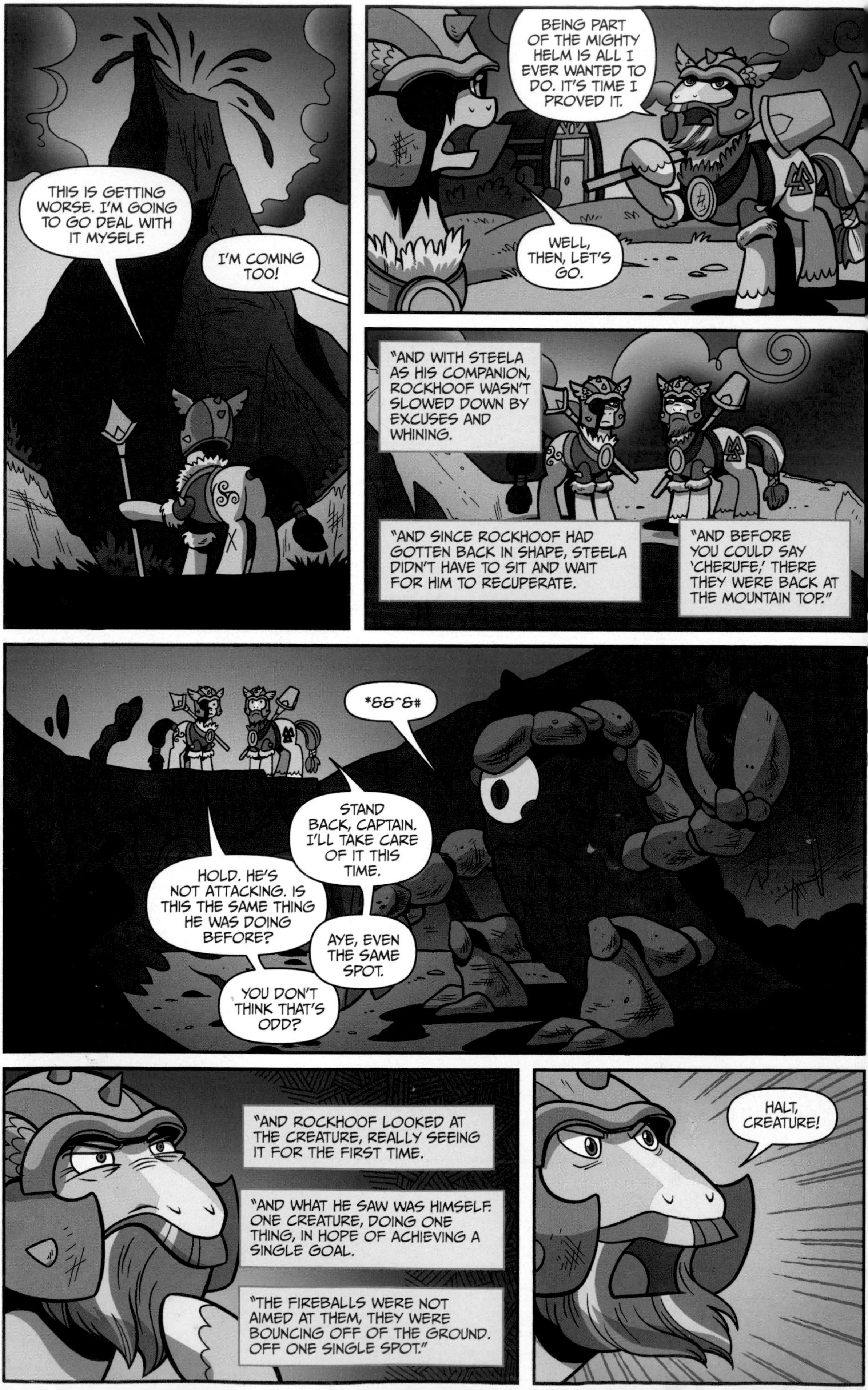

THIS IS GETTING WORSE. I'M GOING TO GO DEAL WITH IT MYSELF.
I'M COMING TOO!
BEING PART OF THE MIGHTY HELM IS ALL I EVER WANTED TO DO. IT'S TIME I PROVED IT.
WELL, THEN, LET'S GO.
"AND WITH STEELA AS HIS COMPANION, ROCKHOOF WASN'T SLOWED DOWN BY EXCUSES AND WHINING.
"AND SINCE ROCKHOOF HAD GOTTEN BACK IN SHAPE, STEELA DIDN'T HAVE TO SIT AND WAIT FOR HIM TO RECUPERATE.
"AND BEFORE YOU COULD SAY 'CHERUFE,' THERE THEY WERE BACK AT THE MOUNTAIN TOP."
*&&^&#
STAND BACK, CAPTAIN. I'LL TAKE CARE OF IT THIS TIME.
HOLD. HE'S NOT ATTACKING. IS THIS THE SAME THING HE WAS DOING BEFORE?
AYE, EVEN THE SAME SPOT.
YOU DON'T THINK THAT'S ODD?
"AND ROCKHOOF LOOKED AT THE CREATURE, REALLY SEEING IT FOR THE FIRST TIME.
"AND WHAT HE SAW WAS HIMSELF. ONE CREATURE, DOING ONE THING, IN HOPE OF ACHIEVING A SINGLE GOAL.
"THE FIREBALLS WERE NOT AIMED AT THEM, THEY WERE BOUNCING OFF OF THE GROUND. OFF ONE SINGLE SPOT."
HALT, CREATURE!

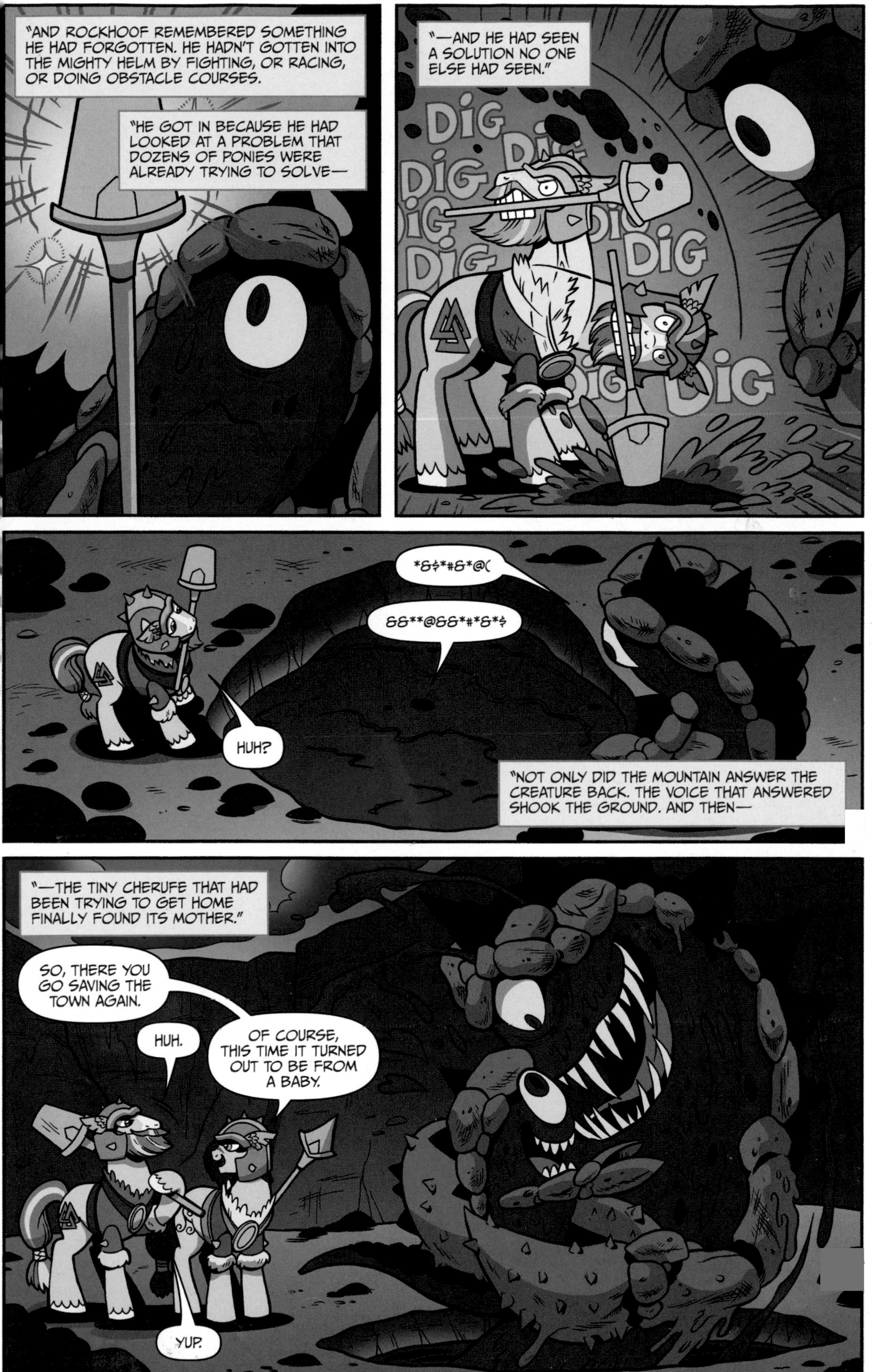
"AND ROCKHOOF REMEMBERED SOMETHING HE HAD FORGOTTEN. HE HADN'T GOTTEN INTO THE MIGHTY HELM BY FIGHTING, OR RACING, OR DOING OBSTACLE COURSES.
"HE GOT IN BECAUSE HE HAD LOOKED AT A PROBLEM THAT DOZENS OF PONIES WERE ALREADY TRYING TO SOLVE—
"—AND HE HAD SEEN A SOLUTION NO ONE ELSE HAD SEEN."
DIG DIG DIG DIG DIG DIG DIG DIG DIG DIG
&$#&*@(
&&**@&&*#*&*$
HUH?
"NOT ONLY DID THE MOUNTAIN ANSWER THE CREATURE BACK. THE VOICE THAT ANSWERED SHOOK THE GROUND. AND THEN—
"—THE TINY CHERUFE THAT HAD BEEN TRYING TO GET HOME FINALLY FOUND ITS MOTHER."
SO, THERE YOU GO SAVING THE TOWN AGAIN.
HUH.
OF COURSE, THIS TIME IT TURNED OUT TO BE FROM A BABY.
YUP.

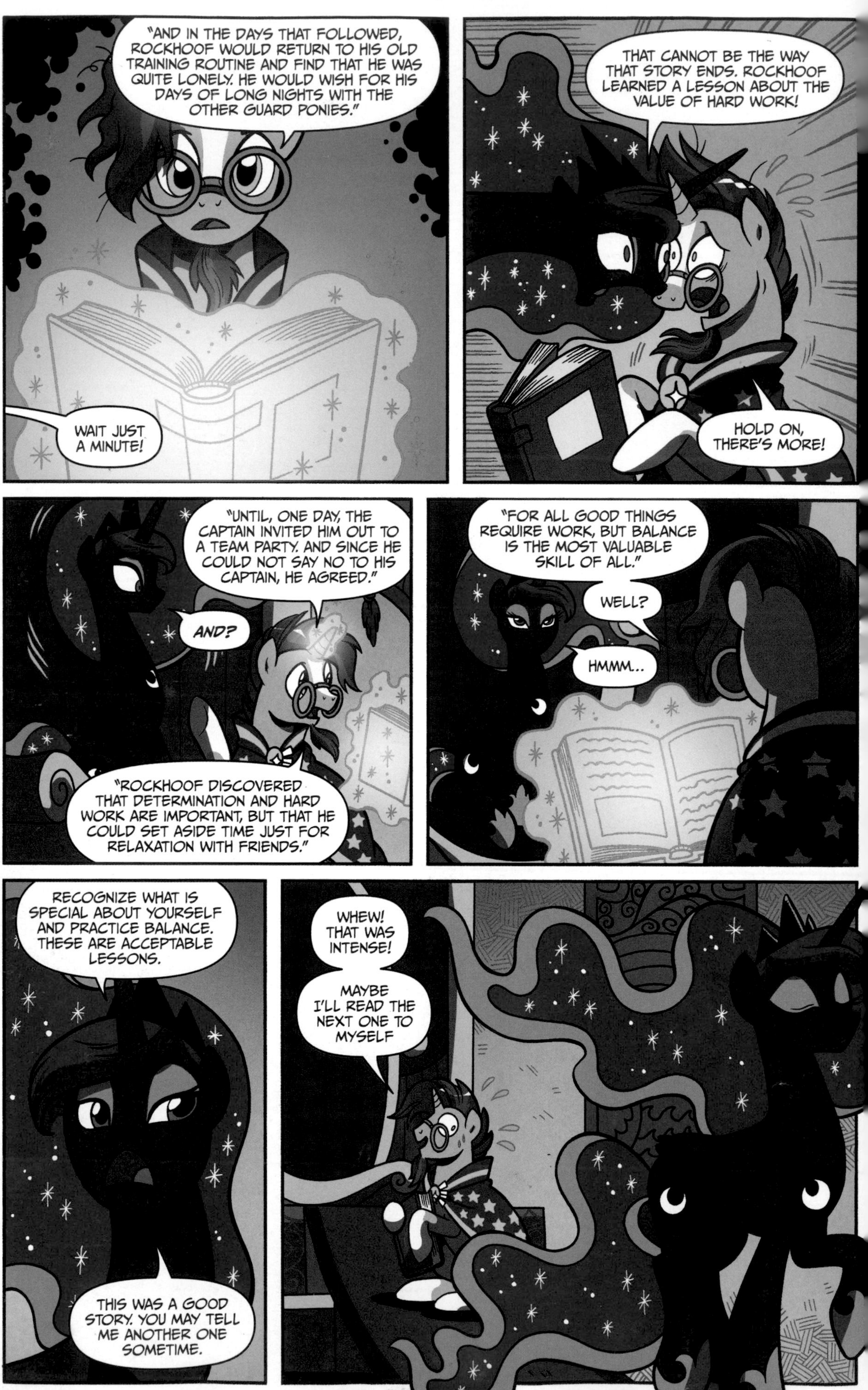
"AND IN THE DAYS THAT FOLLOWED, ROCKHOOF WOULD RETURN TO HIS OLD TRAINING ROUTINE AND FIND THAT HE WAS QUITE LONELY. HE WOULD WISH FOR HIS DAYS OF LONG NIGHTS WITH THE OTHER GUARD PONIES."
WAIT JUST A MINUTE!
THAT CANNOT BE THE WAY THAT STORY ENDS. ROCKHOOF LEARNED A LESSON ABOUT THE VALUE OF HARD WORK!
HOLD ON, THERE'S MORE!
"UNTIL, ONE DAY, THE CAPTAIN INVITED HIM OUT TO A TEAM PARTY. AND SINCE HE COULD NOT SAY NO TO HIS CAPTAIN, HE AGREED."
AND?
"ROCKHOOF DISCOVERED THAT DETERMINATION AND HARD WORK ARE IMPORTANT, BUT THAT HE COULD SET ASIDE TIME JUST FOR RELAXATION WITH FRIENDS."
"FOR ALL GOOD THINGS REQUIRE WORK, BUT BALANCE IS THE MOST VALUABLE SKILL OF ALL."
WELL?
HMMM...
RECOGNIZE WHAT IS SPECIAL ABOUT YOURSELF AND PRACTICE BALANCE. THESE ARE ACCEPTABLE LESSONS.
THIS WAS A GOOD STORY. YOU MAY TELL ME ANOTHER ONE SOMETIME.
WHEW! THAT WAS INTENSE!
MAYBE I'LL READ THE NEXT ONE TO MYSELF

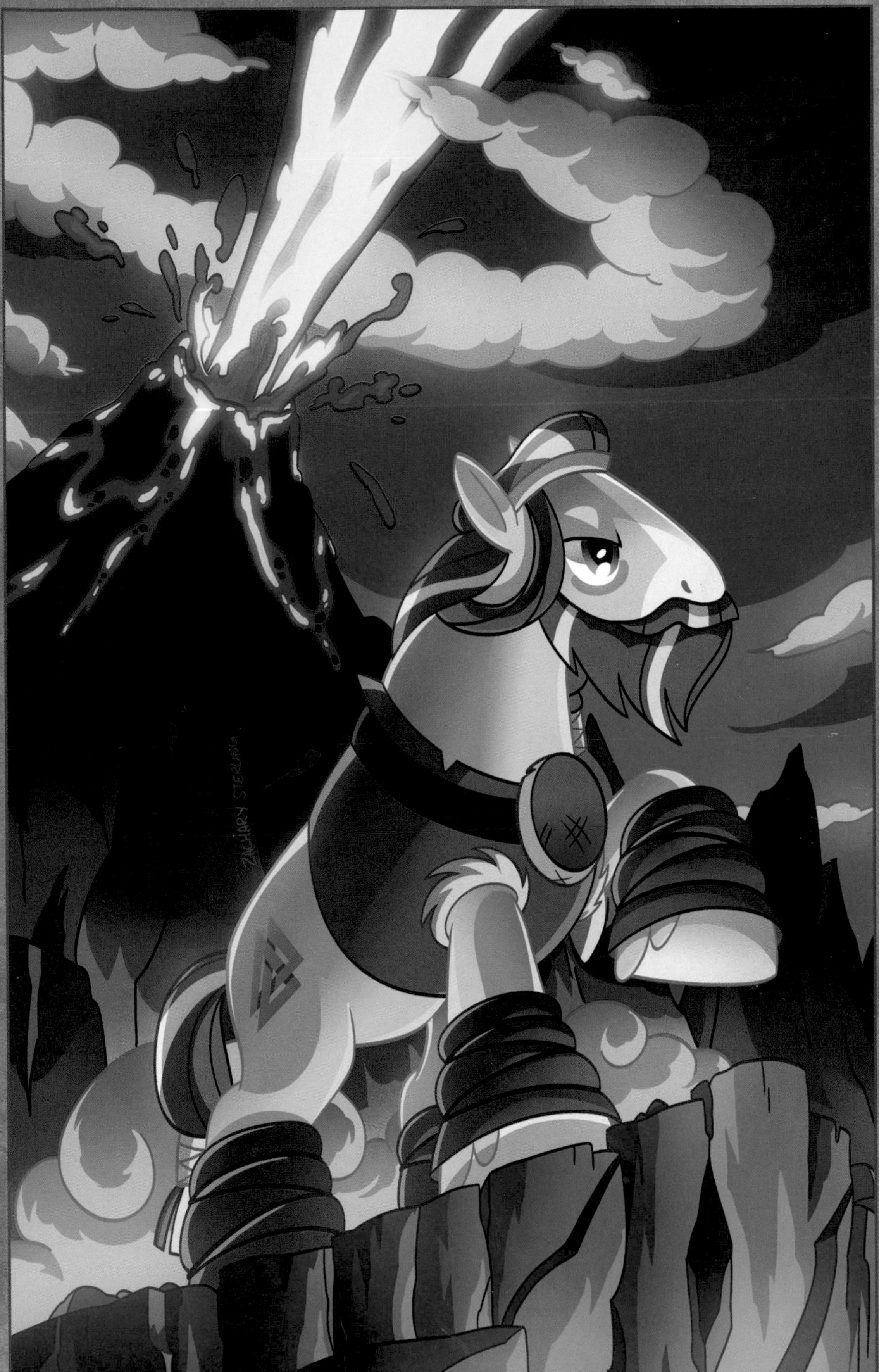
ZACHARY STERLING

ART BY ZACHARY STERLING

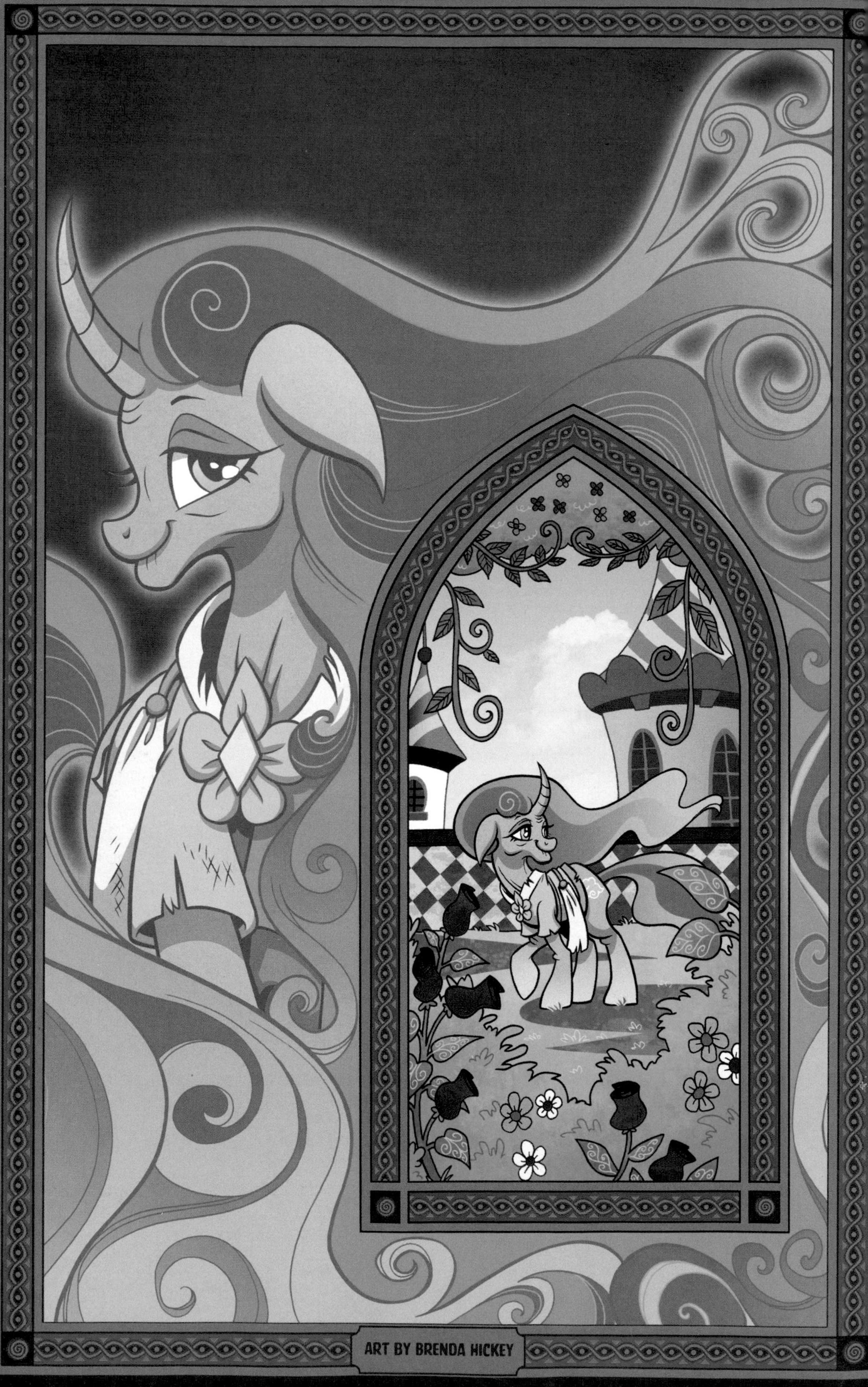
ART BY BRENDA HICKEY

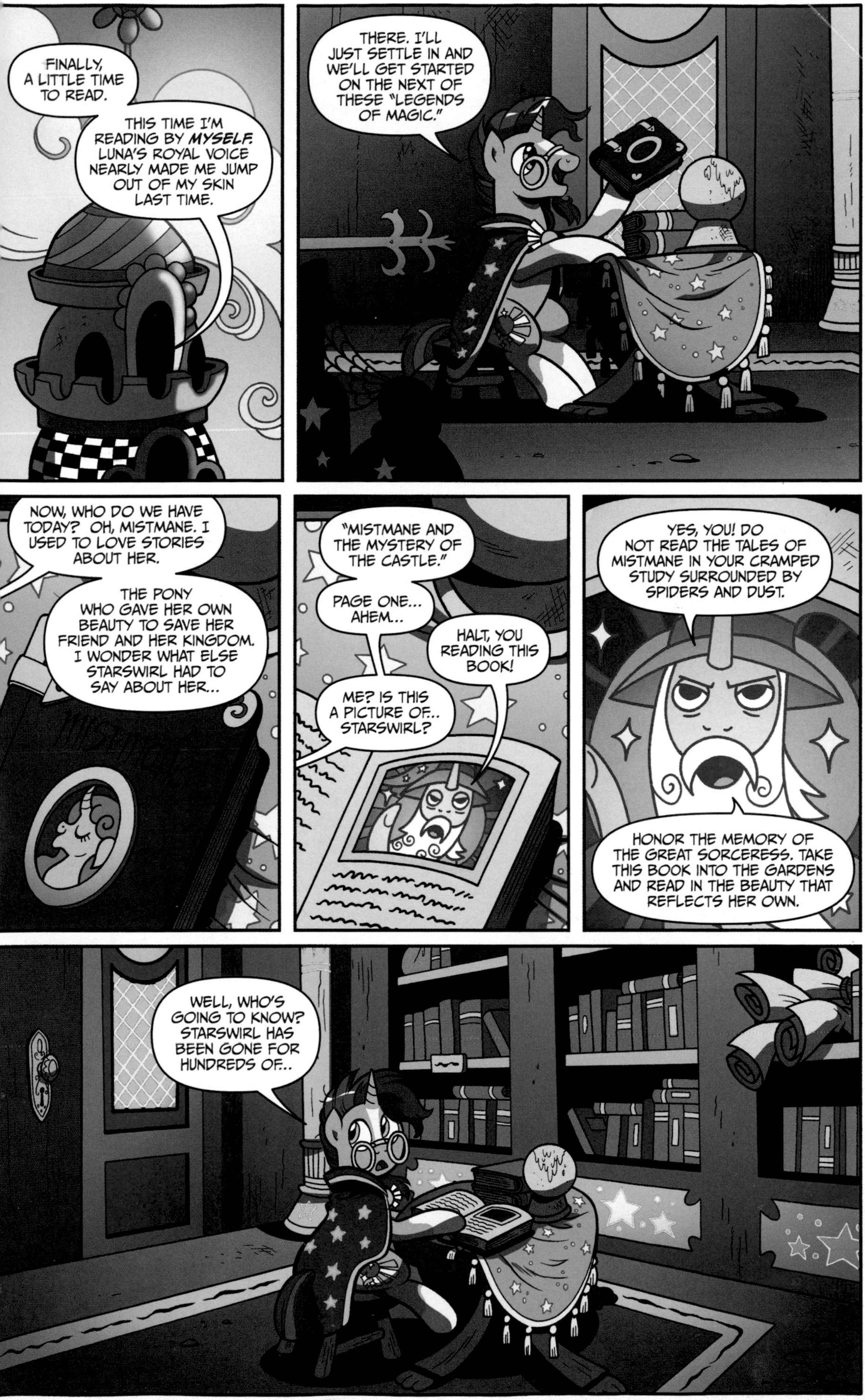

FINALLY, A LITTLE TIME TO READ.
THIS TIME I'M READING BY ***MYSELF.*** LUNA'S ROYAL VOICE NEARLY MADE ME JUMP OUT OF MY SKIN LAST TIME.
THERE. I'LL JUST SETTLE IN AND WE'LL GET STARTED ON THE NEXT OF THESE "LEGENDS OF MAGIC."
NOW, WHO DO WE HAVE TODAY? OH, MISTMANE. I USED TO LOVE STORIES ABOUT HER.
THE PONY WHO GAVE HER OWN BEAUTY TO SAVE HER FRIEND AND HER KINGDOM. I WONDER WHAT ELSE STARSWIRL HAD TO SAY ABOUT HER...
"MISTMANE AND THE MYSTERY OF THE CASTLE."
PAGE ONE... AHEM...
HALT, YOU READING THIS BOOK!
ME? IS THIS A PICTURE OF... STARSWIRL?
YES, YOU! DO NOT READ THE TALES OF MISTMANE IN YOUR CRAMPED STUDY SURROUNDED BY SPIDERS AND DUST.
HONOR THE MEMORY OF THE GREAT SORCERESS. TAKE THIS BOOK INTO THE GARDENS AND READ IN THE BEAUTY THAT REFLECTS HER OWN.
WELL, WHO'S GOING TO KNOW? STARSWIRL HAS BEEN GONE FOR HUNDREDS OF...

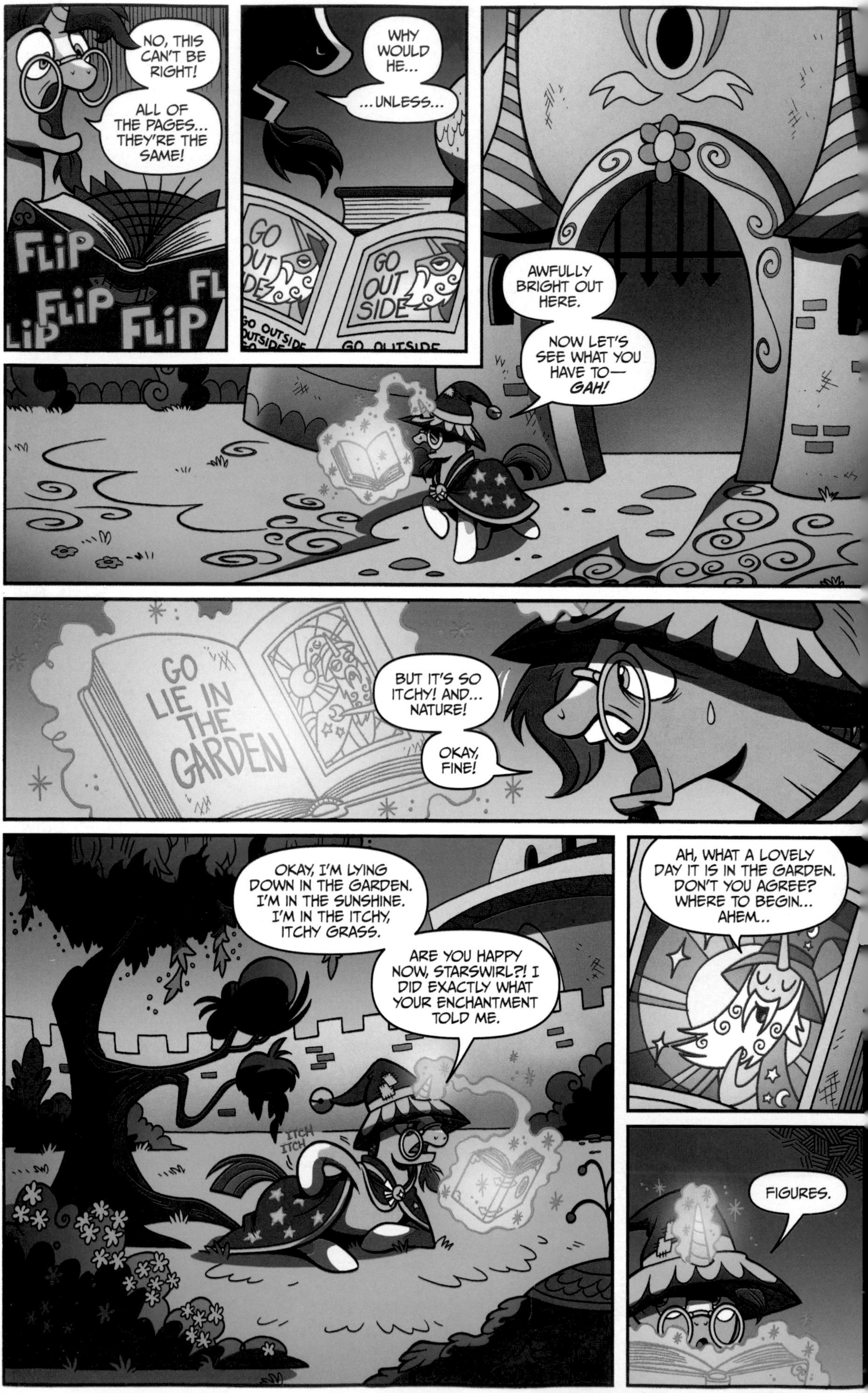
NO, THIS CAN'T BE RIGHT!
ALL OF THE PAGES... THEY'RE THE SAME!
FLIP FLIP FLIP FLIP FLIP FLIP
WHY WOULD HE...
...UNLESS...
GO OUTSIDE
GO OUTSIDE
GO OUTSIDE
GO OUTSIDE
AWFULLY BRIGHT OUT HERE.
NOW LET'S SEE WHAT YOU HAVE TO— GAH!
GO LIE IN THE GARDEN
BUT IT'S SO ITCHY! AND... NATURE!
OKAY, FINE!
OKAY, I'M LYING DOWN IN THE GARDEN. I'M IN THE SUNSHINE. I'M IN THE ITCHY, ITCHY GRASS.
ARE YOU HAPPY NOW, STARSWIRL?! I DID EXACTLY WHAT YOUR ENCHANTMENT TOLD ME.
ITCH ITCH
AH, WHAT A LOVELY DAY IT IS IN THE GARDEN. DON'T YOU AGREE? WHERE TO BEGIN... AHEM...
FIGURES.

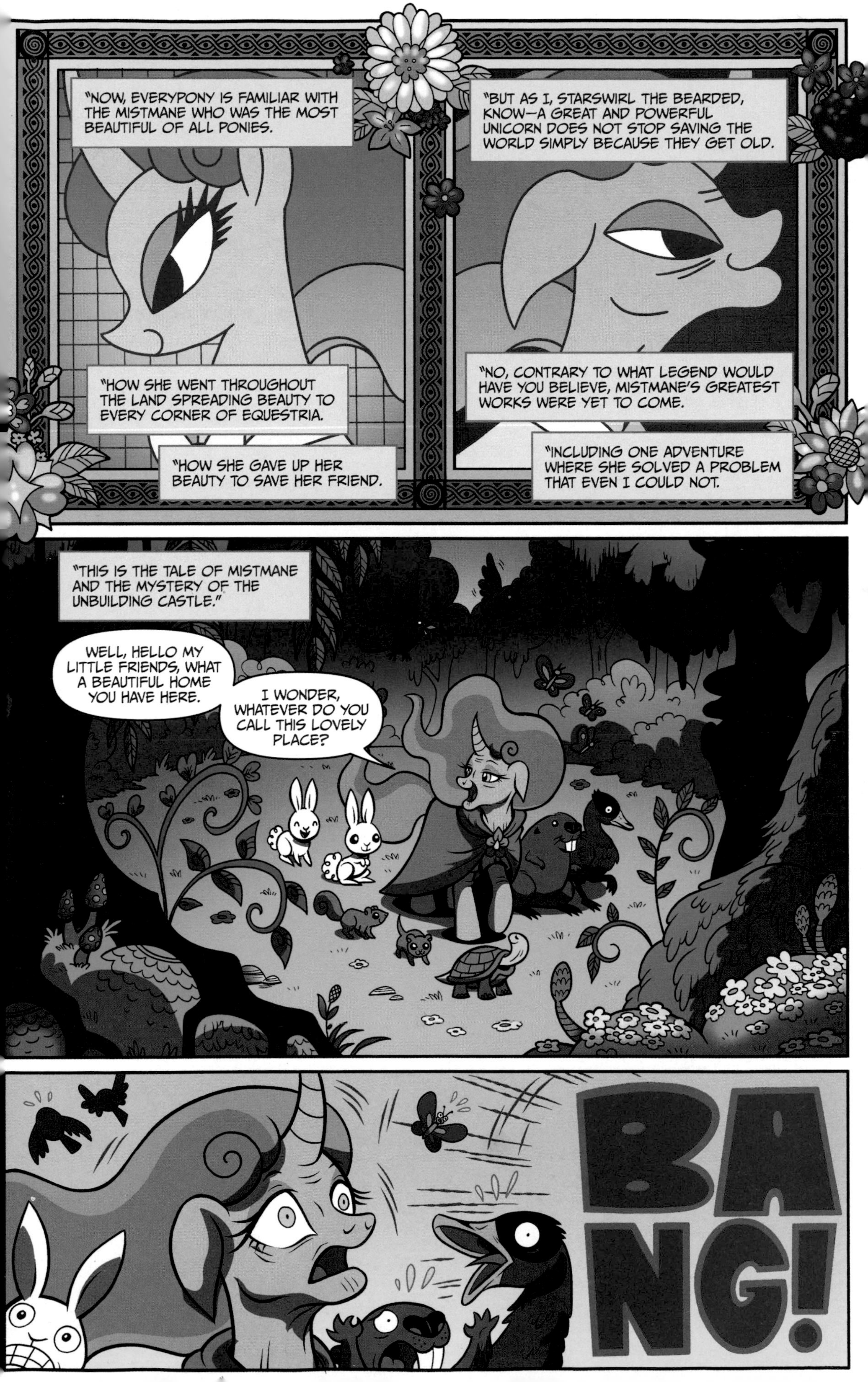
"NOW, EVERYPONY IS FAMILIAR WITH THE MISTMANE WHO WAS THE MOST BEAUTIFUL OF ALL PONIES.
"HOW SHE WENT THROUGHOUT THE LAND SPREADING BEAUTY TO EVERY CORNER OF EQUESTRIA.
"HOW SHE GAVE UP HER BEAUTY TO SAVE HER FRIEND.
"BUT AS I, STARSWIRL THE BEARDED, KNOW—A GREAT AND POWERFUL UNICORN DOES NOT STOP SAVING THE WORLD SIMPLY BECAUSE THEY GET OLD.
"NO, CONTRARY TO WHAT LEGEND WOULD HAVE YOU BELIEVE, MISTMANE'S GREATEST WORKS WERE YET TO COME.
"INCLUDING ONE ADVENTURE WHERE SHE SOLVED A PROBLEM THAT EVEN I COULD NOT.
"THIS IS THE TALE OF MISTMANE AND THE MYSTERY OF THE UNBUILDING CASTLE."
WELL, HELLO MY LITTLE FRIENDS, WHAT A BEAUTIFUL HOME YOU HAVE HERE.
I WONDER, WHATEVER DO YOU CALL THIS LOVELY PLACE?
BANG!

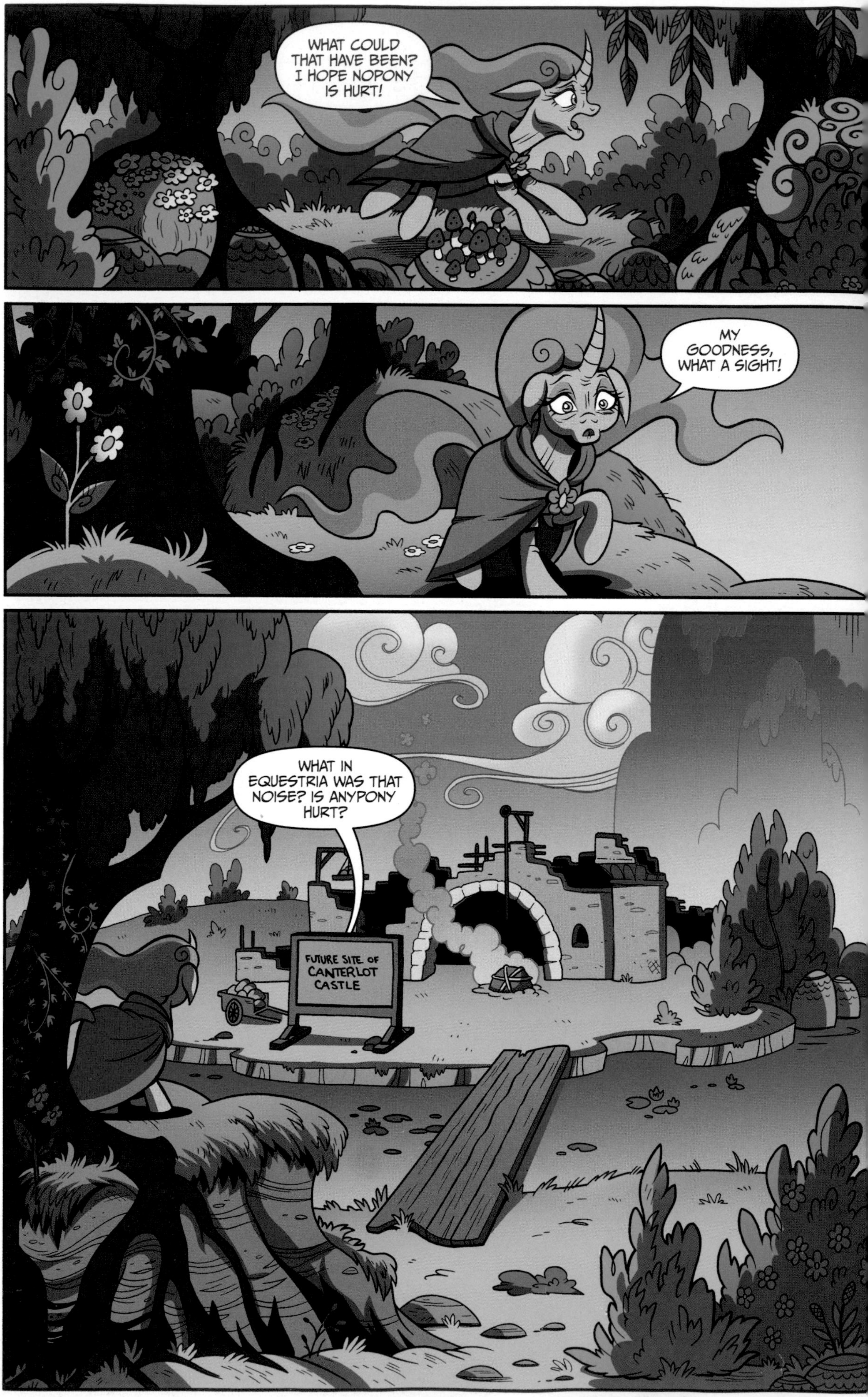
WHAT COULD THAT HAVE BEEN? I HOPE NOPONY IS HURT!
MY GOODNESS, WHAT A SIGHT!
WHAT IN EQUESTRIA WAS THAT NOISE? IS ANYPONY HURT?
FUTURE SITE OF CANTERLOT CASTLE

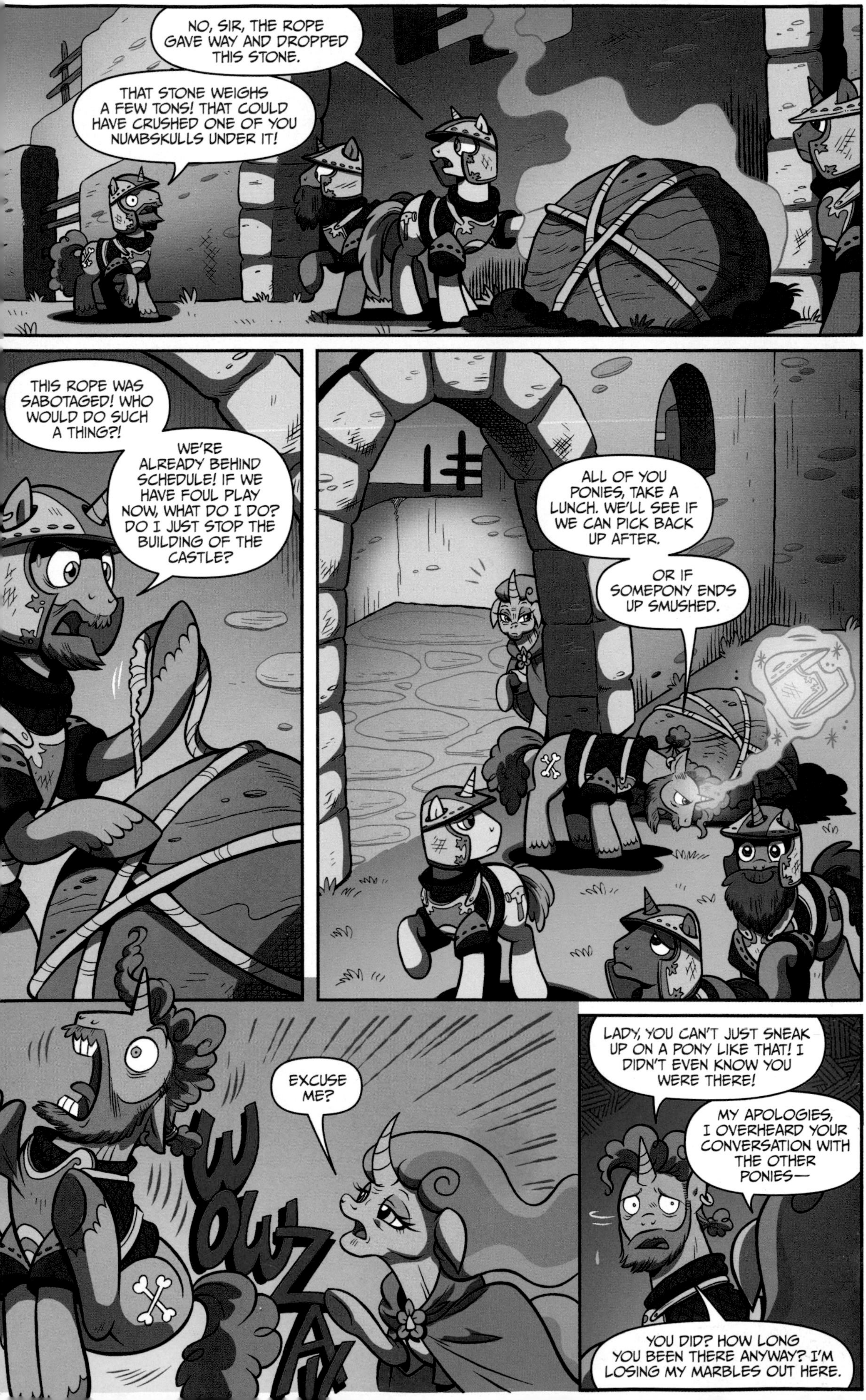

NO, SIR, THE ROPE GAVE WAY AND DROPPED THIS STONE.
THAT STONE WEIGHS A FEW TONS! THAT COULD HAVE CRUSHED ONE OF YOU NUMBSKULLS UNDER IT!
THIS ROPE WAS SABOTAGED! WHO WOULD DO SUCH A THING?!
WE'RE ALREADY BEHIND SCHEDULE! IF WE HAVE FOUL PLAY NOW, WHAT DO I DO? DO I JUST STOP THE BUILDING OF THE CASTLE?
ALL OF YOU PONIES, TAKE A LUNCH. WE'LL SEE IF WE CAN PICK BACK UP AFTER.
OR IF SOMEPONY ENDS UP SMUSHED.
WOWZA
EXCUSE ME?
LADY, YOU CAN'T JUST SNEAK UP ON A PONY LIKE THAT! I DIDN'T EVEN KNOW YOU WERE THERE!
MY APOLOGIES, I OVERHEARD YOUR CONVERSATION WITH THE OTHER PONIES—
YOU DID? HOW LONG YOU BEEN THERE ANYWAY? I'M LOSING MY MARBLES OUT HERE.

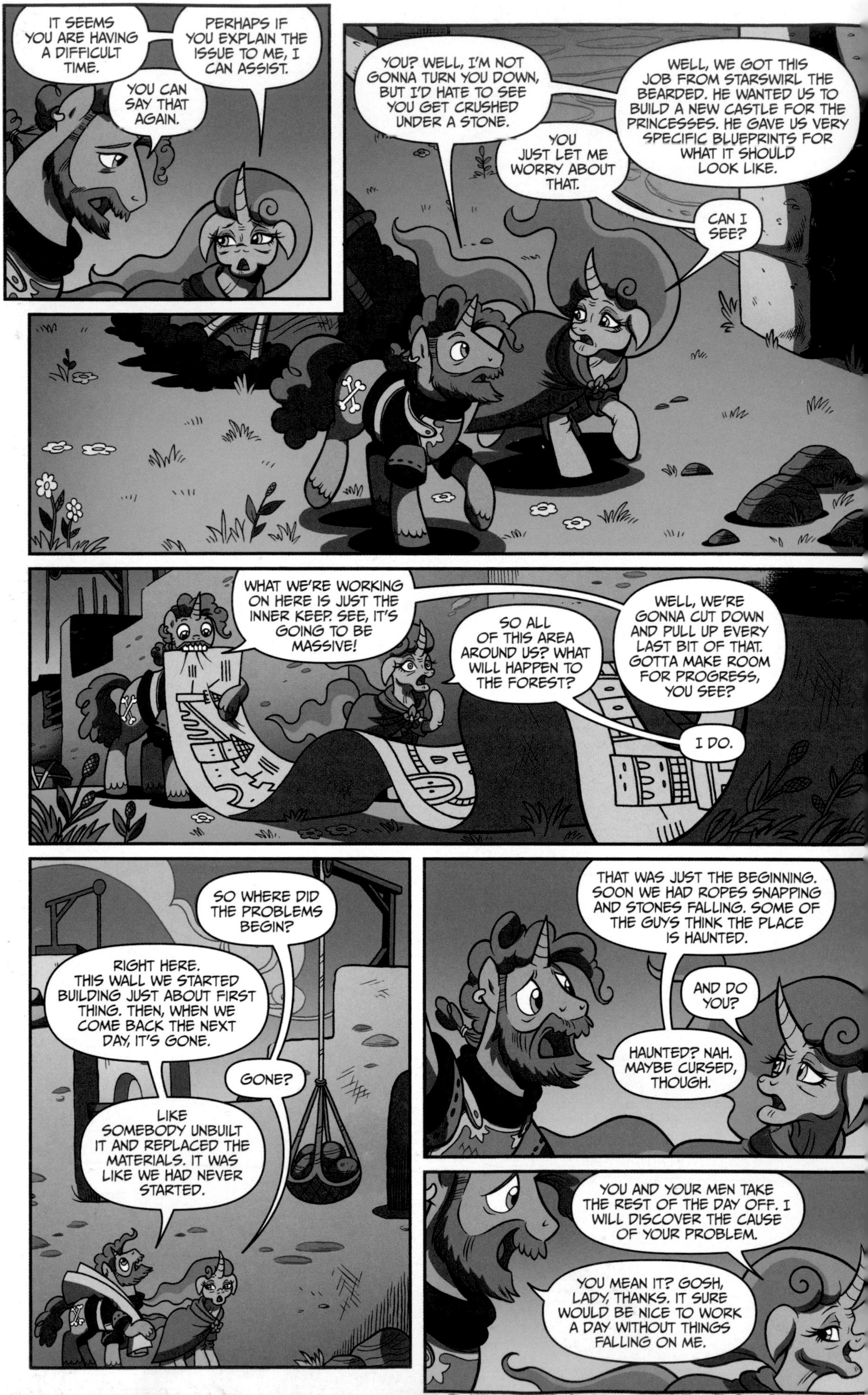
IT SEEMS YOU ARE HAVING A DIFFICULT TIME.
YOU CAN SAY THAT AGAIN.
PERHAPS IF YOU EXPLAIN THE ISSUE TO ME, I CAN ASSIST.
YOU? WELL, I'M NOT GONNA TURN YOU DOWN, BUT I'D HATE TO SEE YOU GET CRUSHED UNDER A STONE.
YOU JUST LET ME WORRY ABOUT THAT.
WELL, WE GOT THIS JOB FROM STARSWIRL THE BEARDED. HE WANTED US TO BUILD A NEW CASTLE FOR THE PRINCESSES. HE GAVE US VERY SPECIFIC BLUEPRINTS FOR WHAT IT SHOULD LOOK LIKE.
CAN I SEE?
WHAT WE'RE WORKING ON HERE IS JUST THE INNER KEEP. SEE, IT'S GOING TO BE MASSIVE!
SO ALL OF THIS AREA AROUND US? WHAT WILL HAPPEN TO THE FOREST?
WELL, WE'RE GONNA CUT DOWN AND PULL UP EVERY LAST BIT OF THAT. GOTTA MAKE ROOM FOR PROGRESS, YOU SEE?
I DO.
SO WHERE DID THE PROBLEMS BEGIN?
RIGHT HERE. THIS WALL WE STARTED BUILDING JUST ABOUT FIRST THING. THEN, WHEN WE COME BACK THE NEXT DAY, IT'S GONE.
GONE?
LIKE SOMEBODY UNBUILT IT AND REPLACED THE MATERIALS. IT WAS LIKE WE HAD NEVER STARTED.
THAT WAS JUST THE BEGINNING. SOON WE HAD ROPES SNAPPING AND STONES FALLING. SOME OF THE GUYS THINK THE PLACE IS HAUNTED.
AND DO YOU?
HAUNTED? NAH. MAYBE CURSED, THOUGH.
YOU AND YOUR MEN TAKE THE REST OF THE DAY OFF. I WILL DISCOVER THE CAUSE OF YOUR PROBLEM.
YOU MEAN IT? GOSH, LADY, THANKS. IT SURE WOULD BE NICE TO WORK A DAY WITHOUT THINGS FALLING ON ME.

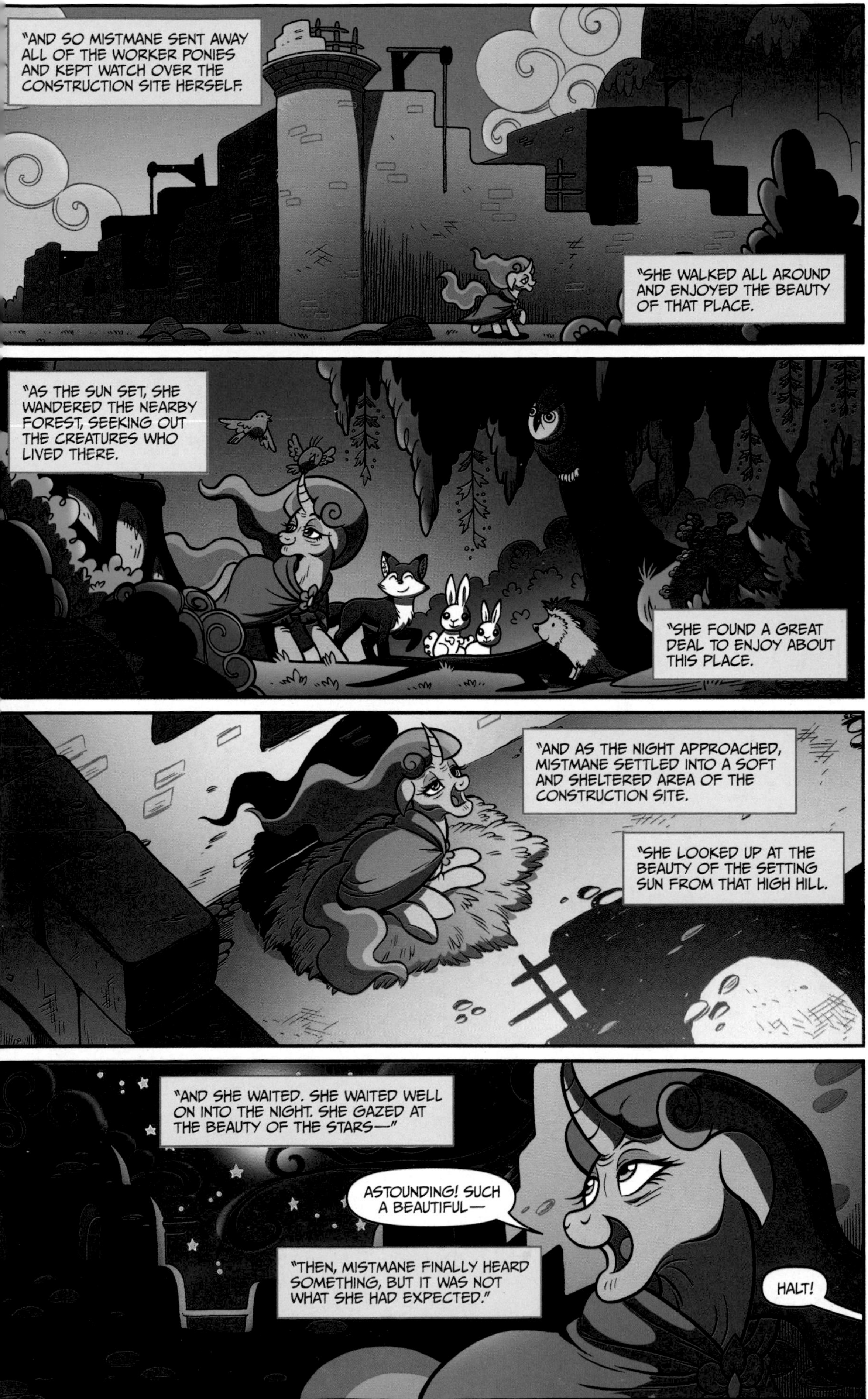
"AND SO MISTMANE SENT AWAY ALL OF THE WORKER PONIES AND KEPT WATCH OVER THE CONSTRUCTION SITE HERSELF.
"SHE WALKED ALL AROUND AND ENJOYED THE BEAUTY OF THAT PLACE.
"AS THE SUN SET, SHE WANDERED THE NEARBY FOREST, SEEKING OUT THE CREATURES WHO LIVED THERE.
"SHE FOUND A GREAT DEAL TO ENJOY ABOUT THIS PLACE.
"AND AS THE NIGHT APPROACHED, MISTMANE SETTLED INTO A SOFT AND SHELTERED AREA OF THE CONSTRUCTION SITE.
"SHE LOOKED UP AT THE BEAUTY OF THE SETTING SUN FROM THAT HIGH HILL.
"AND SHE WAITED. SHE WAITED WELL ON INTO THE NIGHT. SHE GAZED AT THE BEAUTY OF THE STARS—"
ASTOUNDING! SUCH A BEAUTIFUL—
"THEN, MISTMANE FINALLY HEARD SOMETHING, BUT IT WAS NOT WHAT SHE HAD EXPECTED."
HALT!

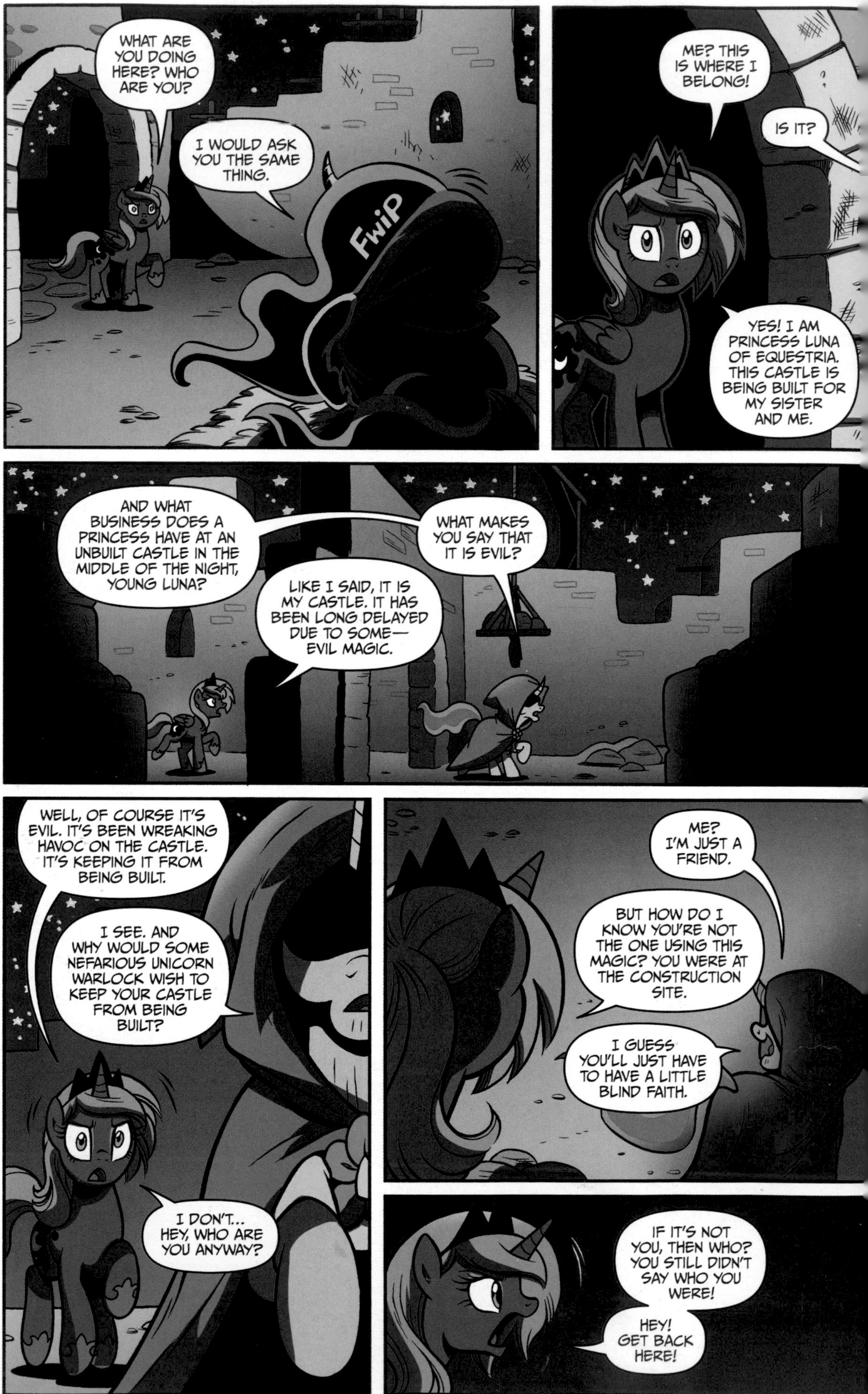
WHAT ARE YOU DOING HERE? WHO ARE YOU?
I WOULD ASK YOU THE SAME THING.
FWIP
ME? THIS IS WHERE I BELONG!
IS IT?
YES! I AM PRINCESS LUNA OF EQUESTRIA. THIS CASTLE IS BEING BUILT FOR MY SISTER AND ME.
AND WHAT BUSINESS DOES A PRINCESS HAVE AT AN UNBUILT CASTLE IN THE MIDDLE OF THE NIGHT, YOUNG LUNA?
LIKE I SAID, IT IS MY CASTLE. IT HAS BEEN LONG DELAYED DUE TO SOME— EVIL MAGIC.
WHAT MAKES YOU SAY THAT IT IS EVIL?
WELL, OF COURSE IT'S EVIL. IT'S BEEN WREAKING HAVOC ON THE CASTLE. IT'S KEEPING IT FROM BEING BUILT.
I SEE. AND WHY WOULD SOME NEFARIOUS UNICORN WARLOCK WISH TO KEEP YOUR CASTLE FROM BEING BUILT?
I DON'T... HEY, WHO ARE YOU ANYWAY?
ME? I'M JUST A FRIEND.
BUT HOW DO I KNOW YOU'RE NOT THE ONE USING THIS MAGIC? YOU WERE AT THE CONSTRUCTION SITE.
I GUESS YOU'LL JUST HAVE TO HAVE A LITTLE BLIND FAITH.
IF IT'S NOT YOU, THEN WHO? YOU STILL DIDN'T SAY WHO YOU WERE!
HEY! GET BACK HERE!

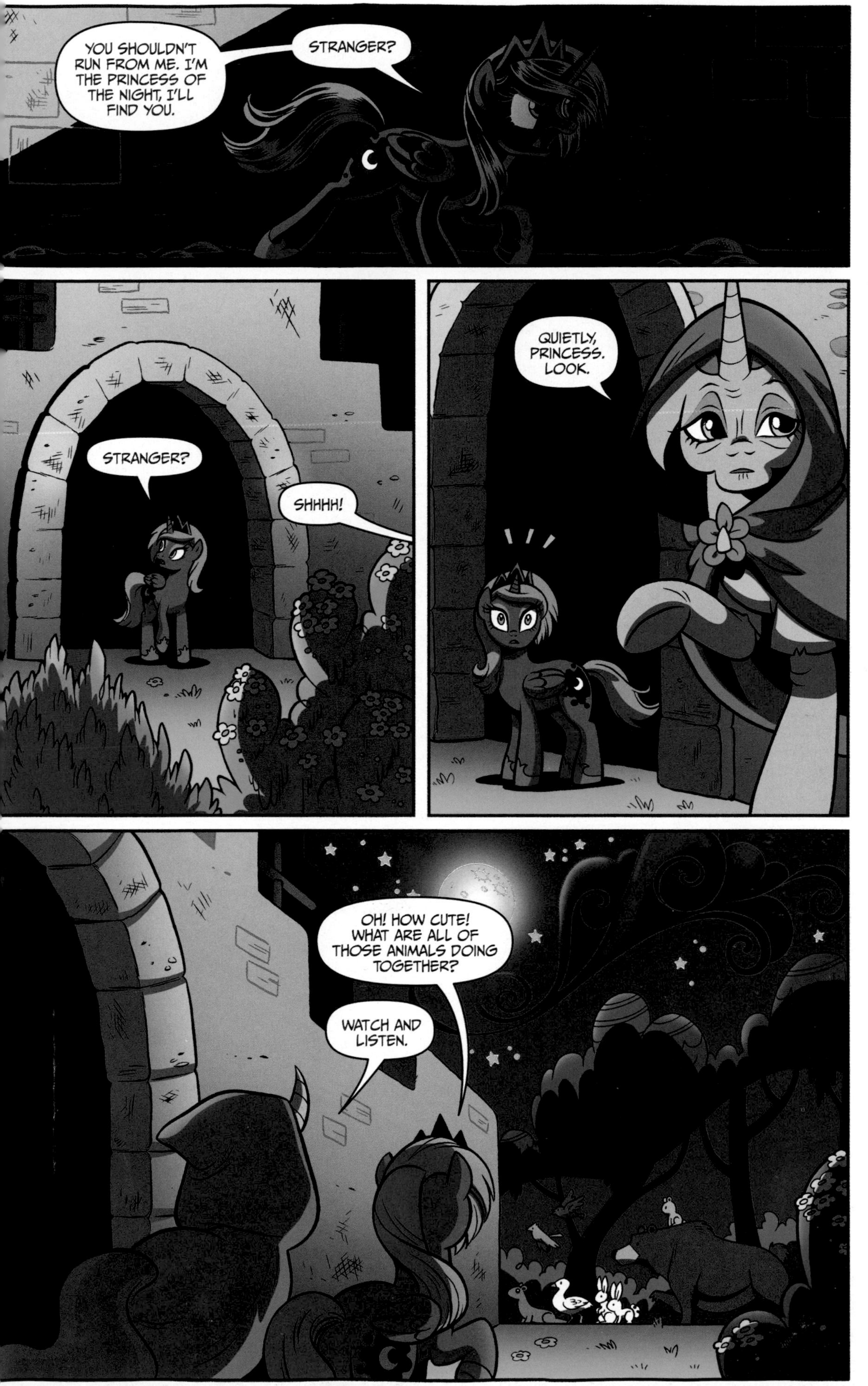
STRANGER?
YOU SHOULDN'T RUN FROM ME. I'M THE PRINCESS OF THE NIGHT, I'LL FIND YOU.
STRANGER?
SHHHH!
QUIETLY, PRINCESS. LOOK.
OH! HOW CUTE! WHAT ARE ALL OF THOSE ANIMALS DOING TOGETHER?
WATCH AND LISTEN.

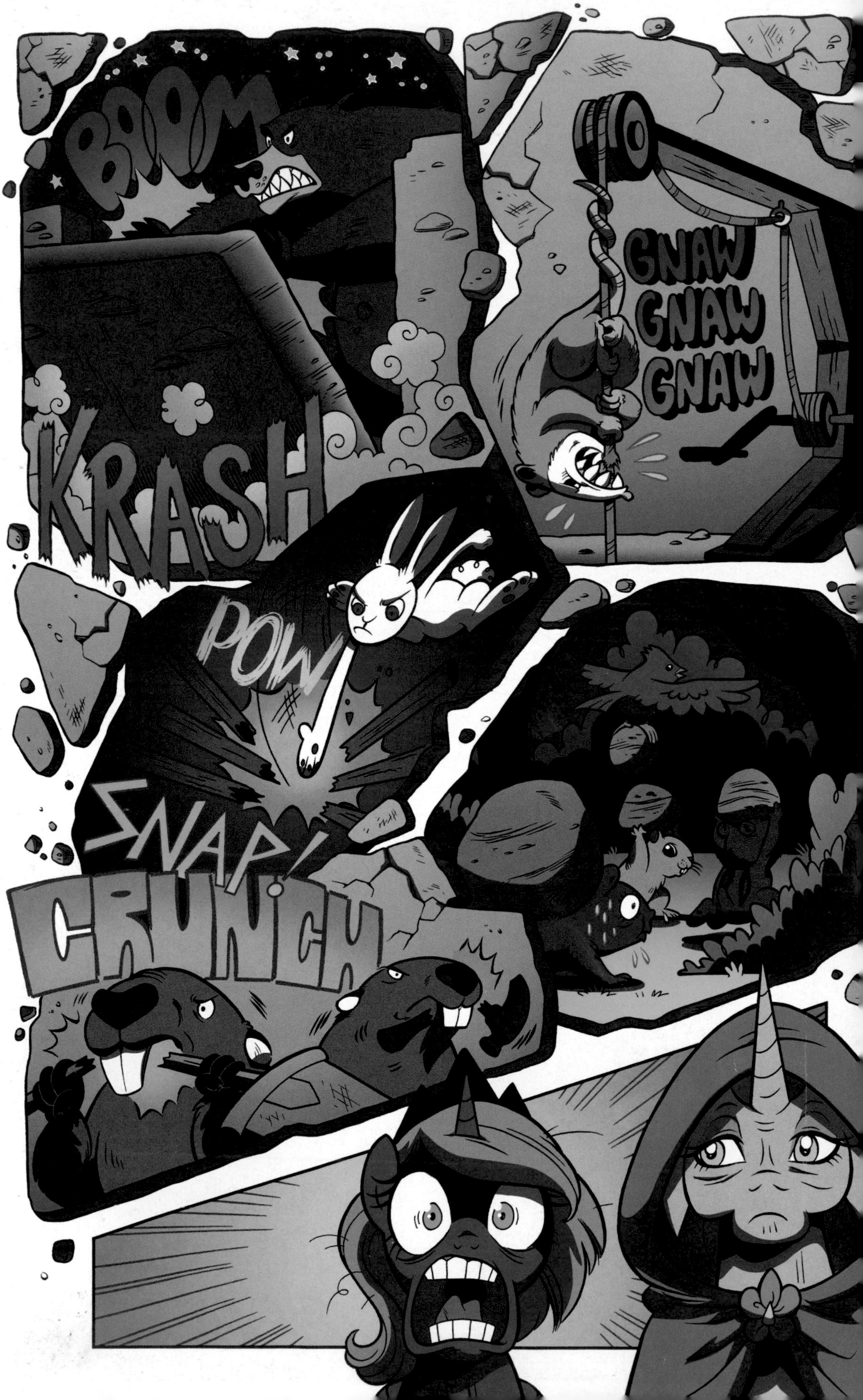
BOOM
GNAW
GNAW
GNAW
KRASH
POW
SNAP!
CRUNCH

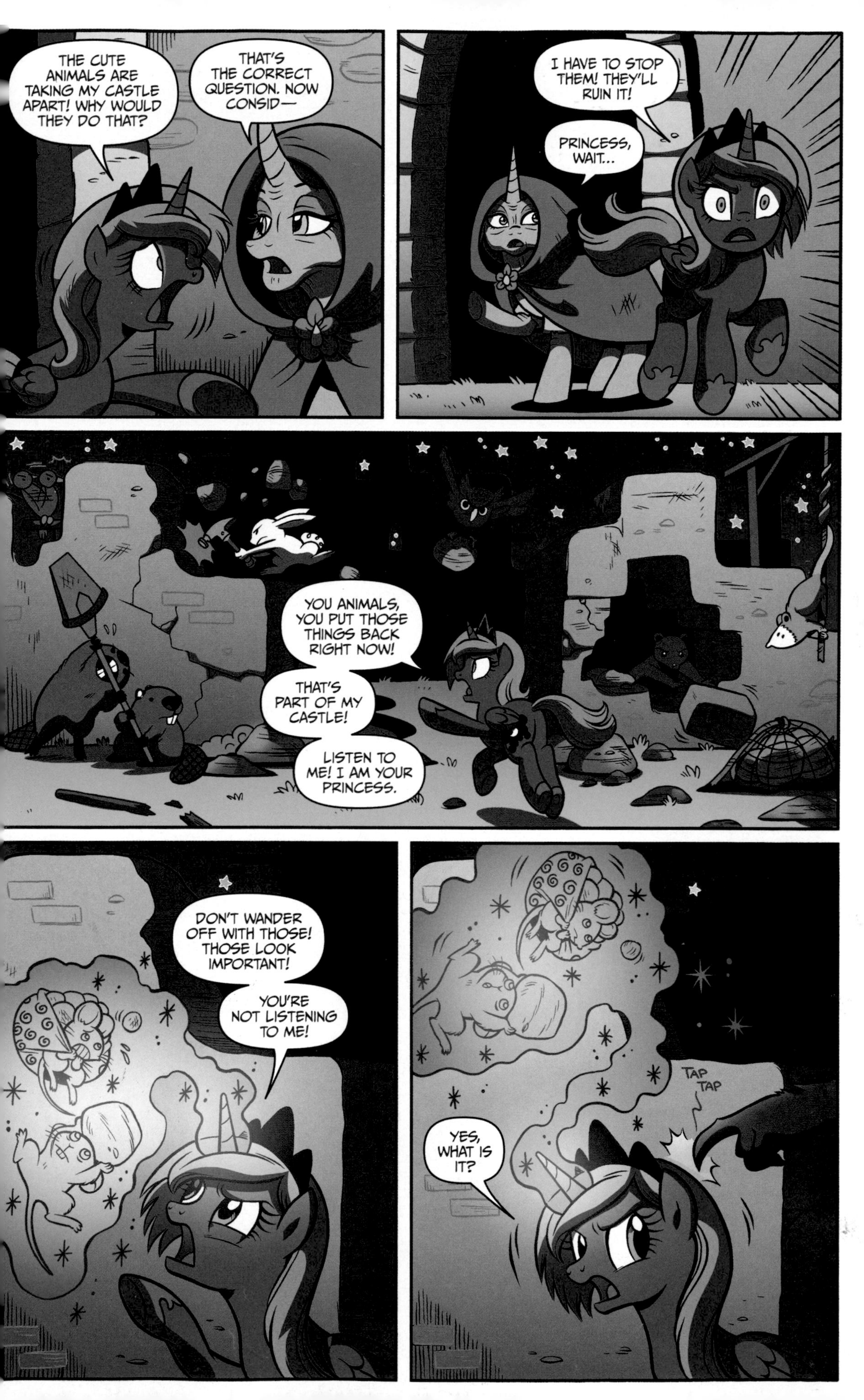
THE CUTE ANIMALS ARE TAKING MY CASTLE APART! WHY WOULD THEY DO THAT?
THAT'S THE CORRECT QUESTION. NOW CONSID—
I HAVE TO STOP THEM! THEY'LL RUIN IT!
PRINCESS, WAIT...
YOU ANIMALS, YOU PUT THOSE THINGS BACK RIGHT NOW!
THAT'S PART OF MY CASTLE!
LISTEN TO ME! I AM YOUR PRINCESS.
DON'T WANDER OFF WITH THOSE! THOSE LOOK IMPORTANT!
YOU'RE NOT LISTENING TO ME!
TAP TAP
YES, WHAT IS IT?

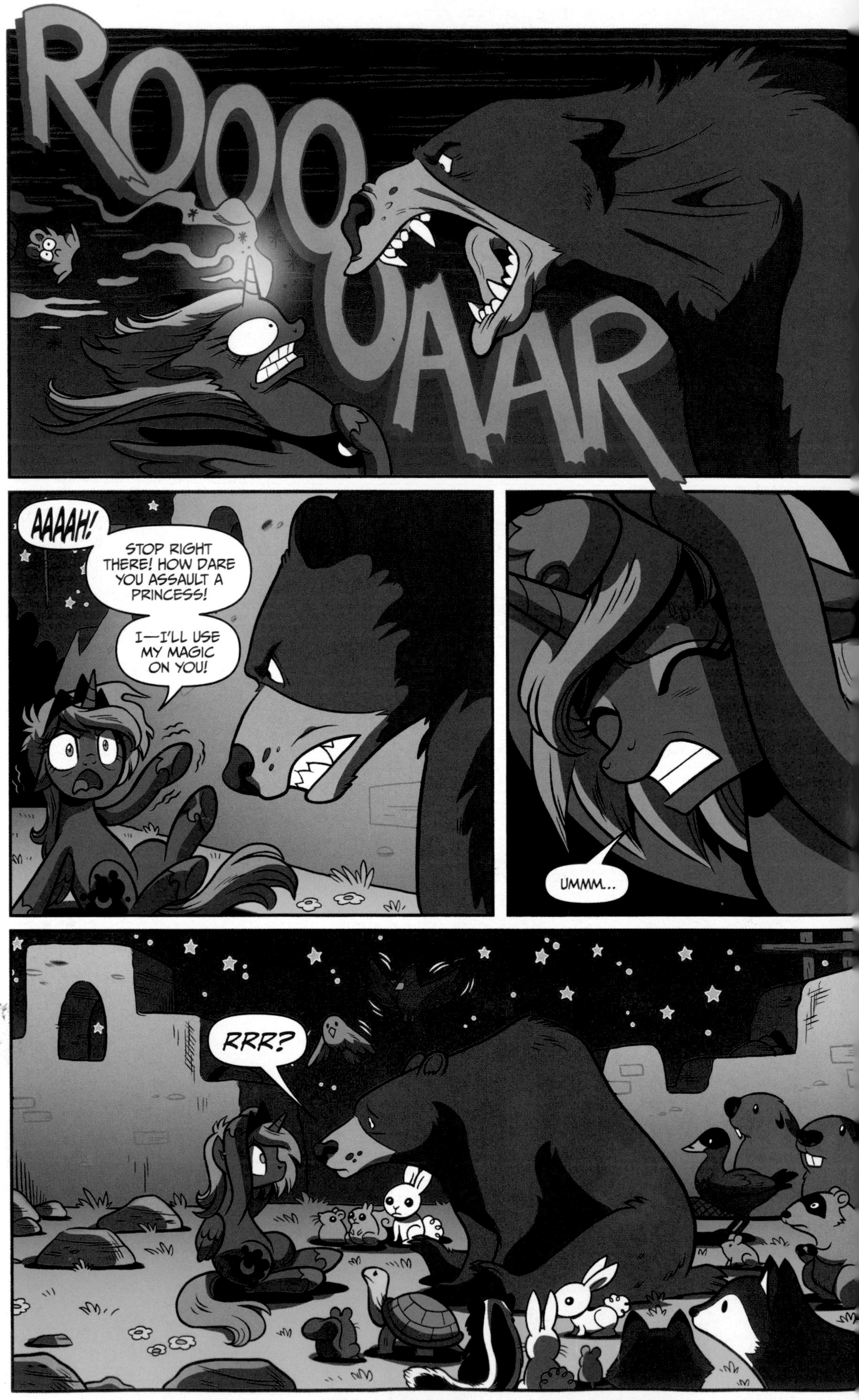
ROOOOAAR
AAAAH!
STOP RIGHT THERE! HOW DARE YOU ASSAULT A PRINCESS!
I—I'LL USE MY MAGIC ON YOU!
UMMM...
RRR?

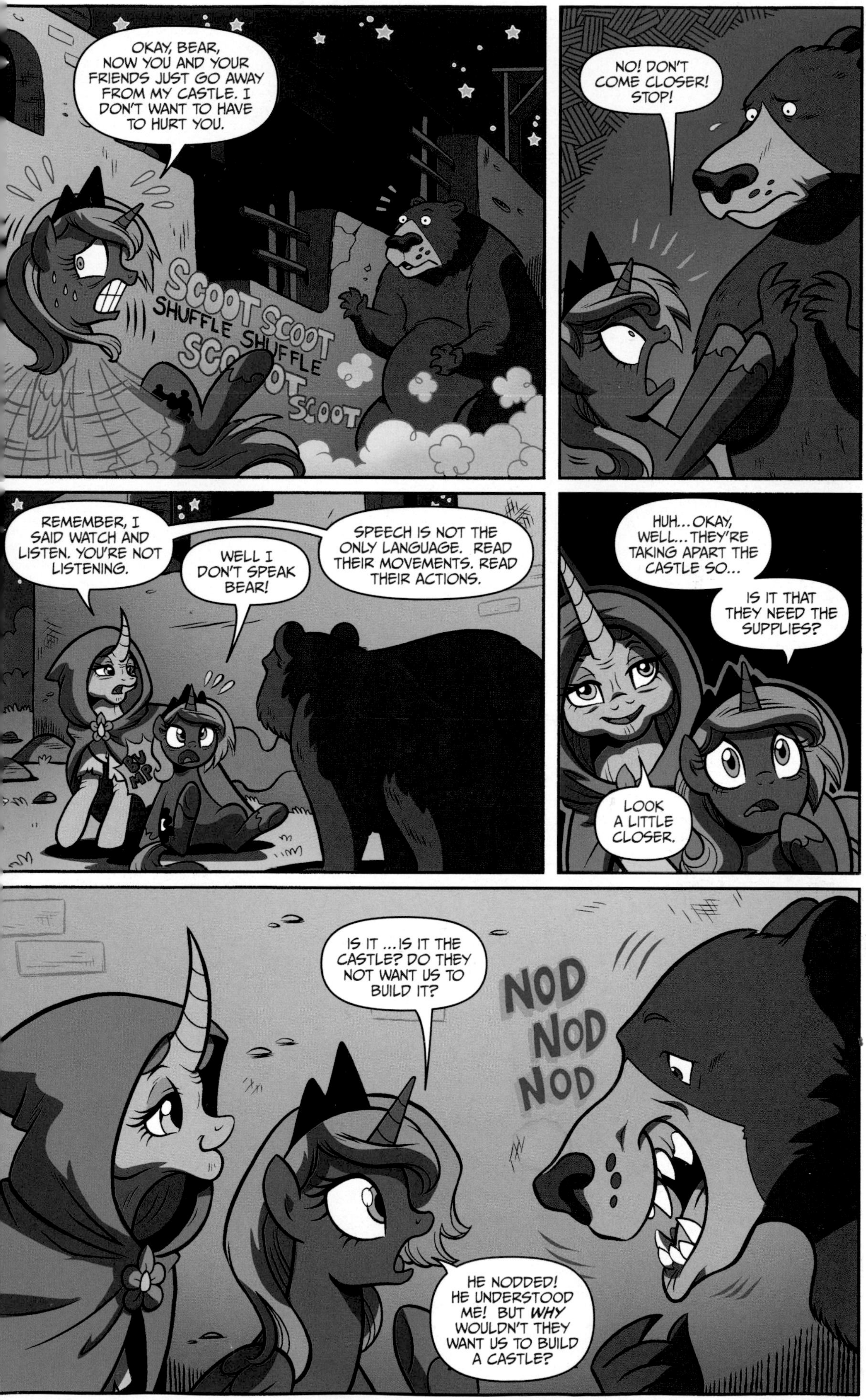
OKAY, BEAR, NOW YOU AND YOUR FRIENDS JUST GO AWAY FROM MY CASTLE. I DON'T WANT TO HAVE TO HURT YOU.
SCOOT SCOOT
SHUFFLE SHUFFLE
SCOOT SCOOT
NO! DON'T COME CLOSER! STOP!
REMEMBER, I SAID WATCH AND LISTEN. YOU'RE NOT LISTENING.
WELL I DON'T SPEAK BEAR!
SPEECH IS NOT THE ONLY LANGUAGE. READ THEIR MOVEMENTS. READ THEIR ACTIONS.
BUMP
HUH...OKAY, WELL...THEY'RE TAKING APART THE CASTLE SO...
IS IT THAT THEY NEED THE SUPPLIES?
LOOK A LITTLE CLOSER.
IS IT ...IS IT THE CASTLE? DO THEY NOT WANT US TO BUILD IT?
NOD NOD NOD
HE NODDED! HE UNDERSTOOD ME! BUT *WHY* WOULDN'T THEY WANT US TO BUILD A CASTLE?

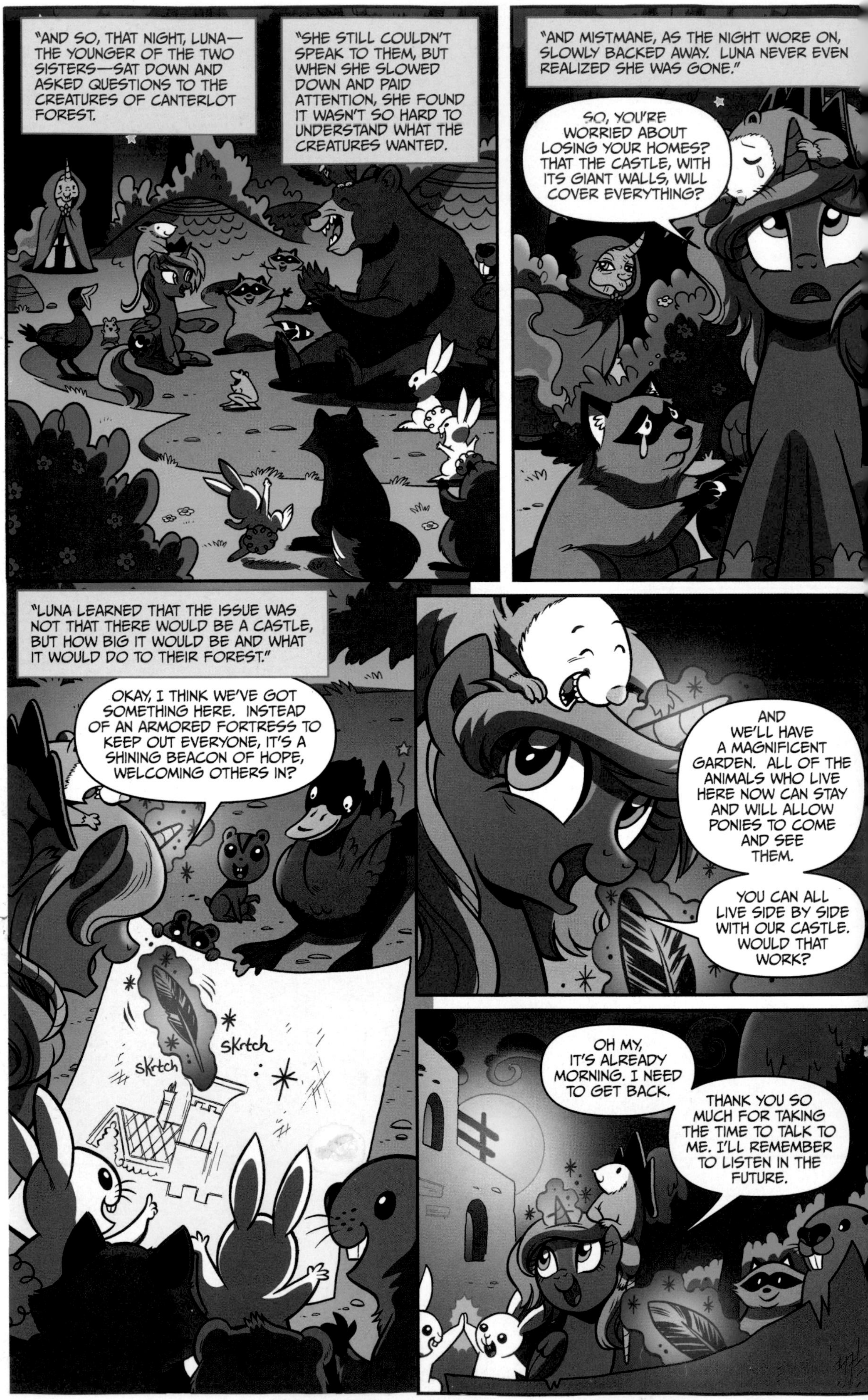
"AND SO, THAT NIGHT, LUNA—THE YOUNGER OF THE TWO SISTERS—SAT DOWN AND ASKED QUESTIONS TO THE CREATURES OF CANTERLOT FOREST.
"SHE STILL COULDN'T SPEAK TO THEM, BUT WHEN SHE SLOWED DOWN AND PAID ATTENTION, SHE FOUND IT WASN'T SO HARD TO UNDERSTAND WHAT THE CREATURES WANTED.
"AND MISTMANE, AS THE NIGHT WORE ON, SLOWLY BACKED AWAY. LUNA NEVER EVEN REALIZED SHE WAS GONE."
SO, YOU'RE WORRIED ABOUT LOSING YOUR HOMES? THAT THE CASTLE, WITH ITS GIANT WALLS, WILL COVER EVERYTHING?
"LUNA LEARNED THAT THE ISSUE WAS NOT THAT THERE WOULD BE A CASTLE, BUT HOW BIG IT WOULD BE AND WHAT IT WOULD DO TO THEIR FOREST."
OKAY, I THINK WE'VE GOT SOMETHING HERE. INSTEAD OF AN ARMORED FORTRESS TO KEEP OUT EVERYONE, IT'S A SHINING BEACON OF HOPE, WELCOMING OTHERS IN?
SKRTCH
SKRTCH
AND WE'LL HAVE A MAGNIFICENT GARDEN. ALL OF THE ANIMALS WHO LIVE HERE NOW CAN STAY AND WILL ALLOW PONIES TO COME AND SEE THEM.
YOU CAN ALL LIVE SIDE BY SIDE WITH OUR CASTLE. WOULD THAT WORK?
OH MY, IT'S ALREADY MORNING. I NEED TO GET BACK.
THANK YOU SO MUCH FOR TAKING THE TIME TO TALK TO ME. I'LL REMEMBER TO LISTEN IN THE FUTURE.

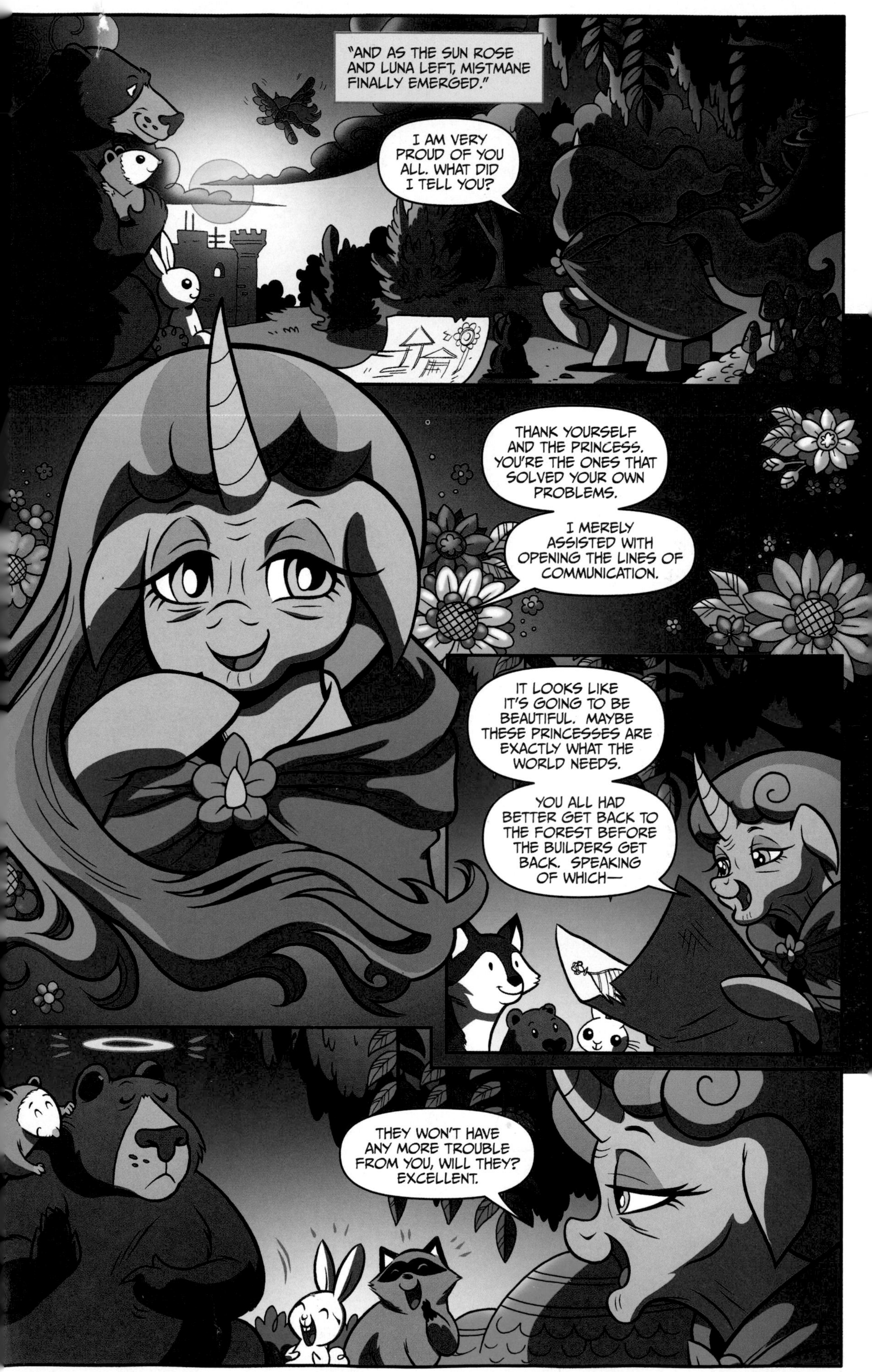
"AND AS THE SUN ROSE AND LUNA LEFT, MISTMANE FINALLY EMERGED."
I AM VERY PROUD OF YOU ALL. WHAT DID I TELL YOU?
THANK YOURSELF AND THE PRINCESS. YOU'RE THE ONES THAT SOLVED YOUR OWN PROBLEMS.
I MERELY ASSISTED WITH OPENING THE LINES OF COMMUNICATION.
IT LOOKS LIKE IT'S GOING TO BE BEAUTIFUL. MAYBE THESE PRINCESSES ARE EXACTLY WHAT THE WORLD NEEDS.
YOU ALL HAD BETTER GET BACK TO THE FOREST BEFORE THE BUILDERS GET BACK. SPEAKING OF WHICH—
THEY WON'T HAVE ANY MORE TROUBLE FROM YOU, WILL THEY? EXCELLENT.

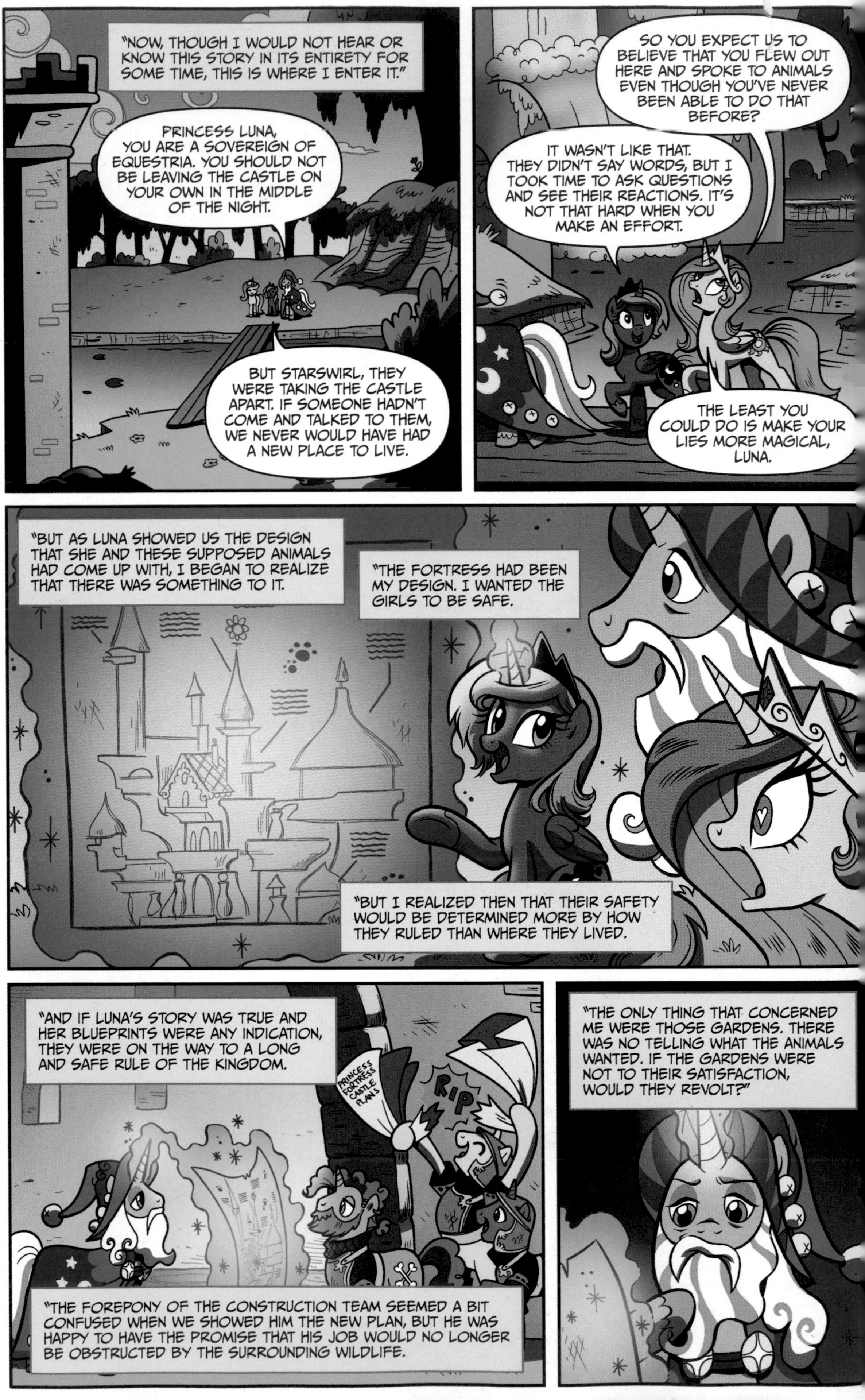
"NOW, THOUGH I WOULD NOT HEAR OR KNOW THIS STORY IN ITS ENTIRETY FOR SOME TIME, THIS IS WHERE I ENTER IT."
PRINCESS LUNA, YOU ARE A SOVEREIGN OF EQUESTRIA. YOU SHOULD NOT BE LEAVING THE CASTLE ON YOUR OWN IN THE MIDDLE OF THE NIGHT.
BUT STARSWIRL, THEY WERE TAKING THE CASTLE APART. IF SOMEONE HADN'T COME AND TALKED TO THEM, WE NEVER WOULD HAVE HAD A NEW PLACE TO LIVE.
SO YOU EXPECT US TO BELIEVE THAT YOU FLEW OUT HERE AND SPOKE TO ANIMALS EVEN THOUGH YOU'VE NEVER BEEN ABLE TO DO THAT BEFORE?
IT WASN'T LIKE THAT. THEY DIDN'T SAY WORDS, BUT I TOOK TIME TO ASK QUESTIONS AND SEE THEIR REACTIONS. IT'S NOT THAT HARD WHEN YOU MAKE AN EFFORT.
THE LEAST YOU COULD DO IS MAKE YOUR LIES MORE MAGICAL, LUNA.
"BUT AS LUNA SHOWED US THE DESIGN THAT SHE AND THESE SUPPOSED ANIMALS HAD COME UP WITH, I BEGAN TO REALIZE THAT THERE WAS SOMETHING TO IT.
"THE FORTRESS HAD BEEN MY DESIGN. I WANTED THE GIRLS TO BE SAFE.
"BUT I REALIZED THEN THAT THEIR SAFETY WOULD BE DETERMINED MORE BY HOW THEY RULED THAN WHERE THEY LIVED.
"AND IF LUNA'S STORY WAS TRUE AND HER BLUEPRINTS WERE ANY INDICATION, THEY WERE ON THE WAY TO A LONG AND SAFE RULE OF THE KINGDOM.
PRINCESS FORTRESS CASTLE PLANS
RIP
"THE FOREPONY OF THE CONSTRUCTION TEAM SEEMED A BIT CONFUSED WHEN WE SHOWED HIM THE NEW PLAN, BUT HE WAS HAPPY TO HAVE THE PROMISE THAT HIS JOB WOULD NO LONGER BE OBSTRUCTED BY THE SURROUNDING WILDLIFE.
"THE ONLY THING THAT CONCERNED ME WERE THOSE GARDENS. THERE WAS NO TELLING WHAT THE ANIMALS WANTED. IF THE GARDENS WERE NOT TO THEIR SATISFACTION, WOULD THEY REVOLT?"

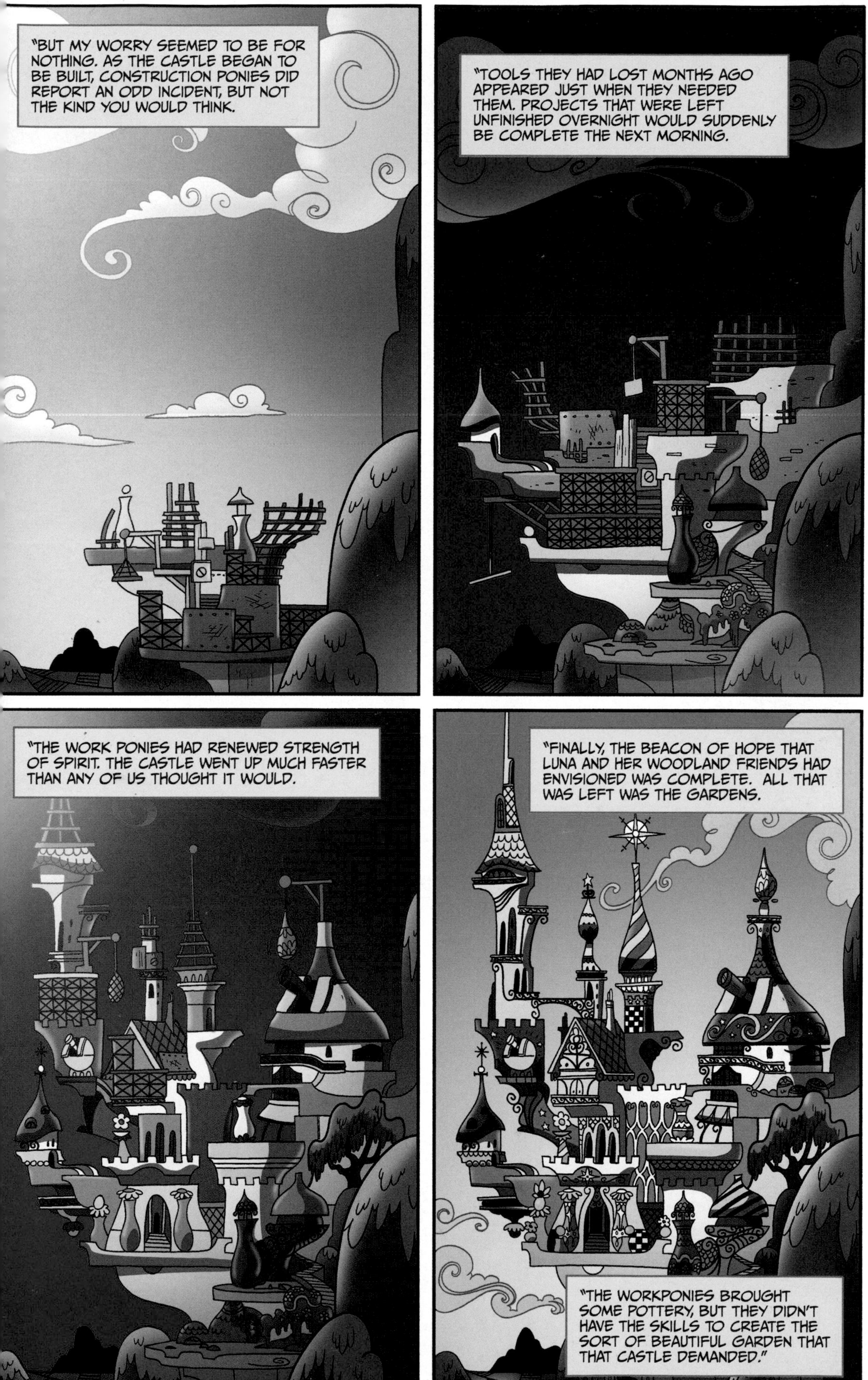
"BUT MY WORRY SEEMED TO BE FOR NOTHING. AS THE CASTLE BEGAN TO BE BUILT, CONSTRUCTION PONIES DID REPORT AN ODD INCIDENT, BUT NOT THE KIND YOU WOULD THINK.
"TOOLS THEY HAD LOST MONTHS AGO APPEARED JUST WHEN THEY NEEDED THEM. PROJECTS THAT WERE LEFT UNFINISHED OVERNIGHT WOULD SUDDENLY BE COMPLETE THE NEXT MORNING.
"THE WORK PONIES HAD RENEWED STRENGTH OF SPIRIT. THE CASTLE WENT UP MUCH FASTER THAN ANY OF US THOUGHT IT WOULD.
"FINALLY, THE BEACON OF HOPE THAT LUNA AND HER WOODLAND FRIENDS HAD ENVISIONED WAS COMPLETE. ALL THAT WAS LEFT WAS THE GARDENS.
"THE WORKPONIES BROUGHT SOME POTTERY, BUT THEY DIDN'T HAVE THE SKILLS TO CREATE THE SORT OF BEAUTIFUL GARDEN THAT THAT CASTLE DEMANDED."

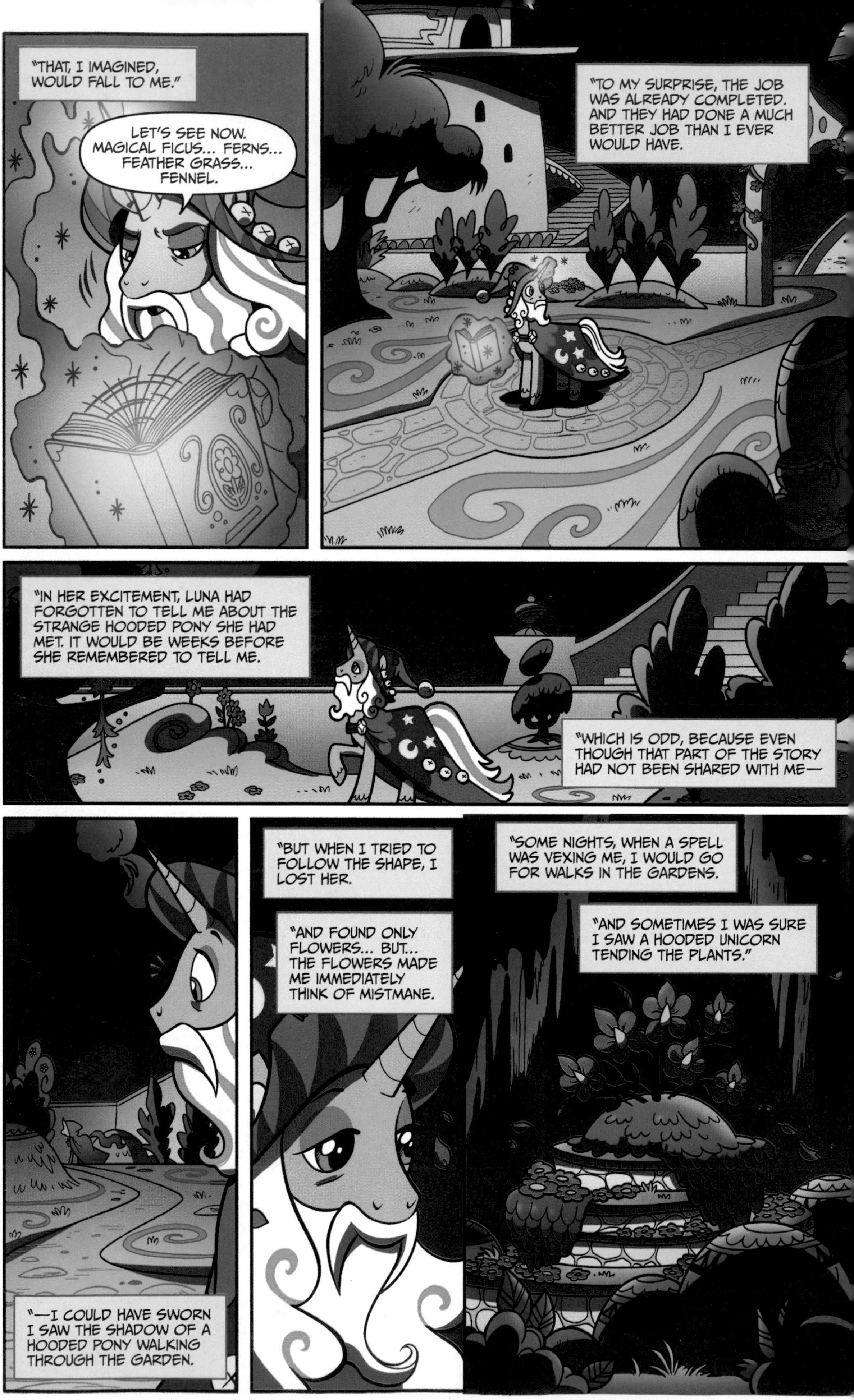
"THAT, I IMAGINED, WOULD FALL TO ME."
LET'S SEE NOW. MAGICAL FICUS... FERNS... FEATHER GRASS... FENNEL.
"TO MY SURPRISE, THE JOB WAS ALREADY COMPLETED. AND THEY HAD DONE A MUCH BETTER JOB THAN I EVER WOULD HAVE.
"IN HER EXCITEMENT, LUNA HAD FORGOTTEN TO TELL ME ABOUT THE STRANGE HOODED PONY SHE HAD MET. IT WOULD BE WEEKS BEFORE SHE REMEMBERED TO TELL ME.
"WHICH IS ODD, BECAUSE EVEN THOUGH THAT PART OF THE STORY HAD NOT BEEN SHARED WITH ME—
"—I COULD HAVE SWORN I SAW THE SHADOW OF A HOODED PONY WALKING THROUGH THE GARDEN.
"BUT WHEN I TRIED TO FOLLOW THE SHAPE, I LOST HER.
"AND FOUND ONLY FLOWERS... BUT... THE FLOWERS MADE ME IMMEDIATELY THINK OF MISTMANE.
"SOME NIGHTS, WHEN A SPELL WAS VEXING ME, I WOULD GO FOR WALKS IN THE GARDENS.
"AND SOMETIMES I WAS SURE I SAW A HOODED UNICORN TENDING THE PLANTS."

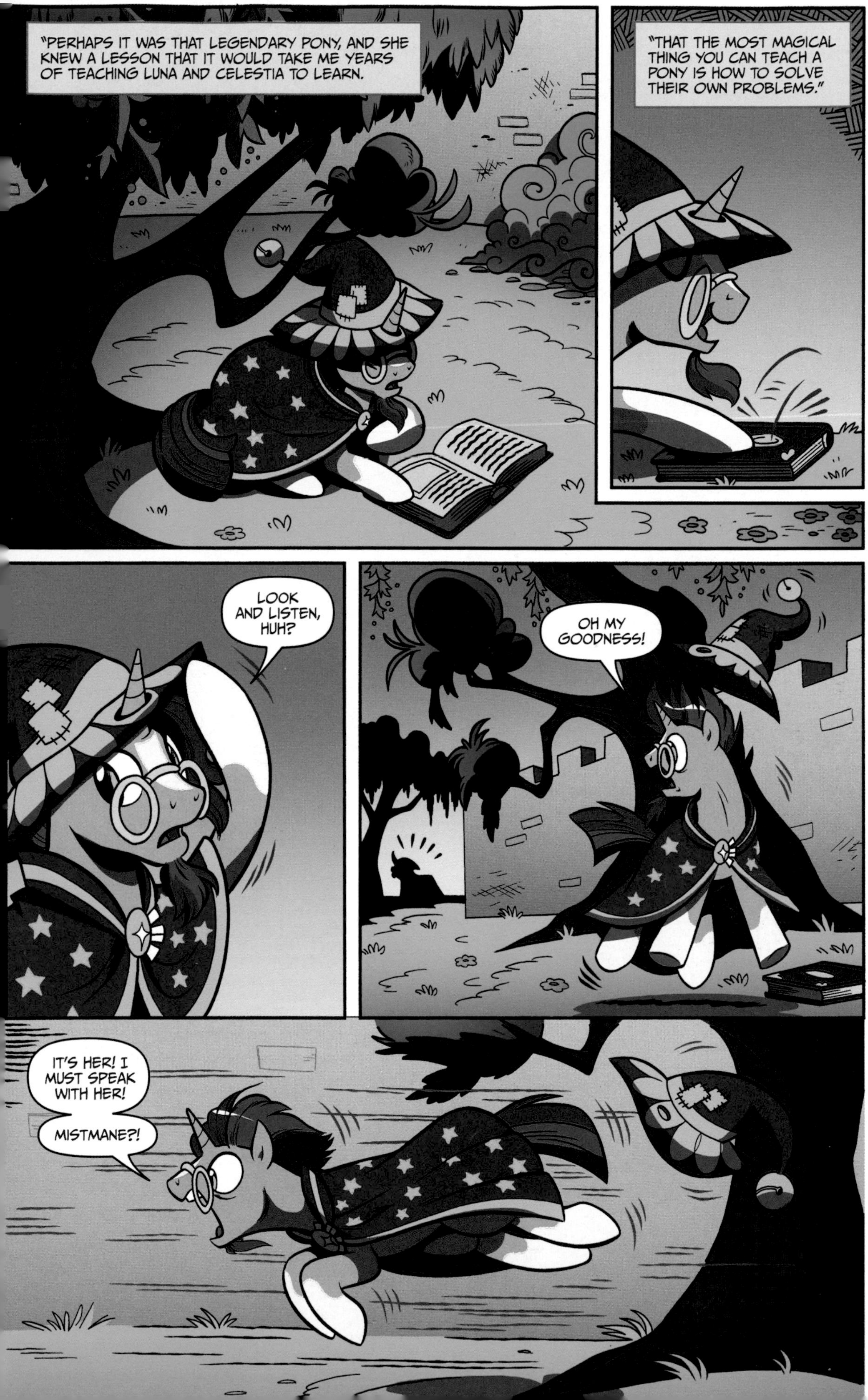
"PERHAPS IT WAS THAT LEGENDARY PONY, AND SHE KNEW A LESSON THAT IT WOULD TAKE ME YEARS OF TEACHING LUNA AND CELESTIA TO LEARN.
"THAT THE MOST MAGICAL THING YOU CAN TEACH A PONY IS HOW TO SOLVE THEIR OWN PROBLEMS."
LOOK AND LISTEN, HUH?
OH MY GOODNESS!
IT'S HER! I MUST SPEAK WITH HER!
MISTMANE?!

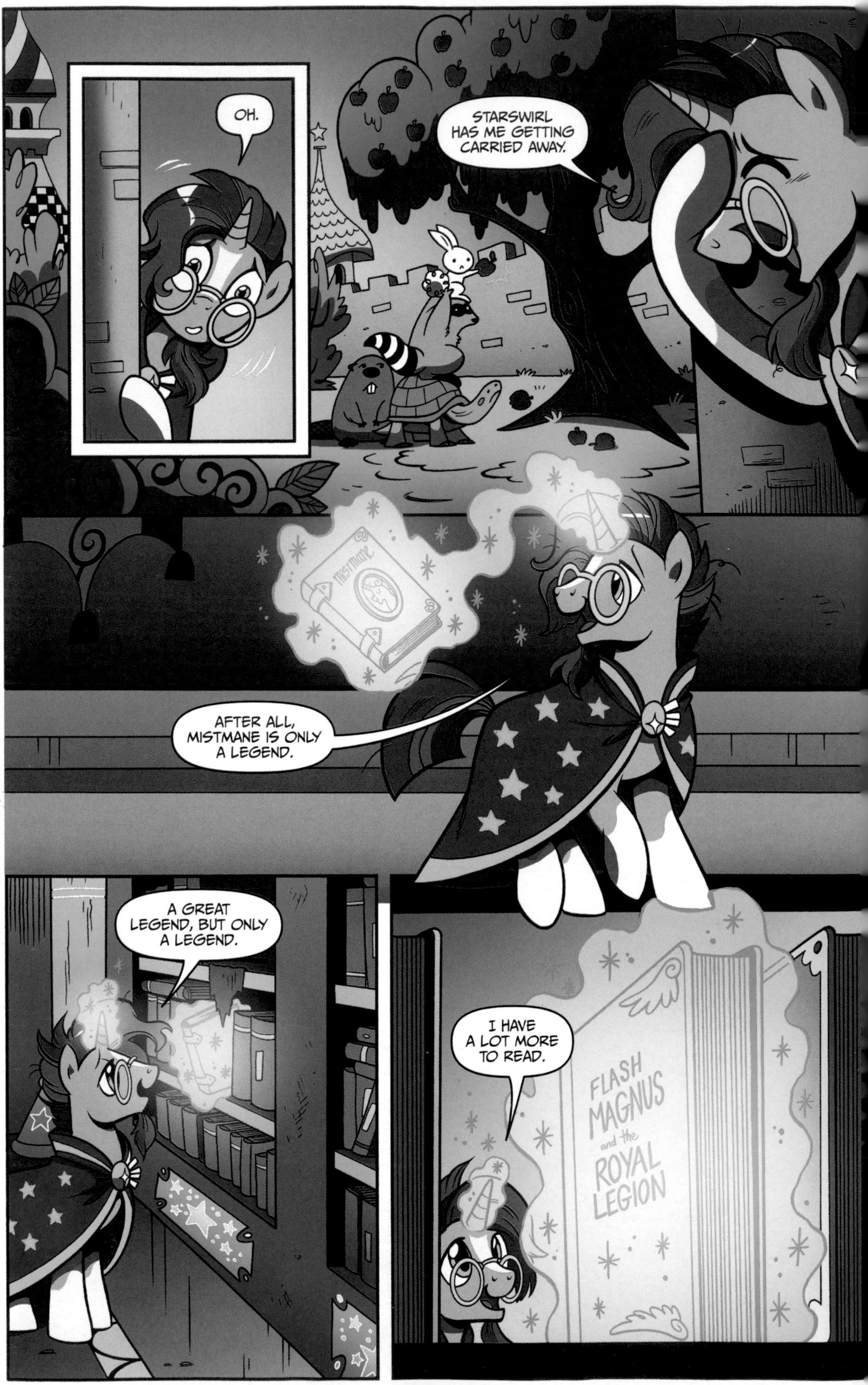
OH.
STARSWIRL HAS ME GETTING CARRIED AWAY.
MISTMANE
AFTER ALL, MISTMANE IS ONLY A LEGEND.
A GREAT LEGEND, BUT ONLY A LEGEND.
I HAVE A LOT MORE TO READ.
FLASH MAGNUS and the ROYAL LEGION

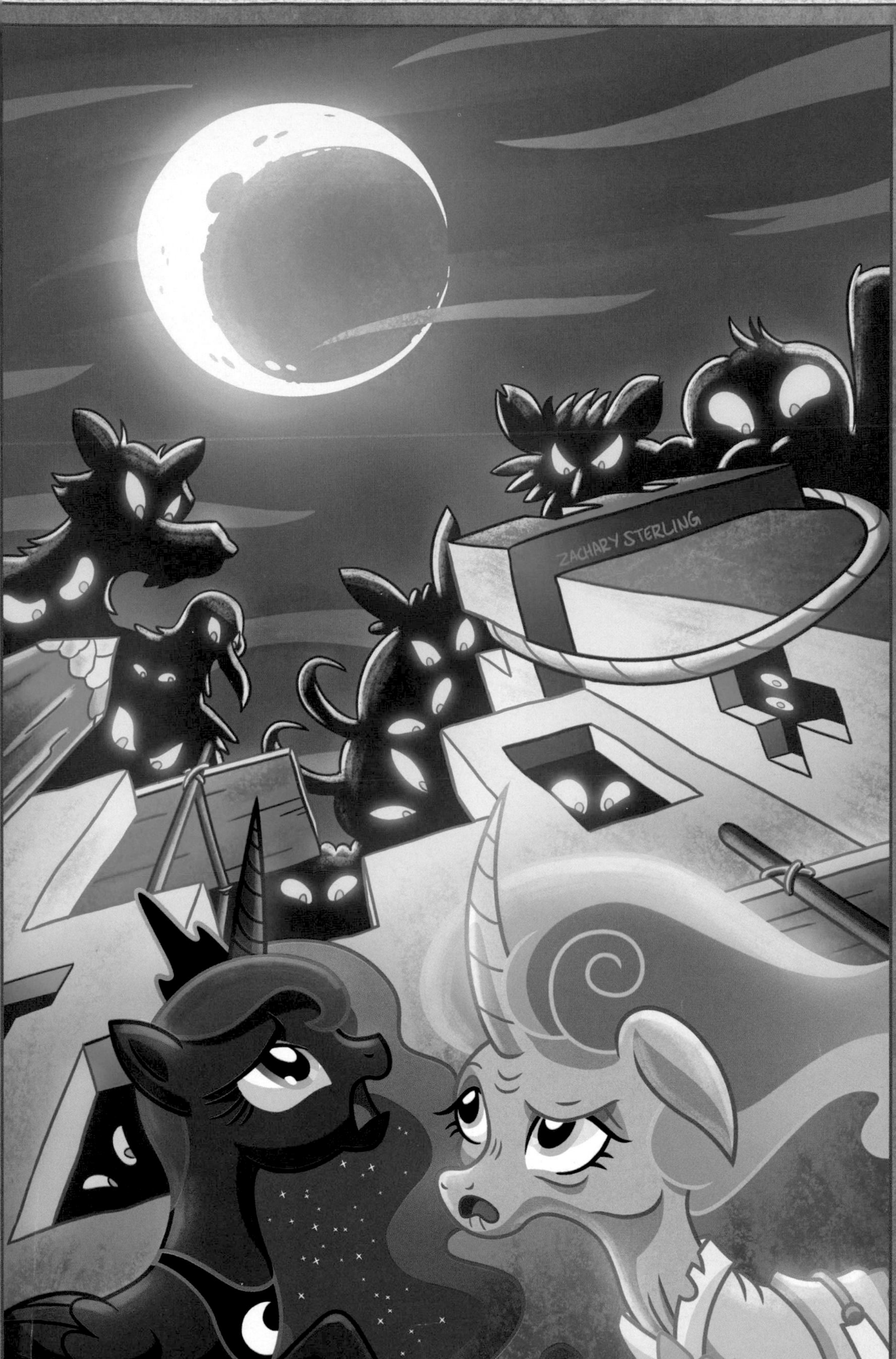
ZACHARY STERLING

ART BY ZACHARY STERLING

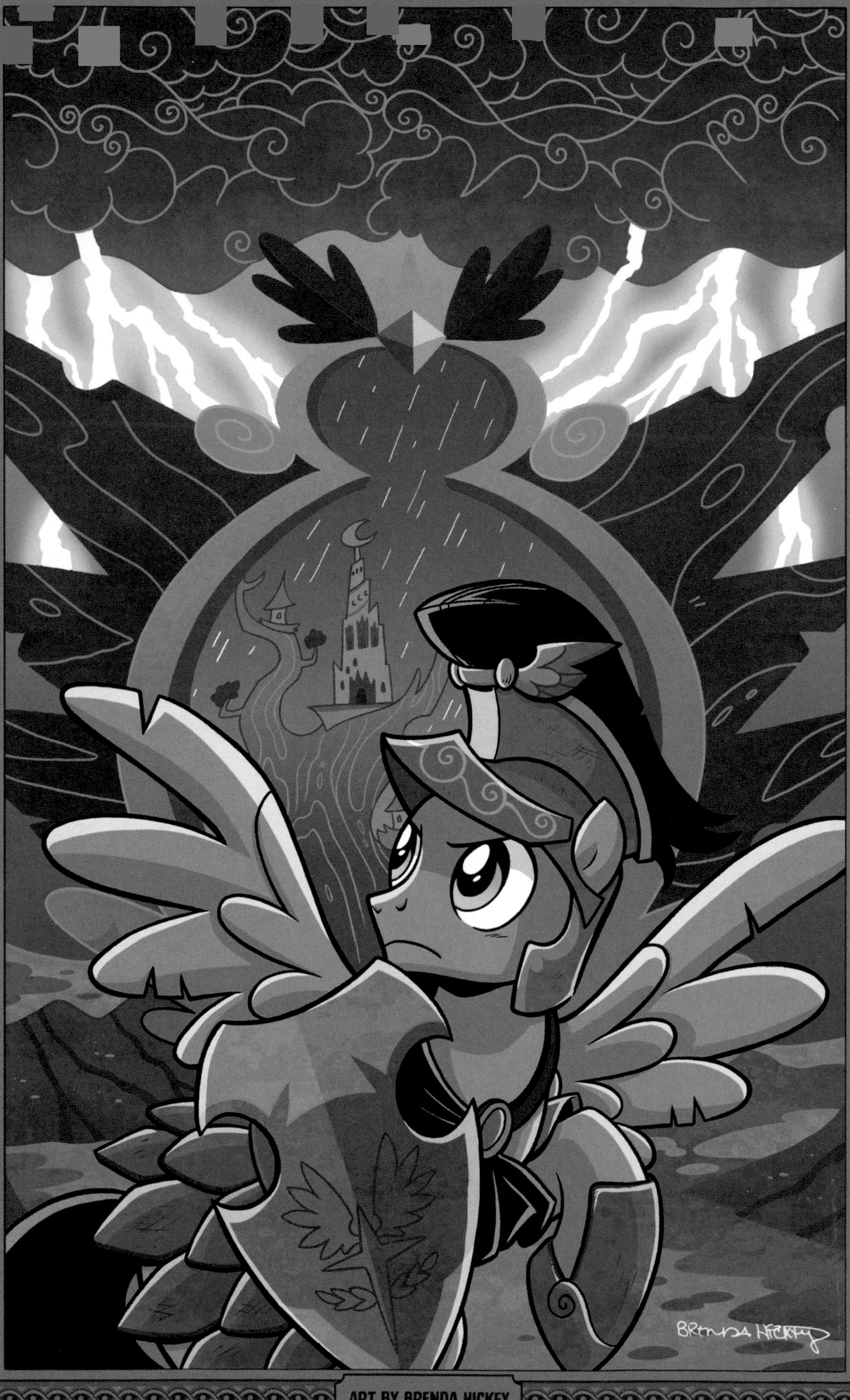

ART BY BRENDA HICKEY

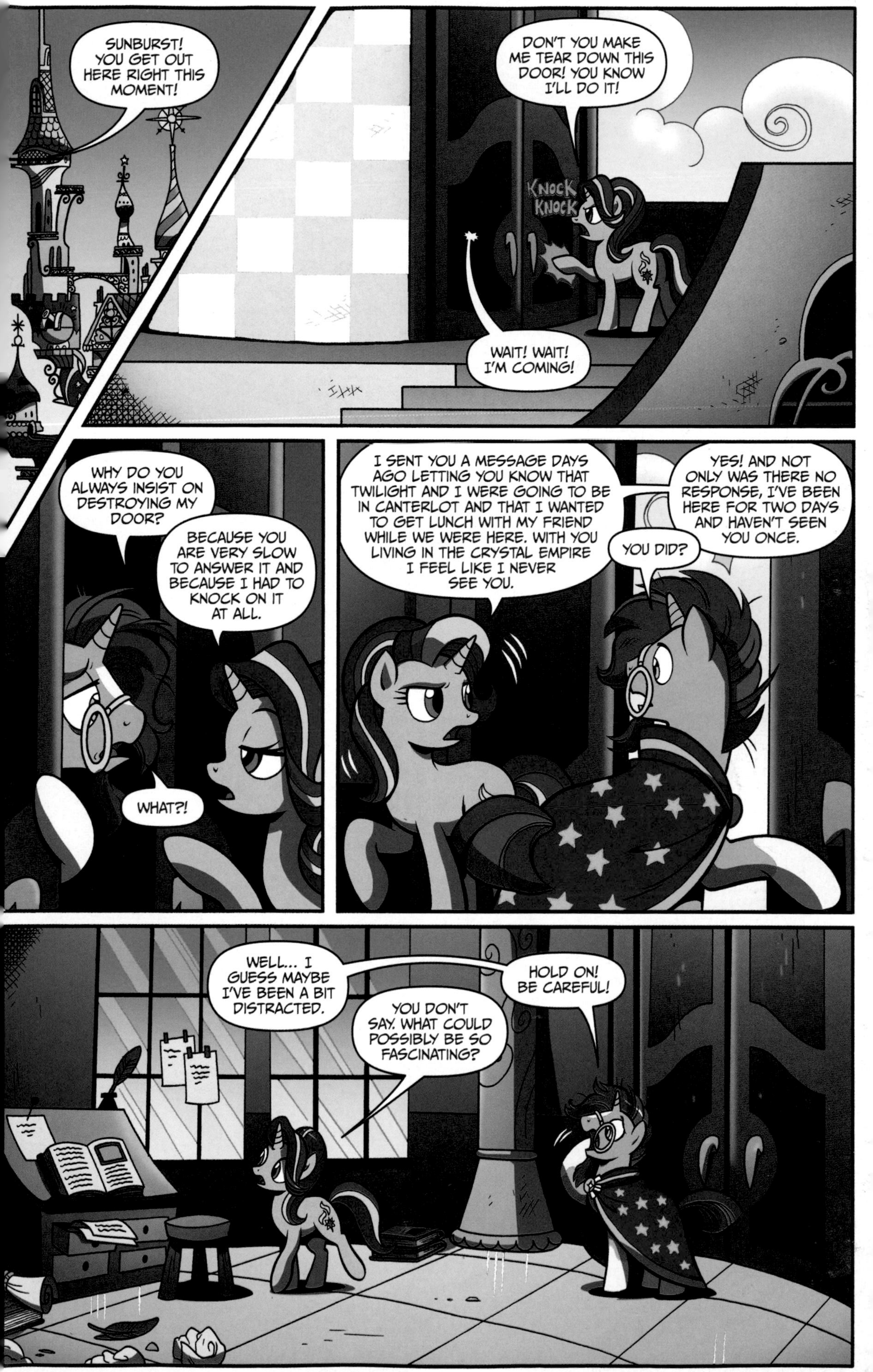
SUNBURST! YOU GET OUT HERE RIGHT THIS MOMENT!
DON'T YOU MAKE ME TEAR DOWN THIS DOOR! YOU KNOW I'LL DO IT!
KNOCK KNOCK
WAIT! WAIT! I'M COMING!
WHY DO YOU ALWAYS INSIST ON DESTROYING MY DOOR?
BECAUSE YOU ARE VERY SLOW TO ANSWER IT AND BECAUSE I HAD TO KNOCK ON IT AT ALL.
WHAT?!
I SENT YOU A MESSAGE DAYS AGO LETTING YOU KNOW THAT TWILIGHT AND I WERE GOING TO BE IN CANTERLOT AND THAT I WANTED TO GET LUNCH WITH MY FRIEND WHILE WE WERE HERE. WITH YOU LIVING IN THE CRYSTAL EMPIRE I FEEL LIKE I NEVER SEE YOU.
YOU DID?
YES! AND NOT ONLY WAS THERE NO RESPONSE, I'VE BEEN HERE FOR TWO DAYS AND HAVEN'T SEEN YOU ONCE.
WELL... I GUESS MAYBE I'VE BEEN A BIT DISTRACTED.
YOU DON'T SAY. WHAT COULD POSSIBLY BE SO FASCINATING?
HOLD ON! BE CAREFUL!

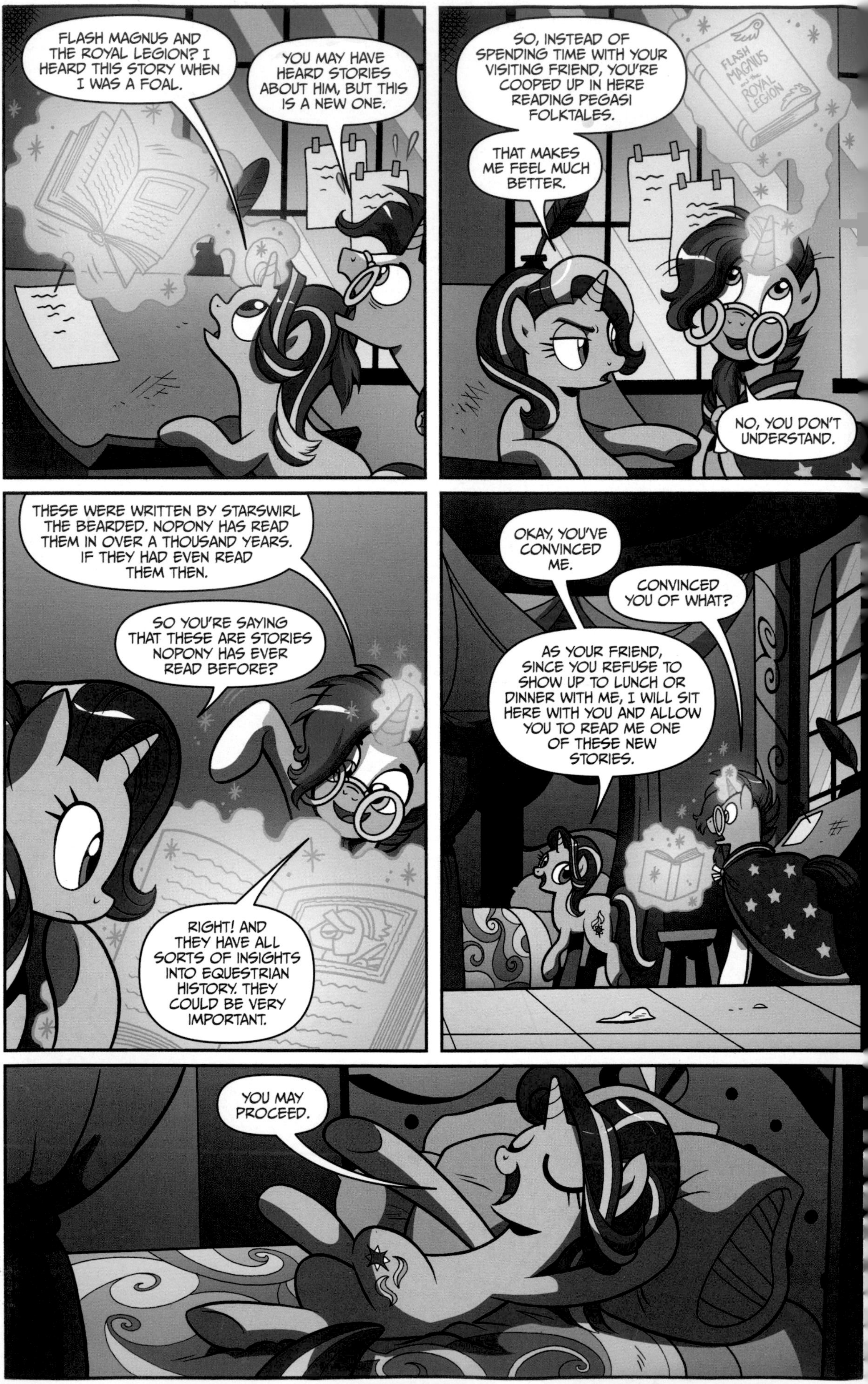
FLASH MAGNUS AND THE ROYAL LEGION? I HEARD THIS STORY WHEN I WAS A FOAL.
YOU MAY HAVE HEARD STORIES ABOUT HIM, BUT THIS IS A NEW ONE.
SO, INSTEAD OF SPENDING TIME WITH YOUR VISITING FRIEND, YOU'RE COOPED UP IN HERE READING PEGASI FOLKTALES.
THAT MAKES ME FEEL MUCH BETTER.
FLASH MAGNUS and the ROYAL LEGION
NO, YOU DON'T UNDERSTAND.
THESE WERE WRITTEN BY STARSWIRL THE BEARDED. NOPONY HAS READ THEM IN OVER A THOUSAND YEARS. IF THEY HAD EVEN READ THEM THEN.
SO YOU'RE SAYING THAT THESE ARE STORIES NOPONY HAS EVER READ BEFORE?
RIGHT! AND THEY HAVE ALL SORTS OF INSIGHTS INTO EQUESTRIAN HISTORY. THEY COULD BE VERY IMPORTANT.
OKAY, YOU'VE CONVINCED ME.
CONVINCED YOU OF WHAT?
AS YOUR FRIEND, SINCE YOU REFUSE TO SHOW UP TO LUNCH OR DINNER WITH ME, I WILL SIT HERE WITH YOU AND ALLOW YOU TO READ ME ONE OF THESE NEW STORIES.
YOU MAY PROCEED.

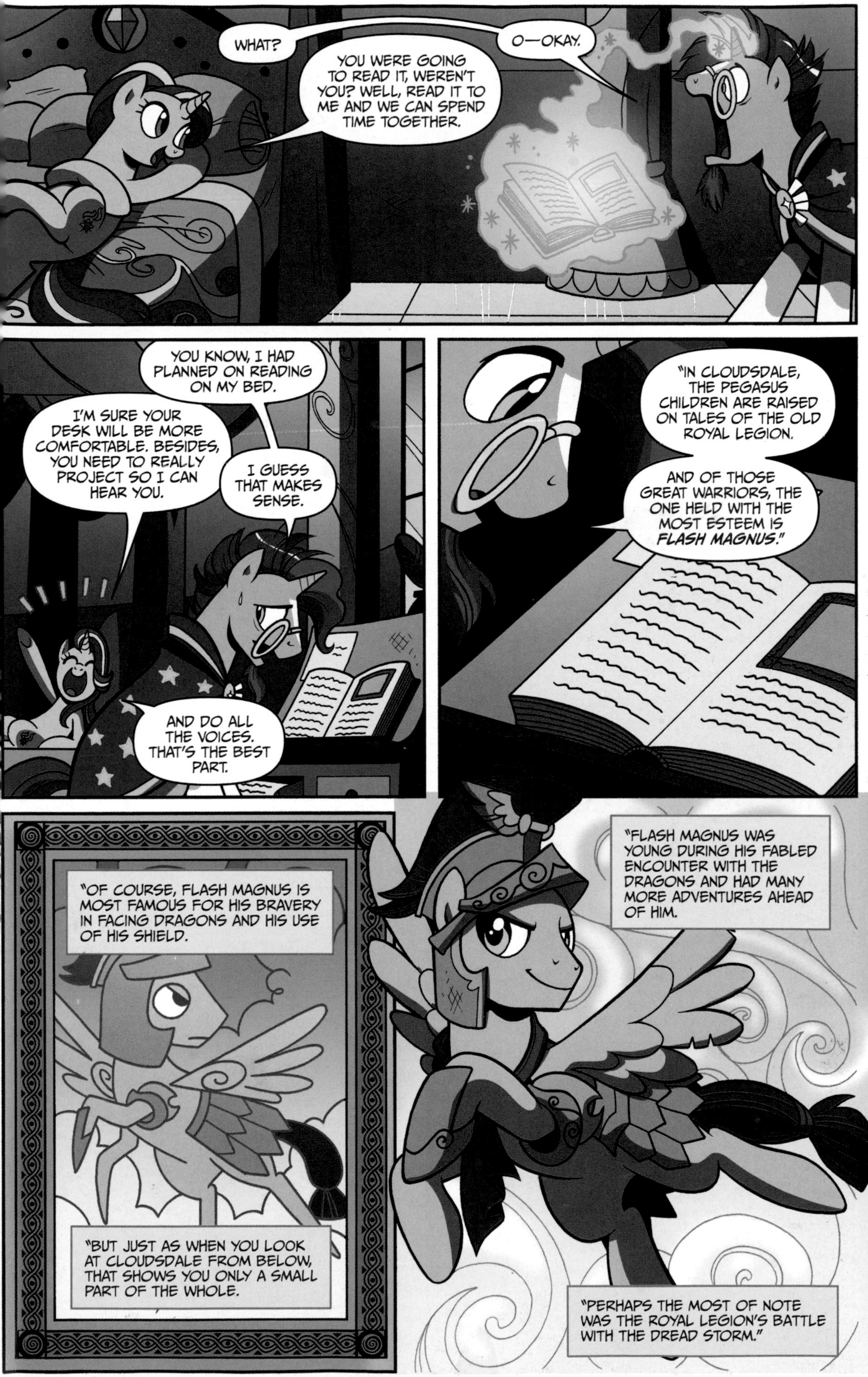
WHAT?
YOU WERE GOING TO READ IT, WEREN'T YOU? WELL, READ IT TO ME AND WE CAN SPEND TIME TOGETHER.
O—OKAY.
YOU KNOW, I HAD PLANNED ON READING ON MY BED.
I'M SURE YOUR DESK WILL BE MORE COMFORTABLE. BESIDES, YOU NEED TO REALLY PROJECT SO I CAN HEAR YOU.
I GUESS THAT MAKES SENSE.
AND DO ALL THE VOICES. THAT'S THE BEST PART.
"IN CLOUDSDALE, THE PEGASUS CHILDREN ARE RAISED ON TALES OF THE OLD ROYAL LEGION.
AND OF THOSE GREAT WARRIORS, THE ONE HELD WITH THE MOST ESTEEM IS *FLASH MAGNUS*."
"OF COURSE, FLASH MAGNUS IS MOST FAMOUS FOR HIS BRAVERY IN FACING DRAGONS AND HIS USE OF HIS SHIELD.
"BUT JUST AS WHEN YOU LOOK AT CLOUDSDALE FROM BELOW, THAT SHOWS YOU ONLY A SMALL PART OF THE WHOLE.
"FLASH MAGNUS WAS YOUNG DURING HIS FABLED ENCOUNTER WITH THE DRAGONS AND HAD MANY MORE ADVENTURES AHEAD OF HIM.
"PERHAPS THE MOST OF NOTE WAS THE ROYAL LEGION'S BATTLE WITH THE DREAD STORM."

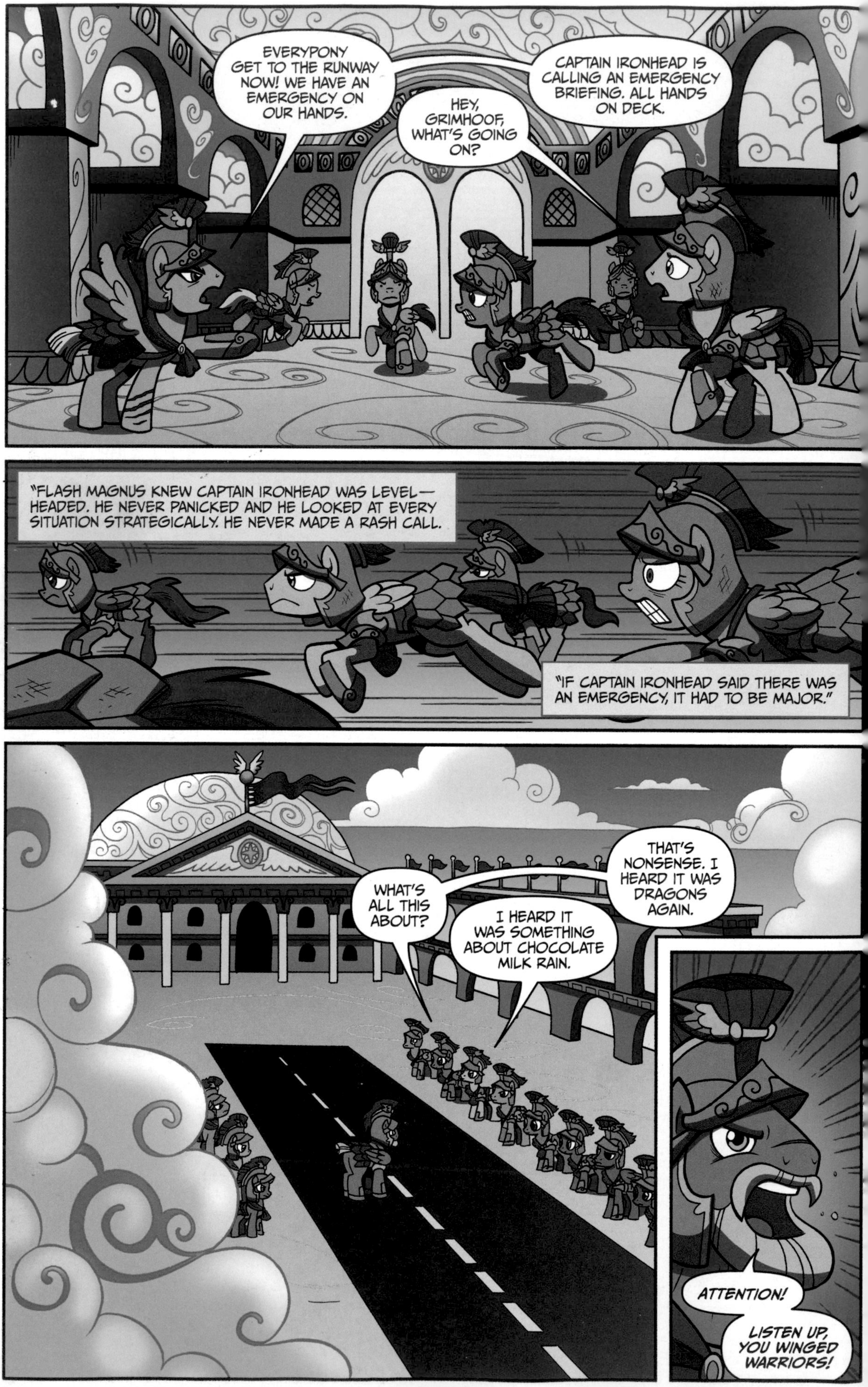
EVERYPONY GET TO THE RUNWAY NOW! WE HAVE AN EMERGENCY ON OUR HANDS.
HEY, GRIMHOOF, WHAT'S GOING ON?
CAPTAIN IRONHEAD IS CALLING AN EMERGENCY BRIEFING. ALL HANDS ON DECK.
"FLASH MAGNUS KNEW CAPTAIN IRONHEAD WAS LEVEL—HEADED. HE NEVER PANICKED AND HE LOOKED AT EVERY SITUATION STRATEGICALLY. HE NEVER MADE A RASH CALL.
"IF CAPTAIN IRONHEAD SAID THERE WAS AN EMERGENCY, IT HAD TO BE MAJOR."
WHAT'S ALL THIS ABOUT?
I HEARD IT WAS SOMETHING ABOUT CHOCOLATE MILK RAIN.
THAT'S NONSENSE. I HEARD IT WAS DRAGONS AGAIN.
ATTENTION!
LISTEN UP, YOU WINGED WARRIORS!

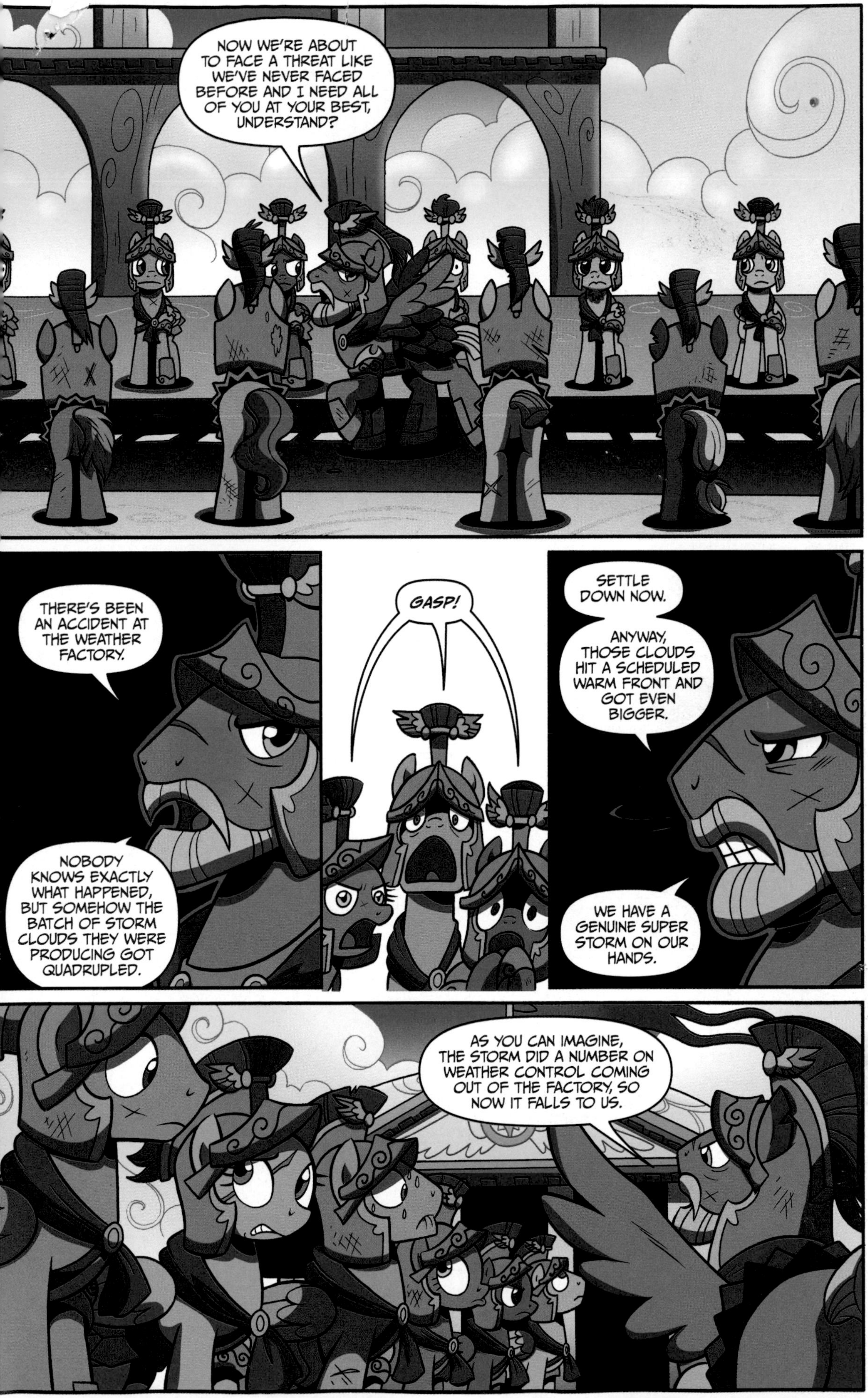
NOW WE'RE ABOUT TO FACE A THREAT LIKE WE'VE NEVER FACED BEFORE AND I NEED ALL OF YOU AT YOUR BEST, UNDERSTAND?
THERE'S BEEN AN ACCIDENT AT THE WEATHER FACTORY.
NOBODY KNOWS EXACTLY WHAT HAPPENED, BUT SOMEHOW THE BATCH OF STORM CLOUDS THEY WERE PRODUCING GOT QUADRUPLED.
GASP!
SETTLE DOWN NOW.
ANYWAY, THOSE CLOUDS HIT A SCHEDULED WARM FRONT AND GOT EVEN BIGGER.
WE HAVE A GENUINE SUPER STORM ON OUR HANDS.
AS YOU CAN IMAGINE, THE STORM DID A NUMBER ON WEATHER CONTROL COMING OUT OF THE FACTORY, SO NOW IT FALLS TO US.

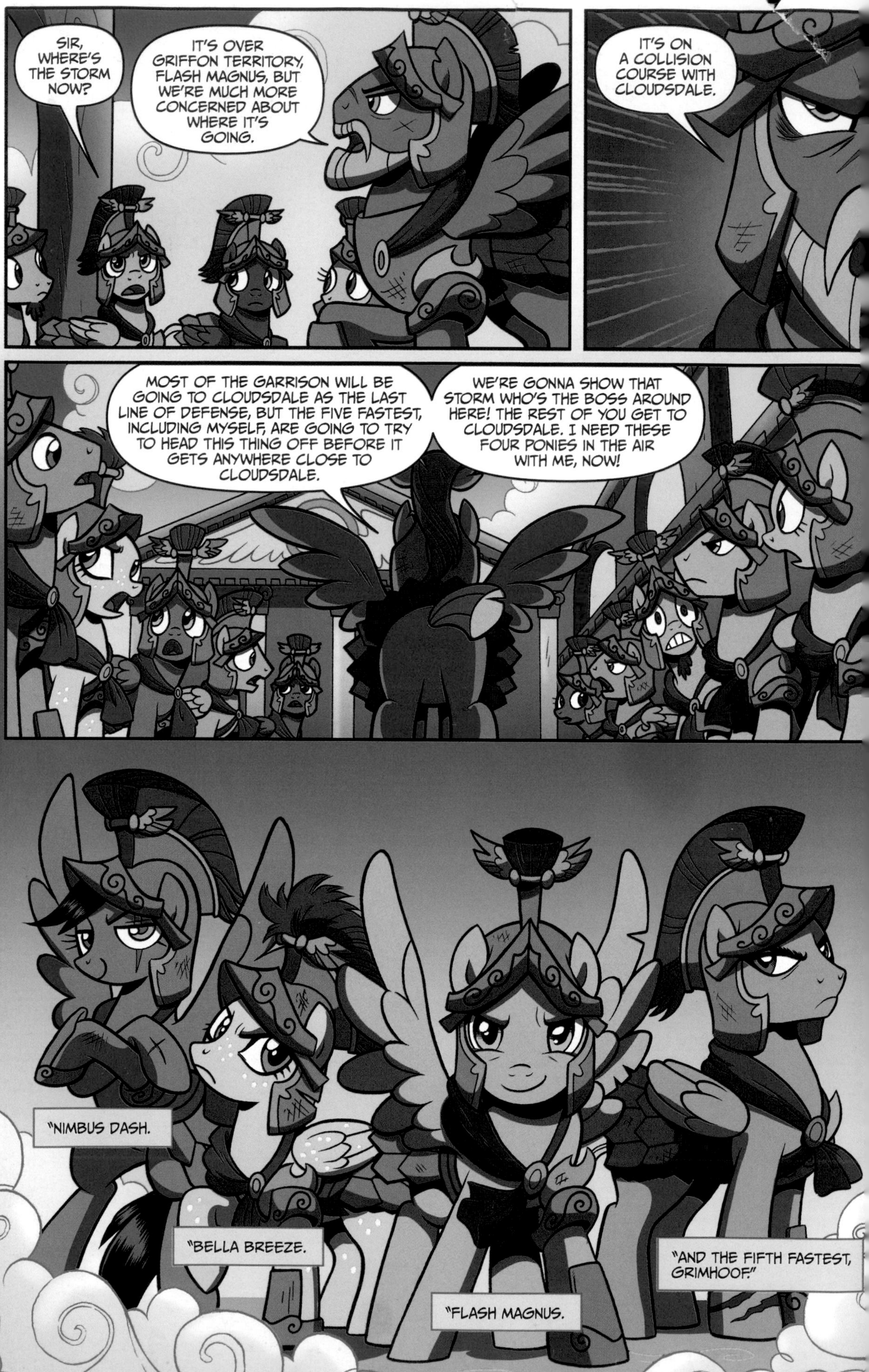
SIR, WHERE'S THE STORM NOW?
IT'S OVER GRIFFON TERRITORY, FLASH MAGNUS, BUT WE'RE MUCH MORE CONCERNED ABOUT WHERE IT'S GOING.
IT'S ON A COLLISION COURSE WITH CLOUDSDALE.
MOST OF THE GARRISON WILL BE GOING TO CLOUDSDALE AS THE LAST LINE OF DEFENSE, BUT THE FIVE FASTEST, INCLUDING MYSELF, ARE GOING TO TRY TO HEAD THIS THING OFF BEFORE IT GETS ANYWHERE CLOSE TO CLOUDSDALE.
WE'RE GONNA SHOW THAT STORM WHO'S THE BOSS AROUND HERE! THE REST OF YOU GET TO CLOUDSDALE. I NEED THESE FOUR PONIES IN THE AIR WITH ME, NOW!
"NIMBUS DASH.
"BELLA BREEZE.
"FLASH MAGNUS.
"AND THE FIFTH FASTEST, GRIMHOOF."

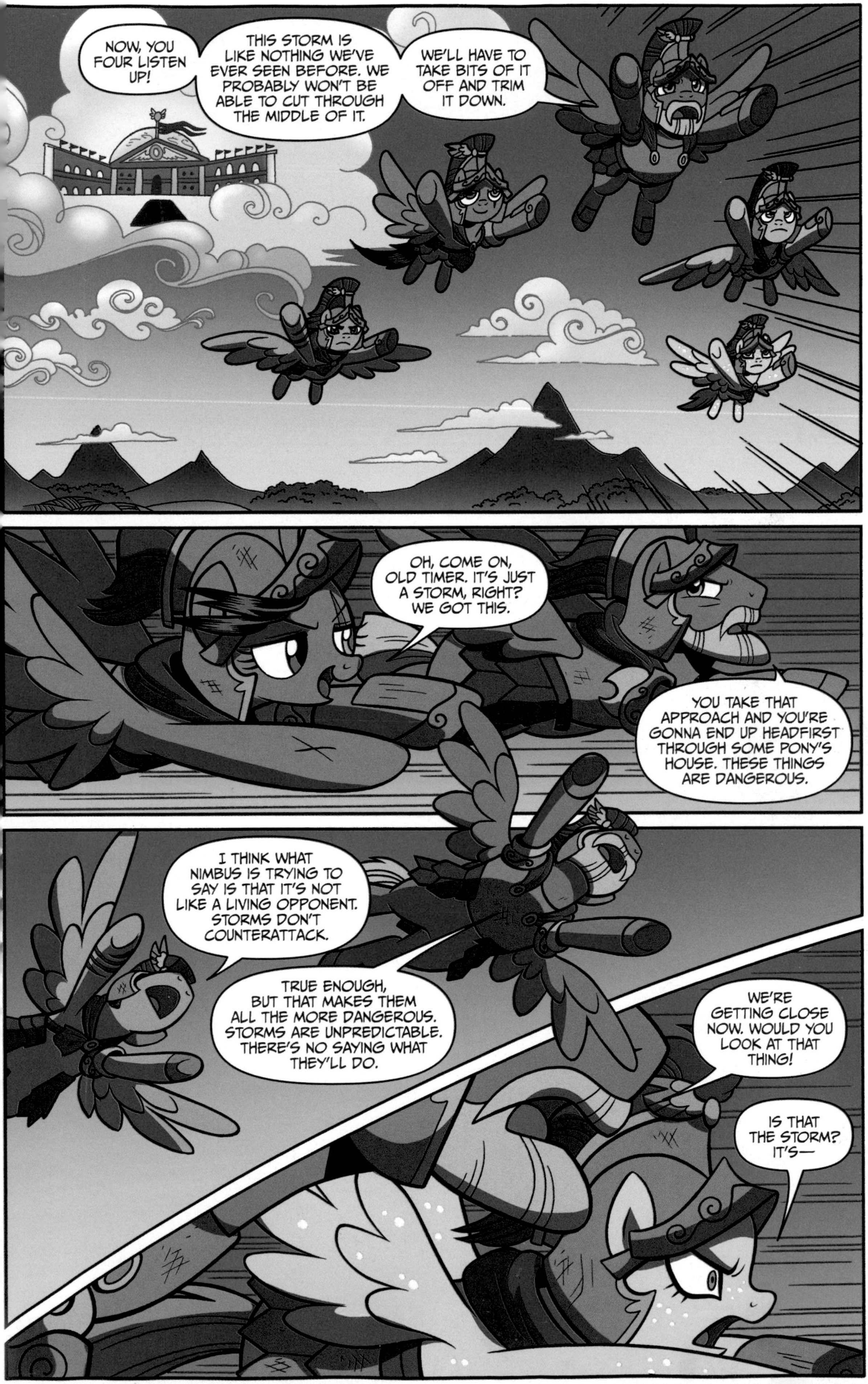
NOW, YOU FOUR LISTEN UP!
THIS STORM IS LIKE NOTHING WE'VE EVER SEEN BEFORE. WE PROBABLY WON'T BE ABLE TO CUT THROUGH THE MIDDLE OF IT.
WE'LL HAVE TO TAKE BITS OF IT OFF AND TRIM IT DOWN.
OH, COME ON, OLD TIMER. IT'S JUST A STORM, RIGHT? WE GOT THIS.
YOU TAKE THAT APPROACH AND YOU'RE GONNA END UP HEADFIRST THROUGH SOME PONY'S HOUSE. THESE THINGS ARE DANGEROUS.
I THINK WHAT NIMBUS IS TRYING TO SAY IS THAT IT'S NOT LIKE A LIVING OPPONENT. STORMS DON'T COUNTERATTACK.
TRUE ENOUGH, BUT THAT MAKES THEM ALL THE MORE DANGEROUS. STORMS ARE UNPREDICTABLE. THERE'S NO SAYING WHAT THEY'LL DO.
WE'RE GETTING CLOSE NOW. WOULD YOU LOOK AT THAT THING!
IS THAT THE STORM? IT'S—

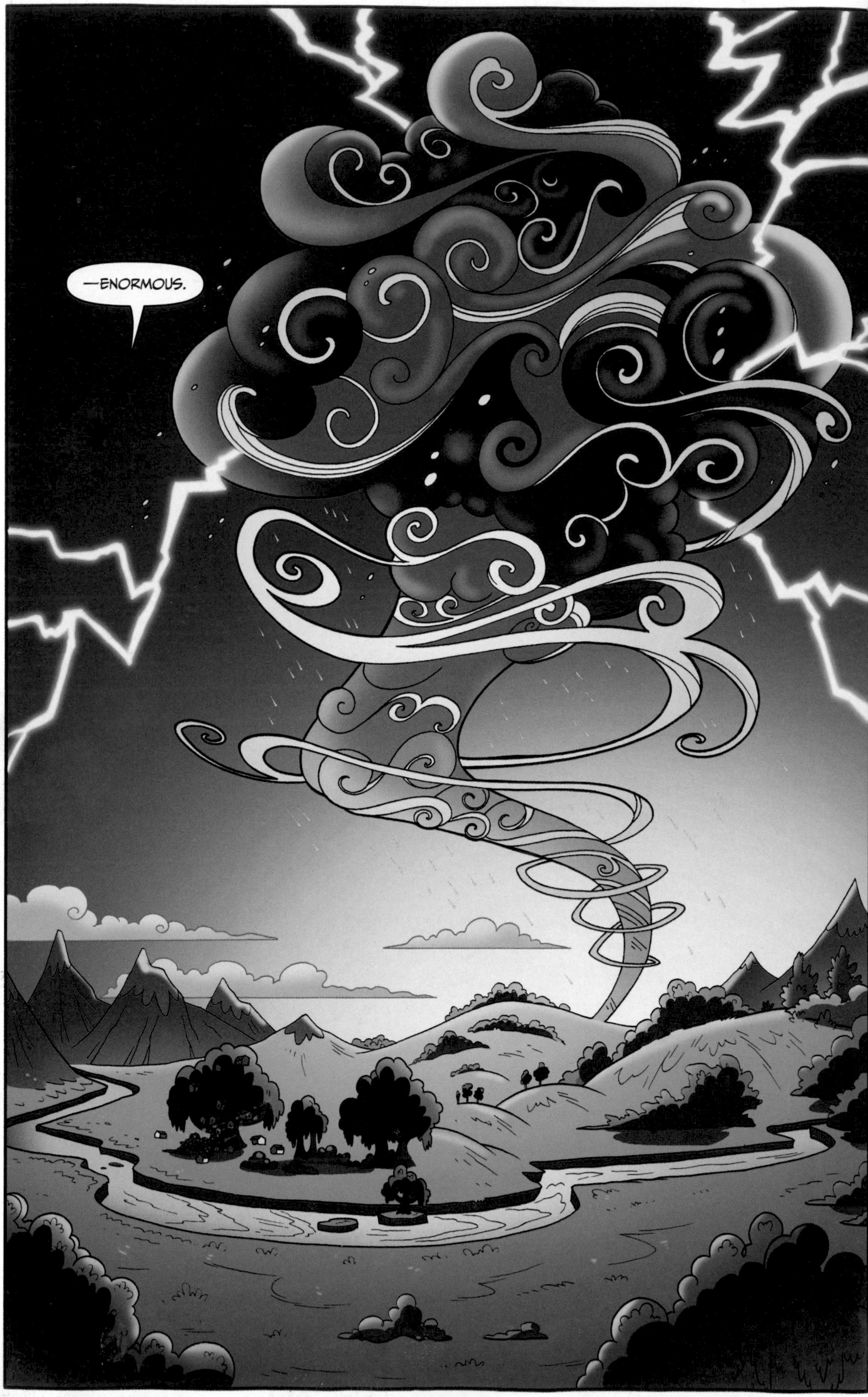
—ENORMOUS.

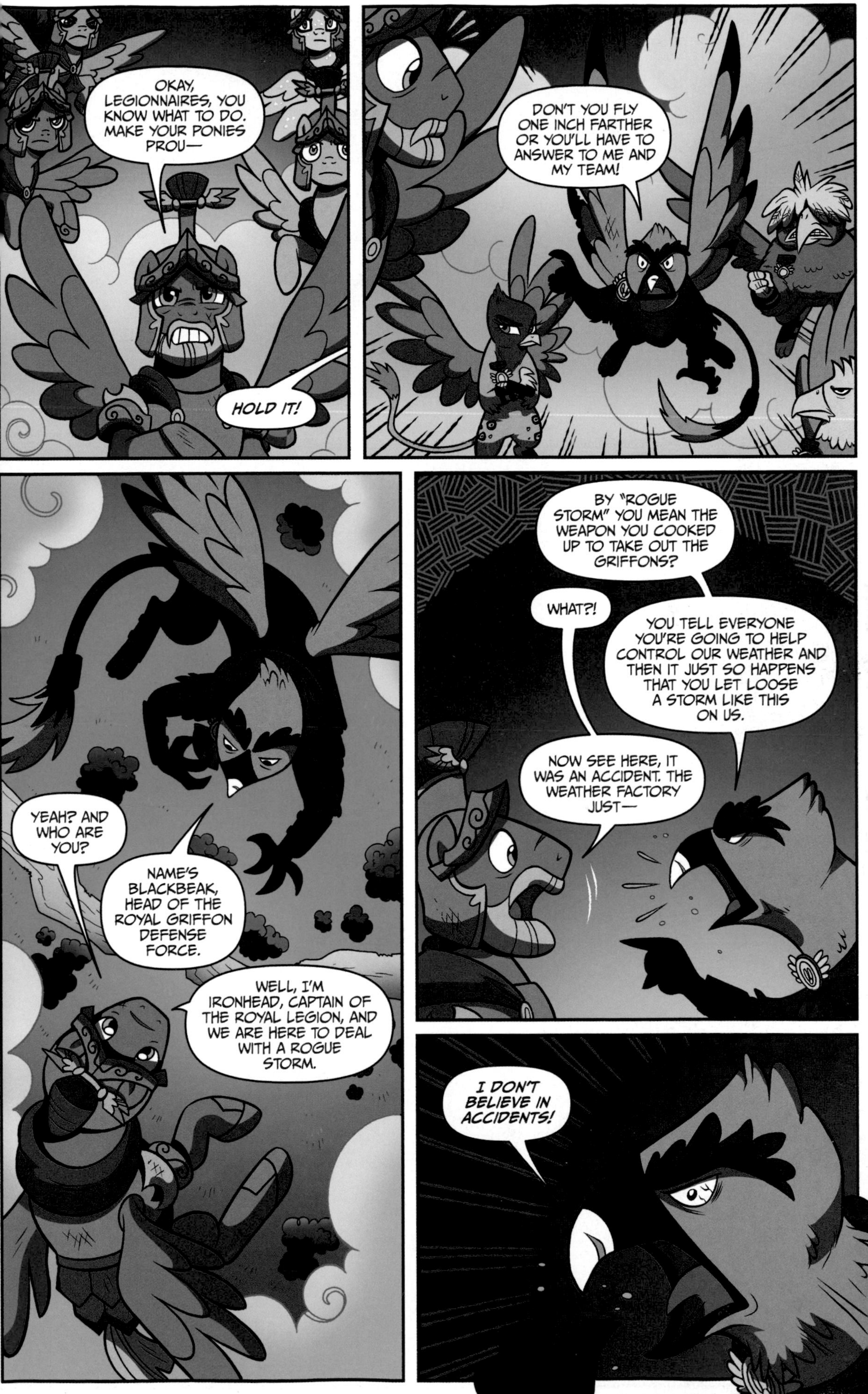
OKAY, LEGIONNAIRES, YOU KNOW WHAT TO DO. MAKE YOUR PONIES PROU—
HOLD IT!
DON'T YOU FLY ONE INCH FARTHER OR YOU'LL HAVE TO ANSWER TO ME AND MY TEAM!
YEAH? AND WHO ARE YOU?
NAME'S BLACKBEAK, HEAD OF THE ROYAL GRIFFON DEFENSE FORCE.
WELL, I'M IRONHEAD, CAPTAIN OF THE ROYAL LEGION, AND WE ARE HERE TO DEAL WITH A ROGUE STORM.
BY "ROGUE STORM" YOU MEAN THE WEAPON YOU COOKED UP TO TAKE OUT THE GRIFFONS?
WHAT?!
YOU TELL EVERYONE YOU'RE GOING TO HELP CONTROL OUR WEATHER AND THEN IT JUST SO HAPPENS THAT YOU LET LOOSE A STORM LIKE THIS ON US.
NOW SEE HERE, IT WAS AN ACCIDENT. THE WEATHER FACTORY JUST—
I DON'T BELIEVE IN ACCIDENTS!

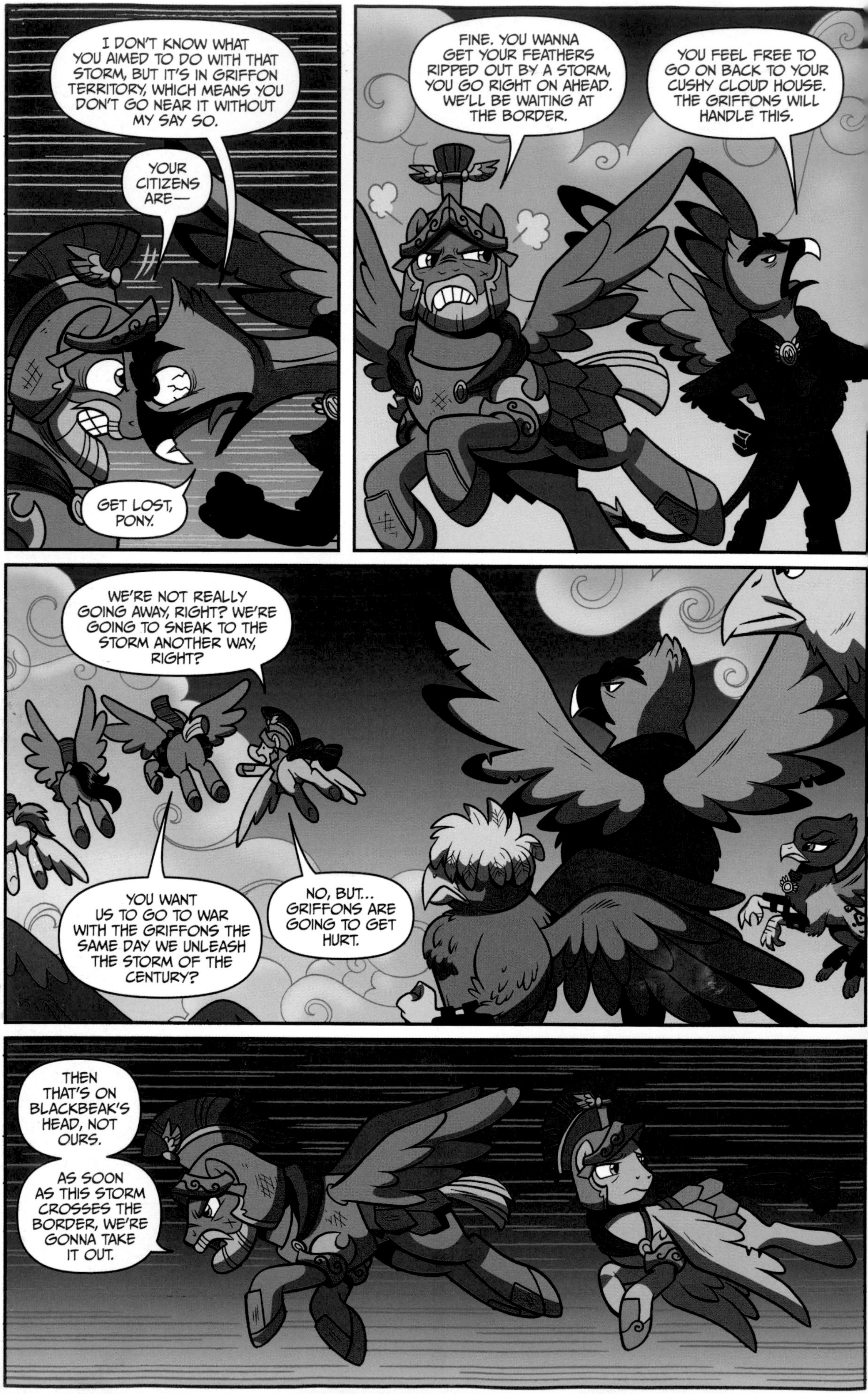
I DON'T KNOW WHAT YOU AIMED TO DO WITH THAT STORM, BUT IT'S IN GRIFFON TERRITORY, WHICH MEANS YOU DON'T GO NEAR IT WITHOUT MY SAY SO.
YOUR CITIZENS ARE—
GET LOST, PONY.
FINE. YOU WANNA GET YOUR FEATHERS RIPPED OUT BY A STORM, YOU GO RIGHT ON AHEAD. WE'LL BE WAITING AT THE BORDER.
YOU FEEL FREE TO GO ON BACK TO YOUR CUSHY CLOUD HOUSE. THE GRIFFONS WILL HANDLE THIS.
WE'RE NOT REALLY GOING AWAY, RIGHT? WE'RE GOING TO SNEAK TO THE STORM ANOTHER WAY, RIGHT?
YOU WANT US TO GO TO WAR WITH THE GRIFFONS THE SAME DAY WE UNLEASH THE STORM OF THE CENTURY?
NO, BUT... GRIFFONS ARE GOING TO GET HURT.
THEN THAT'S ON BLACKBEAK'S HEAD, NOT OURS.
AS SOON AS THIS STORM CROSSES THE BORDER, WE'RE GONNA TAKE IT OUT.

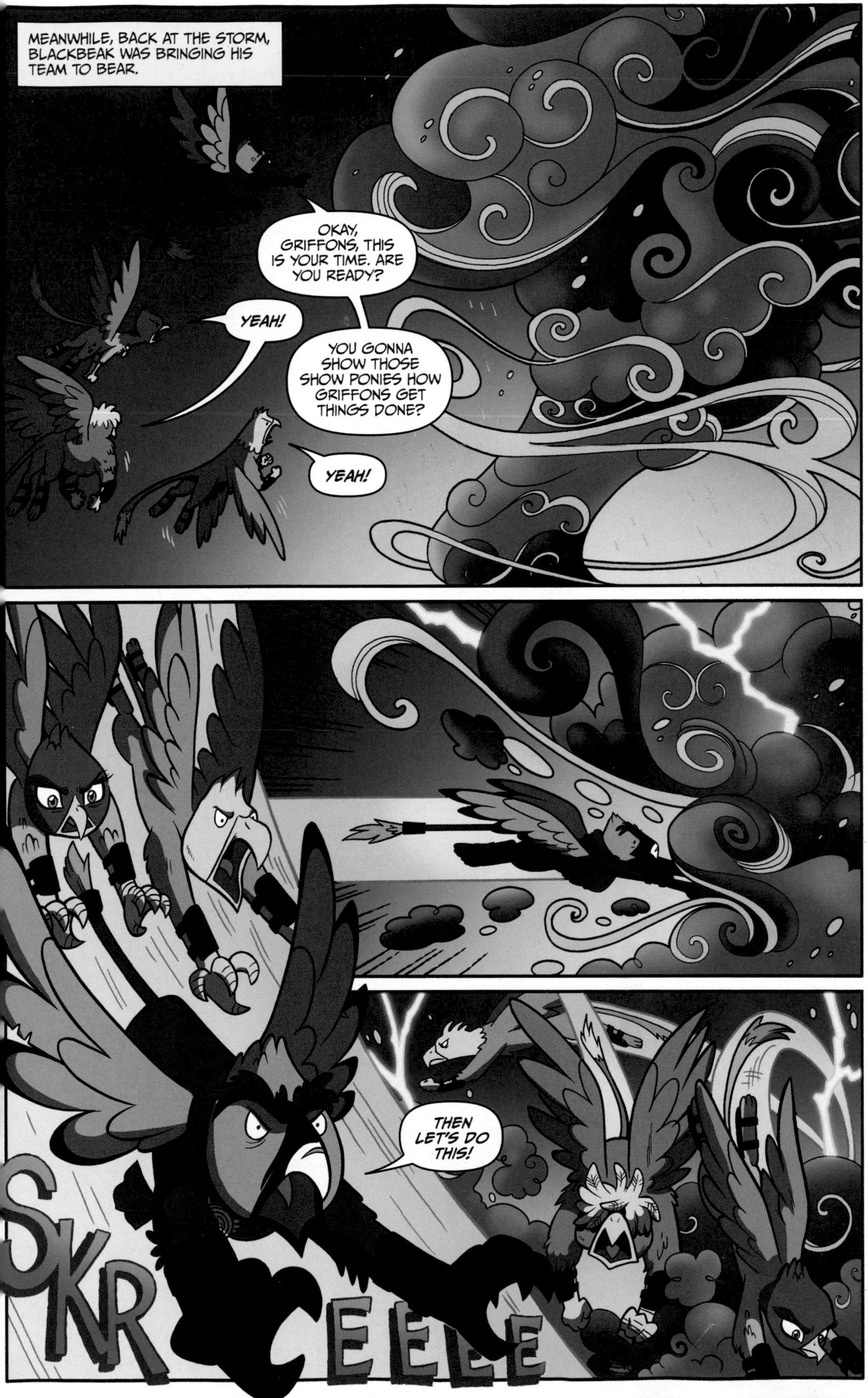
MEANWHILE, BACK AT THE STORM, BLACKBEAK WAS BRINGING HIS TEAM TO BEAR.
OKAY, GRIFFONS, THIS IS YOUR TIME. ARE YOU READY?
YEAH!
YOU GONNA SHOW THOSE SHOW PONIES HOW GRIFFONS GET THINGS DONE?
YEAH!
THEN LET'S DO THIS!
SKREEELE

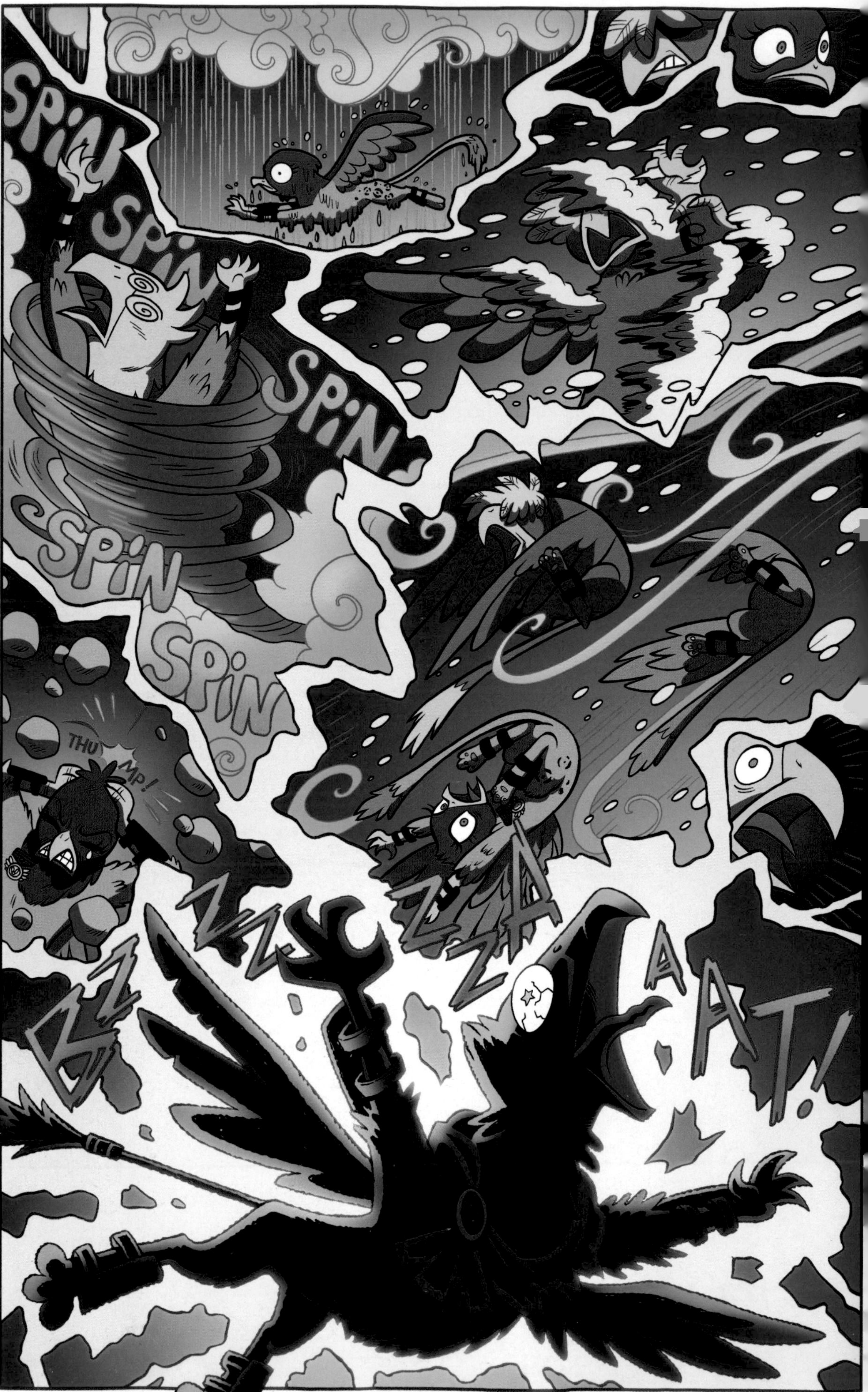
SPIN
SPIN
SPIN
SPIN
SPIN
THUMP!
BZZZZZAAAT!

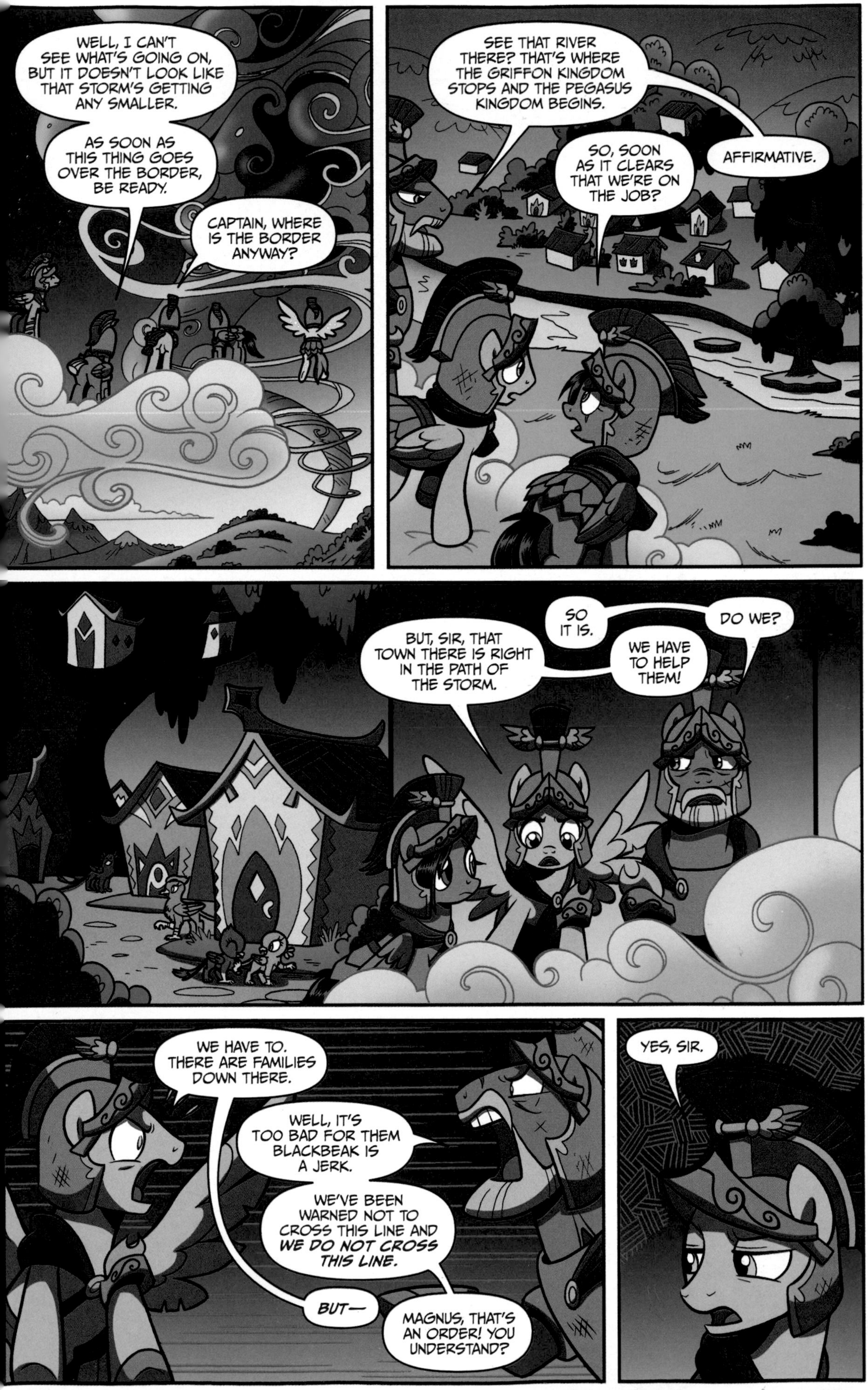
WELL, I CAN'T SEE WHAT'S GOING ON, BUT IT DOESN'T LOOK LIKE THAT STORM'S GETTING ANY SMALLER.
AS SOON AS THIS THING GOES OVER THE BORDER, BE READY.
CAPTAIN, WHERE IS THE BORDER ANYWAY?
SEE THAT RIVER THERE? THAT'S WHERE THE GRIFFON KINGDOM STOPS AND THE PEGASUS KINGDOM BEGINS.
SO, SOON AS IT CLEARS THAT WE'RE ON THE JOB?
AFFIRMATIVE.
BUT, SIR, THAT TOWN THERE IS RIGHT IN THE PATH OF THE STORM.
SO IT IS.
WE HAVE TO HELP THEM!
DO WE?
WE HAVE TO. THERE ARE FAMILIES DOWN THERE.
WELL, IT'S TOO BAD FOR THEM BLACKBEAK IS A JERK.
WE'VE BEEN WARNED NOT TO CROSS THIS LINE AND *WE DO NOT CROSS THIS LINE.*
BUT—
MAGNUS, THAT'S AN ORDER! YOU UNDERSTAND?
YES, SIR.

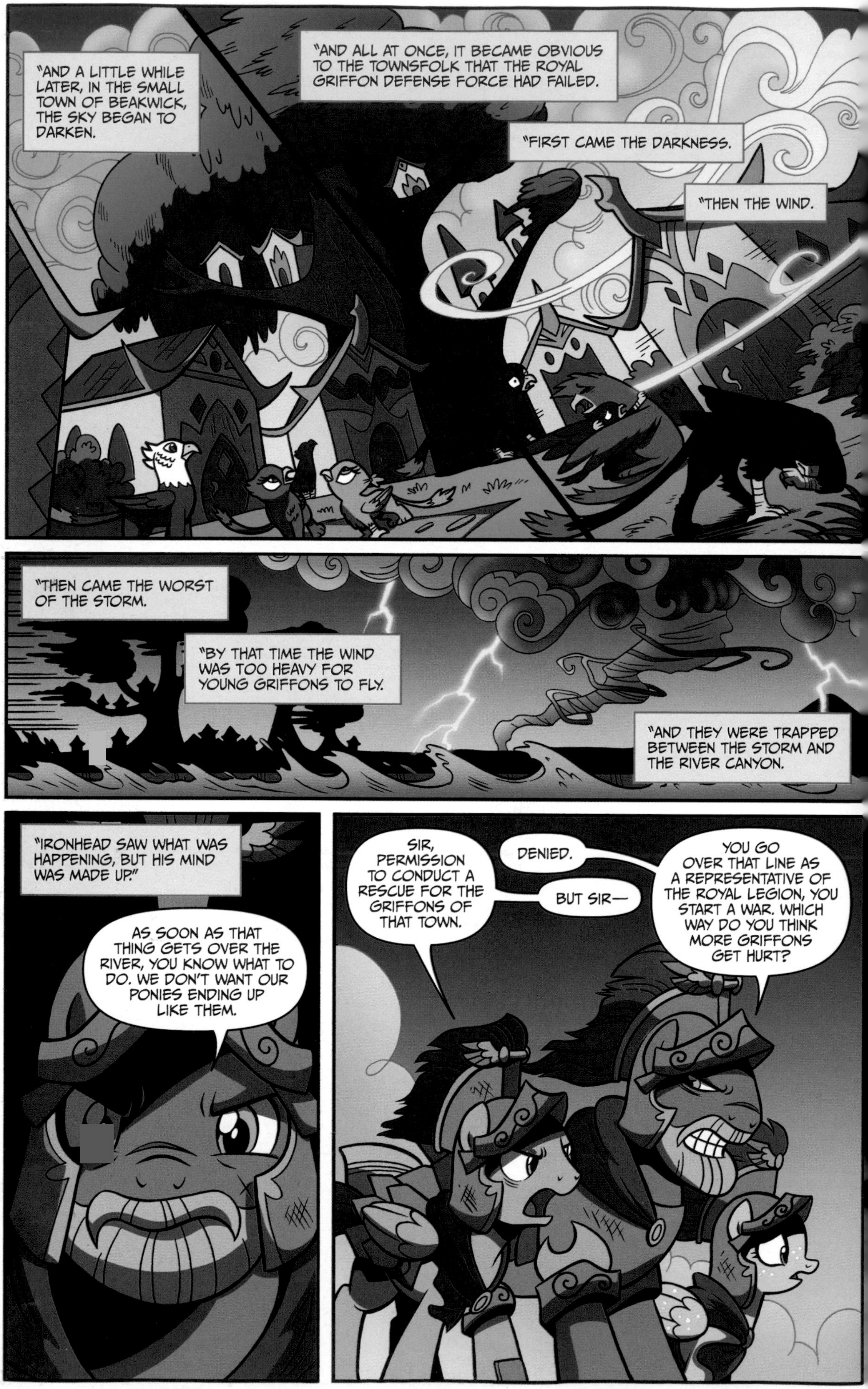
"AND A LITTLE WHILE LATER, IN THE SMALL TOWN OF BEAKWICK, THE SKY BEGAN TO DARKEN.
"AND ALL AT ONCE, IT BECAME OBVIOUS TO THE TOWNSFOLK THAT THE ROYAL GRIFFON DEFENSE FORCE HAD FAILED.
"FIRST CAME THE DARKNESS.
"THEN THE WIND.
"THEN CAME THE WORST OF THE STORM.
"BY THAT TIME THE WIND WAS TOO HEAVY FOR YOUNG GRIFFONS TO FLY.
"AND THEY WERE TRAPPED BETWEEN THE STORM AND THE RIVER CANYON.
"IRONHEAD SAW WHAT WAS HAPPENING, BUT HIS MIND WAS MADE UP."
AS SOON AS THAT THING GETS OVER THE RIVER, YOU KNOW WHAT TO DO. WE DON'T WANT OUR PONIES ENDING UP LIKE THEM.
SIR, PERMISSION TO CONDUCT A RESCUE FOR THE GRIFFONS OF THAT TOWN.
DENIED.
BUT SIR—
YOU GO OVER THAT LINE AS A REPRESENTATIVE OF THE ROYAL LEGION, YOU START A WAR. WHICH WAY DO YOU THINK MORE GRIFFONS GET HURT?

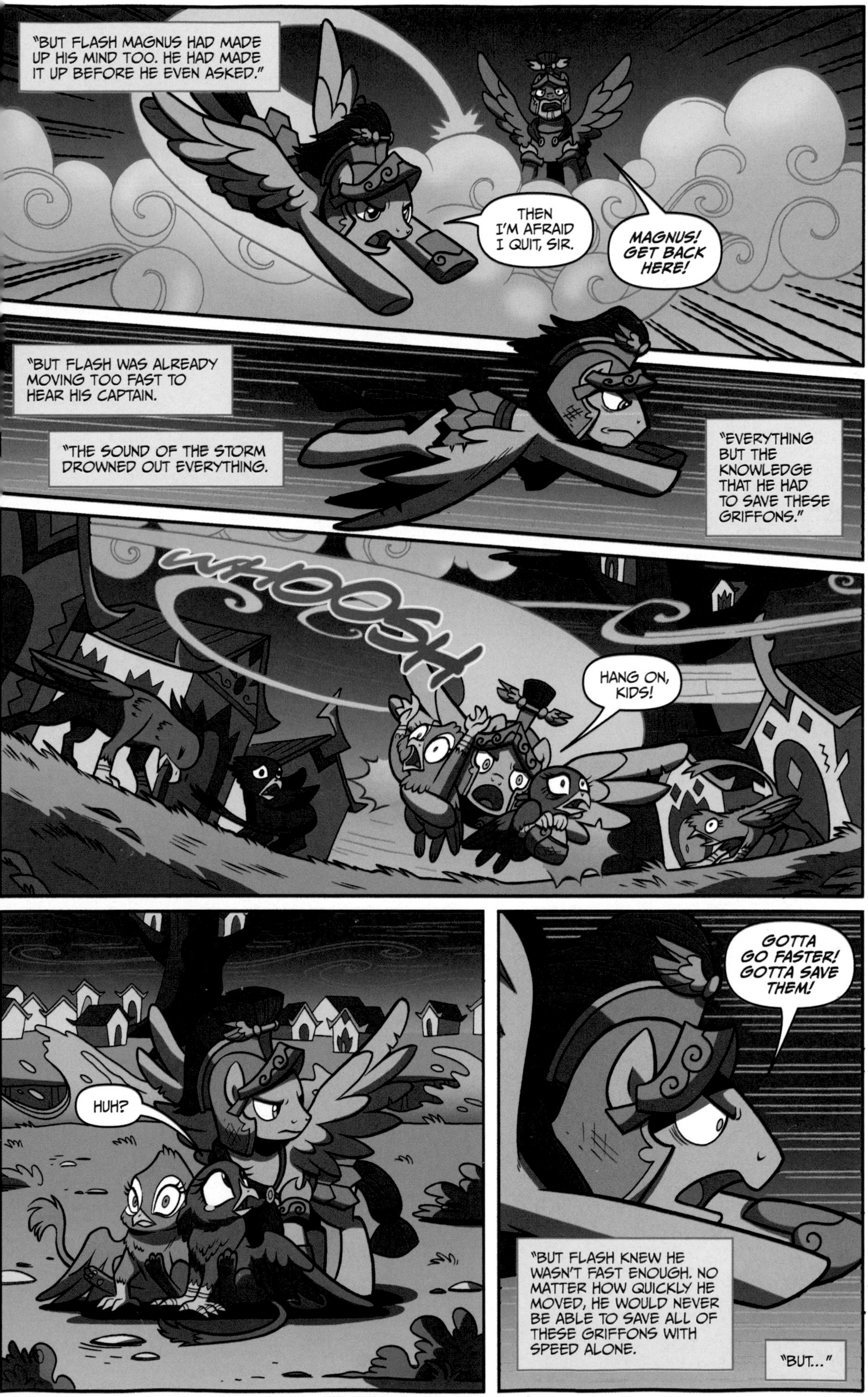
"BUT FLASH MAGNUS HAD MADE UP HIS MIND TOO. HE HAD MADE IT UP BEFORE HE EVEN ASKED."
THEN I'M AFRAID I QUIT, SIR.
MAGNUS! GET BACK HERE!
"BUT FLASH WAS ALREADY MOVING TOO FAST TO HEAR HIS CAPTAIN.
"THE SOUND OF THE STORM DROWNED OUT EVERYTHING.
"EVERYTHING BUT THE KNOWLEDGE THAT HE HAD TO SAVE THESE GRIFFONS."
WHOOSH
HANG ON, KIDS!
HUH?
GOTTA GO FASTER! GOTTA SAVE THEM!
"BUT FLASH KNEW HE WASN'T FAST ENOUGH. NO MATTER HOW QUICKLY HE MOVED, HE WOULD NEVER BE ABLE TO SAVE ALL OF THESE GRIFFONS WITH SPEED ALONE.
"BUT..."

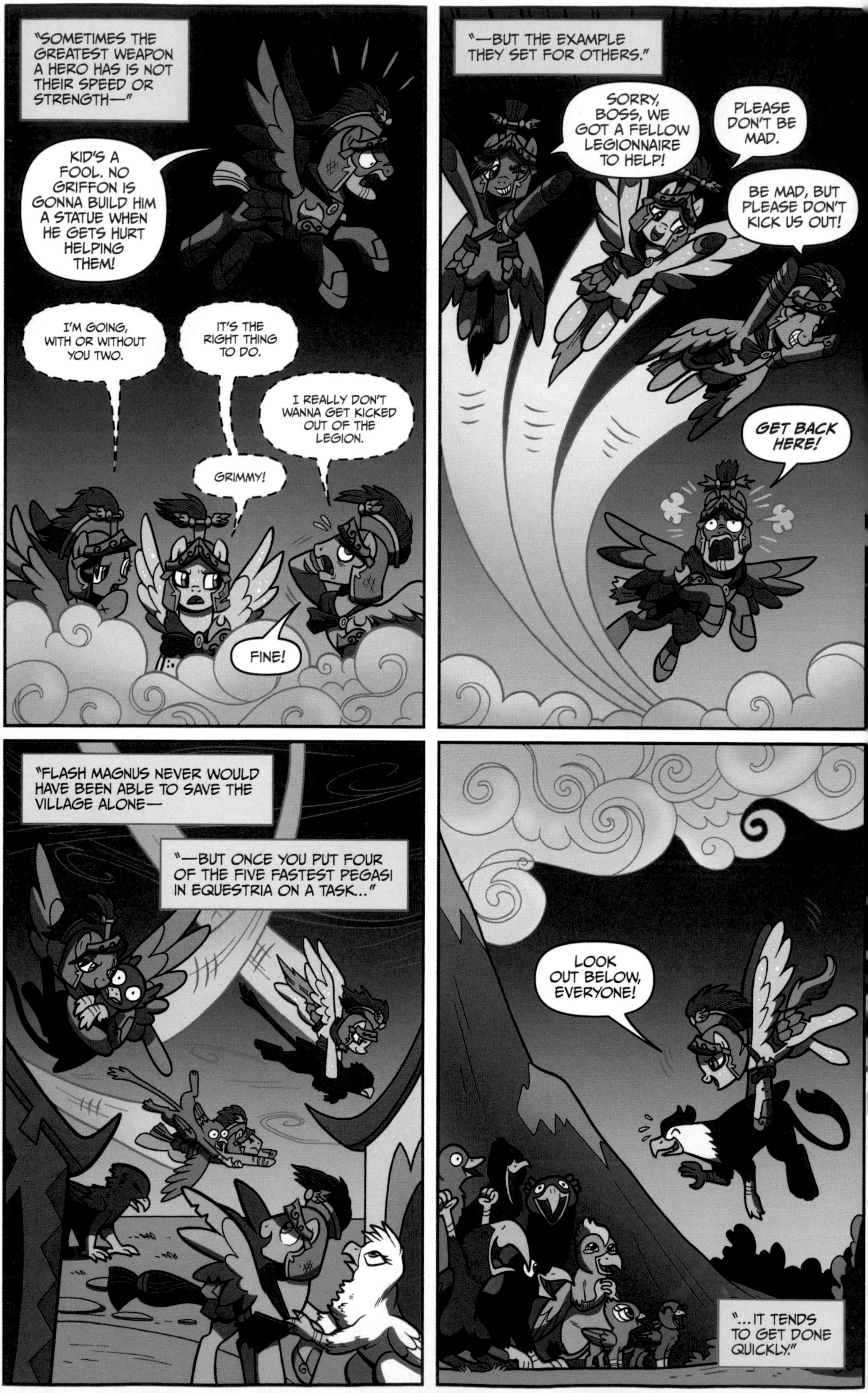
"SOMETIMES THE GREATEST WEAPON A HERO HAS IS NOT THEIR SPEED OR STRENGTH—"
KID'S A FOOL. NO GRIFFON IS GONNA BUILD HIM A STATUE WHEN HE GETS HURT HELPING THEM!
I'M GOING, WITH OR WITHOUT YOU TWO.
IT'S THE RIGHT THING TO DO.
I REALLY DON'T WANNA GET KICKED OUT OF THE LEGION.
GRIMMY!
FINE!
"—BUT THE EXAMPLE THEY SET FOR OTHERS."
SORRY, BOSS, WE GOT A FELLOW LEGIONNAIRE TO HELP!
PLEASE DON'T BE MAD.
BE MAD, BUT PLEASE DON'T KICK US OUT!
GET BACK HERE!
"FLASH MAGNUS NEVER WOULD HAVE BEEN ABLE TO SAVE THE VILLAGE ALONE—
"—BUT ONCE YOU PUT FOUR OF THE FIVE FASTEST PEGASI IN EQUESTRIA ON A TASK..."
LOOK OUT BELOW, EVERYONE!
"...IT TENDS TO GET DONE QUICKLY."

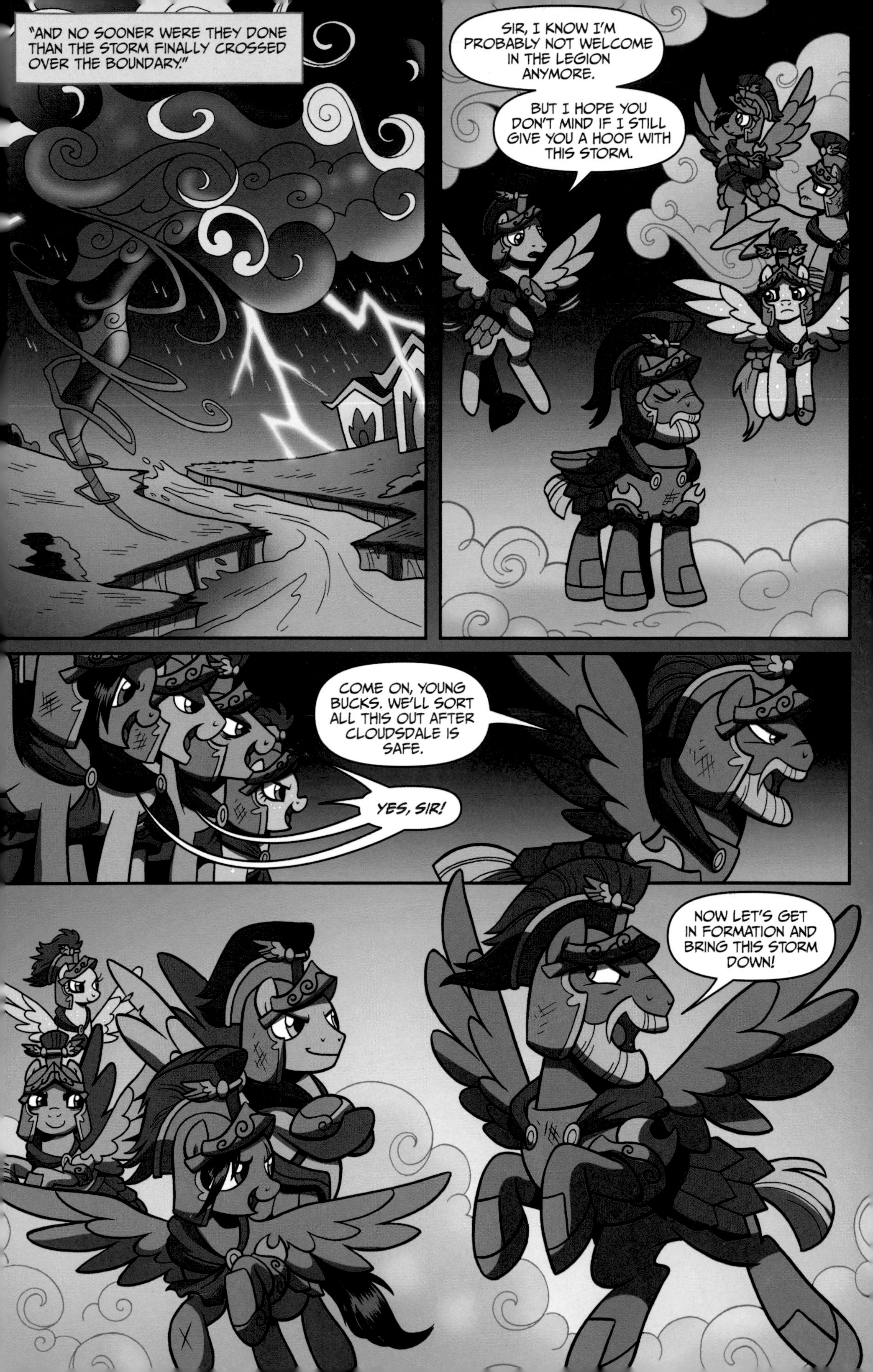
"AND NO SOONER WERE THEY DONE THAN THE STORM FINALLY CROSSED OVER THE BOUNDARY."
SIR, I KNOW I'M PROBABLY NOT WELCOME IN THE LEGION ANYMORE.
BUT I HOPE YOU DON'T MIND IF I STILL GIVE YOU A HOOF WITH THIS STORM.
COME ON, YOUNG BUCKS. WE'LL SORT ALL THIS OUT AFTER CLOUDSDALE IS SAFE.
YES, SIR!
NOW LET'S GET IN FORMATION AND BRING THIS STORM DOWN!

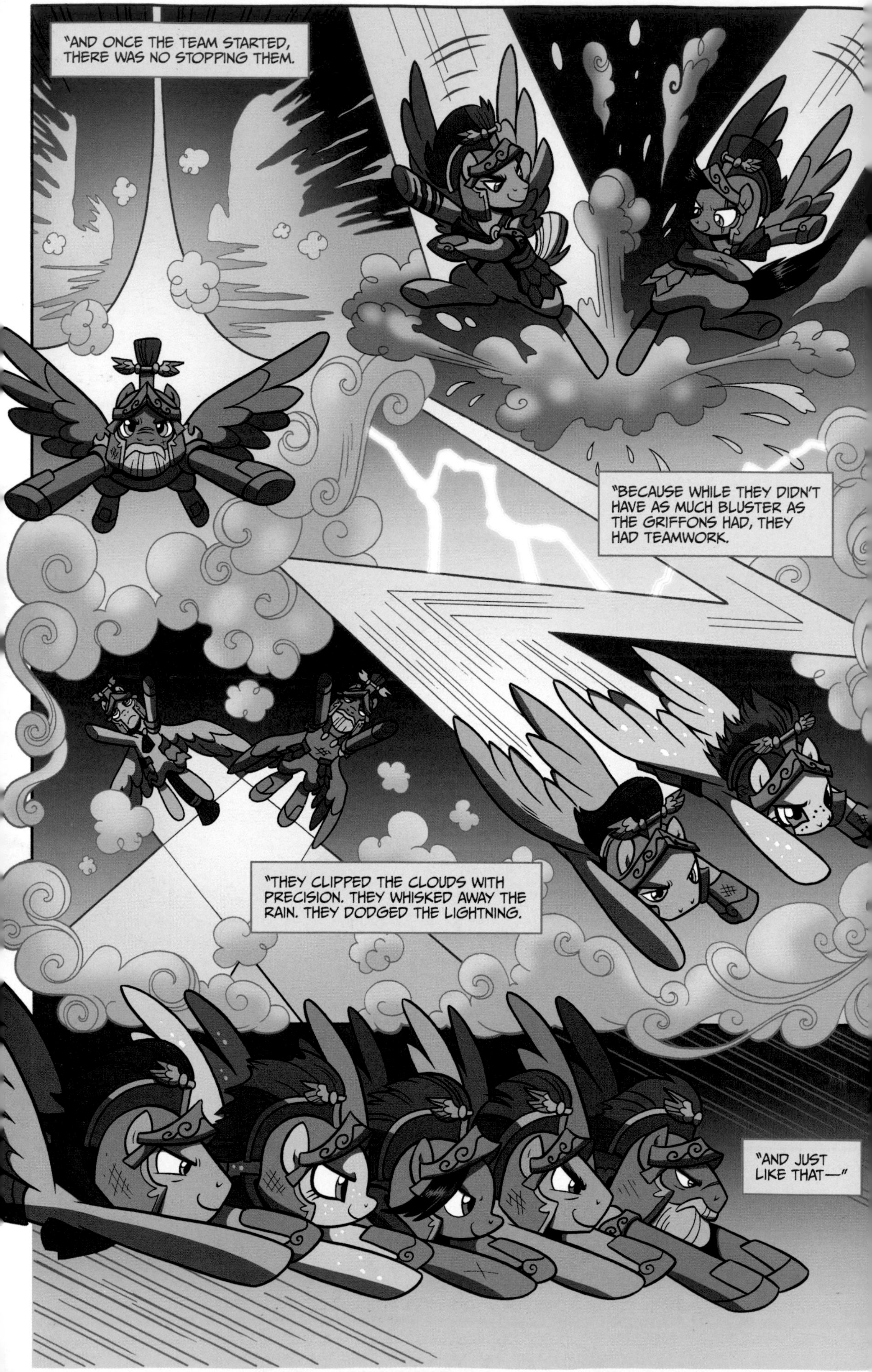
"AND ONCE THE TEAM STARTED, THERE WAS NO STOPPING THEM.
"BECAUSE WHILE THEY DIDN'T HAVE AS MUCH BLUSTER AS THE GRIFFONS HAD, THEY HAD TEAMWORK.
"THEY CLIPPED THE CLOUDS WITH PRECISION. THEY WHISKED AWAY THE RAIN. THEY DODGED THE LIGHTNING.
"AND JUST LIKE THAT—"

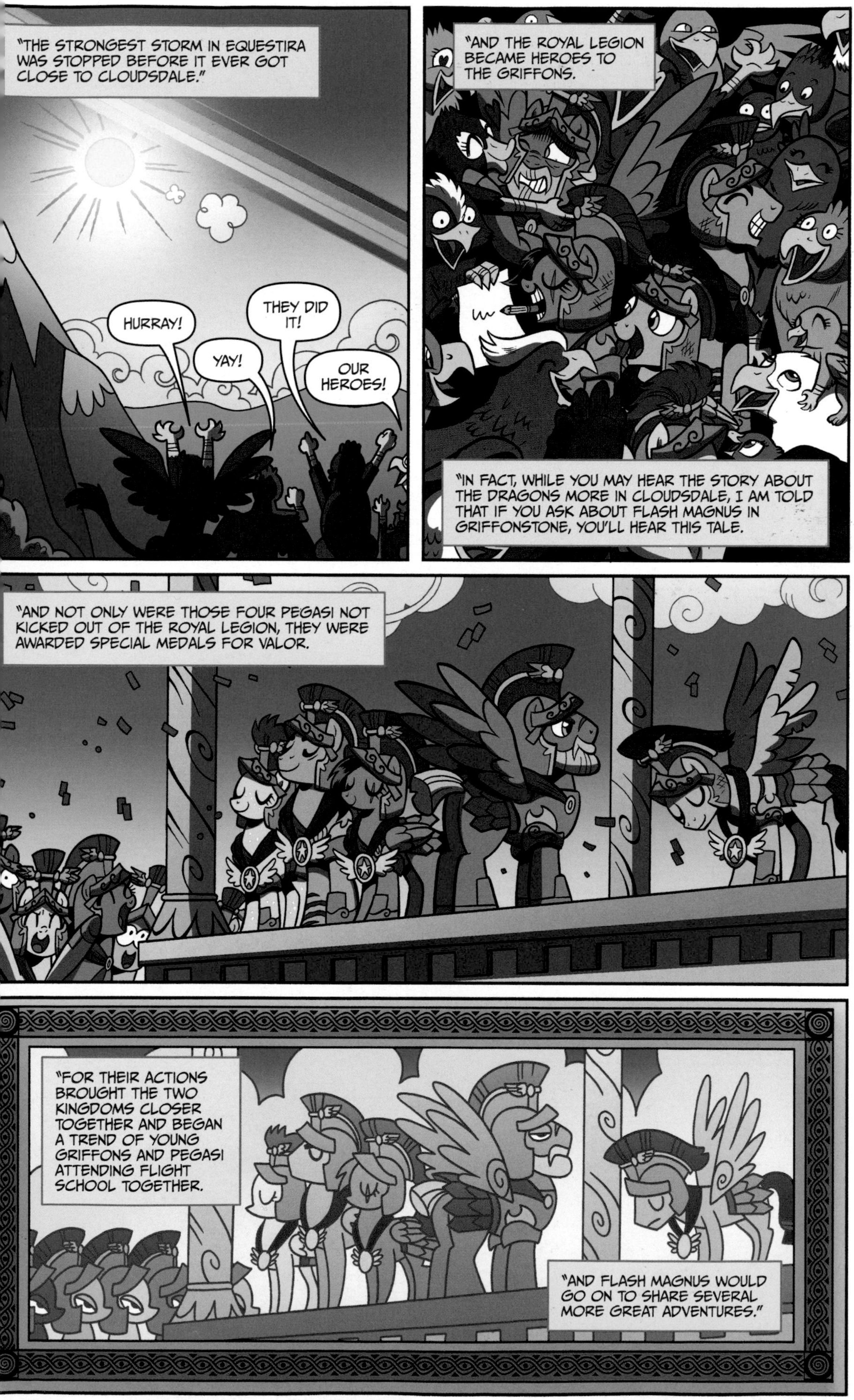
"THE STRONGEST STORM IN EQUESTIRA WAS STOPPED BEFORE IT EVER GOT CLOSE TO CLOUDSDALE."
HURRAY!
THEY DID IT!
YAY!
OUR HEROES!
"AND THE ROYAL LEGION BECAME HEROES TO THE GRIFFONS.
"IN FACT, WHILE YOU MAY HEAR THE STORY ABOUT THE DRAGONS MORE IN CLOUDSDALE, I AM TOLD THAT IF YOU ASK ABOUT FLASH MAGNUS IN GRIFFONSTONE, YOU'LL HEAR THIS TALE.
"AND NOT ONLY WERE THOSE FOUR PEGASI NOT KICKED OUT OF THE ROYAL LEGION, THEY WERE AWARDED SPECIAL MEDALS FOR VALOR.
"FOR THEIR ACTIONS BROUGHT THE TWO KINGDOMS CLOSER TOGETHER AND BEGAN A TREND OF YOUNG GRIFFONS AND PEGASI ATTENDING FLIGHT SCHOOL TOGETHER.
"AND FLASH MAGNUS WOULD GO ON TO SHARE SEVERAL MORE GREAT ADVENTURES."

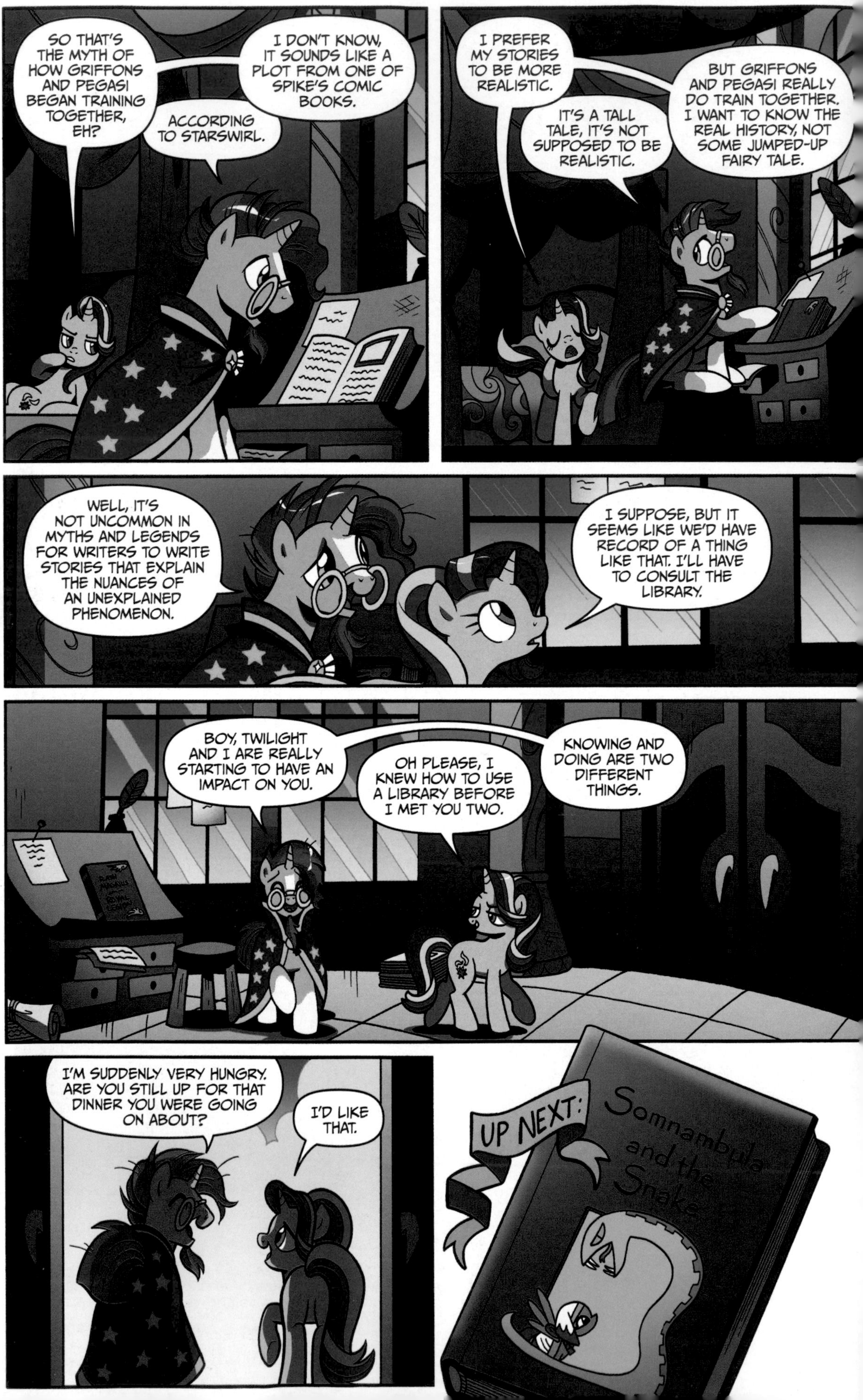
SO THAT'S THE MYTH OF HOW GRIFFONS AND PEGASI BEGAN TRAINING TOGETHER, EH?
ACCORDING TO STARSWIRL.
I DON'T KNOW, IT SOUNDS LIKE A PLOT FROM ONE OF SPIKE'S COMIC BOOKS.
I PREFER MY STORIES TO BE MORE REALISTIC.
IT'S A TALL TALE, IT'S NOT SUPPOSED TO BE REALISTIC.
BUT GRIFFONS AND PEGASI REALLY DO TRAIN TOGETHER. I WANT TO KNOW THE REAL HISTORY, NOT SOME JUMPED-UP FAIRY TALE.
WELL, IT'S NOT UNCOMMON IN MYTHS AND LEGENDS FOR WRITERS TO WRITE STORIES THAT EXPLAIN THE NUANCES OF AN UNEXPLAINED PHENOMENON.
I SUPPOSE, BUT IT SEEMS LIKE WE'D HAVE RECORD OF A THING LIKE THAT. I'LL HAVE TO CONSULT THE LIBRARY.
BOY, TWILIGHT AND I ARE REALLY STARTING TO HAVE AN IMPACT ON YOU.
OH PLEASE, I KNEW HOW TO USE A LIBRARY BEFORE I MET YOU TWO.
KNOWING AND DOING ARE TWO DIFFERENT THINGS.
I'M SUDDENLY VERY HUNGRY. ARE YOU STILL UP FOR THAT DINNER YOU WERE GOING ON ABOUT?
I'D LIKE THAT.
UP NEXT:
Somnambula and the Snake

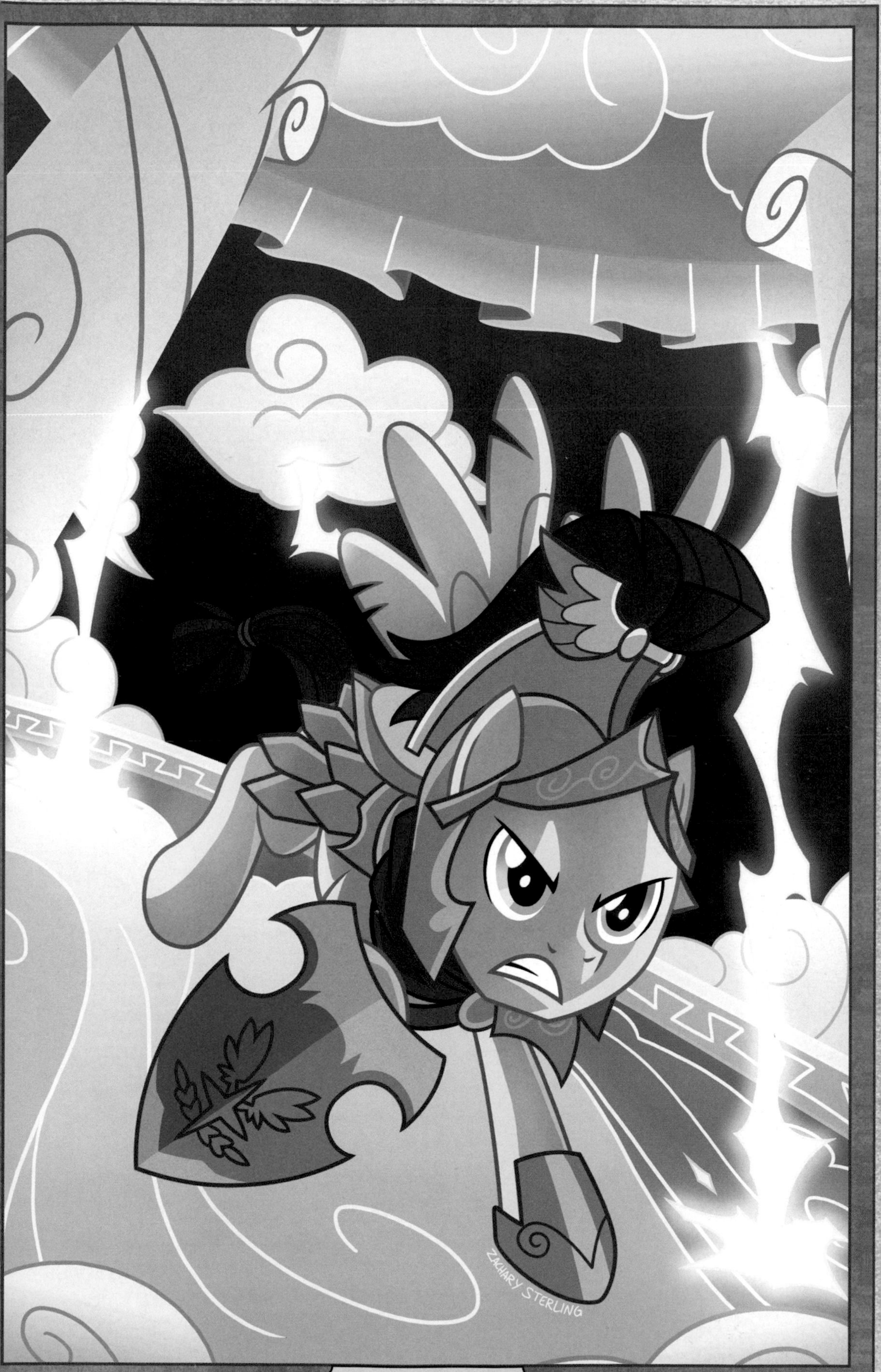
ZACHARY STERLING

ART BY ZACHARY STERLING

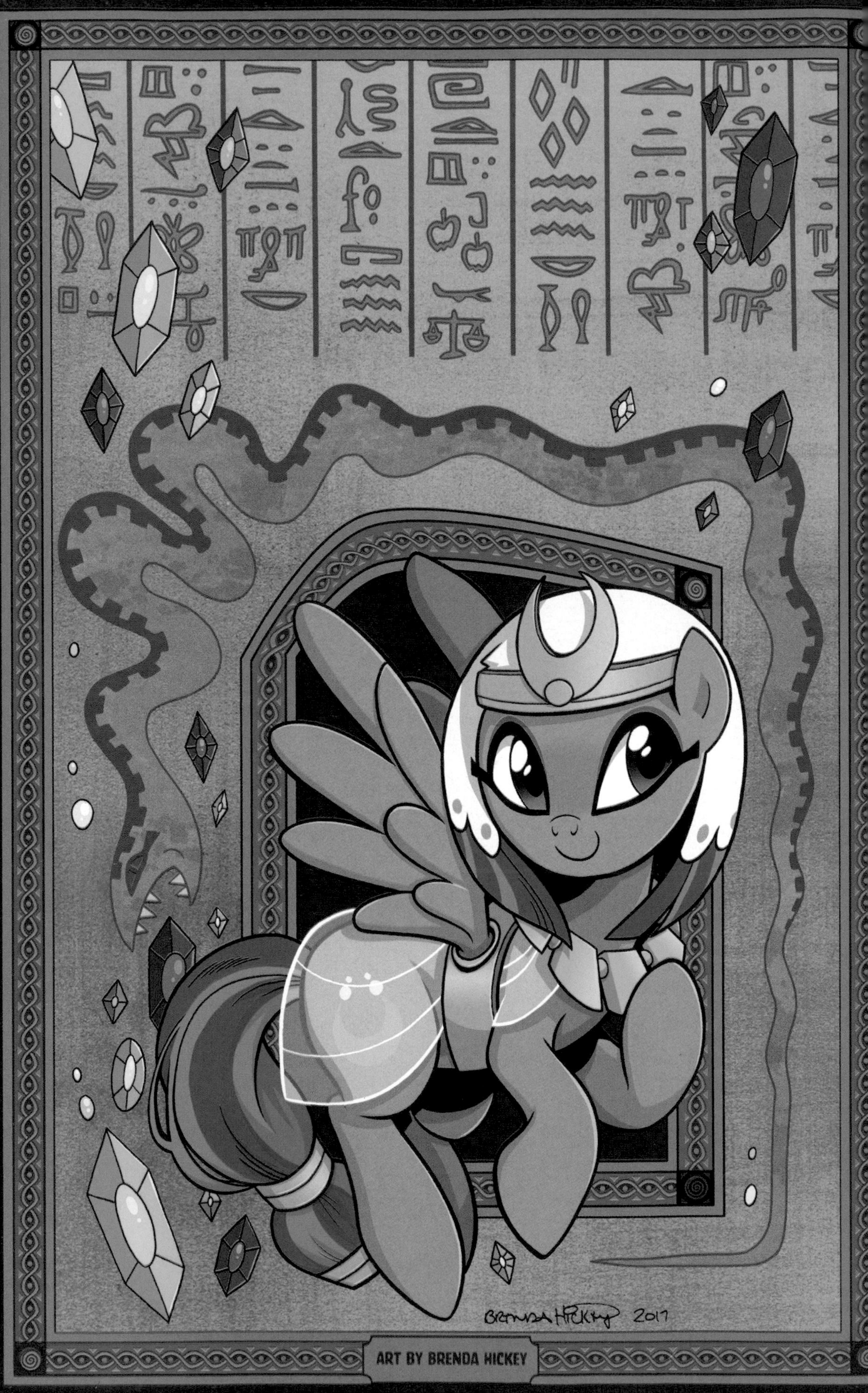
Brenda Hickey 2017
ART BY BRENDA HICKEY

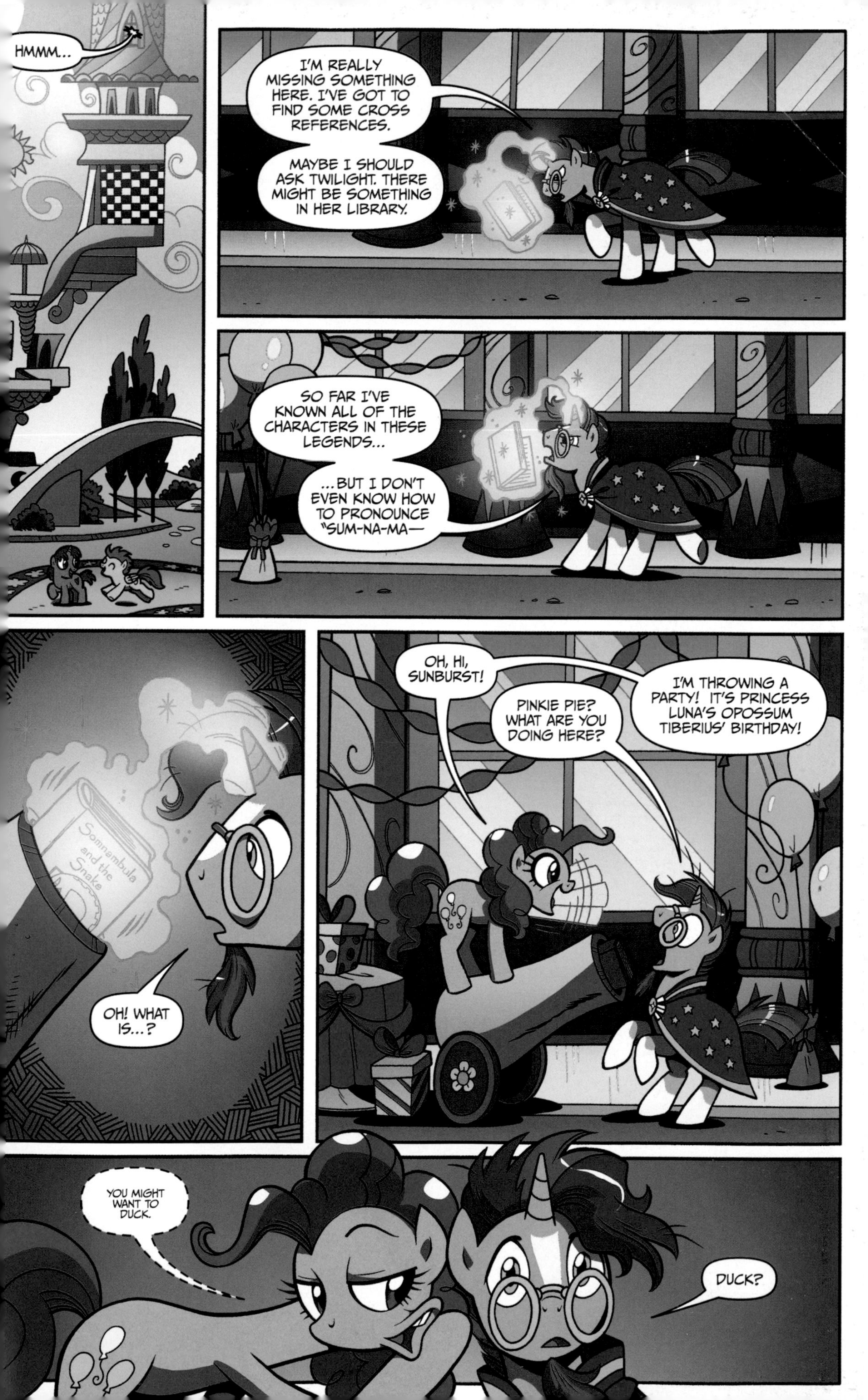
HMMM...
I'M REALLY MISSING SOMETHING HERE. I'VE GOT TO FIND SOME CROSS REFERENCES.
MAYBE I SHOULD ASK TWILIGHT. THERE MIGHT BE SOMETHING IN HER LIBRARY.
SO FAR I'VE KNOWN ALL OF THE CHARACTERS IN THESE LEGENDS...
...BUT I DON'T EVEN KNOW HOW TO PRONOUNCE "SUM-NA-MA—
Somnambula and the Snake
OH! WHAT IS...?
OH, HI, SUNBURST!
PINKIE PIE? WHAT ARE YOU DOING HERE?
I'M THROWING A PARTY! IT'S PRINCESS LUNA'S OPOSSUM TIBERIUS' BIRTHDAY!
YOU MIGHT WANT TO DUCK.
DUCK?

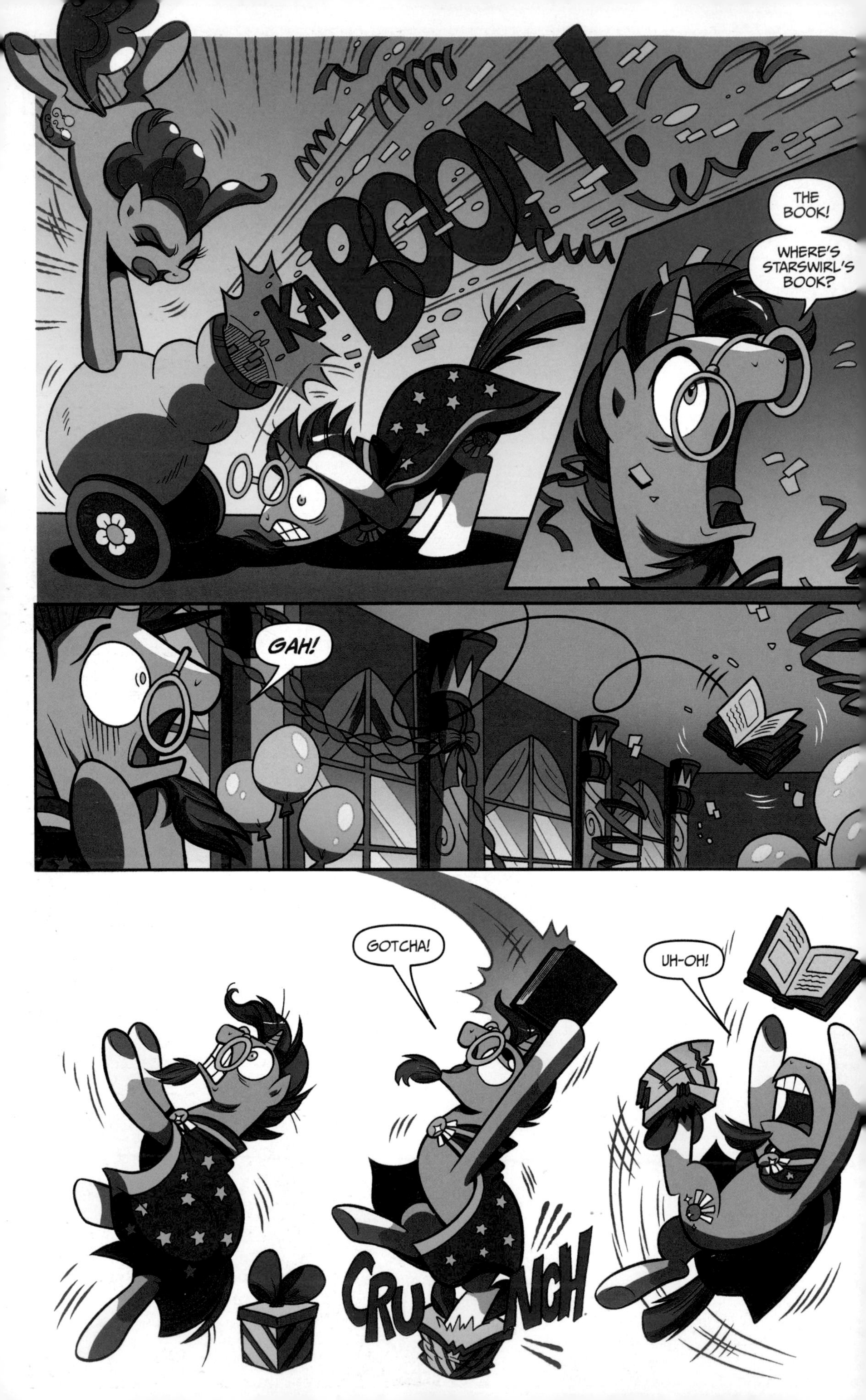
KA BOOM!
THE BOOK!
WHERE'S STARSWIRL'S BOOK?
GAH!
GOTCHA!
UH-OH!
CRUNCH

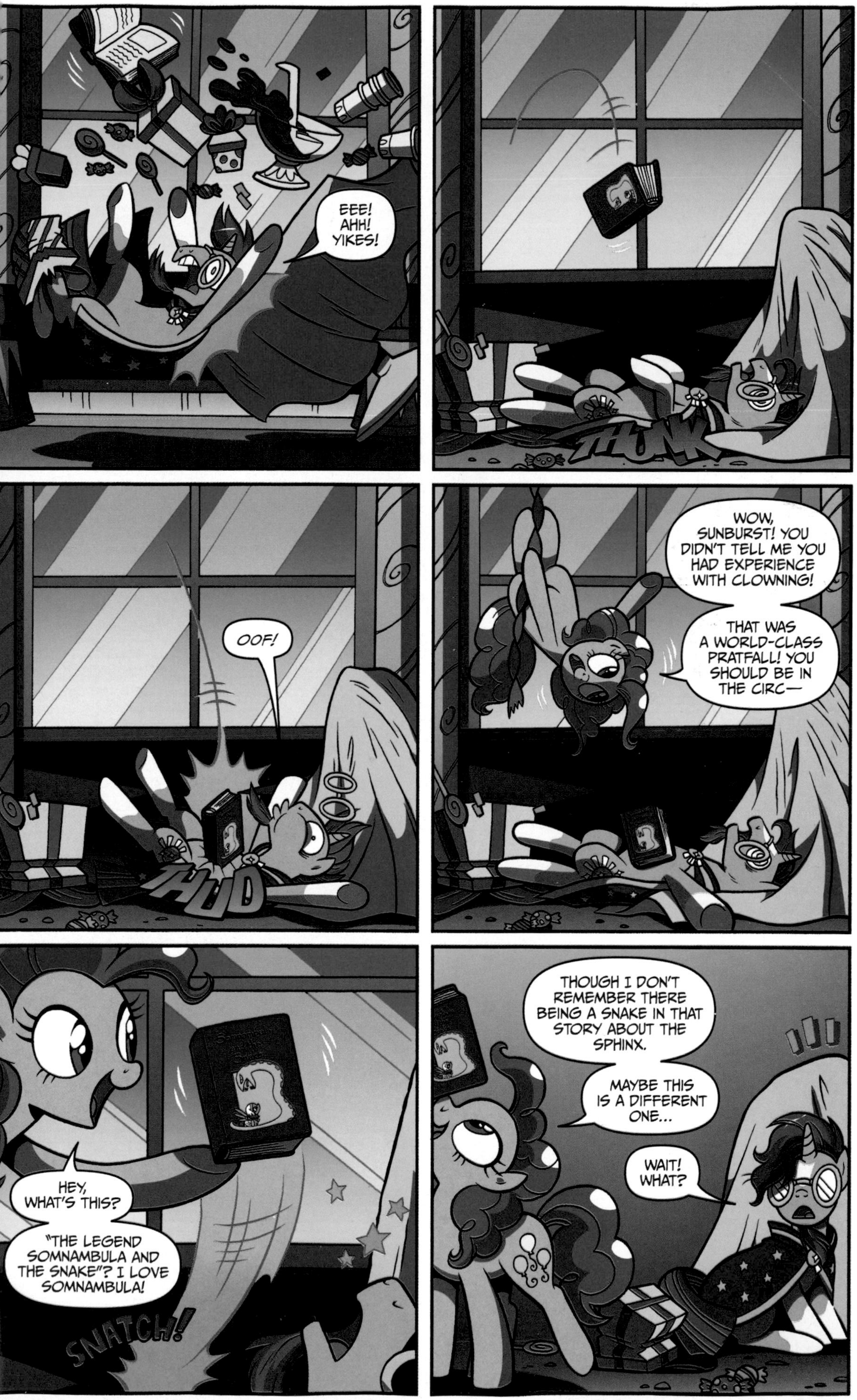
EEE! AHH! YIKES!
THUNK
OOF!
THUD
WOW, SUNBURST! YOU DIDN'T TELL ME YOU HAD EXPERIENCE WITH CLOWNING!
THAT WAS A WORLD-CLASS PRATFALL! YOU SHOULD BE IN THE CIRC—
HEY, WHAT'S THIS?
"THE LEGEND SOMNAMBULA AND THE SNAKE"? I LOVE SOMNAMBULA!
SNATCH!
THOUGH I DON'T REMEMBER THERE BEING A SNAKE IN THAT STORY ABOUT THE SPHINX.
MAYBE THIS IS A DIFFERENT ONE...
WAIT! WHAT?

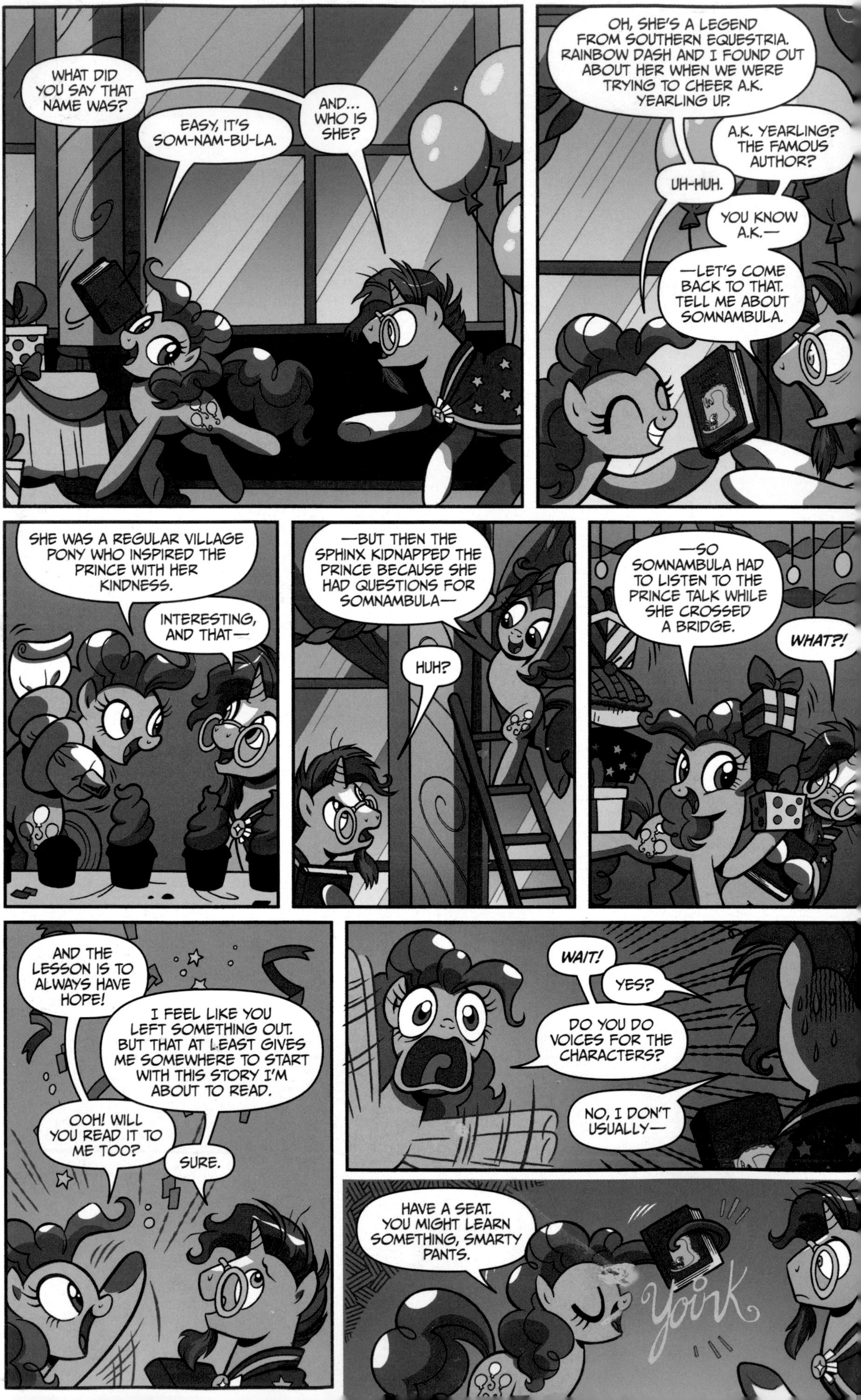
WHAT DID YOU SAY THAT NAME WAS?
EASY, IT'S SOM-NAM-BU-LA.
AND... WHO IS SHE?
OH, SHE'S A LEGEND FROM SOUTHERN EQUESTRIA. RAINBOW DASH AND I FOUND OUT ABOUT HER WHEN WE WERE TRYING TO CHEER A.K. YEARLING UP.
A.K. YEARLING? THE FAMOUS AUTHOR?
UH-HUH.
YOU KNOW A.K.—
—LET'S COME BACK TO THAT. TELL ME ABOUT SOMNAMBULA.
SHE WAS A REGULAR VILLAGE PONY WHO INSPIRED THE PRINCE WITH HER KINDNESS.
INTERESTING, AND THAT—
—BUT THEN THE SPHINX KIDNAPPED THE PRINCE BECAUSE SHE HAD QUESTIONS FOR SOMNAMBULA—
HUH?
—SO SOMNAMBULA HAD TO LISTEN TO THE PRINCE TALK WHILE SHE CROSSED A BRIDGE.
WHAT?!
AND THE LESSON IS TO ALWAYS HAVE HOPE!
I FEEL LIKE YOU LEFT SOMETHING OUT. BUT THAT AT LEAST GIVES ME SOMEWHERE TO START WITH THIS STORY I'M ABOUT TO READ.
OOH! WILL YOU READ IT TO ME TOO?
SURE.
WAIT!
YES?
DO YOU DO VOICES FOR THE CHARACTERS?
NO, I DON'T USUALLY—
HAVE A SEAT. YOU MIGHT LEARN SOMETHING, SMARTY PANTS.
Yoink

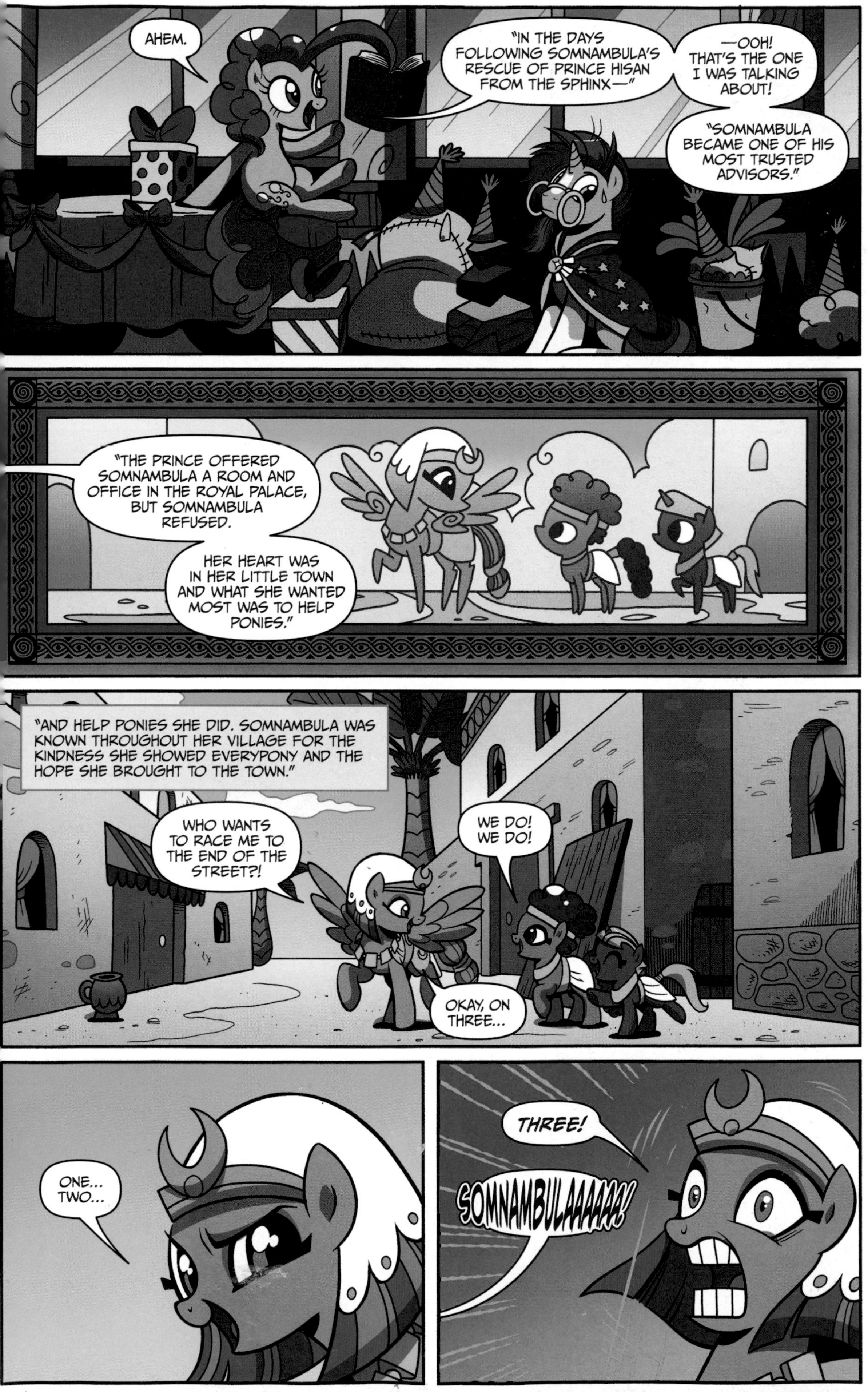
AHEM.
"IN THE DAYS FOLLOWING SOMNAMBULA'S RESCUE OF PRINCE HISAN FROM THE SPHINX—"
—OOH! THAT'S THE ONE I WAS TALKING ABOUT!
"SOMNAMBULA BECAME ONE OF HIS MOST TRUSTED ADVISORS."
"THE PRINCE OFFERED SOMNAMBULA A ROOM AND OFFICE IN THE ROYAL PALACE, BUT SOMNAMBULA REFUSED.
HER HEART WAS IN HER LITTLE TOWN AND WHAT SHE WANTED MOST WAS TO HELP PONIES."
"AND HELP PONIES SHE DID. SOMNAMBULA WAS KNOWN THROUGHOUT HER VILLAGE FOR THE KINDNESS SHE SHOWED EVERYPONY AND THE HOPE SHE BROUGHT TO THE TOWN."
WHO WANTS TO RACE ME TO THE END OF THE STREET?!
WE DO! WE DO!
OKAY, ON THREE...
ONE... TWO...
THREE!
SOMNAMBULAAAAAA!

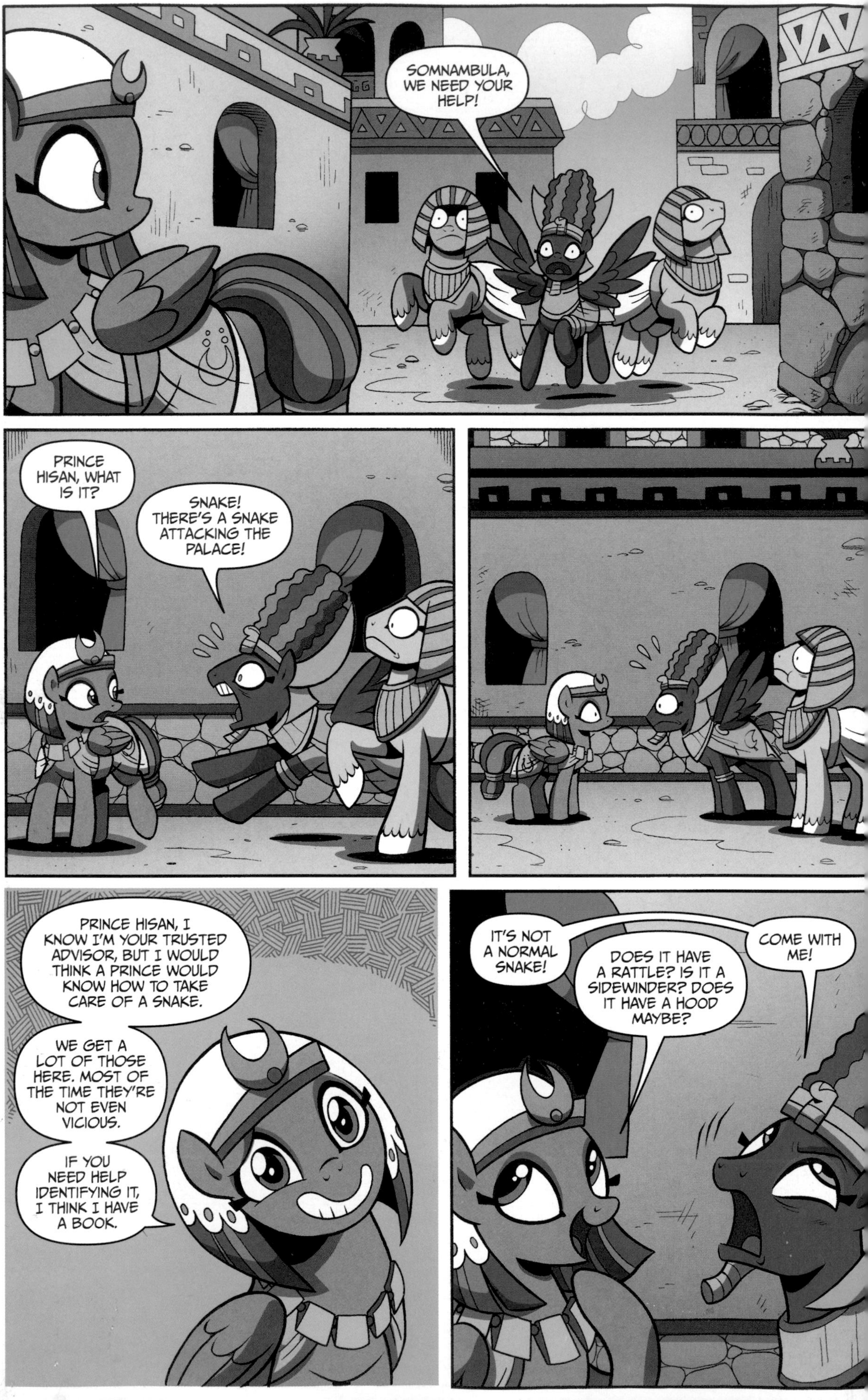
SOMNAMBULA, WE NEED YOUR HELP!
PRINCE HISAN, WHAT IS IT?
SNAKE! THERE'S A SNAKE ATTACKING THE PALACE!
PRINCE HISAN, I KNOW I'M YOUR TRUSTED ADVISOR, BUT I WOULD THINK A PRINCE WOULD KNOW HOW TO TAKE CARE OF A SNAKE.
WE GET A LOT OF THOSE HERE. MOST OF THE TIME THEY'RE NOT EVEN VICIOUS.
IF YOU NEED HELP IDENTIFYING IT, I THINK I HAVE A BOOK.
IT'S NOT A NORMAL SNAKE!
DOES IT HAVE A RATTLE? IS IT A SIDEWINDER? DOES IT HAVE A HOOD MAYBE?
COME WITH ME!

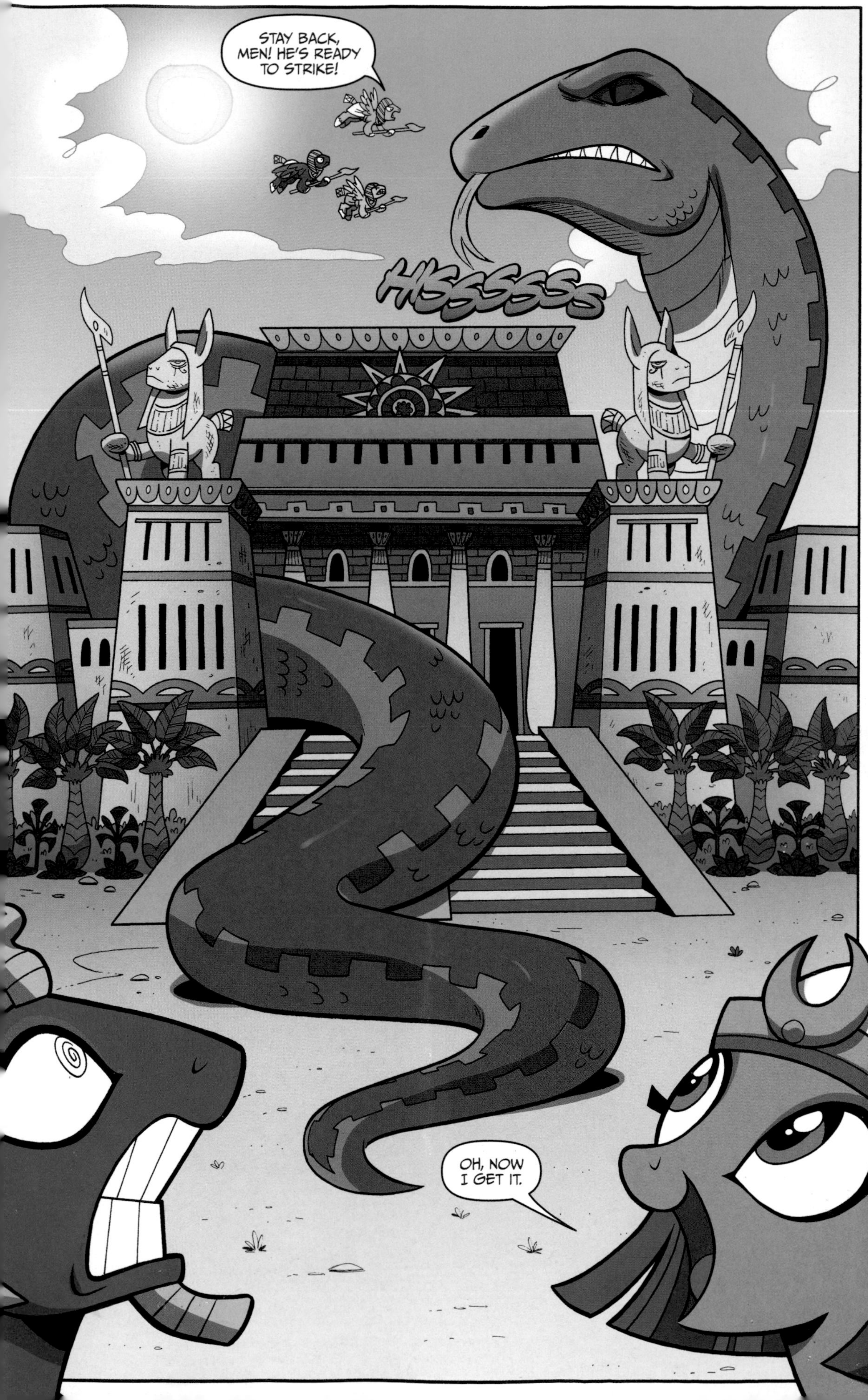
STAY BACK, MEN! HE'S READY TO STRIKE!
HISSSSSS
OH, NOW I GET IT.

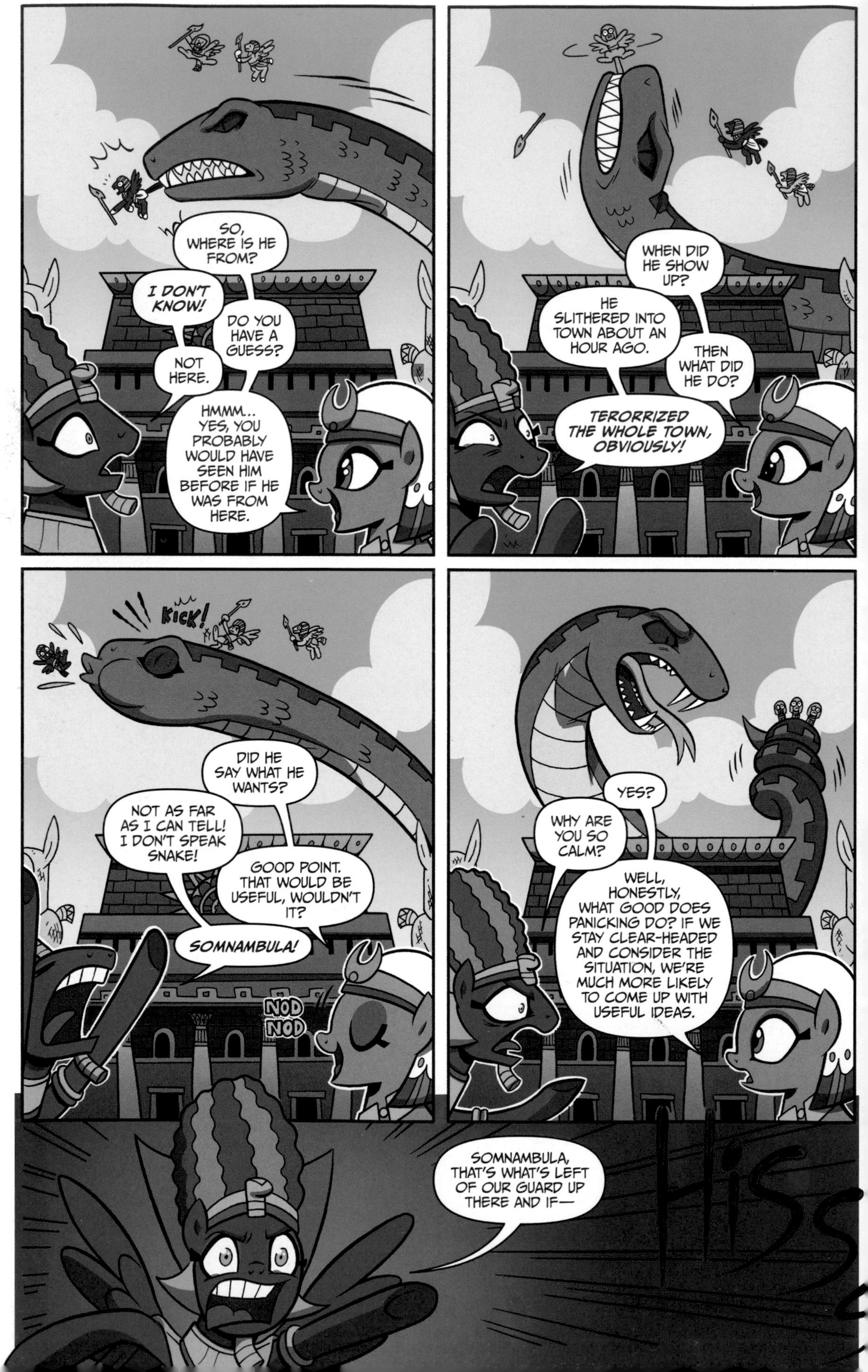
SO, WHERE IS HE FROM?
I DON'T KNOW!
DO YOU HAVE A GUESS?
NOT HERE.
HMMM.. YES, YOU PROBABLY WOULD HAVE SEEN HIM BEFORE IF HE WAS FROM HERE.
WHEN DID HE SHOW UP?
HE SLITHERED INTO TOWN ABOUT AN HOUR AGO.
THEN WHAT DID HE DO?
TERORRIZED THE WHOLE TOWN, OBVIOUSLY!
KICK!
DID HE SAY WHAT HE WANTS?
NOT AS FAR AS I CAN TELL! I DON'T SPEAK SNAKE!
GOOD POINT. THAT WOULD BE USEFUL, WOULDN'T IT?
SOMNAMBULA!
NOD NOD
YES?
WHY ARE YOU SO CALM?
WELL, HONESTLY, WHAT GOOD DOES PANICKING DO? IF WE STAY CLEAR-HEADED AND CONSIDER THE SITUATION, WE'RE MUCH MORE LIKELY TO COME UP WITH USEFUL IDEAS.
SOMNAMBULA, THAT'S WHAT'S LEFT OF OUR GUARD UP THERE AND IF—
HISS

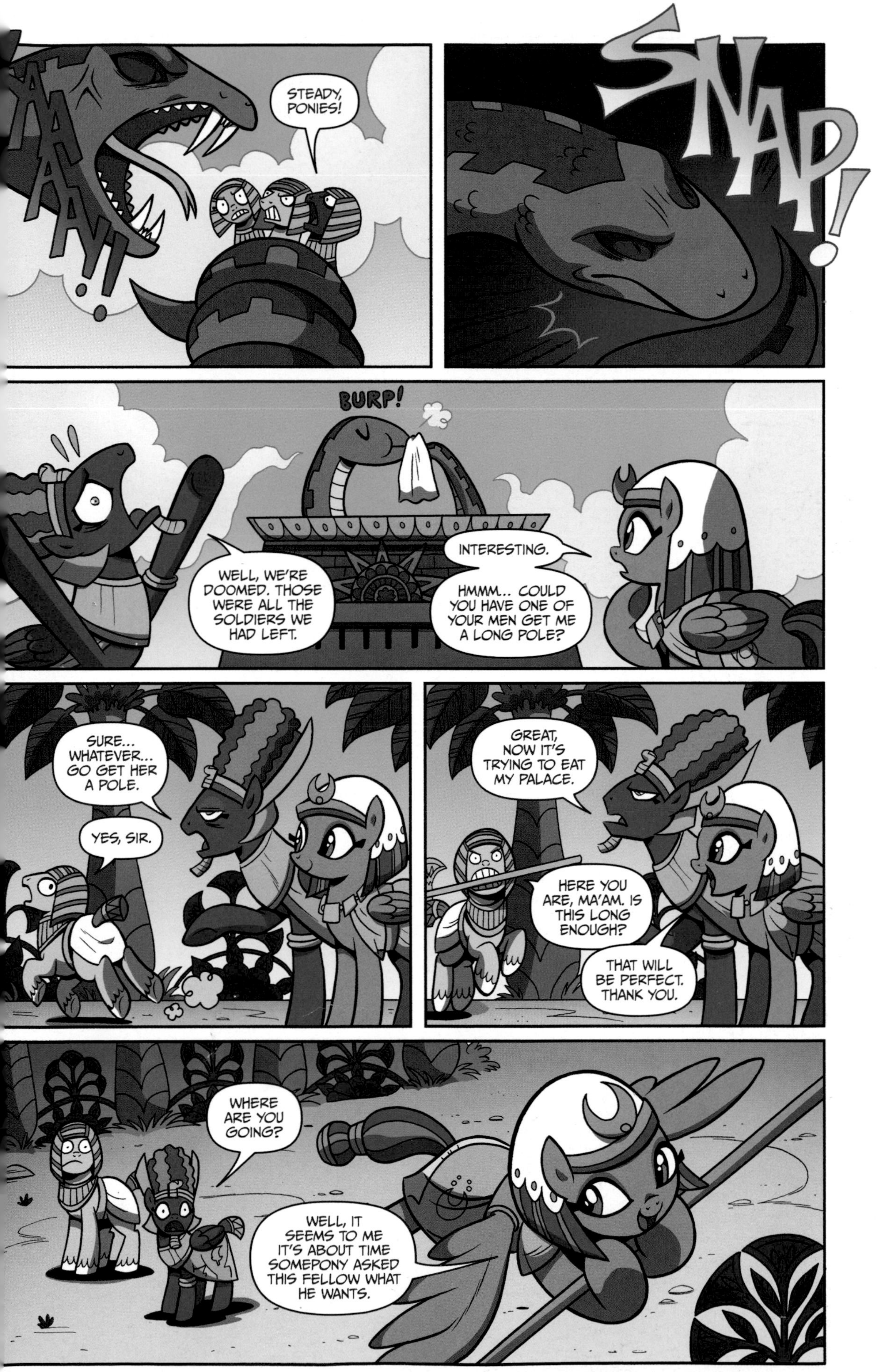
AAAAAH!!
STEADY, PONIES!
SNAP!!
BURP!
WELL, WE'RE DOOMED. THOSE WERE ALL THE SOLDIERS WE HAD LEFT.
INTERESTING.
HMMM... COULD YOU HAVE ONE OF YOUR MEN GET ME A LONG POLE?
SURE... WHATEVER... GO GET HER A POLE.
YES, SIR.
GREAT, NOW IT'S TRYING TO EAT MY PALACE.
HERE YOU ARE, MA'AM. IS THIS LONG ENOUGH?
THAT WILL BE PERFECT. THANK YOU.
WHERE ARE YOU GOING?
WELL, IT SEEMS TO ME IT'S ABOUT TIME SOMEPONY ASKED THIS FELLOW WHAT HE WANTS.

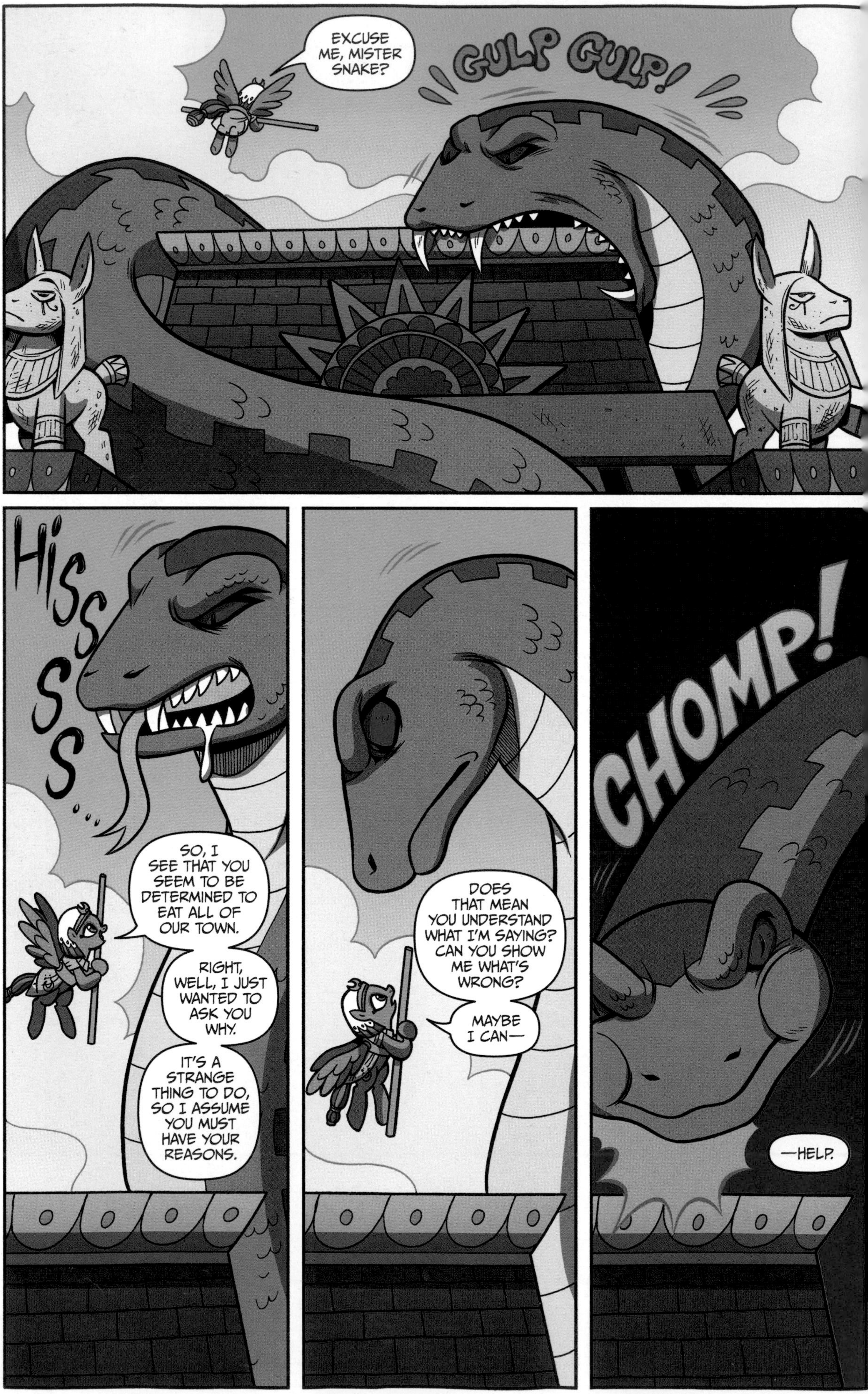
EXCUSE ME, MISTER SNAKE?
GULP GULP!
HISSSS...
SO, I SEE THAT YOU SEEM TO BE DETERMINED TO EAT ALL OF OUR TOWN.
RIGHT, WELL, I JUST WANTED TO ASK YOU WHY.
IT'S A STRANGE THING TO DO, SO I ASSUME YOU MUST HAVE YOUR REASONS.
DOES THAT MEAN YOU UNDERSTAND WHAT I'M SAYING? CAN YOU SHOW ME WHAT'S WRONG?
MAYBE I CAN—
CHOMP!
—HELP.

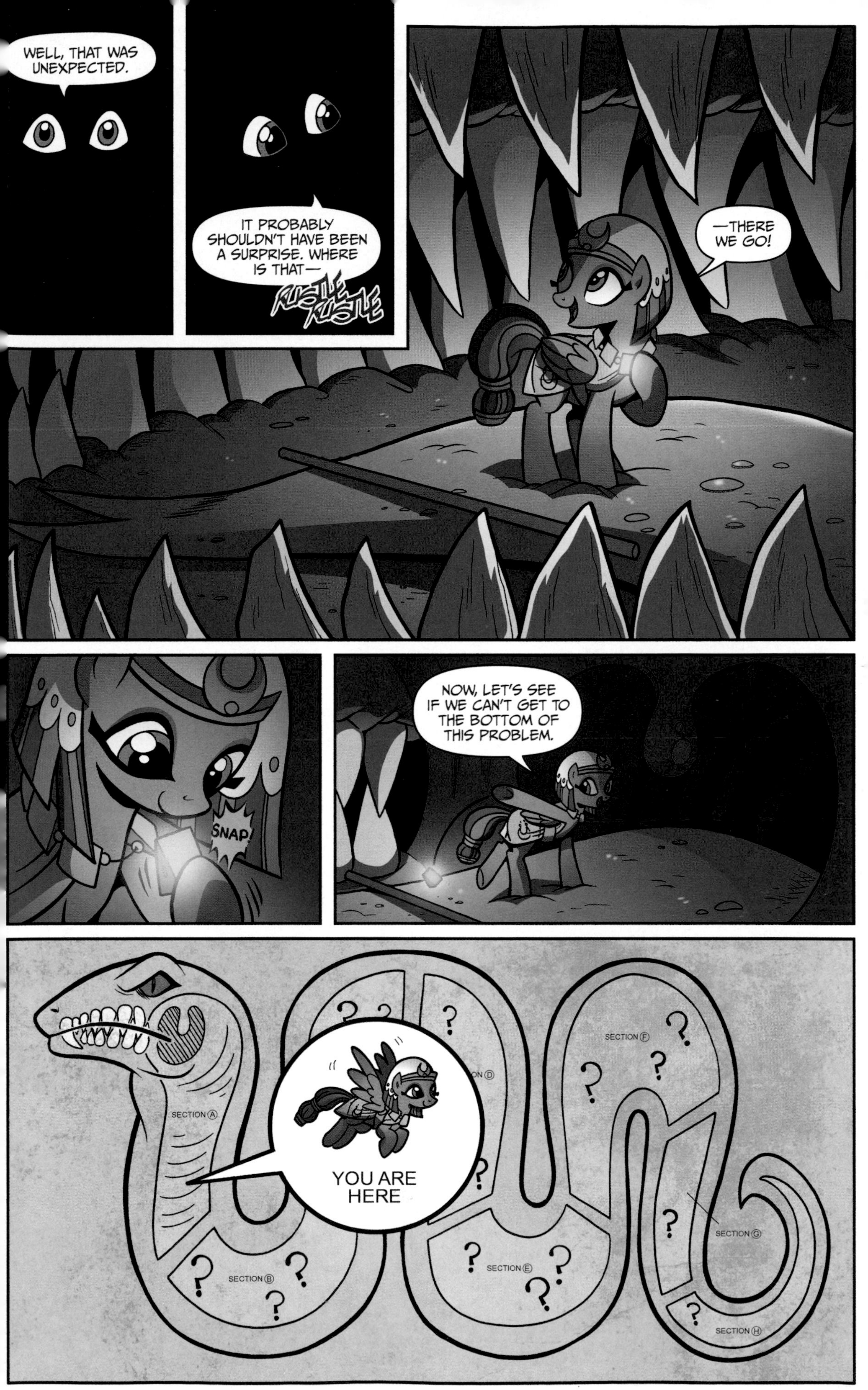
WELL, THAT WAS UNEXPECTED.
IT PROBABLY SHOULDN'T HAVE BEEN A SURPRISE. WHERE IS THAT—
RUSTLE RUSTLE
—THERE WE GO!
SNAP!
NOW, LET'S SEE IF WE CAN'T GET TO THE BOTTOM OF THIS PROBLEM.
SECTION Ⓐ
YOU ARE HERE
SECTION Ⓑ
SECTION Ⓔ
SECTION Ⓕ
SECTION Ⓖ
SECTION Ⓗ

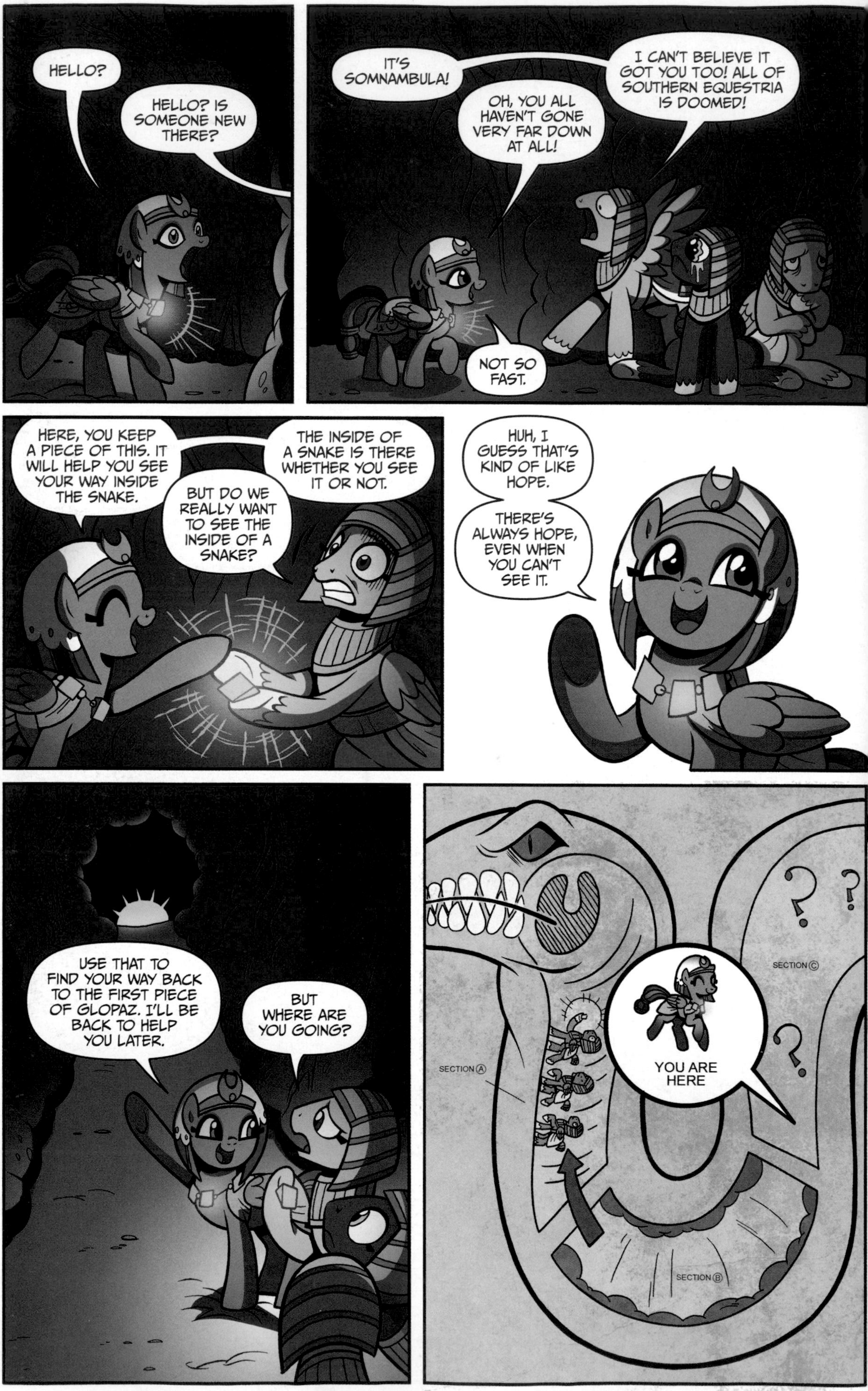
HELLO?
HELLO? IS SOMEONE NEW THERE?
IT'S SOMNAMBULA!
I CAN'T BELIEVE IT GOT YOU TOO! ALL OF SOUTHERN EQUESTRIA IS DOOMED!
OH, YOU ALL HAVEN'T GONE VERY FAR DOWN AT ALL!
NOT SO FAST.
HERE, YOU KEEP A PIECE OF THIS. IT WILL HELP YOU SEE YOUR WAY INSIDE THE SNAKE.
THE INSIDE OF A SNAKE IS THERE WHETHER YOU SEE IT OR NOT.
BUT DO WE REALLY WANT TO SEE THE INSIDE OF A SNAKE?
HUH, I GUESS THAT'S KIND OF LIKE HOPE.
THERE'S ALWAYS HOPE, EVEN WHEN YOU CAN'T SEE IT.
USE THAT TO FIND YOUR WAY BACK TO THE FIRST PIECE OF GLOPAZ. I'LL BE BACK TO HELP YOU LATER.
BUT WHERE ARE YOU GOING?
SECTION Ⓒ
YOU ARE HERE
SECTION Ⓐ
SECTION Ⓑ

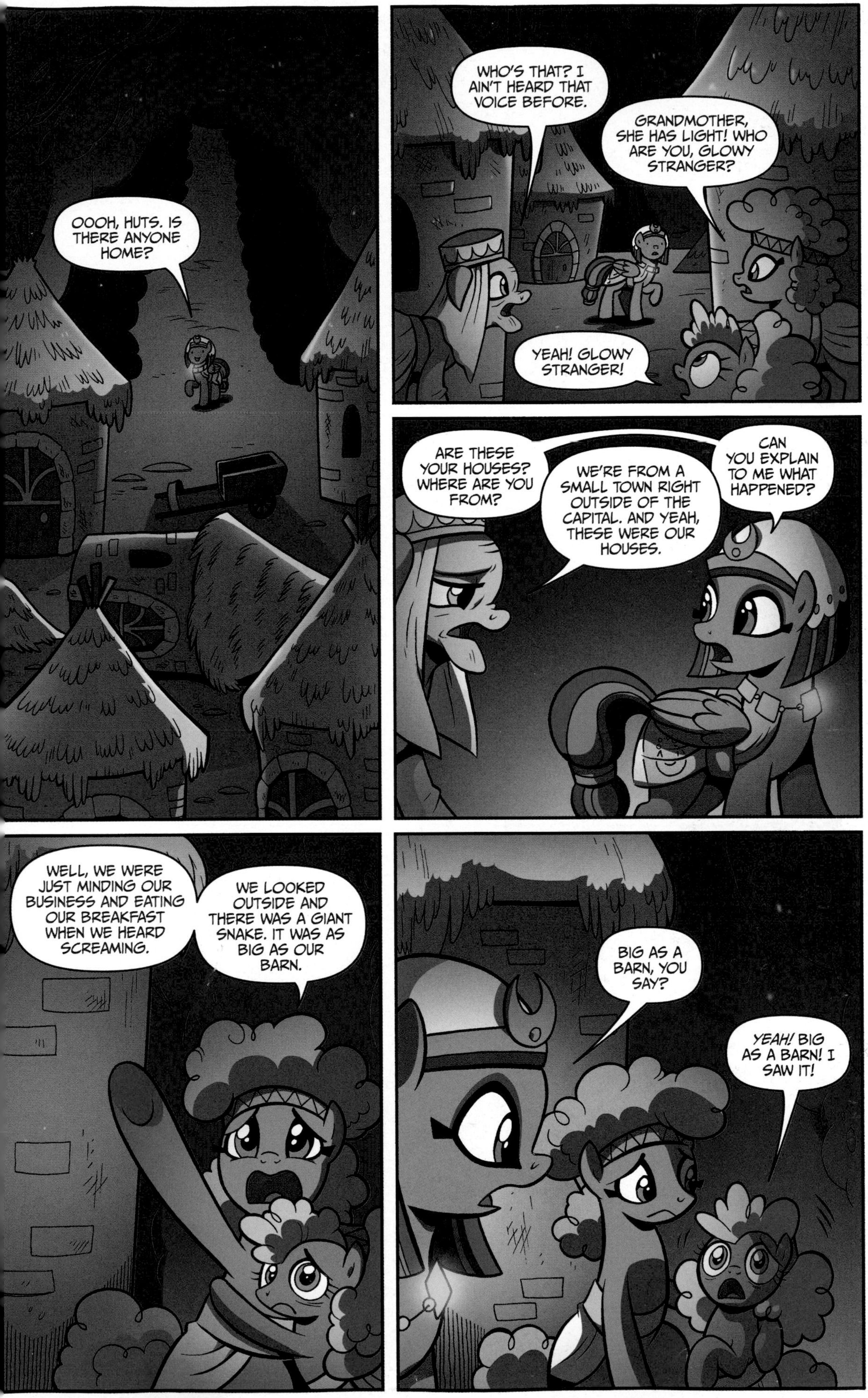
OOOH, HUTS. IS THERE ANYONE HOME?
WHO'S THAT? I AIN'T HEARD THAT VOICE BEFORE.
GRANDMOTHER, SHE HAS LIGHT! WHO ARE YOU, GLOWY STRANGER?
YEAH! GLOWY STRANGER!
ARE THESE YOUR HOUSES? WHERE ARE YOU FROM?
WE'RE FROM A SMALL TOWN RIGHT OUTSIDE OF THE CAPITAL. AND YEAH, THESE WERE OUR HOUSES.
CAN YOU EXPLAIN TO ME WHAT HAPPENED?
WELL, WE WERE JUST MINDING OUR BUSINESS AND EATING OUR BREAKFAST WHEN WE HEARD SCREAMING.
WE LOOKED OUTSIDE AND THERE WAS A GIANT SNAKE. IT WAS AS BIG AS OUR BARN.
BIG AS A BARN, YOU SAY?
YEAH! BIG AS A BARN! I SAW IT!

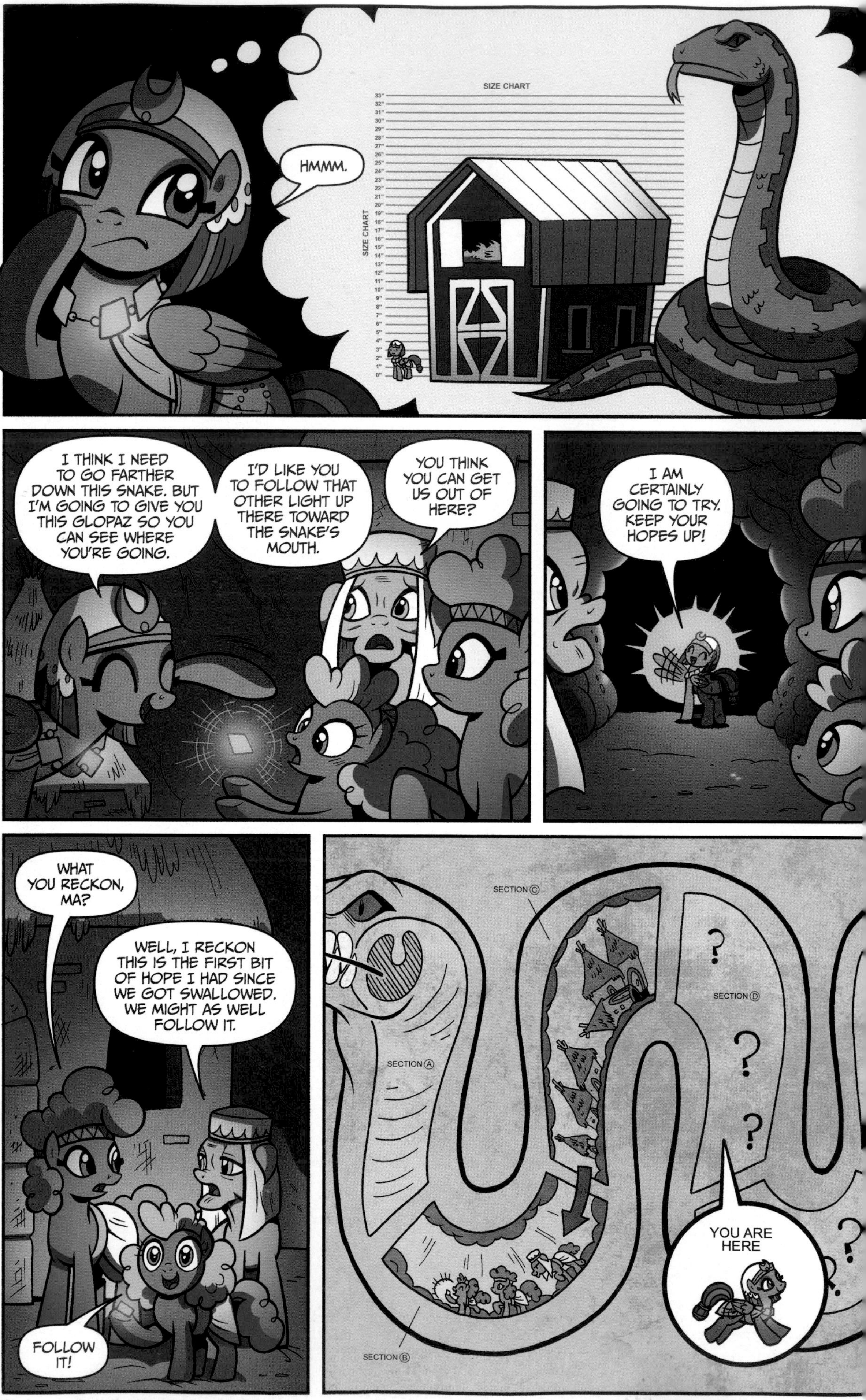
HMMM.
SIZE CHART
SIZE CHART
I THINK I NEED TO GO FARTHER DOWN THIS SNAKE. BUT I'M GOING TO GIVE YOU THIS GLOPAZ SO YOU CAN SEE WHERE YOU'RE GOING.
I'D LIKE YOU TO FOLLOW THAT OTHER LIGHT UP THERE TOWARD THE SNAKE'S MOUTH.
YOU THINK YOU CAN GET US OUT OF HERE?
I AM CERTAINLY GOING TO TRY. KEEP YOUR HOPES UP!
WHAT YOU RECKON, MA?
WELL, I RECKON THIS IS THE FIRST BIT OF HOPE I HAD SINCE WE GOT SWALLOWED. WE MIGHT AS WELL FOLLOW IT.
FOLLOW IT!
SECTION Ⓒ
SECTION Ⓓ
SECTION Ⓐ
SECTION Ⓑ
YOU ARE HERE

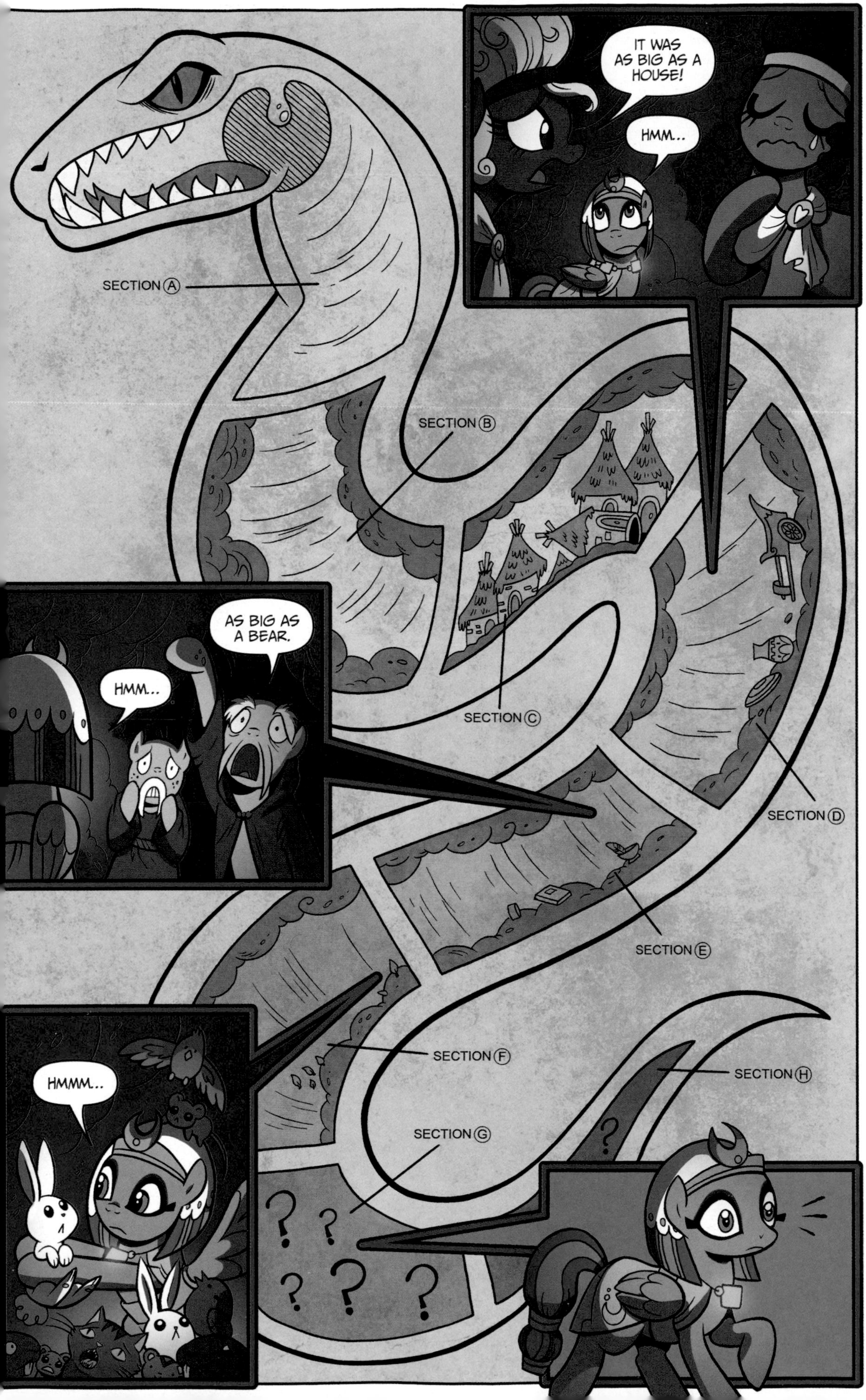

SECTION A
IT WAS AS BIG AS A HOUSE!
HMM...
SECTION B
SECTION C
SECTION D
HMM...
AS BIG AS A BEAR.
SECTION E
SECTION F
HMMM...
SECTION G
SECTION H

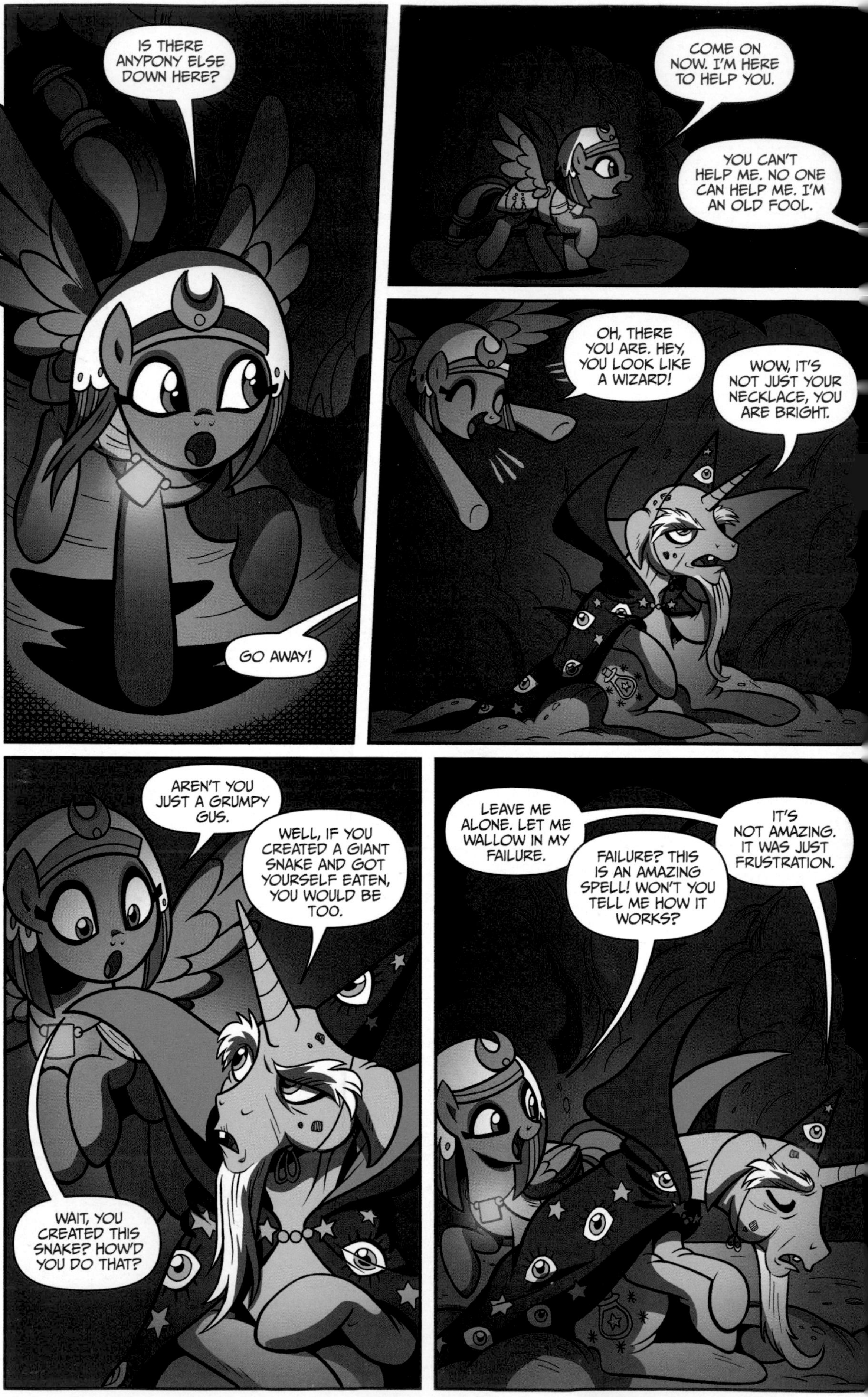
IS THERE ANYPONY ELSE DOWN HERE?
GO AWAY!
COME ON NOW. I'M HERE TO HELP YOU.
YOU CAN'T HELP ME. NO ONE CAN HELP ME. I'M AN OLD FOOL.
OH, THERE YOU ARE. HEY, YOU LOOK LIKE A WIZARD!
WOW, IT'S NOT JUST YOUR NECKLACE, YOU ARE BRIGHT.
AREN'T YOU JUST A GRUMPY GUS.
WELL, IF YOU CREATED A GIANT SNAKE AND GOT YOURSELF EATEN, YOU WOULD BE TOO.
WAIT, YOU CREATED THIS SNAKE? HOW'D YOU DO THAT?
LEAVE ME ALONE. LET ME WALLOW IN MY FAILURE.
FAILURE? THIS IS AN AMAZING SPELL! WON'T YOU TELL ME HOW IT WORKS?
IT'S NOT AMAZING. IT WAS JUST FRUSTRATION.

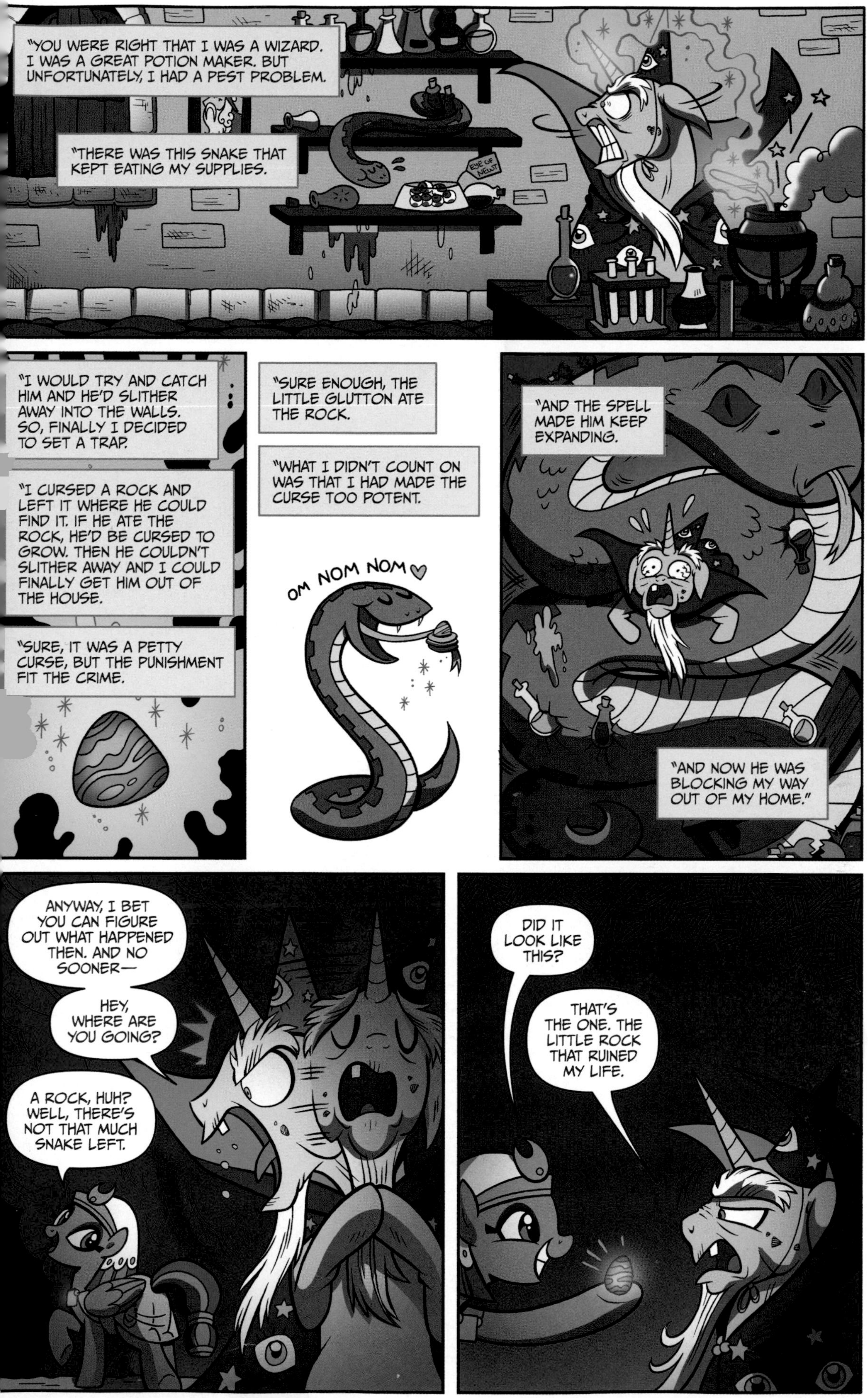

"YOU WERE RIGHT THAT I WAS A WIZARD. I WAS A GREAT POTION MAKER. BUT UNFORTUNATELY, I HAD A PEST PROBLEM.
"THERE WAS THIS SNAKE THAT KEPT EATING MY SUPPLIES.
EYE OF NEWT
"I WOULD TRY AND CATCH HIM AND HE'D SLITHER AWAY INTO THE WALLS. SO, FINALLY I DECIDED TO SET A TRAP.
"I CURSED A ROCK AND LEFT IT WHERE HE COULD FIND IT. IF HE ATE THE ROCK, HE'D BE CURSED TO GROW. THEN HE COULDN'T SLITHER AWAY AND I COULD FINALLY GET HIM OUT OF THE HOUSE.
"SURE, IT WAS A PETTY CURSE, BUT THE PUNISHMENT FIT THE CRIME.
"SURE ENOUGH, THE LITTLE GLUTTON ATE THE ROCK.
"WHAT I DIDN'T COUNT ON WAS THAT I HAD MADE THE CURSE TOO POTENT.
OM NOM NOM ♥
"AND THE SPELL MADE HIM KEEP EXPANDING.
"AND NOW HE WAS BLOCKING MY WAY OUT OF MY HOME."
ANYWAY, I BET YOU CAN FIGURE OUT WHAT HAPPENED THEN. AND NO SOONER—
HEY, WHERE ARE YOU GOING?
A ROCK, HUH? WELL, THERE'S NOT THAT MUCH SNAKE LEFT.
DID IT LOOK LIKE THIS?
THAT'S THE ONE. THE LITTLE ROCK THAT RUINED MY LIFE.

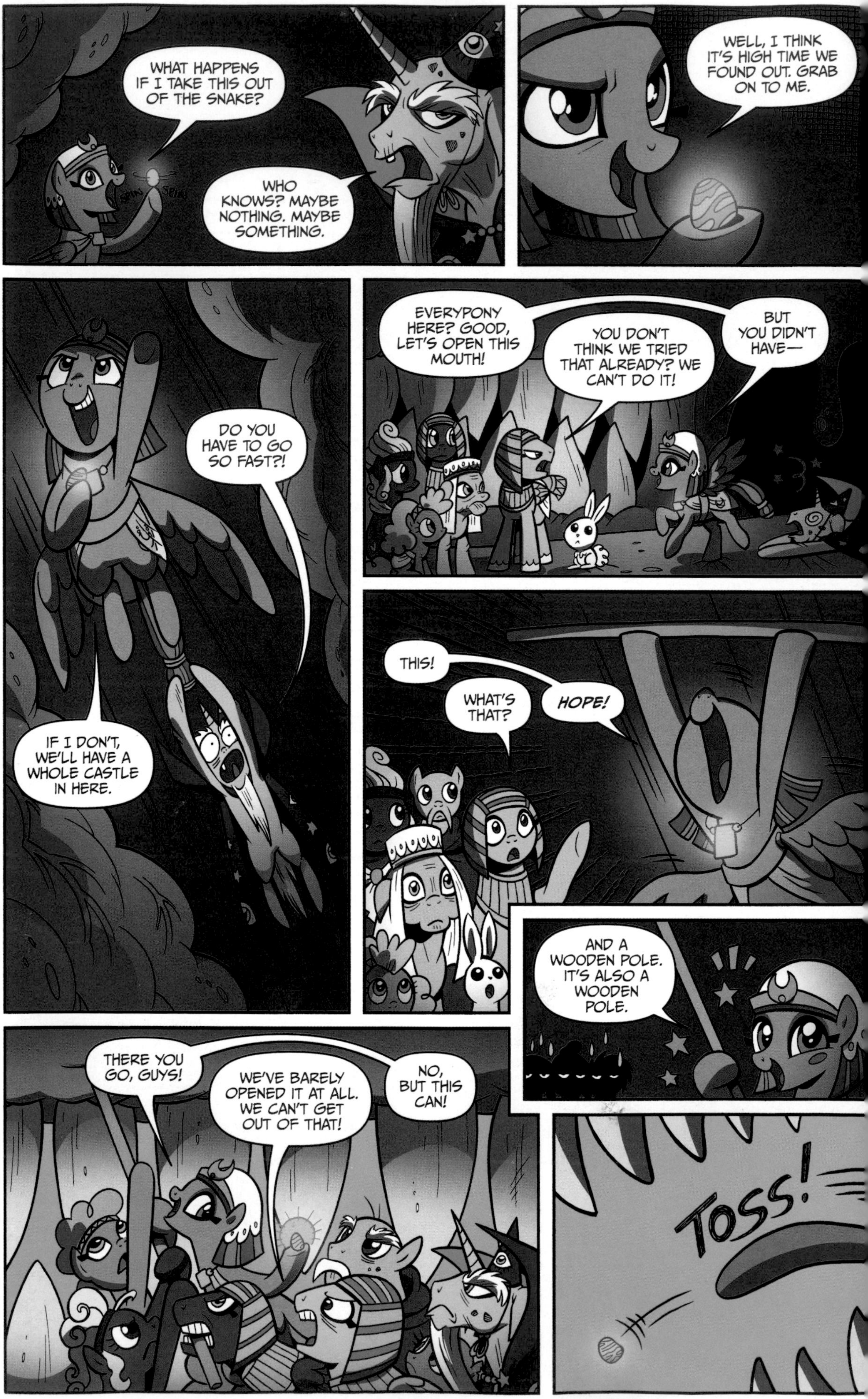
WHAT HAPPENS IF I TAKE THIS OUT OF THE SNAKE?
SPIN SPIN
WHO KNOWS? MAYBE NOTHING. MAYBE SOMETHING.
WELL, I THINK IT'S HIGH TIME WE FOUND OUT. GRAB ON TO ME.
DO YOU HAVE TO GO SO FAST?!
IF I DON'T, WE'LL HAVE A WHOLE CASTLE IN HERE.
EVERYPONY HERE? GOOD, LET'S OPEN THIS MOUTH!
YOU DON'T THINK WE TRIED THAT ALREADY? WE CAN'T DO IT!
BUT YOU DIDN'T HAVE—
THIS!
WHAT'S THAT?
HOPE!
AND A WOODEN POLE. IT'S ALSO A WOODEN POLE.
THERE YOU GO, GUYS!
WE'VE BARELY OPENED IT AT ALL. WE CAN'T GET OUT OF THAT!
NO, BUT THIS CAN!
TOSS!

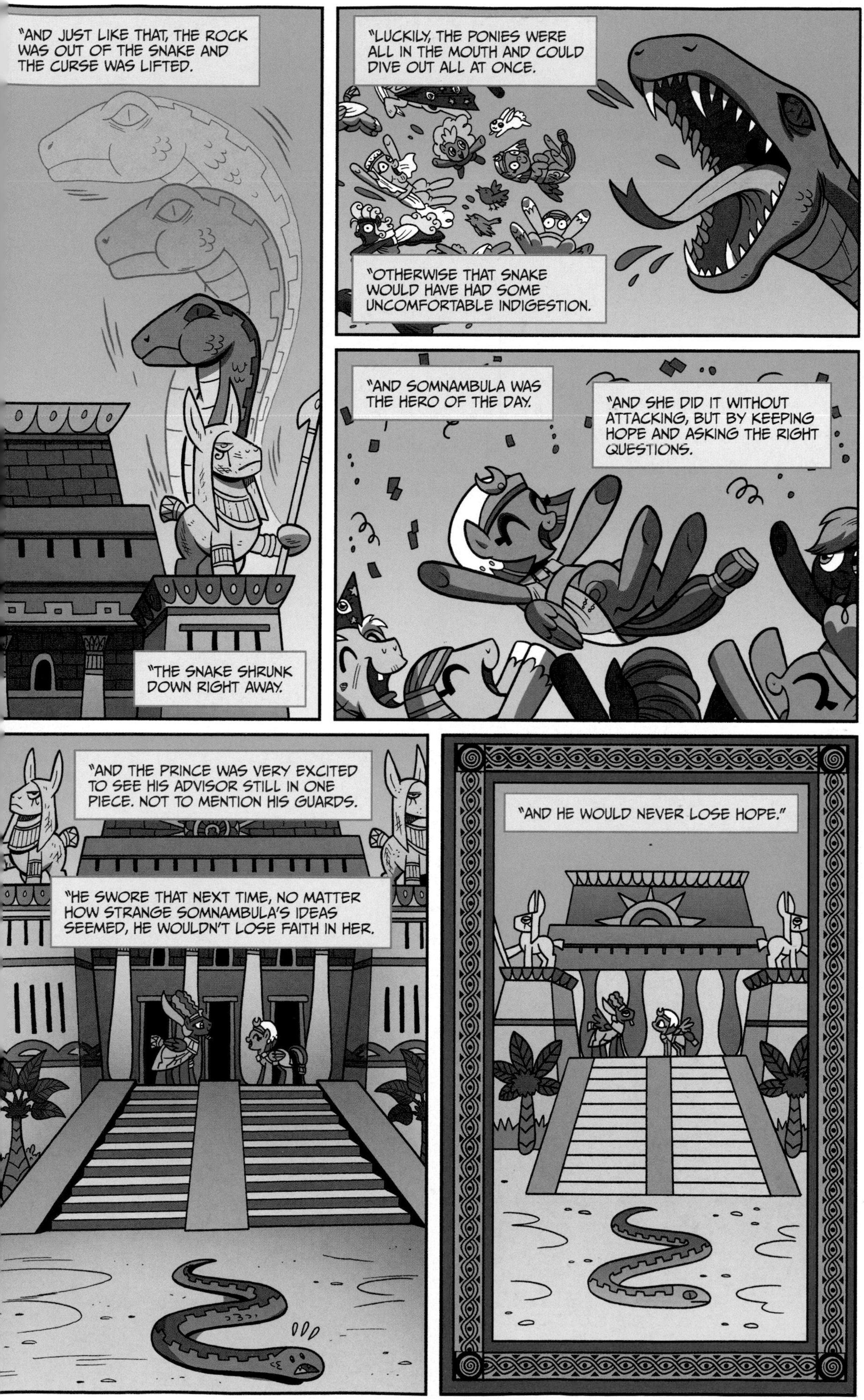
"AND JUST LIKE THAT, THE ROCK WAS OUT OF THE SNAKE AND THE CURSE WAS LIFTED.
"THE SNAKE SHRUNK DOWN RIGHT AWAY.
"LUCKILY, THE PONIES WERE ALL IN THE MOUTH AND COULD DIVE OUT ALL AT ONCE.
"OTHERWISE THAT SNAKE WOULD HAVE HAD SOME UNCOMFORTABLE INDIGESTION.
"AND SOMNAMBULA WAS THE HERO OF THE DAY.
"AND SHE DID IT WITHOUT ATTACKING, BUT BY KEEPING HOPE AND ASKING THE RIGHT QUESTIONS.
"AND THE PRINCE WAS VERY EXCITED TO SEE HIS ADVISOR STILL IN ONE PIECE. NOT TO MENTION HIS GUARDS.
"HE SWORE THAT NEXT TIME, NO MATTER HOW STRANGE SOMNAMBULA'S IDEAS SEEMED, HE WOULDN'T LOSE FAITH IN HER.
"AND HE WOULD NEVER LOSE HOPE."

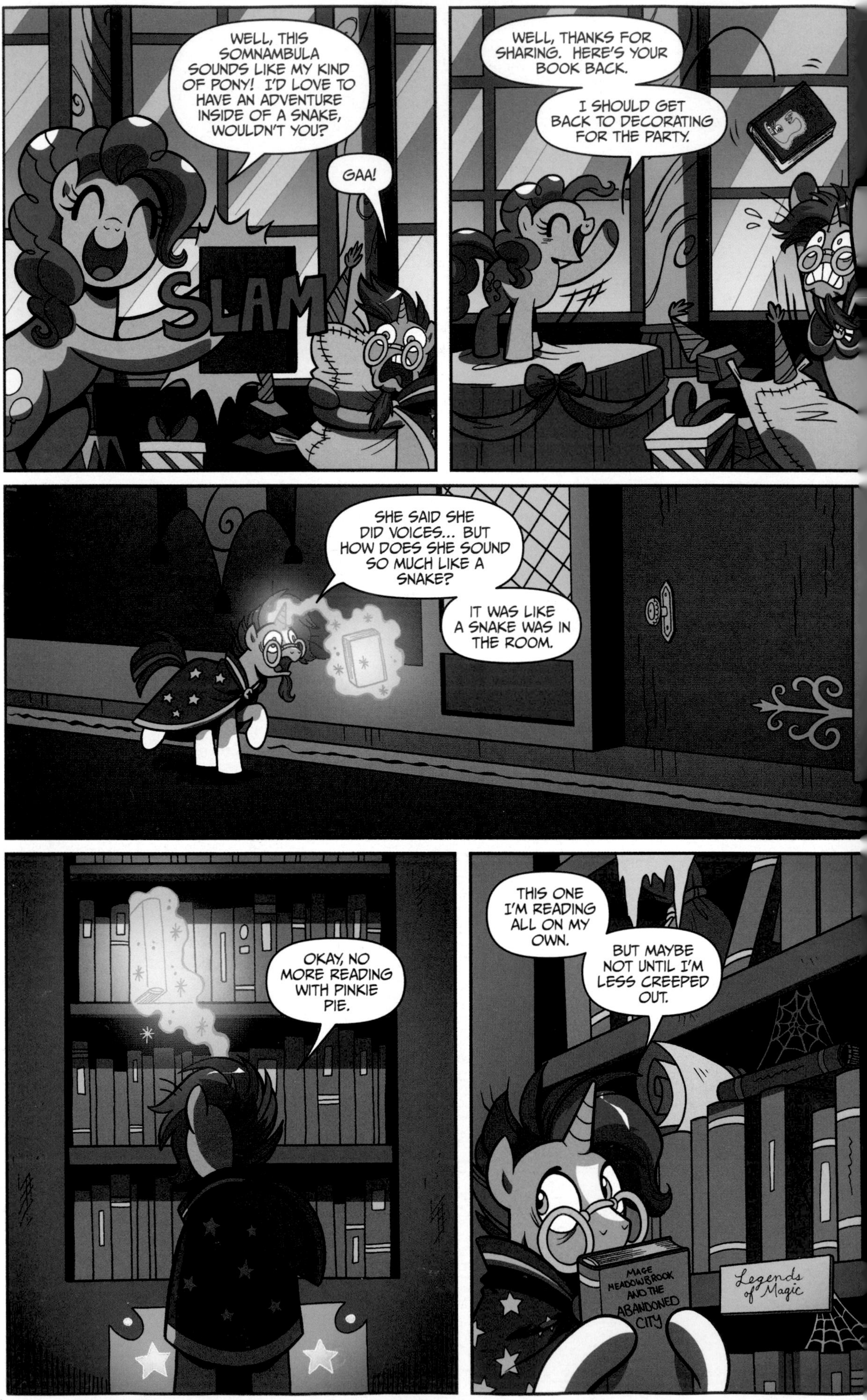
WELL, THIS SOMNAMBULA SOUNDS LIKE MY KIND OF PONY! I'D LOVE TO HAVE AN ADVENTURE INSIDE OF A SNAKE, WOULDN'T YOU?
SLAM
GAA!
WELL, THANKS FOR SHARING. HERE'S YOUR BOOK BACK.
I SHOULD GET BACK TO DECORATING FOR THE PARTY.
SHE SAID SHE DID VOICES... BUT HOW DOES SHE SOUND SO MUCH LIKE A SNAKE?
IT WAS LIKE A SNAKE WAS IN THE ROOM.
OKAY, NO MORE READING WITH PINKIE PIE.
THIS ONE I'M READING ALL ON MY OWN.
BUT MAYBE NOT UNTIL I'M LESS CREEPED OUT.
MAGE MEADOWBROOK AND THE ABANDONED CITY
Legends of Magic

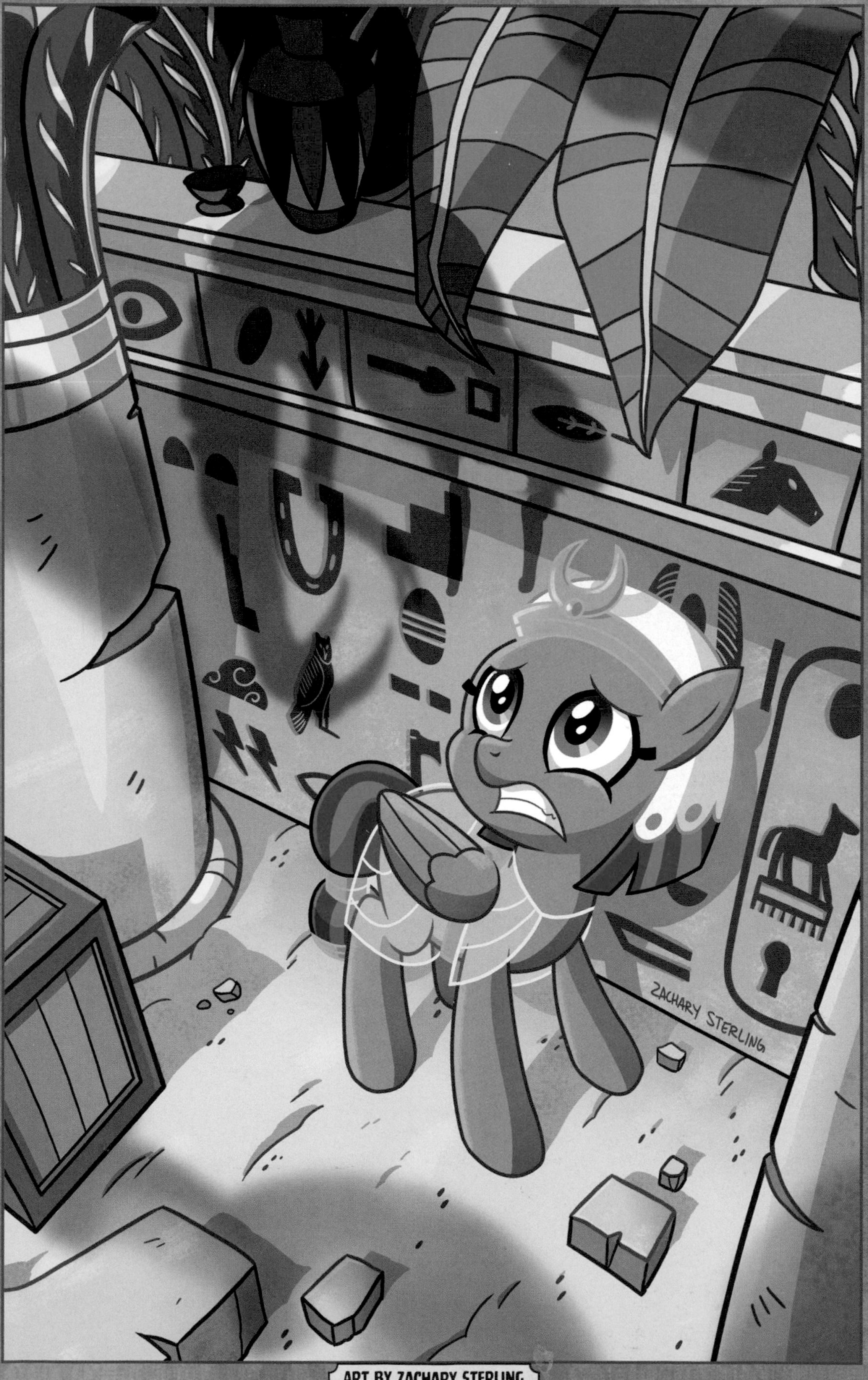
ZACHARY STERLING

ART BY ZACHARY STERLING

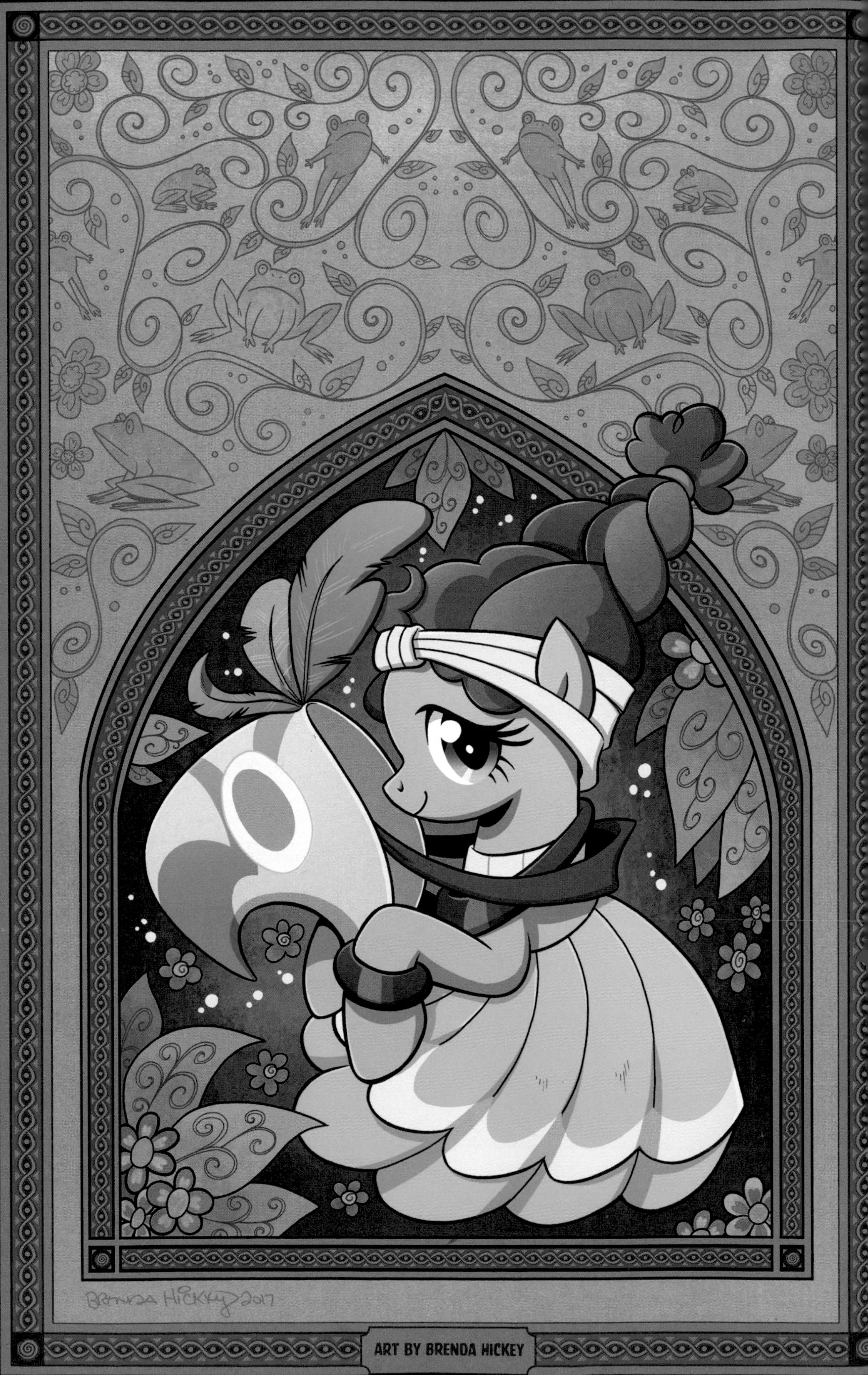
BRENDA HICKEY 2017
ART BY BRENDA HICKEY

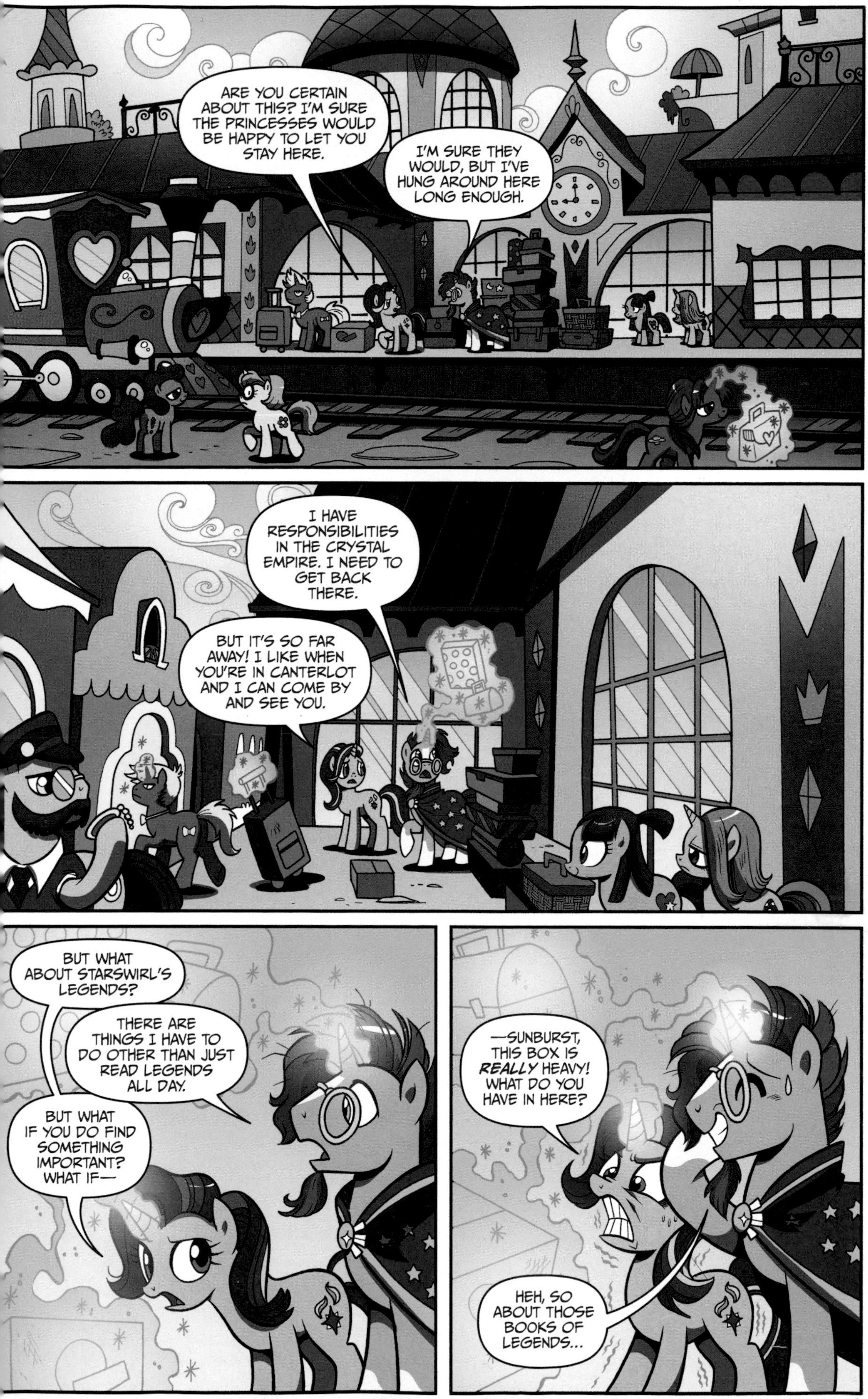

ARE YOU CERTAIN ABOUT THIS? I'M SURE THE PRINCESSES WOULD BE HAPPY TO LET YOU STAY HERE.
I'M SURE THEY WOULD, BUT I'VE HUNG AROUND HERE LONG ENOUGH.
I HAVE RESPONSIBILITIES IN THE CRYSTAL EMPIRE. I NEED TO GET BACK THERE.
BUT IT'S SO FAR AWAY! I LIKE WHEN YOU'RE IN CANTERLOT AND I CAN COME BY AND SEE YOU.
BUT WHAT ABOUT STARSWIRL'S LEGENDS?
THERE ARE THINGS I HAVE TO DO OTHER THAN JUST READ LEGENDS ALL DAY.
BUT WHAT IF YOU DO FIND SOMETHING IMPORTANT? WHAT IF—
—SUNBURST, THIS BOX IS *REALLY* HEAVY! WHAT DO YOU HAVE IN HERE?
HEH, SO ABOUT THOSE BOOKS OF LEGENDS...

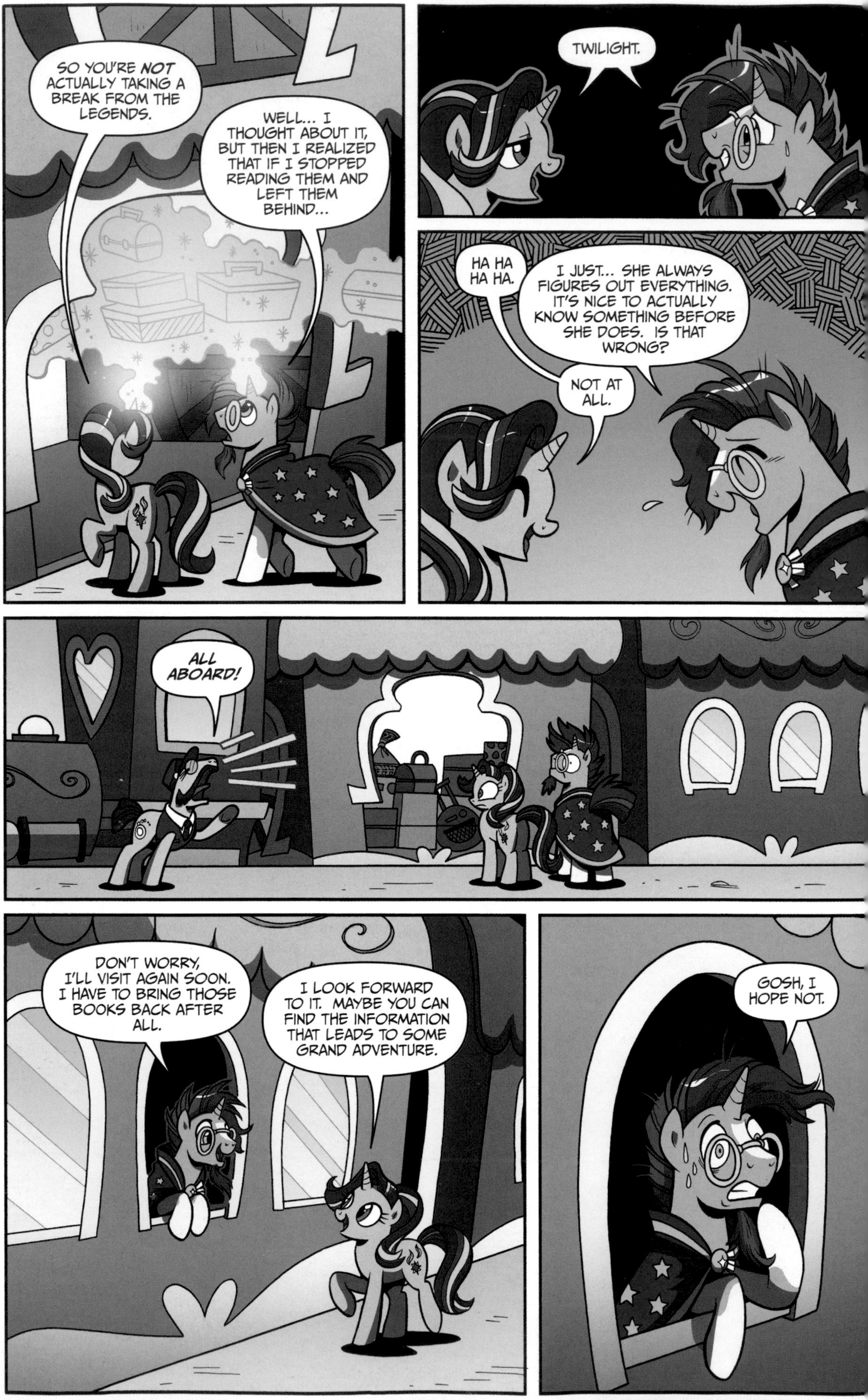
SO YOU'RE *NOT* ACTUALLY TAKING A BREAK FROM THE LEGENDS.
WELL... I THOUGHT ABOUT IT, BUT THEN I REALIZED THAT IF I STOPPED READING THEM AND LEFT THEM BEHIND...
TWILIGHT.
HA HA HA HA.
I JUST... SHE ALWAYS FIGURES OUT EVERYTHING. IT'S NICE TO ACTUALLY KNOW SOMETHING BEFORE SHE DOES. IS THAT WRONG?
NOT AT ALL.
ALL ABOARD!
DON'T WORRY, I'LL VISIT AGAIN SOON. I HAVE TO BRING THOSE BOOKS BACK AFTER ALL.
I LOOK FORWARD TO IT. MAYBE YOU CAN FIND THE INFORMATION THAT LEADS TO SOME GRAND ADVENTURE.
GOSH, I HOPE NOT.

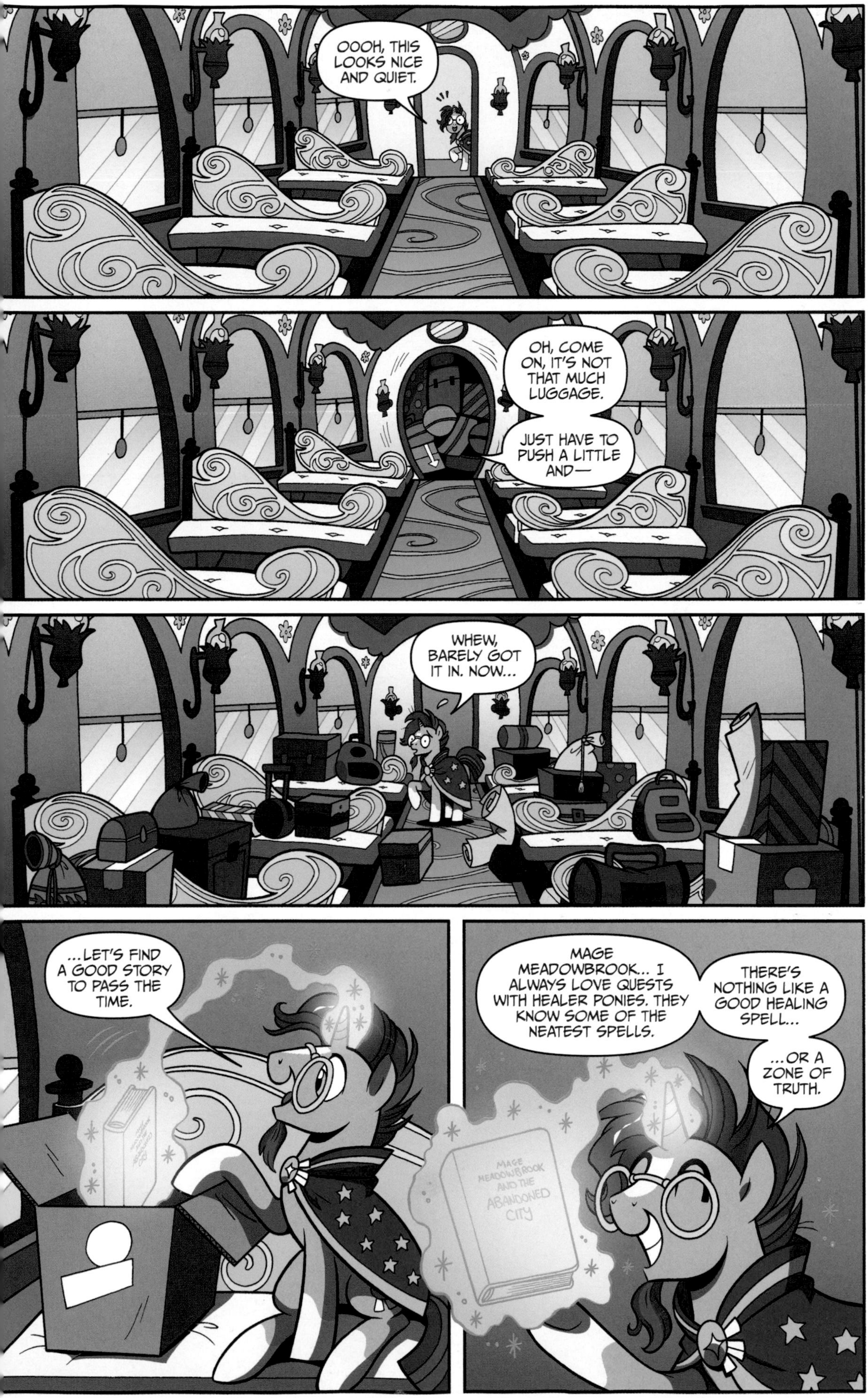
OOOH, THIS LOOKS NICE AND QUIET.
OH, COME ON, IT'S NOT THAT MUCH LUGGAGE.
JUST HAVE TO PUSH A LITTLE AND—
WHEW, BARELY GOT IT IN. NOW...
...LET'S FIND A GOOD STORY TO PASS THE TIME.
MAGE MEADOWBROOK... I ALWAYS LOVE QUESTS WITH HEALER PONIES. THEY KNOW SOME OF THE NEATEST SPELLS.
THERE'S NOTHING LIKE A GOOD HEALING SPELL...
...OR A ZONE OF TRUTH.
MAGE MEADOWBROOK AND THE ABANDONED CITY

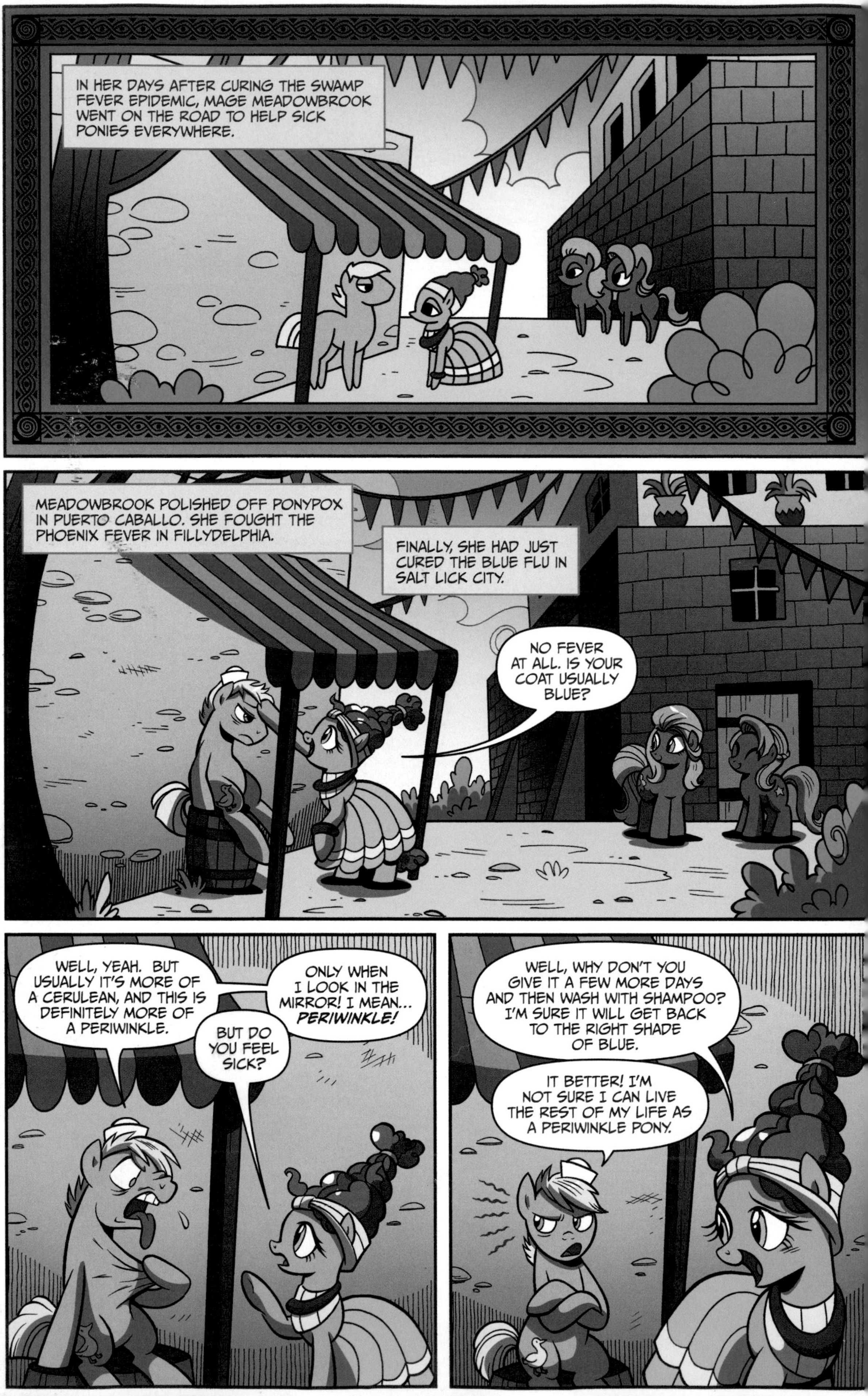
IN HER DAYS AFTER CURING THE SWAMP FEVER EPIDEMIC, MAGE MEADOWBROOK WENT ON THE ROAD TO HELP SICK PONIES EVERYWHERE.
MEADOWBROOK POLISHED OFF PONYPOX IN PUERTO CABALLO. SHE FOUGHT THE PHOENIX FEVER IN FILLYDELPHIA.
FINALLY, SHE HAD JUST CURED THE BLUE FLU IN SALT LICK CITY.
NO FEVER AT ALL. IS YOUR COAT USUALLY BLUE?
WELL, YEAH. BUT USUALLY IT'S MORE OF A CERULEAN, AND THIS IS DEFINITELY MORE OF A PERIWINKLE.
BUT DO YOU FEEL SICK?
ONLY WHEN I LOOK IN THE MIRROR! I MEAN... PERIWINKLE!
WELL, WHY DON'T YOU GIVE IT A FEW MORE DAYS AND THEN WASH WITH SHAMPOO? I'M SURE IT WILL GET BACK TO THE RIGHT SHADE OF BLUE.
IT BETTER! I'M NOT SURE I CAN LIVE THE REST OF MY LIFE AS A PERIWINKLE PONY.

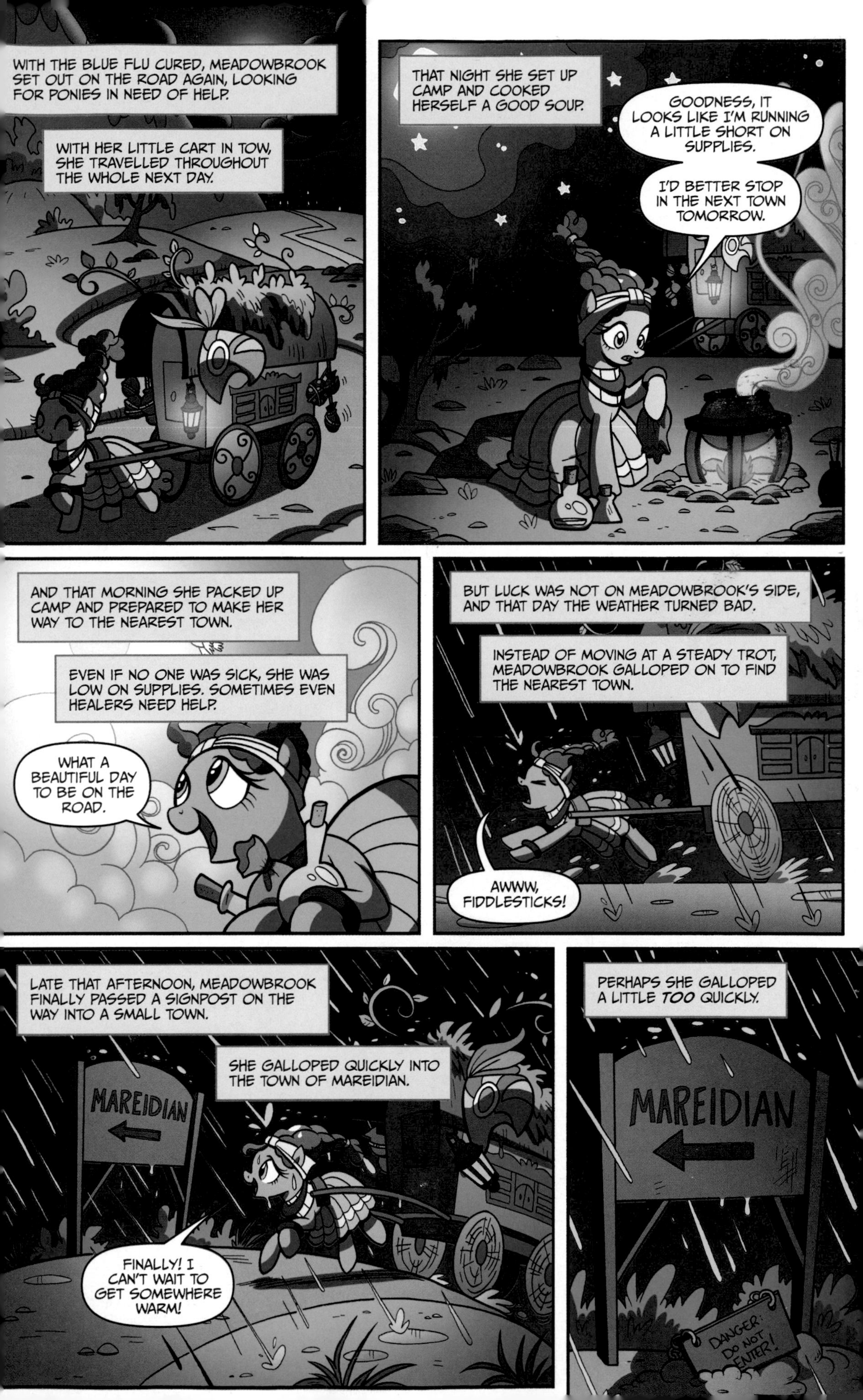

WITH THE BLUE FLU CURED, MEADOWBROOK SET OUT ON THE ROAD AGAIN, LOOKING FOR PONIES IN NEED OF HELP.
WITH HER LITTLE CART IN TOW, SHE TRAVELLED THROUGHOUT THE WHOLE NEXT DAY.
THAT NIGHT SHE SET UP CAMP AND COOKED HERSELF A GOOD SOUP.
GOODNESS, IT LOOKS LIKE I'M RUNNING A LITTLE SHORT ON SUPPLIES.
I'D BETTER STOP IN THE NEXT TOWN TOMORROW.
AND THAT MORNING SHE PACKED UP CAMP AND PREPARED TO MAKE HER WAY TO THE NEAREST TOWN.
EVEN IF NO ONE WAS SICK, SHE WAS LOW ON SUPPLIES. SOMETIMES EVEN HEALERS NEED HELP.
WHAT A BEAUTIFUL DAY TO BE ON THE ROAD.
BUT LUCK WAS NOT ON MEADOWBROOK'S SIDE, AND THAT DAY THE WEATHER TURNED BAD.
INSTEAD OF MOVING AT A STEADY TROT, MEADOWBROOK GALLOPED ON TO FIND THE NEAREST TOWN.
AWWW, FIDDLESTICKS!
LATE THAT AFTERNOON, MEADOWBROOK FINALLY PASSED A SIGNPOST ON THE WAY INTO A SMALL TOWN.
MAREIDIAN
SHE GALLOPED QUICKLY INTO THE TOWN OF MAREIDIAN.
FINALLY! I CAN'T WAIT TO GET SOMEWHERE WARM!
PERHAPS SHE GALLOPED A LITTLE *TOO* QUICKLY.
MAREIDIAN
DANGER: DO NOT ENTER!

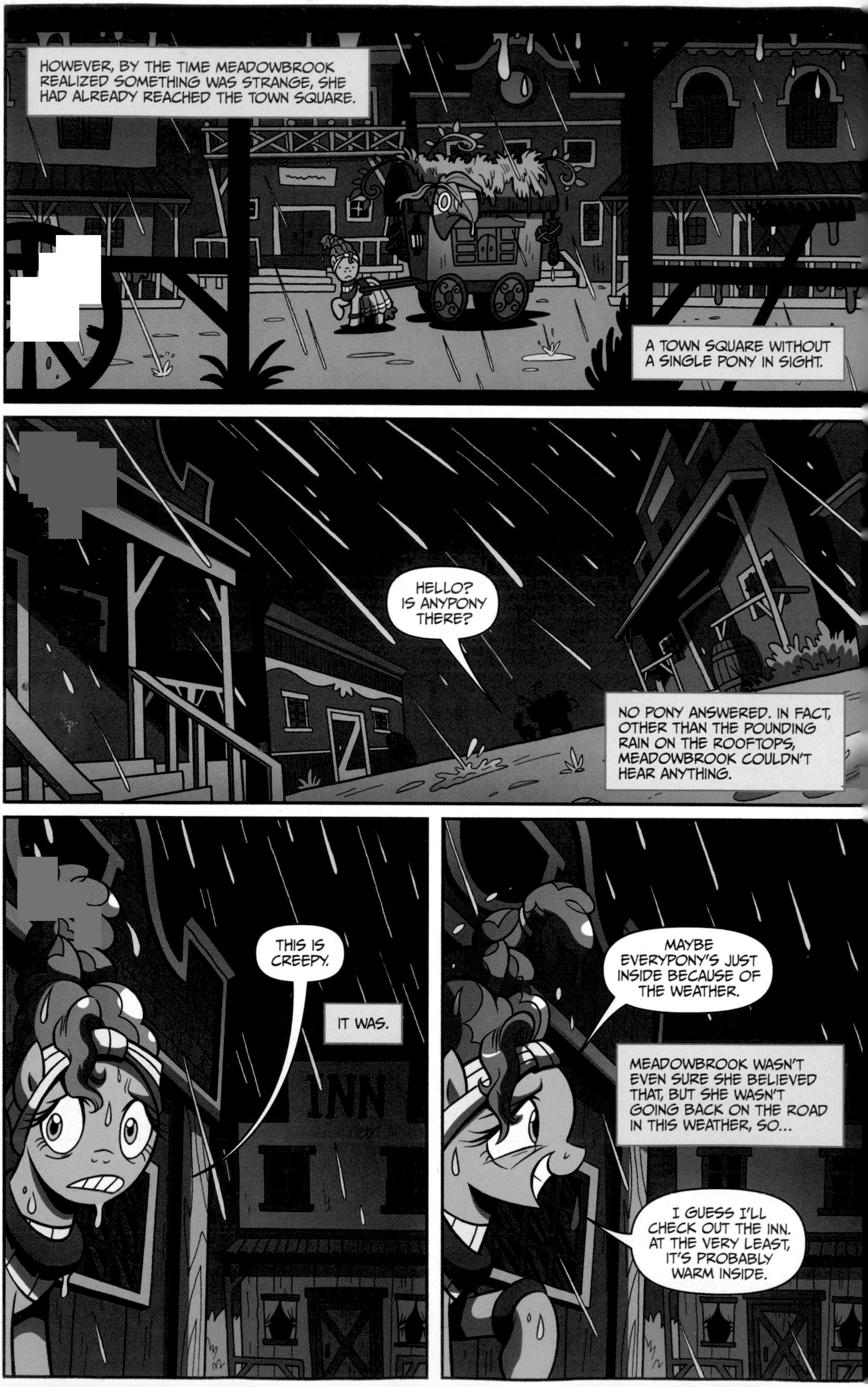

HOWEVER, BY THE TIME MEADOWBROOK REALIZED SOMETHING WAS STRANGE, SHE HAD ALREADY REACHED THE TOWN SQUARE.
A TOWN SQUARE WITHOUT A SINGLE PONY IN SIGHT.
HELLO? IS ANYPONY THERE?
NO PONY ANSWERED. IN FACT, OTHER THAN THE POUNDING RAIN ON THE ROOFTOPS, MEADOWBROOK COULDN'T HEAR ANYTHING.
THIS IS CREEPY.
IT WAS.
INN
MAYBE EVERYPONY'S JUST INSIDE BECAUSE OF THE WEATHER.
MEADOWBROOK WASN'T EVEN SURE SHE BELIEVED THAT, BUT SHE WASN'T GOING BACK ON THE ROAD IN THIS WEATHER, SO...
I GUESS I'LL CHECK OUT THE INN. AT THE VERY LEAST, IT'S PROBABLY WARM INSIDE.

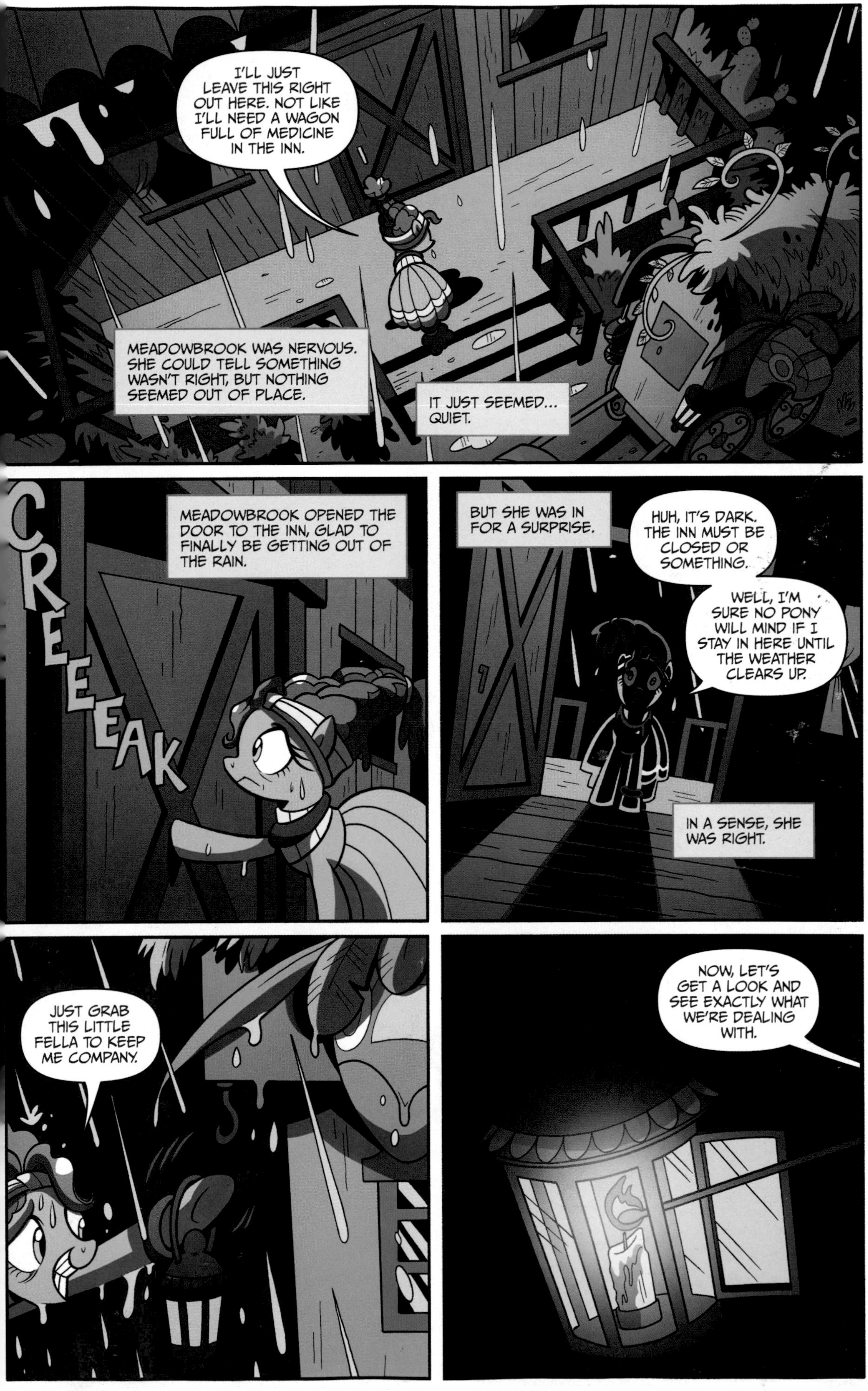

I'LL JUST LEAVE THIS RIGHT OUT HERE. NOT LIKE I'LL NEED A WAGON FULL OF MEDICINE IN THE INN.
MEADOWBROOK WAS NERVOUS. SHE COULD TELL SOMETHING WASN'T RIGHT, BUT NOTHING SEEMED OUT OF PLACE.
IT JUST SEEMED... QUIET.
MEADOWBROOK OPENED THE DOOR TO THE INN, GLAD TO FINALLY BE GETTING OUT OF THE RAIN.
CREEEAK
BUT SHE WAS IN FOR A SURPRISE.
HUH, IT'S DARK. THE INN MUST BE CLOSED OR SOMETHING.
WELL, I'M SURE NO PONY WILL MIND IF I STAY IN HERE UNTIL THE WEATHER CLEARS UP.
IN A SENSE, SHE WAS RIGHT.
JUST GRAB THIS LITTLE FELLA TO KEEP ME COMPANY.
NOW, LET'S GET A LOOK AND SEE EXACTLY WHAT WE'RE DEALING WITH.

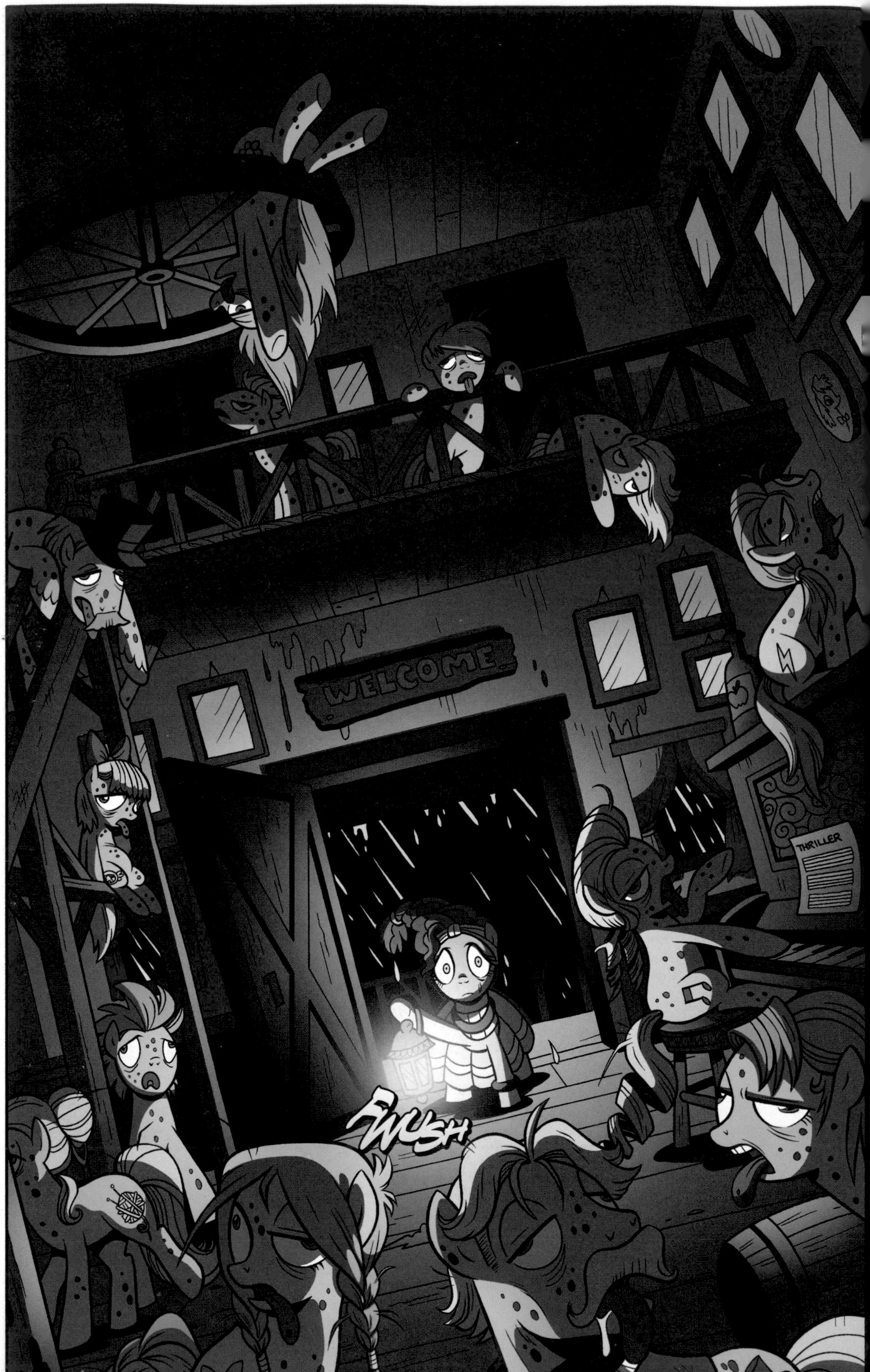
WELCOME
THRILLER
FWUSH

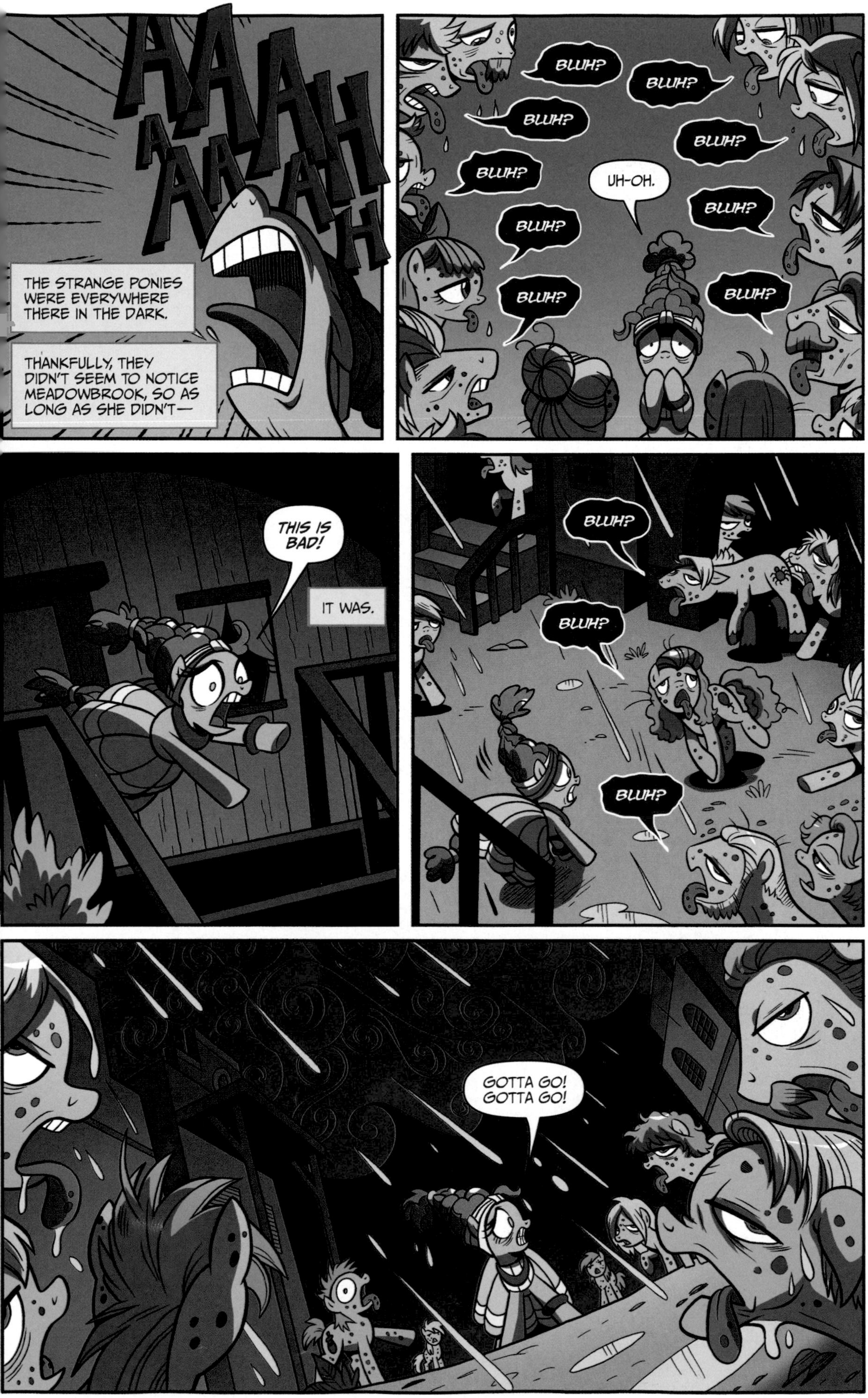
AAAAH AAAAAH
THE STRANGE PONIES WERE EVERYWHERE THERE IN THE DARK.
THANKFULLY, THEY DIDN'T SEEM TO NOTICE MEADOWBROOK, SO AS LONG AS SHE DIDN'T—
BLUH?
BLUH?
BLUH?
BLUH?
BLUH?
UH-OH.
BLUH?
BLUH?
BLUH?
BLUH?
THIS IS BAD!
IT WAS.
BLUH?
BLUH?
BLUH?
GOTTA GO! GOTTA GO!

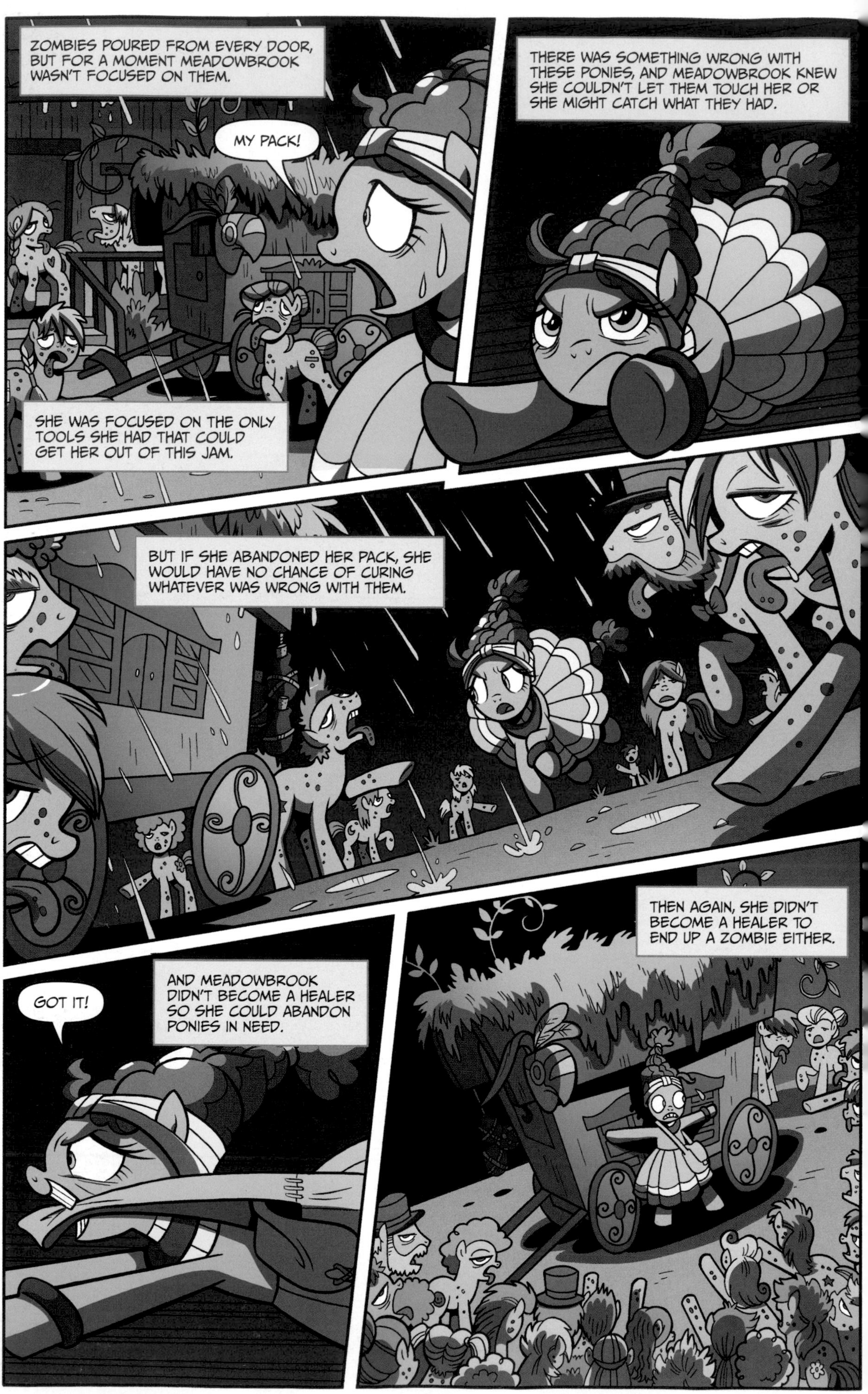
ZOMBIES POURED FROM EVERY DOOR, BUT FOR A MOMENT MEADOWBROOK WASN'T FOCUSED ON THEM.
MY PACK!
SHE WAS FOCUSED ON THE ONLY TOOLS SHE HAD THAT COULD GET HER OUT OF THIS JAM.
THERE WAS SOMETHING WRONG WITH THESE PONIES, AND MEADOWBROOK KNEW SHE COULDN'T LET THEM TOUCH HER OR SHE MIGHT CATCH WHAT THEY HAD.
BUT IF SHE ABANDONED HER PACK, SHE WOULD HAVE NO CHANCE OF CURING WHATEVER WAS WRONG WITH THEM.
GOT IT!
AND MEADOWBROOK DIDN'T BECOME A HEALER SO SHE COULD ABANDON PONIES IN NEED.
THEN AGAIN, SHE DIDN'T BECOME A HEALER TO END UP A ZOMBIE EITHER.

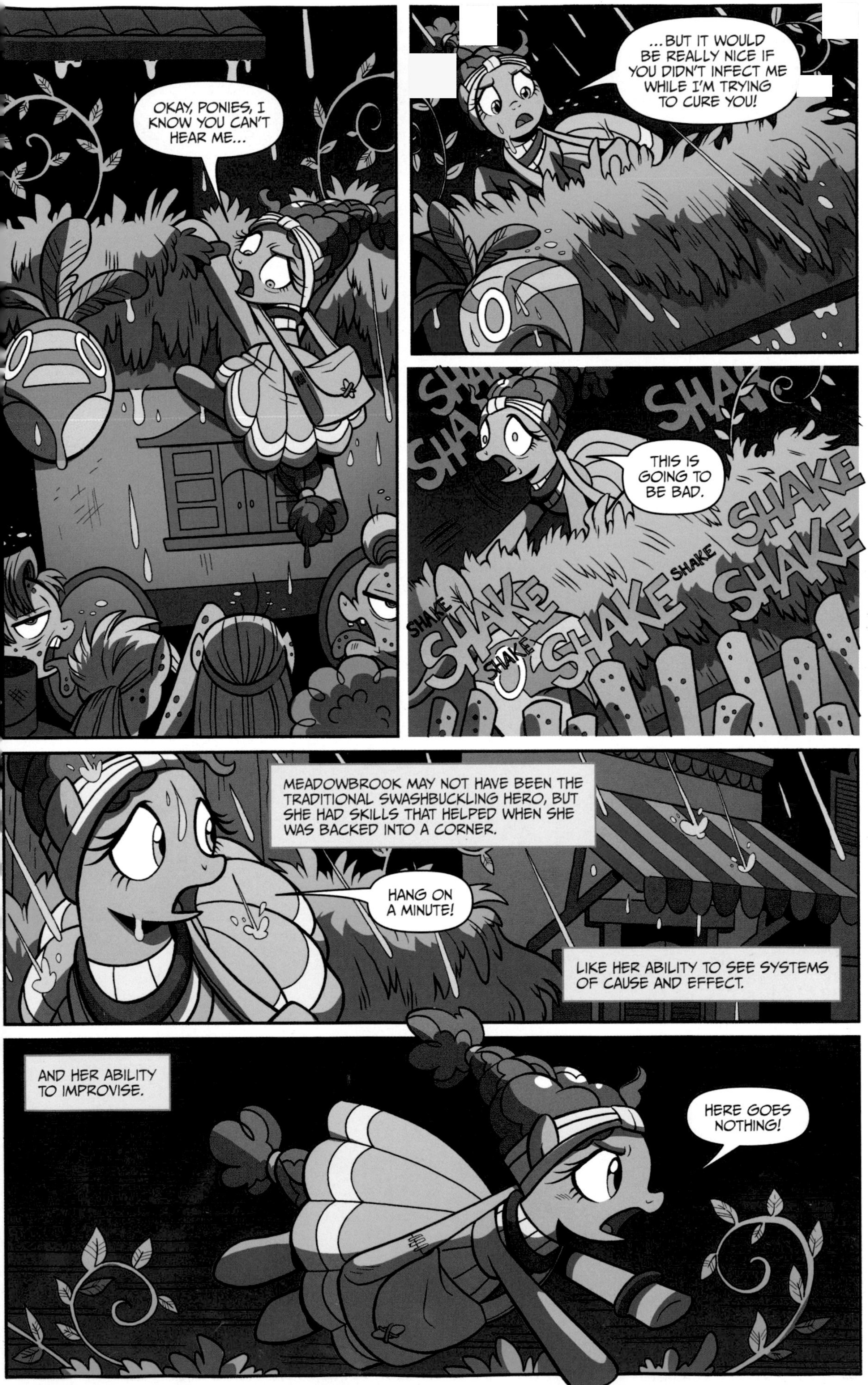
OKAY, PONIES, I KNOW YOU CAN'T HEAR ME...
...BUT IT WOULD BE REALLY NICE IF YOU DIDN'T INFECT ME WHILE I'M TRYING TO CURE YOU!
SHAKE
SHAKE
SHAKE
THIS IS GOING TO BE BAD.
SHAKE
SHAKE
SHAKE
SHAKE
SHAKE
SHAKE
SHAKE
SHAKE
MEADOWBROOK MAY NOT HAVE BEEN THE TRADITIONAL SWASHBUCKLING HERO, BUT SHE HAD SKILLS THAT HELPED WHEN SHE WAS BACKED INTO A CORNER.
HANG ON A MINUTE!
LIKE HER ABILITY TO SEE SYSTEMS OF CAUSE AND EFFECT.
AND HER ABILITY TO IMPROVISE.
HERE GOES NOTHING!

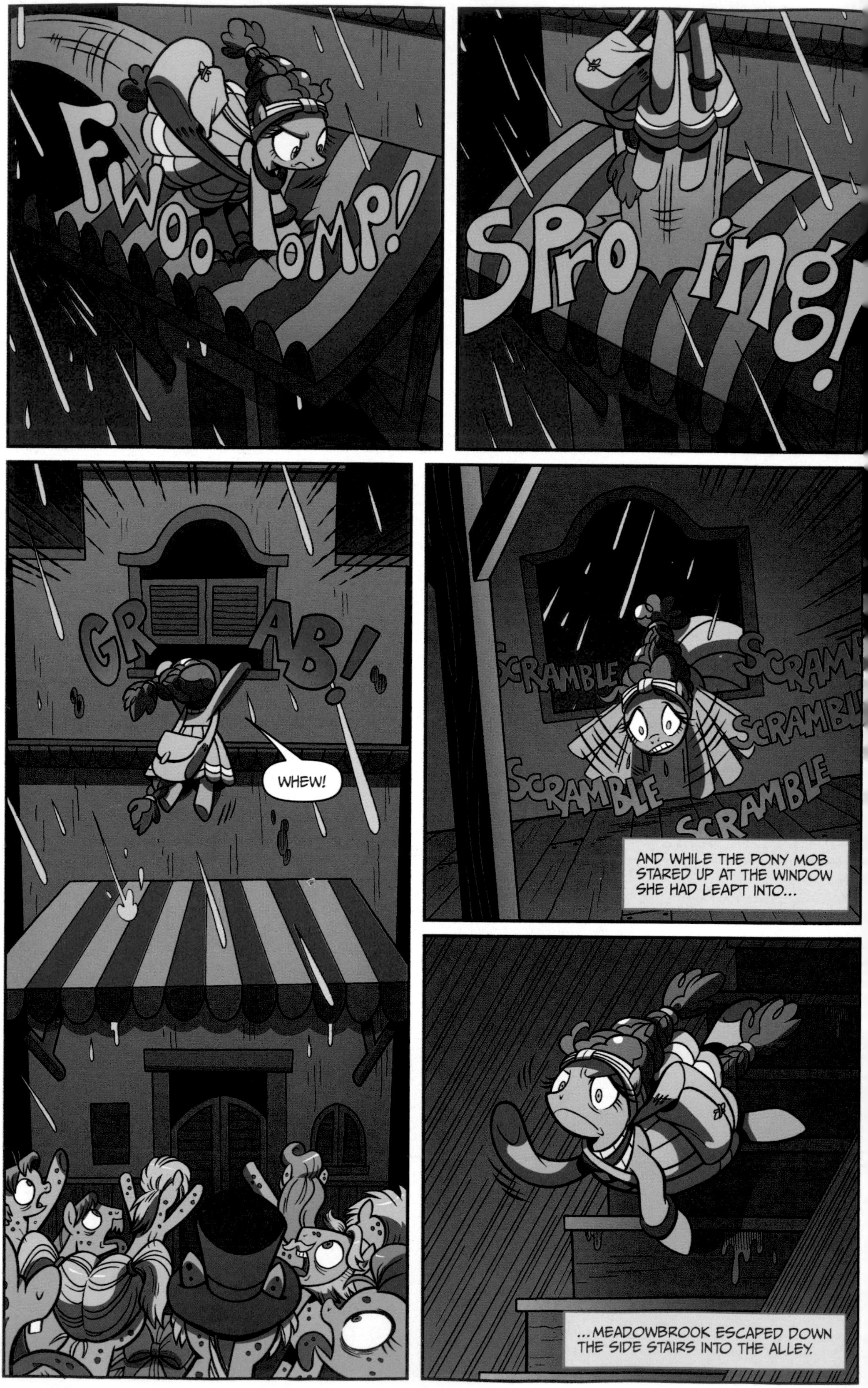
FWOOOMP!
SPROING!
GRAB!
WHEW!
SCRAMBLE
SCRAMBLE
SCRAMBLE
SCRAMBLE
SCRAMBLE
SCRAMBLE
AND WHILE THE PONY MOB STARED UP AT THE WINDOW SHE HAD LEAPT INTO...
...MEADOWBROOK ESCAPED DOWN THE SIDE STAIRS INTO THE ALLEY.

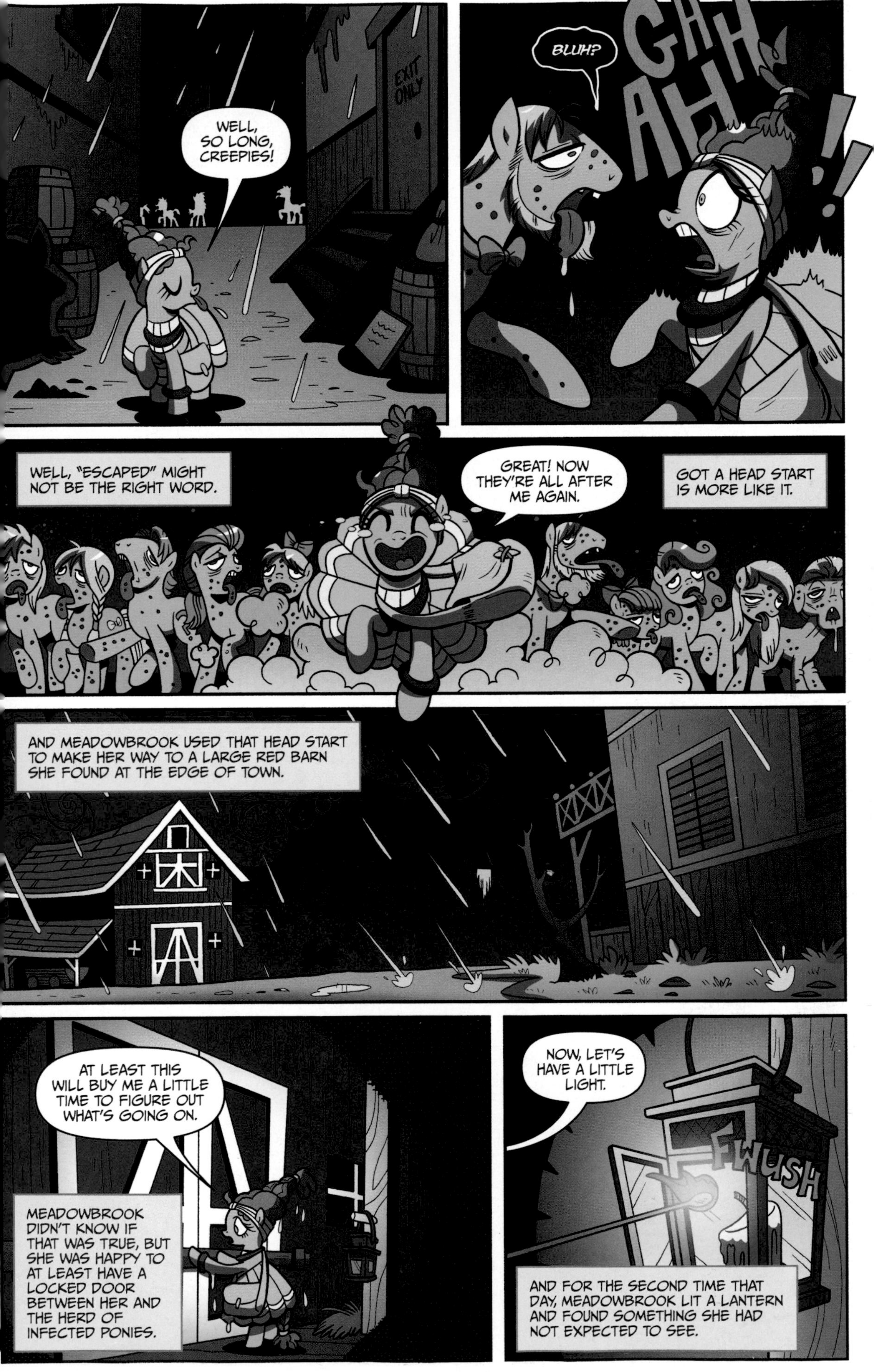
EXIT ONLY
WELL, SO LONG, CREEPIES!
BLUH?
GAHAH!!
WELL, "ESCAPED" MIGHT NOT BE THE RIGHT WORD.
GREAT! NOW THEY'RE ALL AFTER ME AGAIN.
GOT A HEAD START IS MORE LIKE IT.
AND MEADOWBROOK USED THAT HEAD START TO MAKE HER WAY TO A LARGE RED BARN SHE FOUND AT THE EDGE OF TOWN.
AT LEAST THIS WILL BUY ME A LITTLE TIME TO FIGURE OUT WHAT'S GOING ON.
MEADOWBROOK DIDN'T KNOW IF THAT WAS TRUE, BUT SHE WAS HAPPY TO AT LEAST HAVE A LOCKED DOOR BETWEEN HER AND THE HERD OF INFECTED PONIES.
NOW, LET'S HAVE A LITTLE LIGHT.
FWUSH
AND FOR THE SECOND TIME THAT DAY, MEADOWBROOK LIT A LANTERN AND FOUND SOMETHING SHE HAD NOT EXPECTED TO SEE.

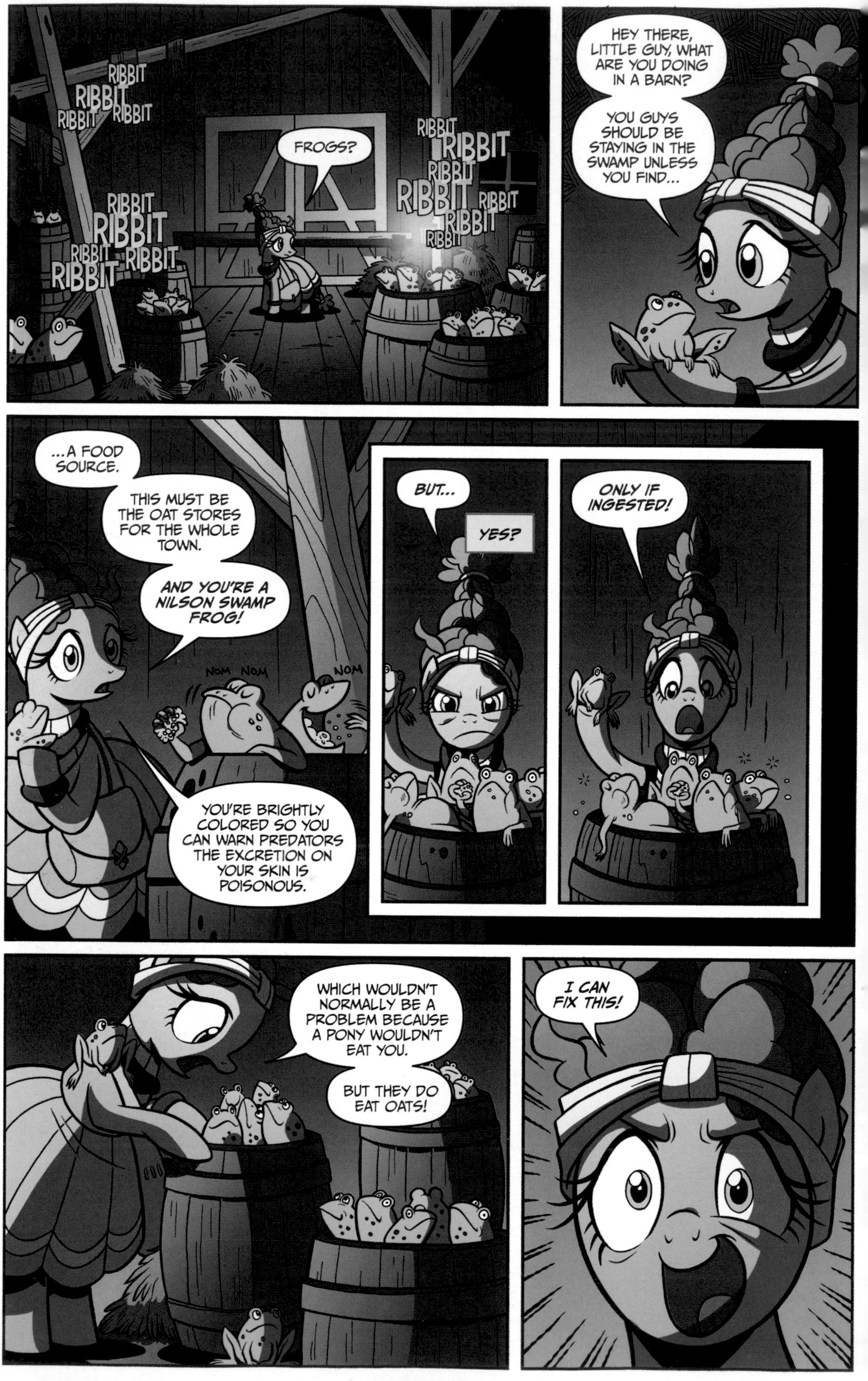
RIBBIT
RIBBIT
RIBBIT RIBBIT
RIBBIT
RIBBIT
RIBBIT RIBBIT
RIBBIT
FROGS?
RIBBIT
RIBBIT
RIBBIT
RIBBIT RIBBIT
RIBBIT
RIBBIT
HEY THERE, LITTLE GUY, WHAT ARE YOU DOING IN A BARN?
YOU GUYS SHOULD BE STAYING IN THE SWAMP UNLESS YOU FIND...
...A FOOD SOURCE.
THIS MUST BE THE OAT STORES FOR THE WHOLE TOWN.
AND YOU'RE A NILSON SWAMP FROG!
NOM NOM
NOM
YOU'RE BRIGHTLY COLORED SO YOU CAN WARN PREDATORS THE EXCRETION ON YOUR SKIN IS POISONOUS.
BUT...
YES?
ONLY IF INGESTED!
WHICH WOULDN'T NORMALLY BE A PROBLEM BECAUSE A PONY WOULDN'T EAT YOU.
BUT THEY DO EAT OATS!
I CAN FIX THIS!

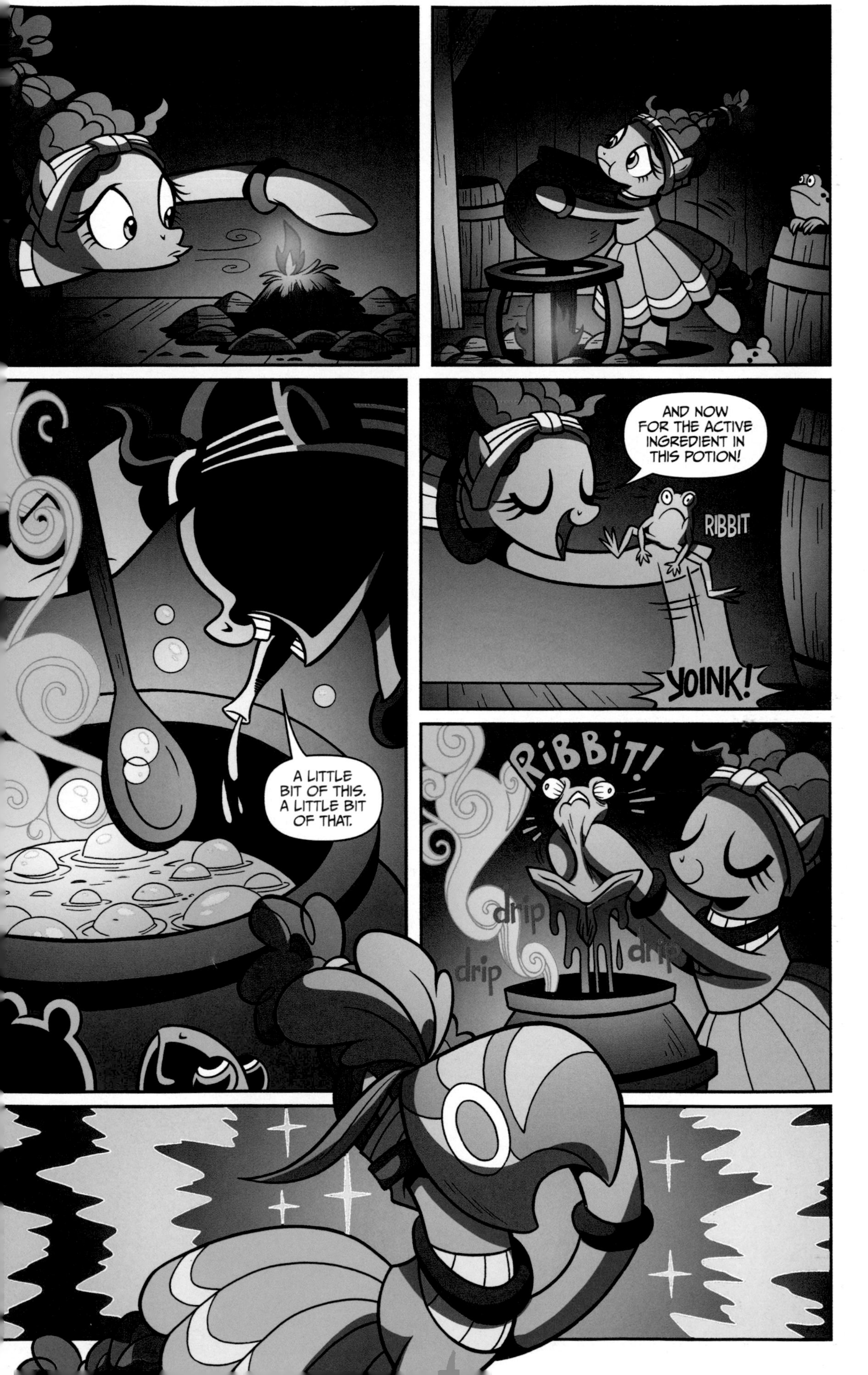
AND NOW FOR THE ACTIVE INGREDIENT IN THIS POTION!
RIBBIT
YOINK!
A LITTLE BIT OF THIS. A LITTLE BIT OF THAT.
RIBBIT!
drip
drip
drip

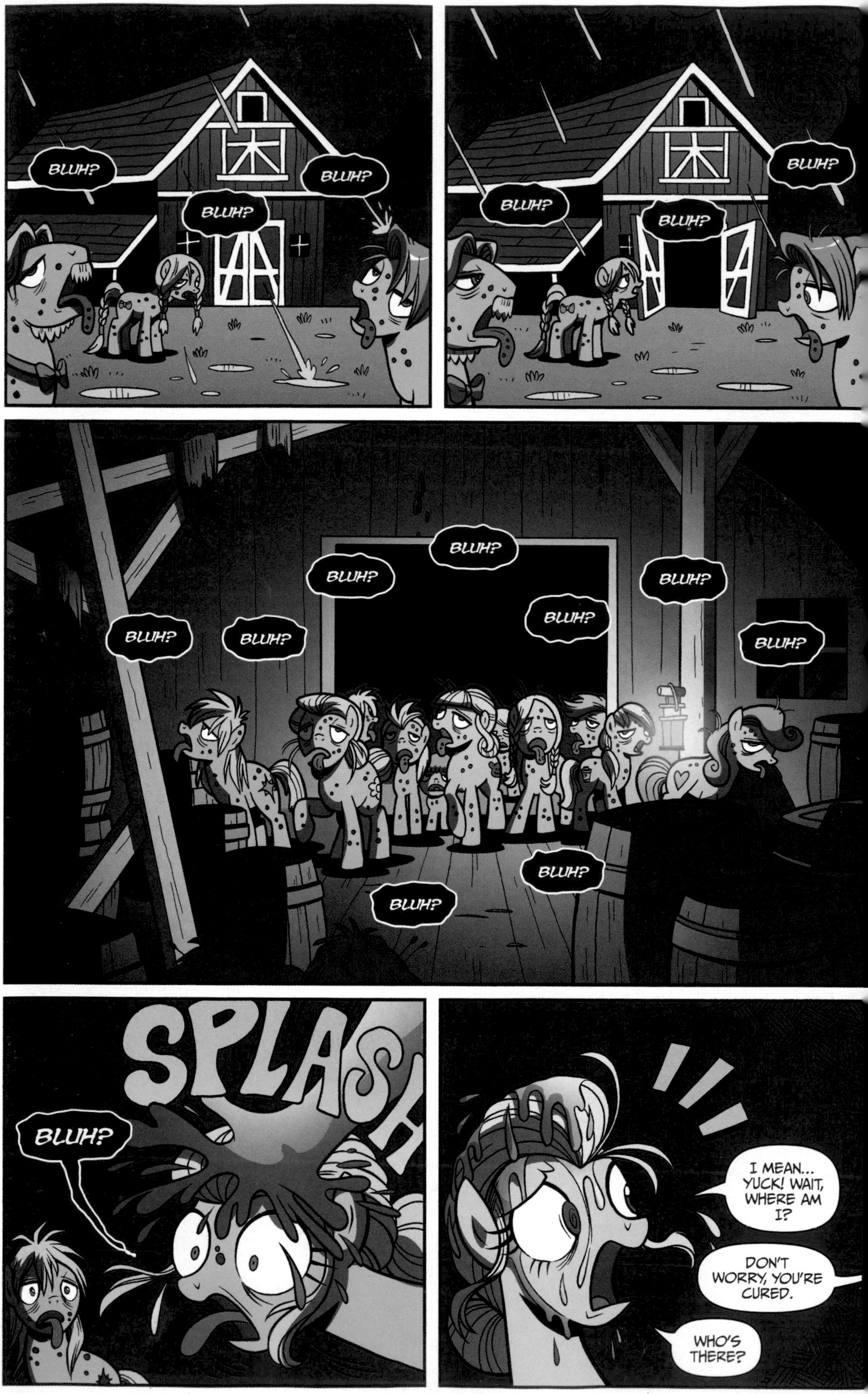
BLUH?
BLUH?
BLUH?
BLUH?
BLUH?
BLUH?
BLUH?
BLUH?
BLUH?
BLUH?
BLUH?
BLUH?
BLUH?
BLUH?
BLUH?
SPLASH
BLUH?
I MEAN... YUCK! WAIT, WHERE AM I?
DON'T WORRY, YOU'RE CURED.
WHO'S THERE?

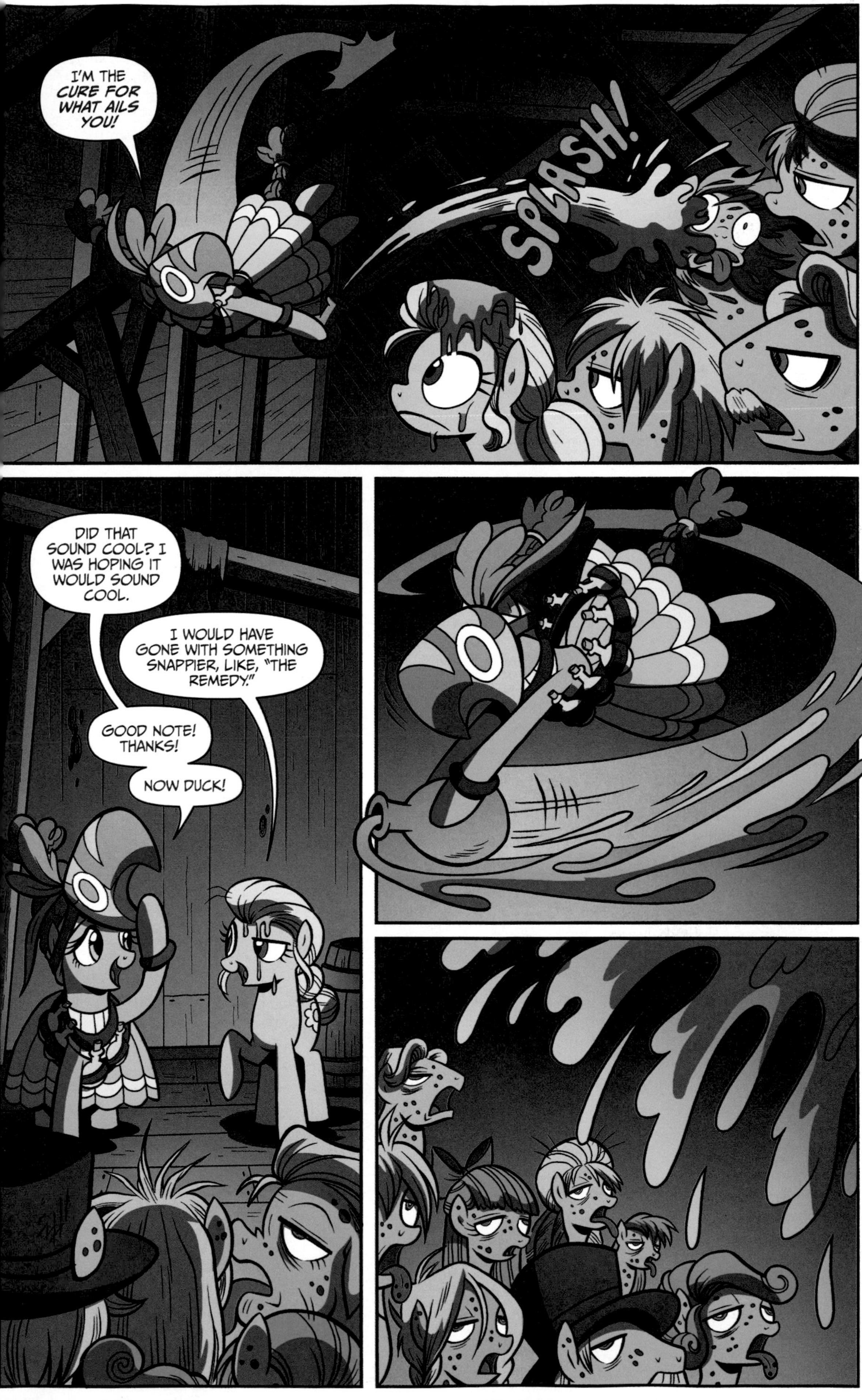
I'M THE CURE FOR WHAT AILS YOU!
SPLASH!
DID THAT SOUND COOL? I WAS HOPING IT WOULD SOUND COOL.
I WOULD HAVE GONE WITH SOMETHING SNAPPIER, LIKE, "THE REMEDY."
GOOD NOTE! THANKS!
NOW DUCK!

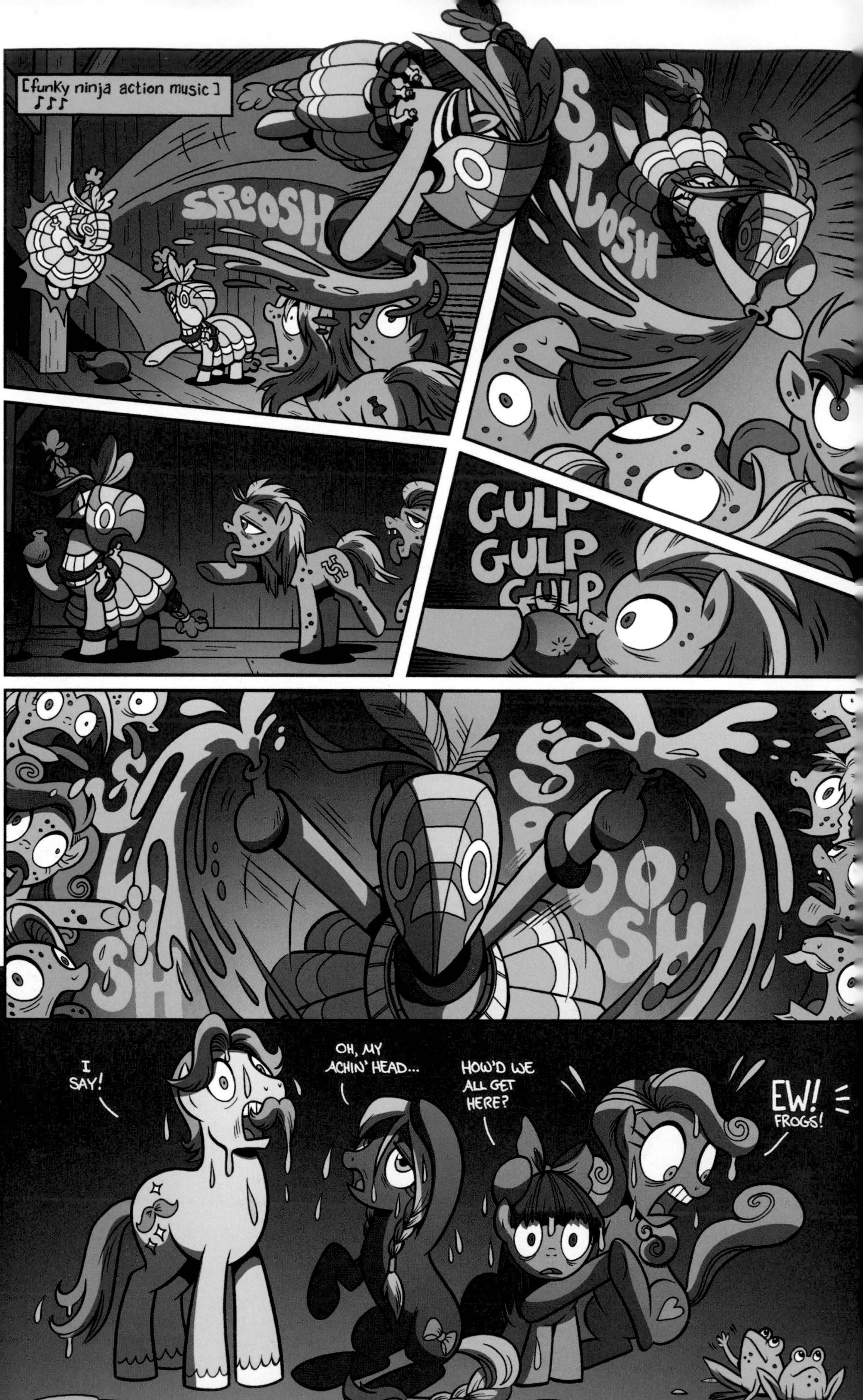
[funky ninja action music]
♪♪♪
SPLOOSH
SPLOOSH
GULP
GULP
GULP
SPLOOSH
SPLOOSH
I SAY!
OH, MY ACHIN' HEAD...
HOW'D WE ALL GET HERE?
EW! FROGS!

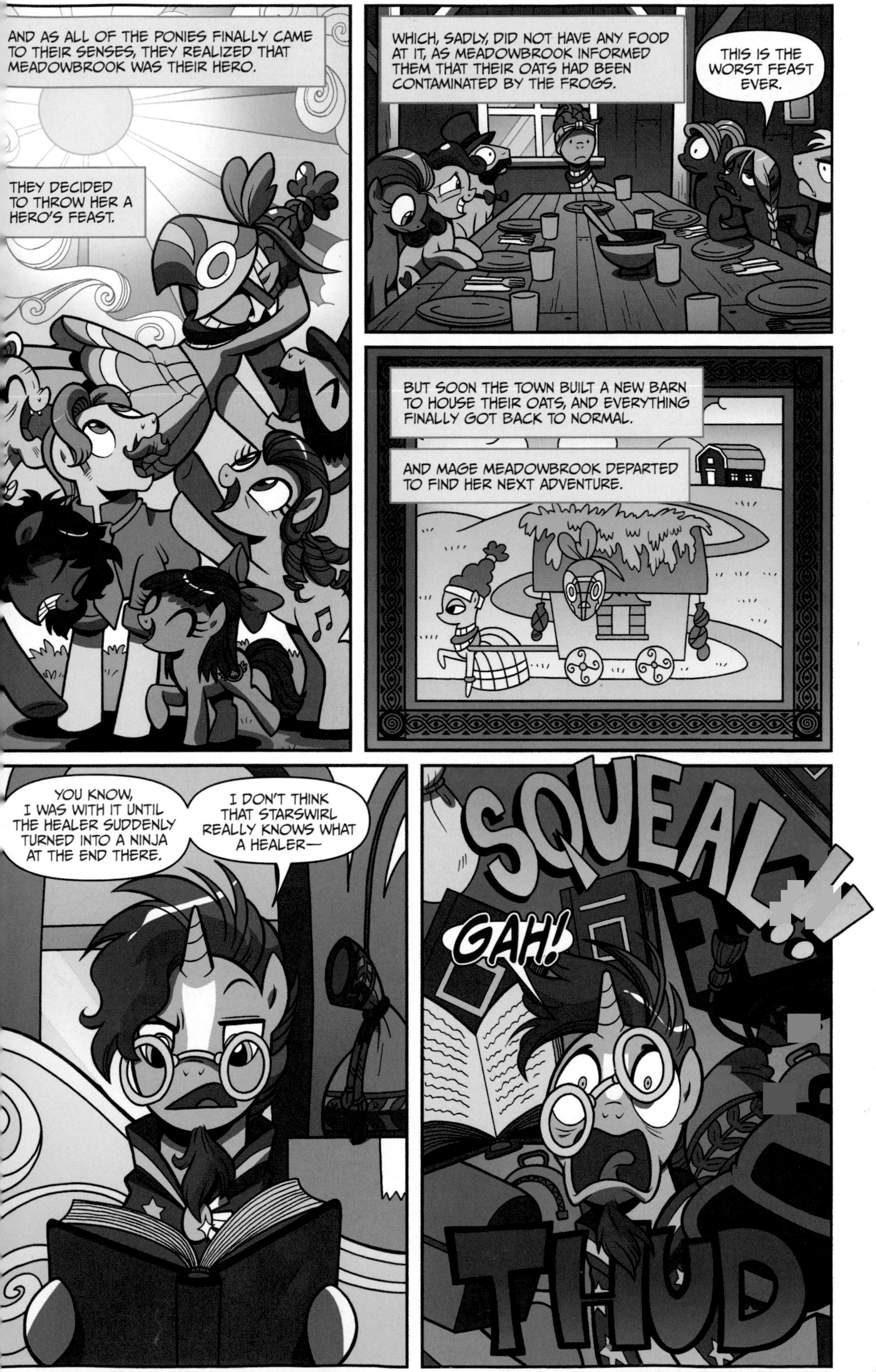
AND AS ALL OF THE PONIES FINALLY CAME TO THEIR SENSES, THEY REALIZED THAT MEADOWBROOK WAS THEIR HERO.
THEY DECIDED TO THROW HER A HERO'S FEAST.
WHICH, SADLY, DID NOT HAVE ANY FOOD AT IT, AS MEADOWBROOK INFORMED THEM THAT THEIR OATS HAD BEEN CONTAMINATED BY THE FROGS.
THIS IS THE WORST FEAST EVER.
BUT SOON THE TOWN BUILT A NEW BARN TO HOUSE THEIR OATS, AND EVERYTHING FINALLY GOT BACK TO NORMAL.
AND MAGE MEADOWBROOK DEPARTED TO FIND HER NEXT ADVENTURE.
YOU KNOW, I WAS WITH IT UNTIL THE HEALER SUDDENLY TURNED INTO A NINJA AT THE END THERE.
I DON'T THINK THAT STARSWIRL REALLY KNOWS WHAT A HEALER—
SQUEAL!
GAH!
THUD

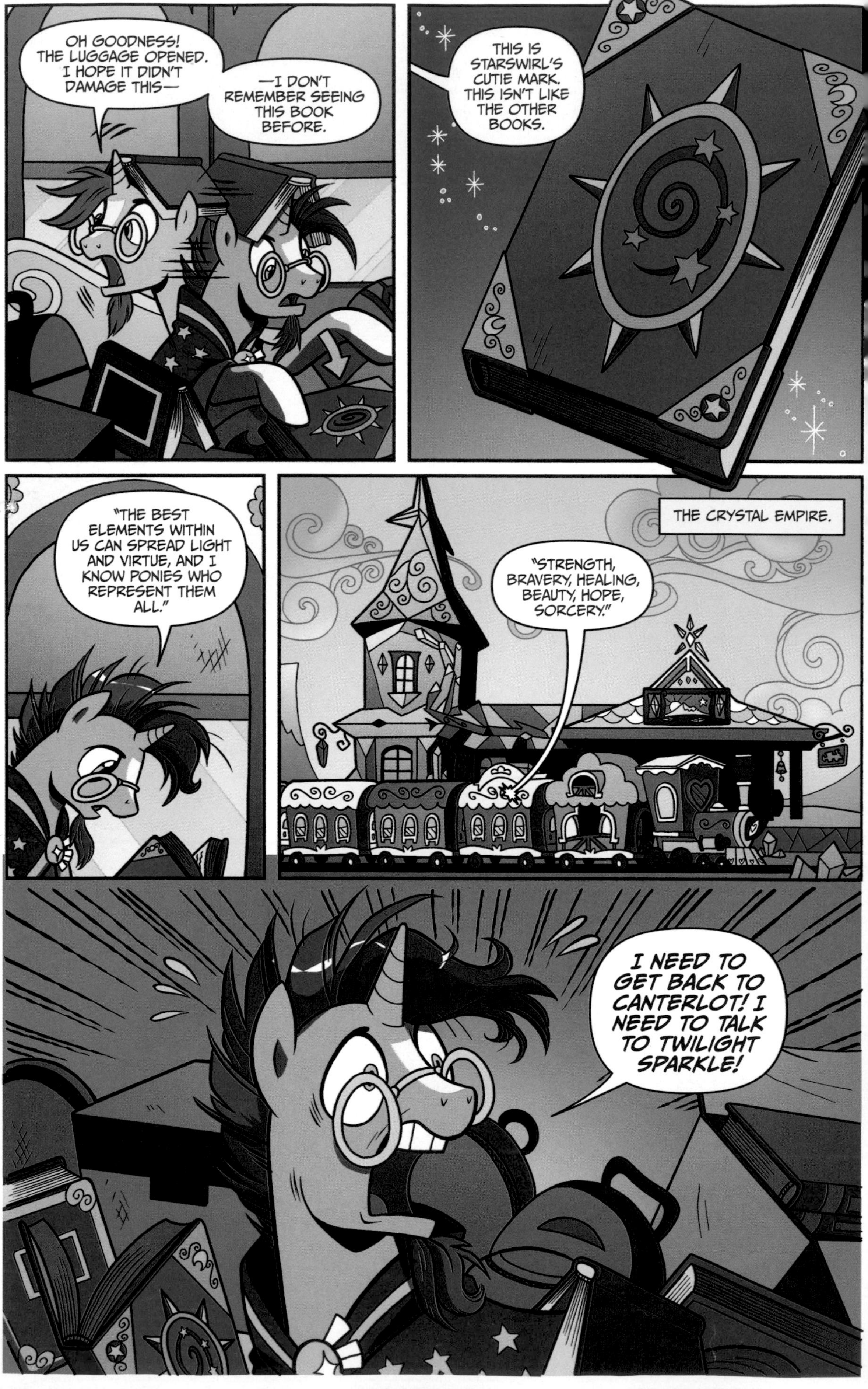
OH GOODNESS! THE LUGGAGE OPENED. I HOPE IT DIDN'T DAMAGE THIS—
—I DON'T REMEMBER SEEING THIS BOOK BEFORE.
THIS IS STARSWIRL'S CUTIE MARK. THIS ISN'T LIKE THE OTHER BOOKS.
"THE BEST ELEMENTS WITHIN US CAN SPREAD LIGHT AND VIRTUE, AND I KNOW PONIES WHO REPRESENT THEM ALL."
THE CRYSTAL EMPIRE.
"STRENGTH, BRAVERY, HEALING, BEAUTY, HOPE, SORCERY."
I NEED TO GET BACK TO CANTERLOT! I NEED TO TALK TO TWILIGHT SPARKLE!

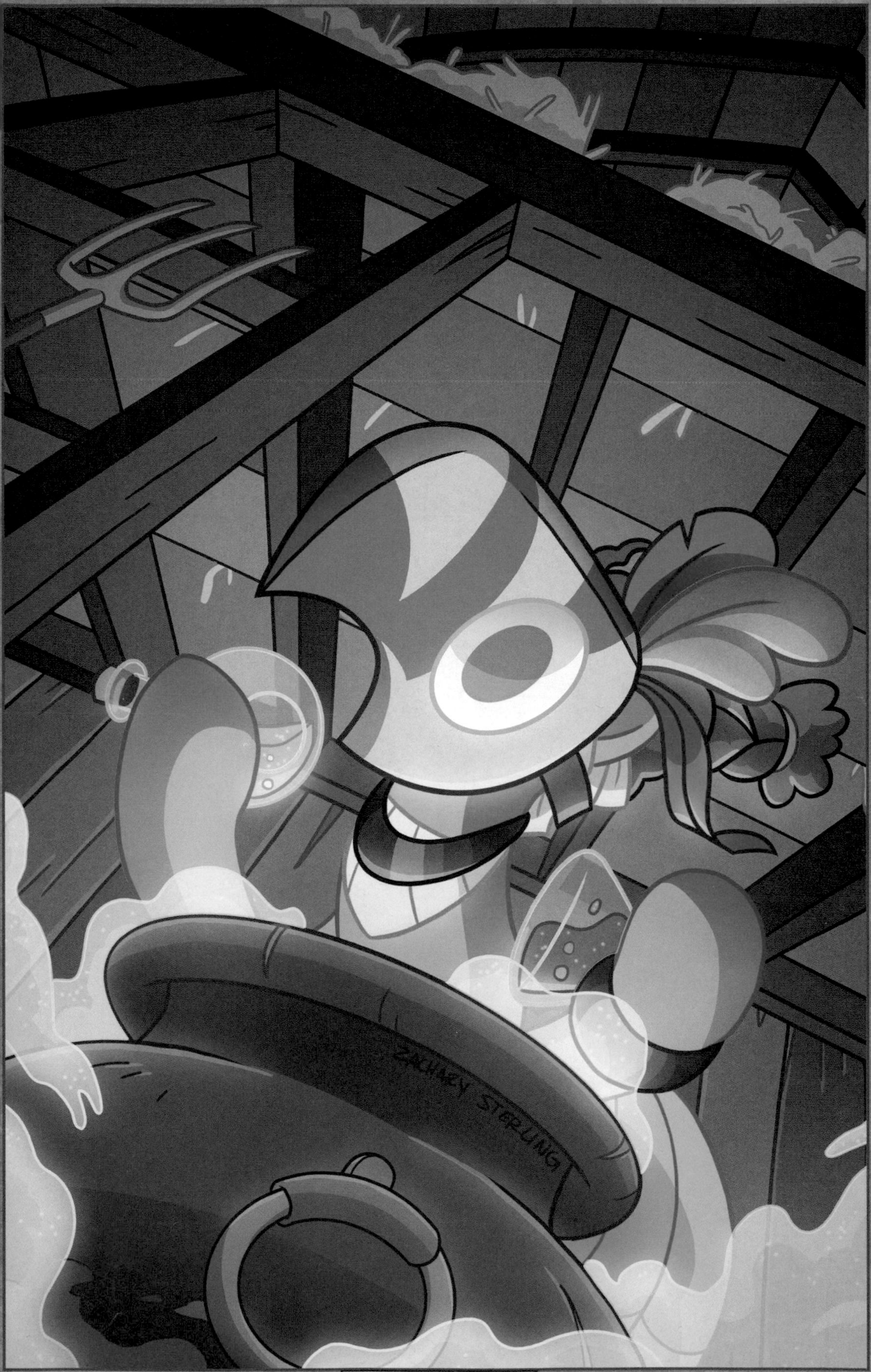
ZACHARY STERLING

ART BY ZACHARY STERLING

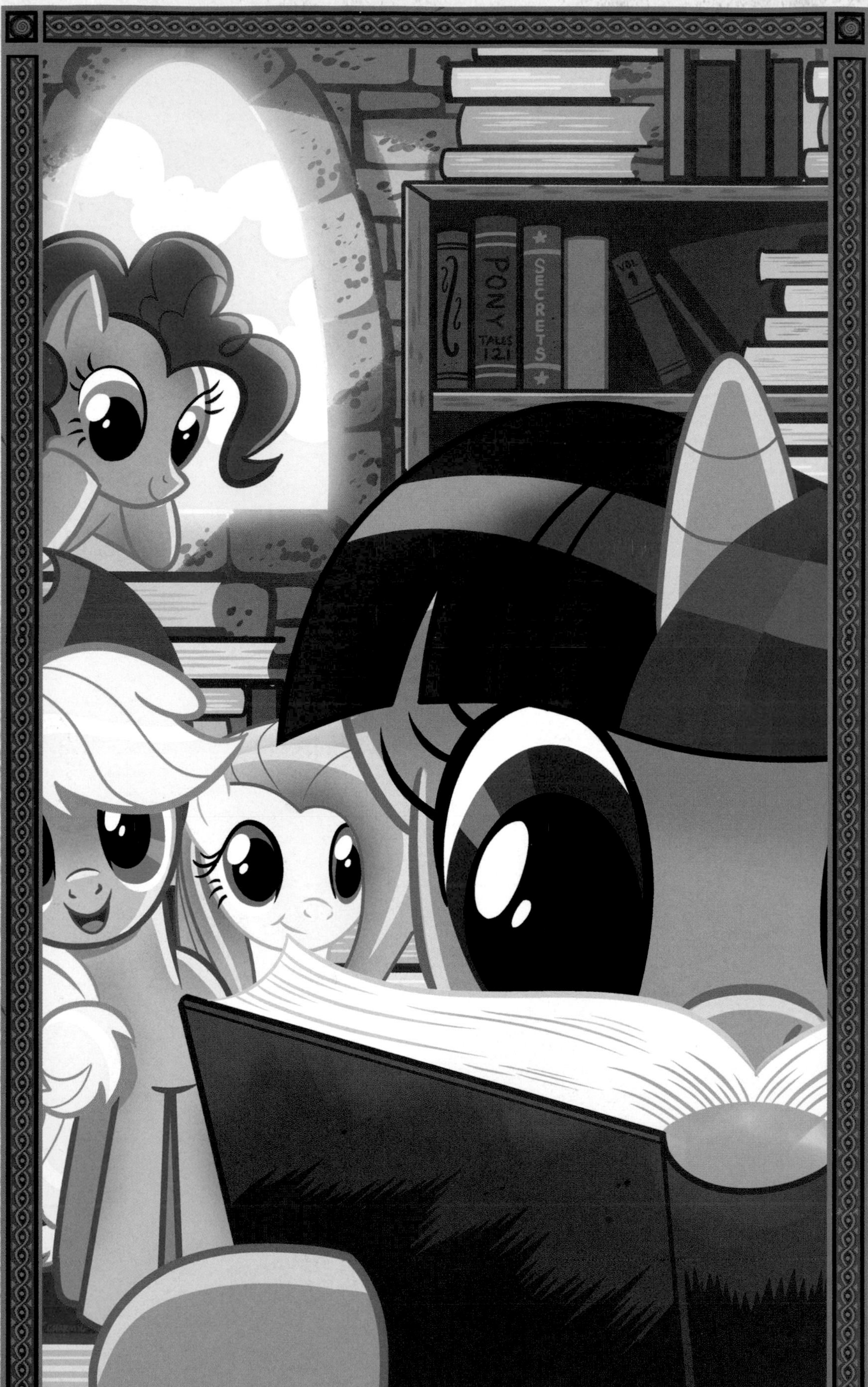
PONY
TALES 121
SECRETS
VOL 1

ART BY DEREK CHARM

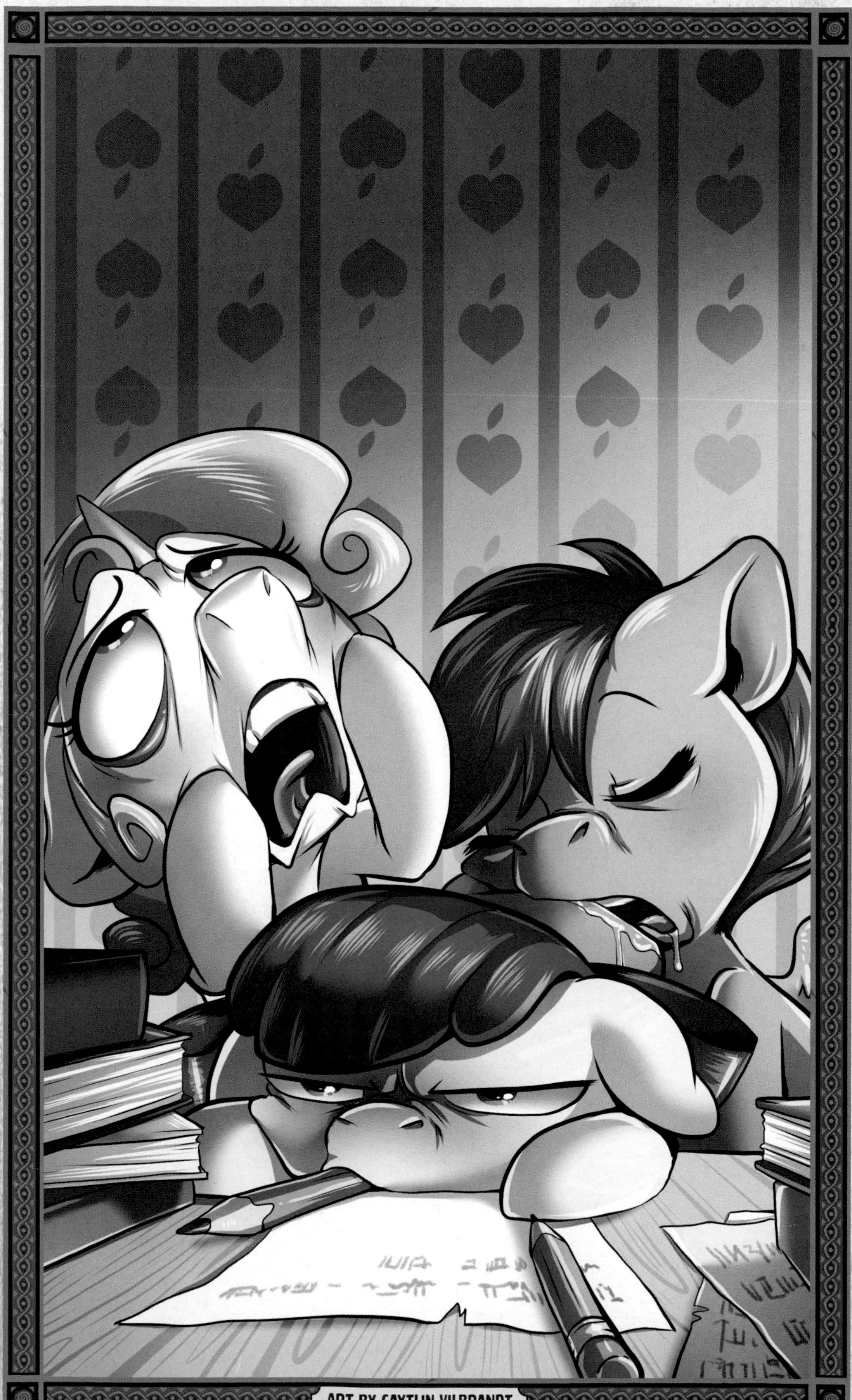
ART BY CAYTLIN VILBRANDT

ART BY PAUL ABTRUSE, COLORS BY EDDIE SWAN

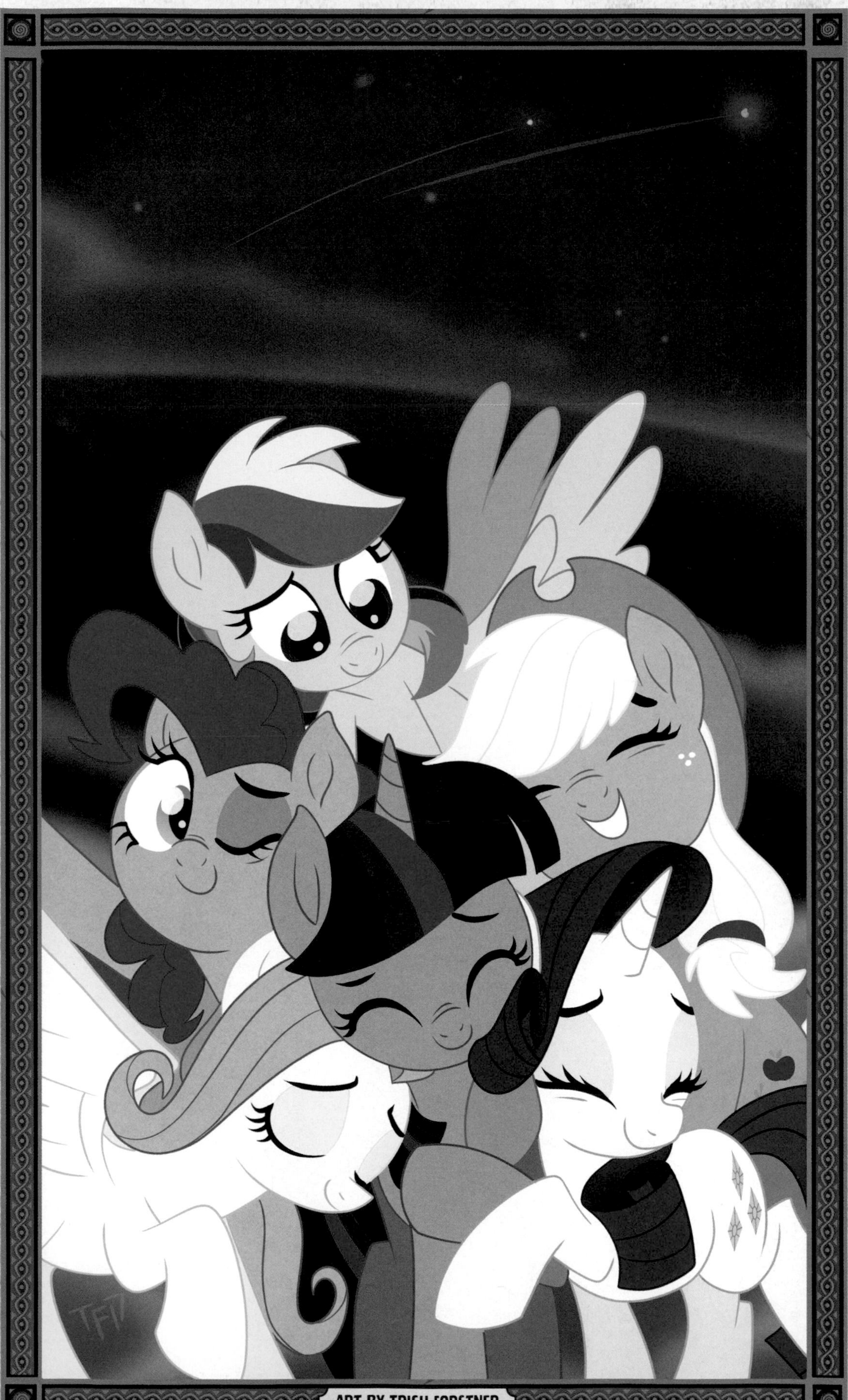
TF17

ART BY TRISH FORSTNER

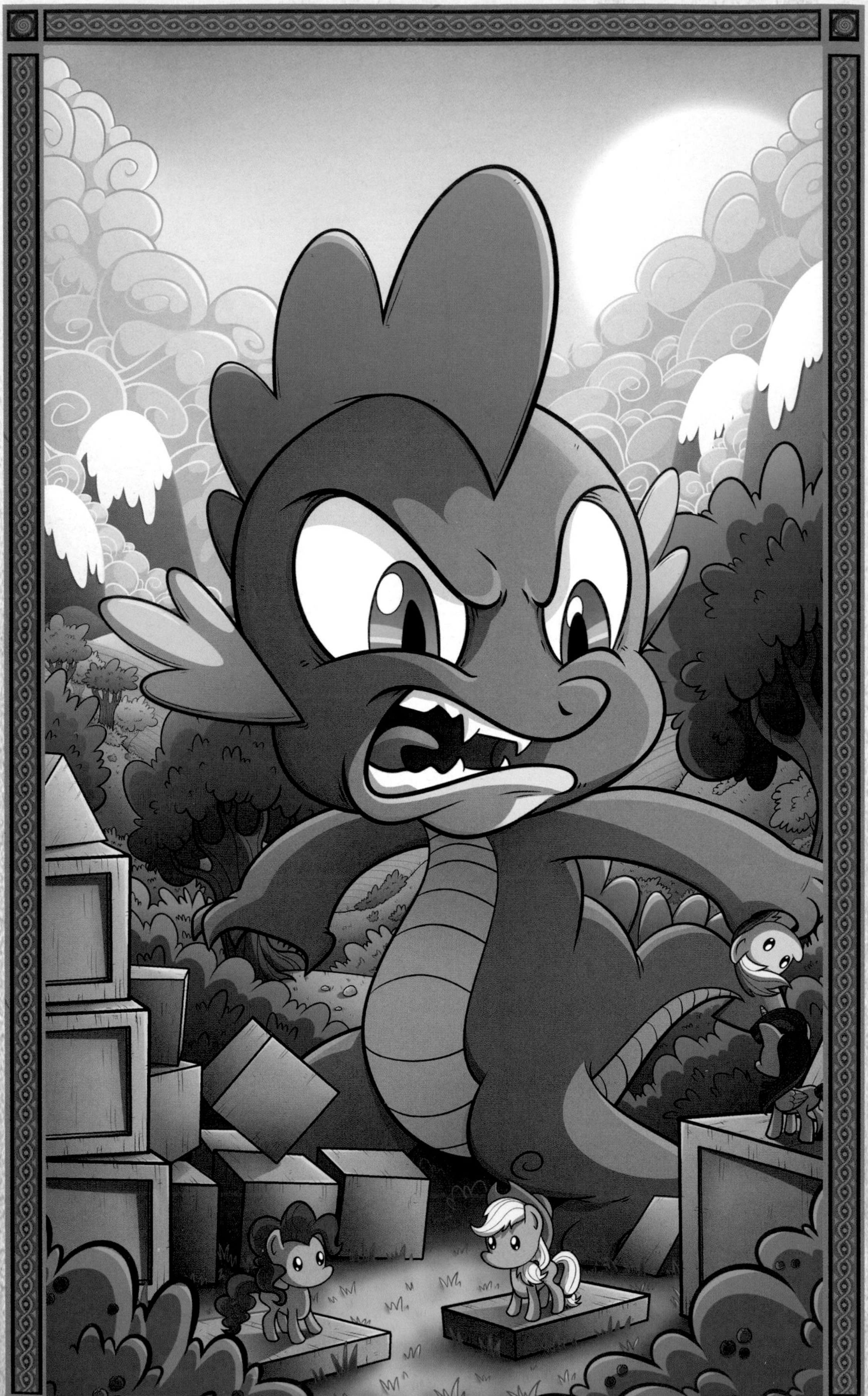
ART BY MIKE VASQUEZ

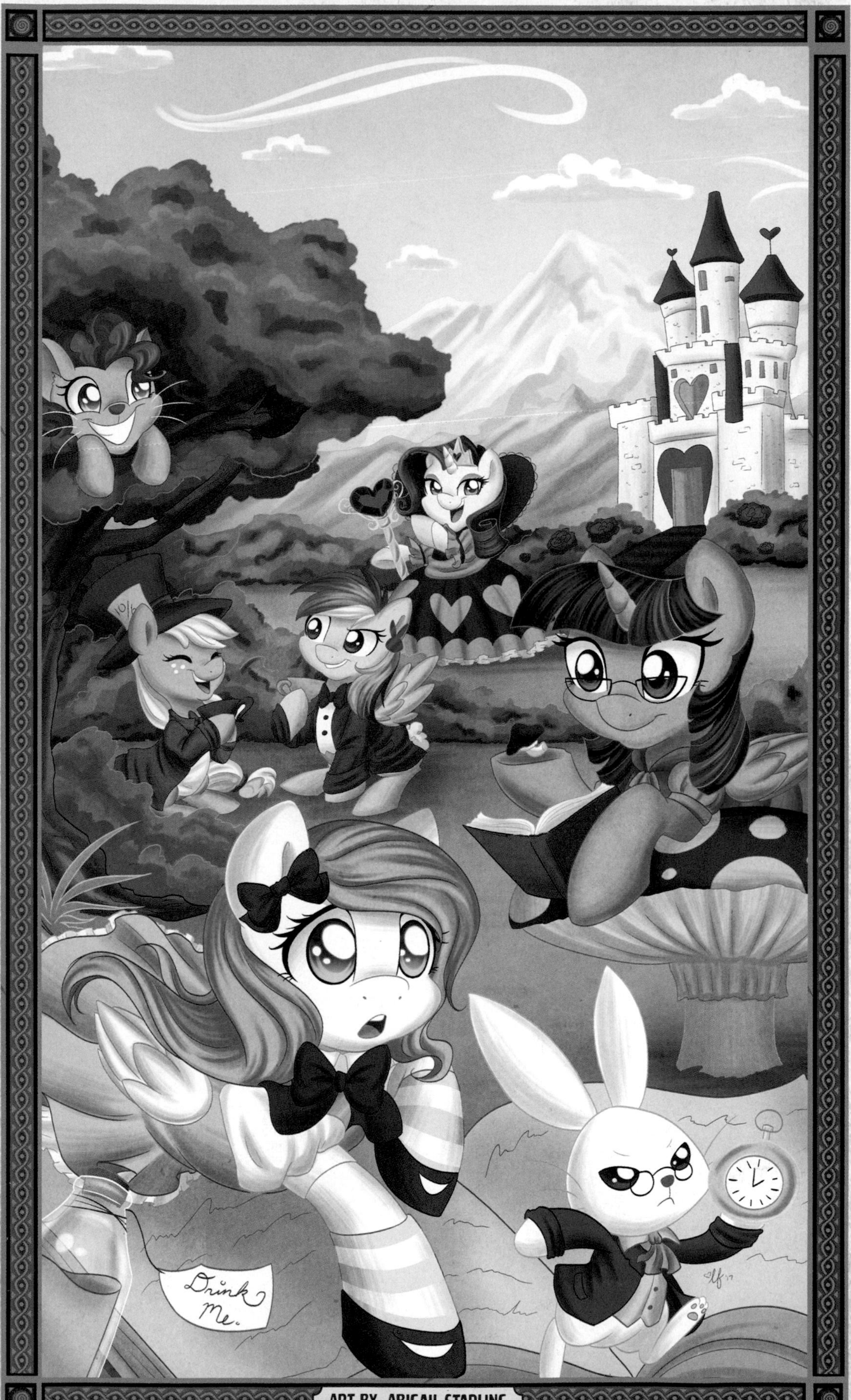
10/6
Drink Me.

ART BY ABIGAIL STARLING

The official prequel to the blockbuster feature film!

MY LITTLE PONY
THE MOVIE
prequel

my LITTLE PONY
Legends of Magic

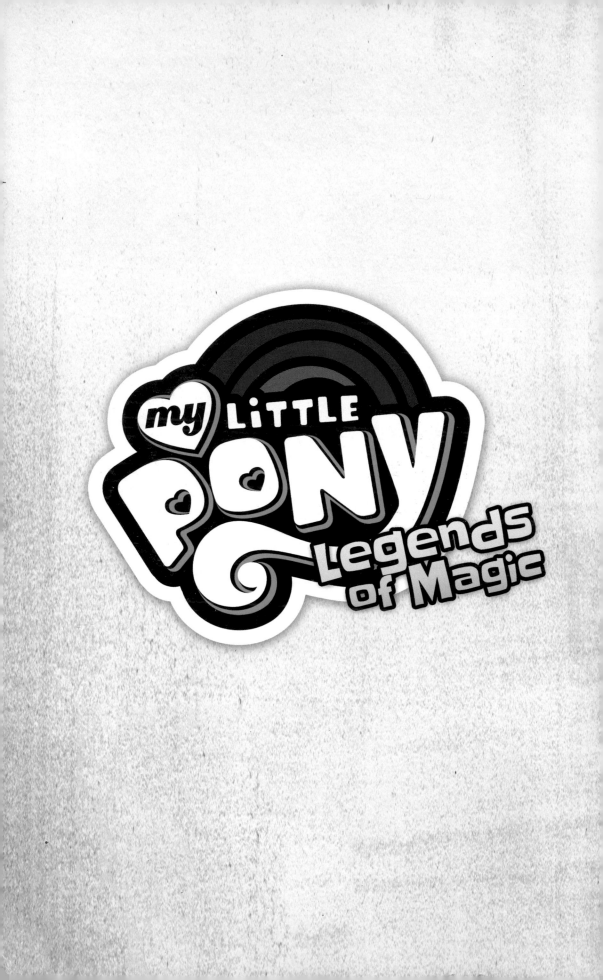